MINOTAUR

BOOKS

CENTAUR

PRAISE FOR JOAN HESS
AND THE CLAIRE MALLOY SERIES

"A good substitute for a trip to Egypt."
—*Deadly Pleasures* on *Mummy Dearest*

"Lively, sharp, irreverent."
—*The New York Times Book Review* on *Poisoned Pins*

"Hess fans will find much to entertain them..."
—*Publishers Weekly* on *Damsels in Distress*

"Larcenous shenanigans...breezy throughout."
—*Chicago Tribune* on *Poisoned Pins*

"With her wry asides, Claire makes a most engaging narrator. The author deftly juggles the various plot strands...the surprising denouement comes off with éclat."
—*Publishers Weekly* on *Out on a Limb*

"A winning blend of soft-core feminism, trendy sub-plots, and a completely irreverent style that characterizes both the series and the sleuth."
—*Houston Chronicle*

"Refreshing...blends humor, eccentric characters, familiar emotions, and plot twists into an enjoyable lark."
—*Nashville Banner* on *Poisoned Pins*

"A colorful kaleidoscope of plotting and clues... undeniably funny."
—*Arkansas Democrat-Gazette* on *Poisoned Pins*

"A wildly entertaining series."
—*Mystery Scene*

MORE...

THE CLAIRE MALLOY MYSTERIES
BY JOAN HESS

MUMMY DEAREST

Joan Hess

St. Martin's Paperbacks

This is a work of fiction. All of the characters, organizations and events portrayed in this novel are either products of the author's imagination or are used fictitiously.

MUMMY DEAREST

Copyright © 2008 by Joan Hess.
Excerpt from *Busy Bodies* copyright © 2009 by Joan Hess.

For information address St. Martin's Press, 175 Fifth Avenue, New York, NY 10010.

Library of Congress Catalog Card Number: 2007051831

ISBN: 0-312-36565-9
EAN: 978-0-312-36565-3

Printed in the United States of America

St. Martin's Press hardcover edition / April 2008
St. Martin's Paperbacks edition / February 2009

St. Martin's Paperbacks are published by St. Martin's Press, 175 Fifth Avenue, New York, NY 10010.

10 9 8 7 6 5 4 3 2 1

*This book is dedicated
with love and respect to Barbara Mertz
(who also goes by the aliases Elizabeth Peters and
Barbara Michaels)*

ACKNOWLEDGMENTS

I would like to express my gratitude to the following, who willingly or unwittingly provided me with knowledge and opportunities to learn about aspects of Egypt unavailable to most travelers:

Dr. Barbara Mertz, Ph.D. in Egyptology, University of Chicago; Dr. W. Ray Smith, Director, Chicago House, Luxor; Dennis Forbes, editor of *KMT: A Modern Journal of Ancient Egypt;* Joel Cole, artist and steadying hand on arduous treks; Dr. Otto Schaden, excavator of KV63; Dr. Salima Ikram, American University in Cairo; Bill and Nancy Petty of Museum Tours; Dr. Marjorie Fisher, Adjunct Assistant Professor of Egyptology, Department of Near East Studies, University of Michigan; and Charles Roberts, who bears sole responsibility for coercing me onto that blasted camel.

CHAPTER 1

"Those Do Not look like camels to me."

"That's because they're horses."

"Where are the camels?"

"How should I know?"

"You're the one who said there'd be camels all over the place."

"I did not!"

"You did so!"

What a dandy way to start a honeymoon, I thought as I came into the parlor of the suite. My daughter, Caron, and her best friend, Inez, were on the balcony, engaged in what was clearly an argument of cosmic significance. I felt as if I'd been flattened by a giant waffle iron. The three of us had left Farberville many hours ago, possibly even days ago. We'd flown to Dallas, then Atlanta, then Frankfurt, followed by a six-hour layover and a flight to Cairo. After an interminable time snaking through customs at that airport, we'd flown on to Luxor. A lovely man whose name I did not remember had met us at the gate, collected our luggage, and whisked us to the hotel. Although the sun was still shining, I'd brushed my teeth and collapsed in bed.

Now, showered and wearing the terry-cloth bathrobe I'd found in the bathroom, I joined the girls on the balcony. The view was dazzling. Below us were terraces delineated with marble rails, a lush garden of shady grass and cheerful flowers, and beyond those the corniche, a boulevard that ran alongside the Nile. The medians were dotted with palm trees, shrubs, and minimal litter. Boxy metal cruise ships were docked at a large concrete pier, and small boats with triangular sails sliced through the brown water. On the other side of the river, hostile mountains dominated the horizon. There was no trace of vegetation on the slopes, only rocks and sheer cliffs. The fabled West Bank, with its Valley of the Kings and, somewhere to the south, the Valley of the Queens. The pharaohs, it seemed, preferred separate accommodations, even in the next world.

"Horse-drawn carriages and frenetic little cars," I said, "but no camels. Camels have humps."

Inez coughed delicately. "What one would expect to see here are dromedaries, or Arabian camels. They have one hump. Bactrian camels are indigenous to Asia and have two humps. Camels can go for two weeks without water, and a month without food. Contrary to popular belief, they don't store water in their humps. The fatty tissue metabolizes with—"

"Hump, hump, harrumph." Caron sat down on one of the padded chairs. "We were about to call for the paramedics, Mother. You slept for fifteen hours."

"Don't worry, Ms. Malloy," Inez said earnestly. "It's classic jet lag, and at your age, it—" She stopped and stared. "I guess I should call you Ms. Rosen, shouldn't I? I'll try, but it still sounds really weird. I've always called you Ms. Malloy."

"I'm not going to change my name," I said.

Caron snorted. "Yeah, all that paperwork. What does Peter think about it—or did you bother to ask him? Where is he, anyway?"

I leaned against the marble rail. "It's my decision, not his. As for his whereabouts, they are unknown. He was supposed to be here when we arrived. He must have been tied up in a meeting in Cairo." I was relieved when neither girl persisted with questions. I'd intentionally been vague about the trip in general, saying only that Peter might be asked to discuss police matters while we were there. I did not want them to know the extent of his involvement, and frankly, I didn't want to know, either. He'd attended a training session at what I blithely had called FBI summer camp and, after a brief furlough, returned to the East Coast for six weeks of further tutelage in the delicacies of international skulduggery. He'd had three days off to come home to give me tickets and travel information, confer with the captain of the Farberville Police Department—and show up at our wedding. Two days later Peter left for final briefings, and I hadn't seen him since. I suspected the CIA, Interpol, and the Department of Homeland Security were behind all this, but Peter hadn't volunteered any information and I hadn't asked.

However, because of whoever it was, we had an all-expenses-paid honeymoon to an exotic locale. We had a suite in the Winter Palace, where the idle rich had come for more than a hundred years to play whist, gingerly poke around dusty tombs, and enjoy the balmy fall and winter weather. Situated at one end of the third floor, the suite had a large parlor with fiercely floral upholstered sofas and chairs, and an eclectic mix of antique (sideboard, framed paintings, gaudy vases) and contemporary (mini-bar, TV) furnishings. Massive arrangements of flowers and a tray of fresh and dried fruit had awaited us. I had not yet seen the girls' bedroom, but the master bedroom had a fireplace, a sitting area, and a bathroom with a stall shower, a marble vanity, and a bathtub in which one might swim laps.

There was a knock. Caron hurried past me to the front door of the parlor.

"She ordered coffee from room service while you were taking a shower," Inez explained.

"Oh," I murmured, somewhat unnerved by their display of thoughtfulness. Although Caron was still plagued by fits of adolescent pique, she was beginning to show more frequent outbursts of maturity. I didn't know if it was due to the arrival of her seventeenth birthday, her ascendancy to status of an upperclassman, or my marriage. September had been a month fraught with significance for all of us.

Caron came out to the balcony and whispered, "Am I supposed to tip him?"

I looked back at the elderly man in a white coat, who was gathering up orange and banana peels from the coffee table. He was bald, his scalp dappled with dark blemishes; his face was creased like a walnut shell. "I don't know," I said, "so let's not worry about it now. I'll ask Peter when he gets here."

"This was delivered to the front desk," she said, handing me an envelope. Peter's meticulously proper prep school handwriting on the front was easy to identify. "The guy in there brought it for you. This is a bizarre honeymoon, Mother. I mean, what's the point if all the two of you are going to do is correspond? We could have stayed home."

Ignoring her, I went into the parlor and nodded at the man. "Thank you."

He smiled. "It is my pleasure. My name is Abdullah, and I will be your houseman for your time with us. If there is any little thing I can do to make your stay most pleasant, please call the desk and they will send me here. Are your rooms to your liking?"

"Everything is lovely," I said.

"Would madam care to order breakfast, or will you prefer the buffet on the patio adjoining the restaurant? It is served until ten o'clock."

Caron gave him a wary look. "I don't know about this buffet. I need something more substantial than pickled onions and hummus."

"Oh no, miss," Abdullah said. "Many of our guests are British or American. You will find toast and eggs, cereal, and fruit, and also cold meats and cheeses. The bacon and sausages are made of turkey meat, but I am told they are tasty."

Inez sounded disappointed as she said, "No traditional Arab dishes?"

"Those, also," he said, smiling at her.

"We'll go down to the buffet," I said to Abdullah. "I don't believe there's anything else we need right now. Thank you very much for the coffee."

After he'd left, I poured myself a cup of coffee. I opened

the envelope and read Peter's note, then said, "He apologizes for missing our arrival, but will be here in time to take us out to dinner. He suggests we spend the day resting or exploring the area around the hotel. There are plenty of shops within a block or two. We can have lunch here."

"Is that all?" asked Caron.

"The rest is personal." I tucked the note in my bathrobe pocket. "Give me ten minutes to get dressed; then we'll go downstairs for breakfast." The girls were wearing shorts, T-shirts, and sandals. The guidebooks had sworn that such attire was suitable for tourist activities, with the exception of holy Muslim sites. I opted for slacks and a cotton blouse, ran a comb through my red curls, and put the heavy room key in my purse.

When we reached the multi-leveled lobby, with its impressively high ceiling, plush carpets, brass urns holding plants, and grandiose staircase, the manager hurried over. I vaguely recognized him from the previous afternoon when we'd staggered into the hotel, bleary and shell-shocked.

"Good morning, *Sitt* Malloy-Rosen," he said, beaming at me. "I hope you had a nice long sleep and that the traffic did not disturb you. Some nights the drivers honk their cars and drummers gather on the pier. In the old days, our valued guests were obliged to endure only the clopping of horses as they pulled carriages along the corniche. Now, the youths have radios that blare more loudly than braying camels. We at the Winter Palace can only apologize and beg your forgiveness."

It seemed to me that "in the old days" the manager was more likely to have been wearing diapers instead of a black suit and a striped tie. "It's not a problem," I said. "All cities are noisy."

"Yes, you are so very correct. Cairo is much, much worse. Here we have only one hundred and fifty thousand citizens. Cairo has ten million, with air that smells very bad and much poverty and crime. You and Mr. Rosen are wise to bring your young ladies here to Luxor. I do hope he will be joining you soon."

The final remark was more of a request for information than a sentiment. I chose to overlook it. "We're looking forward to seeing all the wonderful archeological wonders of Luxor, but right now we're more interested in breakfast. If you'll be so kind as to point us in the right direction . . ."

"I shall escort you." He barked something in Arabic to a desk clerk, then gestured at a short flight of steps up to a hallway. "The restaurants and patio dining are in the New Winter Palace, which was added to accommodate those who are unable to afford the Winter Palace. You are in the Presidential Suite. Directly across the hall is a stairwell that will take you to the New Winter Palace. This will save you the necessity of walking down the corridor to the elevators to come through the lobby. The entrance is not so grand there, but you may find it convenient. We at the Winter Palace are very proud of our marble staircases from the driveway to the lobby, which have been shown in many American movies. Perhaps you have seen *Death on the Nile,* based on a novel by Agatha Christie? She was a very fine writer of mystery novels. She visited Cairo when she was a girl, and her second husband was a noted archeologist. Many famous archeologists have stayed here at the Winter Palace, including Howard Carter, who found King Tut's tomb almost ninety years ago. You will see many photographs of him and his benefactor, the Earl of Carnarvon, in our bar."

I silently vowed to avoid the lobby in the future. Behind me I heard a noise that was either rumbling or grumbling, which suggested I was not the only one with the same idea. By the time we reached the patio door, I knew that the manager's name was Ahmed, that he was born in Luxor, learned English as a purser on an British ship, had a cousin in Milwaukee, and would die in order to protect us from speeding taxis. I stopped him before he could seat us at a table and drape napkins on our laps, and sent him away as graciously as possible. The girls and I perused the buffet and returned to our table with standard American fare.

"That man is a menace," Caron said as she spread jam on a roll.

Inez nodded. "It's tempting to go stand in the middle of the corniche and see if he keeps his word."

"He's just trying to be helpful," I said. "Egyptians are friendly, and they cherish tourists, who are vital to the economy. Ever since the—" I caught myself before I blurted out the phrase "terrorist attacks."

"Ever since what?" demanded Caron.

"The discovery of the tomb of King Tutankhamun," I said quickly. "In 1922, by Howard Carter. Nearly ten million tourists come to Egypt every year."

Inez gazed at me. Unlike Caron, whose sole preparation for the trip had been to watch *Lawrence of Arabia* and shop for sunglasses, Inez had read everything I had at my bookstore, then moved on to the Farber College library. I'd overheard her trying to teach Caron a few words of Arabic. I could tell from Inez's expression that she knew about the terrorist attack at the Temple of Hatshepsut in 1997 and the more recent incidents at resorts on the Red Sea. She also knew how Caron would respond if the topic was aired.

"Oh yeah," Caron said, examining the omelet on her plate for any hint that an alien ingredient might have been slipped inside it despite her vigilance.

I asked a waiter to bring me a pot of tea, then forced myself to eat a piece of toast and a few bites of melon. The tedious trip had not only exhausted me, but also confused my body. We'd been plied with food and drink along the way, although not with any reference to my internal rhythm. It would be wise, I thought, to take things easy for a day or two until I was acclimatized. Caron and Inez appeared to have already done so, but they were seventeen and thought nothing of staying up all night to watch movies, feast on junk food, and paint their toenails cerise.

"Howdy, ma'am and little ladies. You reckon I might join you?" The speaker, a tall man with thick gray hair combed into a sculpted pompadour, pulled out a chair and sat down across from me. He wore a white suit, ornately detailed leather boots, and a bolo tie; all that was missing was a broad-brimmed hat with a rattlesnake band. "Please send me off with my tail between my legs if I'm interrupting, ma'am. I've spent the last week minglin' with the natives, and I was thinking it would be right nice to talk to some Americans for a change. Name's Sittermann, from Houston in the great state of Texas. I'm what you call an entrepreneur. I'm lookin' into building a theme park outside of Cairo, with a roller coaster, water slides, rides, and costumed characters like King Tut and Cleopatra."

"You're welcome to join us," I said inanely, since he already had and was waving at a waiter.

"This your first time in Egypt?" he asked.

Caron and Inez were both glaring at him. I frowned at them, then said, "Yes, it is, Mr. Sittermann, but not yours, I gather."

He spoke in Arabic to the waiter, then sat back and said, "You're very astute, Mrs. . . . ?"

"Malloy. This is my daughter, Caron, and her friend, Inez."

"I hope you enjoy yourselves. There's all sorts of places to see in Luxor, presuming you like to look at old rocks. The Temple of Luxor's right next to the hotel, but you got to walk a good ways to the entrance to go inside."

Inez regained control of herself. "Primarily built by Amenhotep, from 1390 to 1352 B.C., on the site of a sanctuary built by Hatshepsut and dedicated to the deities Amun, Mut, and Khons. Amun was the most important god of Thebes, later worshipped as Amun-Ra."

Caron threw her napkin on the table. "Enough, okay? I am not going to spend the next two weeks in a dreary documentary that drones on and on about every stupid little name and date. I would rather throw myself off the balcony. Mother, promise that you'll take my body home for a proper burial. I don't want to spend eternity being gnawed by jackals." She shoved back her chair. "I'm going up to the room to see what's on TV. I'm sure Egyptian cable will be more fascinating than this."

She stalked into the hotel. After a moment, Inez placed her napkin next to her plate and followed her. A waiter

swept in and removed their glasses and plates. A nondescript brown bird fluttered to the table and began to peck at
crumbs.

"We're all tired," I said to Sittermann. "We arrived late
yesterday afternoon."

"No need to apologize, Mrs. Malloy. I know how it is
with young folks. One minute they're all courteous and
charming, and the next minute they're spoiled brats. Jet lag
brings out the worst side in some folks."

"They are not spoiled brats," I said with a trace of cold-
ness, not mentioning that this was hardly their worst side.

"Why, I'd never imply they were. I was just making a
general observation. I'm sure that your young ladies will recover their good spirits when they've rested up." He refilled
his coffee cup from the small pot. "Will Mr. Malloy be joining you soon?"

Only as a mummy, I thought, resisting the urge to giggle
at the image that popped into my mind. Carlton Malloy, my
first husband, was residing in the cemetery in Farberville,
due to an unfortunately close encounter with a chicken truck
on a snowy mountain road, and, more unfortunately, in the
company of one of his more curvaceous blond students. The
scandalous details had been hushed up by the college ad-
ministration, but their exposure by a romance writer had
resulted in murder. Lieutenant Peter Rosen had had the audacity to suspect me, then almost crossed the line by accus-
ing me of flouncing. It had made for a tenuous start to our
relationship. "I very much doubt that," I said, then took a sip
of tea.

"It's brave of you to travel without a man to watch out for
you. Egypt's not as bad as some of the Arab countries, but
pretty women like yourself are liable to attract unwanted attention."

"I'm sure they do," I said, "but the girls and I are capable
of taking care of ourselves."

"All the same, I'd be honored to escort you all on any of
your excursions. I've been doing business over here for a
long while. I can't say that I understand how they think, but

I know for a fact that they're more than willing to take advantage of single women, especially Westerners. Be real careful about being overcharged, even by the hotel staff. Any man who so much as opens a door for you will expect baksheesh, but just brush 'em off like flies. Don't ever get in a taxi without settling on a price first."

"Thank you for your advice," I said, wondering if he was distantly related to the hotel manager. "However, my husband will be joining us this evening, so you need not concern yourself further."

I expected my boorish companion to question this, but he merely shrugged. "That takes a load off my mind, Mrs. Malloy. I just didn't want to think about you and the little fillies being pestered and cheated on account of your sex. How long will you be staying here in Luxor?"

"I really couldn't say, Mr. Sittermann. If you'll excuse me, I'd like to check on the girls. It's a long drop from the balcony, and my daughter is capable of almost anything."

"You must be staying in the Presidential Suite. I hear it's right fancy."

"Good day," I said, then went into the hotel. After a brief debate, I tackled the stairwell and arrived, albeit panting, on the third floor across the hall from our suite. As I opened the door, I heard Inez's voice from their bedroom.

" 'Her heart began to pound as she studied his cruel gray eyes and the sneer that tugged at his lips. She knew he was watching her while he twirled the jewel-encrusted dagger in his calloused hands, watching for any sign of weakness from her. What more could he want from her? He'd brutally ravished her that first horrible night. She felt heat color her face as she remembered how he'd torn off her blouse, and then seized her breasts as if he owned them. Despite her cries of protest, he'd overpowered her and forced her to surrender to his despicable desires until the sun rose over the dunes.' "

Inez turned the page of the book she held, oblivious to my intrusion. " 'She vowed, as she had done every waking moment since he'd kidnapped her at the oasis, that she would never bend beneath his piercing stare, nor submit willingly to his brutish demands. He could have his way with her body, she thought bitterly, but she would never allow him to forget that he was a filthy native, a dark-skinned heathen worthy of nothing more than her contempt, while she was a lady of breeding. No, she would never give him the satisfaction of seeing her weep or plead for mercy.' "

"What are you reading?" I asked, appalled.

"The Savage Sheik."

Caron, who was flopped across the bed, raised her head. "It should be called *Gone with the Sirocco.* I'm sure it must have titillated the upper-class British ladies back in the nineteen-twenties, but it's impossibly silly these days. She practically swoons every time he exhales."

Inez pulled off her glasses and cleaned them on her shirt. "Then I won't bore you with it anymore."

"Fine with me." Caron flopped back across the bed and fluttered her hands. "Bring me my smelling salts. I am overwhelmed with repressed lust for the filthy native and his deadly dagger. Ravage me, you savage!"

"You have no concept of period literature," Inez said huffily.

I decided both of them needed a nap before they lapsed any further into hostility. I could not suggest such a juvenile thing, so I opted for tact. "Why don't we go out for a little while? I need to change some money, and there's a bank right outside the hotel entrance. We can wander around and look in some of the shops, then come back here for lunch and a rest. Then, if you'd like, we can have tea on the terrace and wait for Peter."

Caron brightened at the idea of shopping and began to rummage through her suitcase. Inez reluctantly put down her book and disappeared into the bathroom. I went to the master bedroom, noting that the bed had been made and the bathroom supplied with fresh towels, and made sure I had my passport and a few hundred dollars in traveler's checks. Even though I'd been dazed when we arrived at the hotel, I had noticed the shops' windows cluttered with jewelry and

designer fashions. I am not miserly by nature, but I'd struggled to earn a living from my beloved bookstore. It had
seemed like a dream when I'd leased the old depot and
carefully stocked it with racks and shelves of books. Within
three months, reality had settled in like a bad head cold. My
competition came from the chain bookstores at the mall and,
more recently, from online sources. I relied on the campus
community and a decreasing number of regular customers
with eclectic taste or a fondness for pop fiction genres they
preferred to purchase discreetly.

In this situation, which was admittedly peculiar since
very few couples take teenagers with them on a honeymoon,
Peter insisted on loading me up with traveler's checks.
When I protested, he countered with the price of a single airplane ticket to Luxor. There was a flaw in the logic, but I'd
acquiesced with a becoming blush. Even brides slightly over
forty years of age are allowed such things, as long as they
don't flutter their eyelashes and simper. Or swoon.

"Let's use the stairs and go out through the New Winter
Palace lobby," I suggested as we went into the hall. I spotted
Abdullah watching us from behind a cart laden with cleaning supplies. I gave him a small wave, then followed the
girls down to the less impressive lobby. Several of the male
employees (I'd yet to see a female one), all dressed in white
coats and red fezzes, nodded at us as we went outside.

Within the walls of the hotel compound was a walkway
lined with shops. Caron and Inez paused at a window filled
with T-shirts and hats, while I went into a tiny bank branch
and armed myself with a thick stack of Egyptian pound
notes. I caught up with the girls at a shop selling scarves and
perfume.

"This stuff is so expensive," Caron said morosely. "Some
of the T-shirts are eighty pounds. There are some cute sandals for a hundred pounds. I know Peter wants us to buy
things, but this is ridiculous."

"Divide by five for dollars," I said. "Before you get too
carried away with these shops, let's look into some local
ones. There's a mall of sorts just past the corner."

"A mall?" echoed Inez.

"More like an alley," I said. "The man at the bank told me about it. This is a tourist area, so the prices will still be on the high side. We might as well have a look, though." I did not add that we would pass by a bookstore on the way. It's an addiction that cannot be easily explained and can rarely be overcome.

The temperature was warm but comfortable, as promised by the guidebook. We strolled along the side of the corniche, ignoring the carriage drivers and shoeshine boys clamoring for our attention. Shop owners came out and begged us to consider their offerings, which were, of course, available at the best prices in Luxor. Inside a newsstand, two boys were playing a game on a computer. An ancient man shaped like a pear sat on a folding stool, scowling at his Arabic newspaper and puffing on a water pipe. Many of the men wore long white robes and some had sweat-stained cloths tied around their heads. A gaggle of schoolgirls passed us, wearing dark scarves and long skirts but also sandals adorned with plastic flowers and glass beads.

A sandwich board announced the so-called mall. We turned into the passageway crowded with souvenir shops and racks of T-shirts. I looked around curiously as the girls cooed over plush toy camels and plastic sphinxes. I had managed to walk by the bookstore without a whimper, but I could feel its seductive allure. I decided I could interest the girls in postcards on our way back to the hotel. I drifted away from the T-shirt racks and began to look at jewelry in a window. I needed to take back a gift for Sergeant Jorgeson and his wife, who'd hosted our wedding in their garden, and one for Luanne Bradshaw, my best friend and confidante. I needed to find something that was either hysterically tacky or incredibly tasteful for her. A piece of antique jewelry might fit either category.

Caron caught my elbow and dragged me into a tiny shop overpowered with shelves of tablecloths and tea towels. "Mother," she whispered, "I think we're being followed."

"I'm sure we are, dear. We're tourists. We might as well

have bull's-eyes pinned on our backs proclaiming us to be rich and foolish."

"No, I saw him at the hotel, too. He was sitting near the exit, pretending to read a newspaper."

"Maybe he *was* reading a newspaper," I said.

"He looked right at us when we walked by him."

I grinned. "He may be planning on making an offer for you. How many camels are you worth? A hundred? Should I hold out for more?"

Caron's lower lip shot out. "You are So Not Funny. What if he's trying to figure out how to kidnap us?"

Inez scuttled into the shop and began to wheeze. "He spoke to me," she said between gasps. "I was looking at this really cute puppet when he brushed against me and said, '*Ahlan wa-sahlan.*' I think that's what he said, anyway. I almost screamed."

I frowned. "Any idea what it meant?"

She gulped. "If I heard it right, it means 'hello.'"

"And then . . . ?" I said.

"He turned away and said something to the owner, who laughed and said something back. I know they were talking about me."

"What are you going to do, Mother?" demanded Caron.

Gazing solemnly at them, I said, "I'm going to pop in that bookstore and see if they carry books in English. If they do, I may browse for an hour and perhaps buy some postcards. After that, I'm going to go back to the hotel and have a light lunch on the patio. Would you two care to join me?"

"What if he's stalking us?" demanded Caron.

"That's a strong word," I said, shaking my head. "Is he Egyptian?"

Inez shrugged. "Arab, anyway, with a droopy mustache and a scar across his cheek. He has on sunglasses, a plaid sport jacket, and wrinkled trousers. He looks like the villain in an old movie like *Casablanca*."

I glanced out the shop window. "I don't see anybody who looks remotely like that." The shopkeeper was moving in on us, his eyes bright and his smile painfully broad. I nudged

the girls toward the door. "Let's go to the bookstore. If you
spot this man, you can point him out to me."

"Then you believe us?" Caron said.

I didn't, but I also didn't want to linger and end up with
a tablecloth and matching napkins. "I believe you captured
the attention of an Arab gentleman who most likely thinks
the two of you are attractive and charming, and is hoping
for an opportunity to make your acquaintance." I lowered
my voice. "Then fling you across his camel and carry you to
his oasis, where he will ravish you nightly and force you to
wear emeralds in your navels."

"Mother!"

I allowed them to sputter while I herded them back to the
bookstore. Neither claimed to see their less-than-dashing
sheik, and eventually they began to look at postcards. The
bookstore was much mustier than mine, and dusty enough
to elicit several explosive sneezes from me. I dabbed my
eyes with a handkerchief while I examined the shelves of
worn covers and titles in a bewildering array of languages. I
was looking at an ornithology guide when Caron and Inez
tracked me down and admitted they were tired.

The two salesclerks did not look up as we left. We turned
onto the corniche and headed for the hotel. The grand staircase that led up to the lobby of the Winter Palace looked
daunting, so we continued past the low wall to the entrance
of the New Winter Palace.

Abruptly Caron stopped. "There he is!" she squeaked.
"Going in the lobby! Do you see him, Mother? The same
man!"

I paused. "I see a businessman returning to his hotel."

"That's the man," Inez said, squeaking less vehemently
than Caron but doing her best. "The one who has been following us."

"Now's your chance to reciprocate," I said, "unless you
want to stand out here and dither the rest of the day. I'm not
in the mood for lunch. I'm going to buy a newspaper and go
up to our suite. You can either eat lunch downstairs or come
up and order room service."

Ten minutes later I was on the balcony, reading the previous day's newspaper and listening to snores from the bedroom on the far side of the parlor.

Thus far, my honeymoon had been less than romantic—but the moon had yet to rise above the Nile.

CHAPTER 2

Caron, Inez, and I were having tea on the terrace when Peter arrived. He was accompanied by an Egyptian man in a rumpled suit, who waited at a polite distance while Peter greeted me as warmly as he dared in front of the girls. "I hope you all made it with a minimum of fuss," he said.

"It took forever," said Caron, not yet recovered from her nap. "Ten thousand miles, at least. Maybe more."

Inez put down her teacup and stared solemnly at him. "It's slightly less than seven thousand, if one travels in a straight line. Since we flew through Frankfurt, it was actually—"

"A very long way," I said. "Would you and your friend care to join us?"

Peter, who was rather tan for someone who supposedly had been in meetings for two weeks, gestured to the man. "This is Chief Inspector Mahmoud el-Habachi, of the local tourist security office. Mahmoud, this is my wife, Claire Malloy, her daughter, Caron, and Inez Thornton, our resident scholar. Mahmoud and his wife, Aisha, have invited me for meals at their home several times. Aisha is looking forward to meeting you."

We exchanged pleasantries as Mahmoud sat down. Although a relatively young man, Mahmoud had the same air of resignation as that of Peter's beleaguered sergeant in the Farberville PD. Bureaucracies seem to breed gray hairs and weary smiles, as if they were standard issue along with badges. Both Mahmoud and Peter needed to have their hair trimmed and their suits sent to a dry cleaner. A waiter in a starchy white jacket materialized at the table. Peter requested a gin and tonic, and I acknowledged that I might enjoy one as well.

Mahmoud opted for a glass of lemonade. "I am Muslim and do not drink alcoholic beverages. I do not object when others do, although it grieves me to see our younger generation sneering at the old traditions and ignoring their religious training." He laughed ruefully. "I suppose that is precisely what my parents said about me and my friends, and their parents said about them. It is now the twenty-first century. We must all adapt, or so my children keep telling me when they're not playing their computer games or downloading music."

Caron and Inez rolled their eyes at each other, then realized I was looking at them and returned their attention to the platters of sandwiches and cakes.

"Peter tells me that you two were married quite recently," Mahmoud continued. "Aisha and I have been married for nearly twelve years, but she still complains that I work too late and never have time for her and our three children. One day she will be complaining that I never have time for our grandchildren. I can see that you are not as naive as she is, *Sitt* Malloy."

"Call me Claire, please. Peter managed to show up for the ceremony, but we haven't had much time together since then. I hope he'll be able to show us around. I'm particularly excited at the chance to see the Valley of the Kings."

Mahmoud gave Peter one of those indecipherable male glances, then said, "You have at your disposal a car and driver." He took a card out of his wallet and handed it to me. "Please call this number half an hour before you wish to depart. Bakr will be available day or evening to take you to your chosen destination and wait while you take all the time you wish to appreciate the sites. He will also run errands and make purchases for you, although it might be best to write down specifically what you want. Bakr speaks English fairly well, but he is no better than any man when it comes to ladies' cosmetics and toiletries. To us, shampoo is shampoo. I know my wife has exacting preferences as to brands."

"Thank you very much," I said. "Do we have any idea about an itincrary, Peter?"

My darling husband, with his lovely brown eyes and dazzling smile (all of which could have a profound effect on me in amorous moments), reached over and held my hand. "I have nothing on my schedule tomorrow. You seem a little tired from the trip, so I thought you might prefer to spend a restful day at the hotel. Bakr can take Caron and Inez to the temples at Karnak and arrange for a private tour." He smiled at the girls, who were looking leery at the idea of a lengthy lecture on history. "Whenever you've had enough, Bakr will take you to a café for ice cream or whatever you wish. Later you can return for the sound-and-light show. How does that sound?"

Caron grimaced. "It sounds like you're trying to get rid of us for the day."

"Yes, I am," Peter said. "I haven't seen my wife for a month."

"Karnak is cool," Inez volunteered before Caron could respond. "It has a hypostyle hall and a sacred lake, and all sorts of reliefs and hieroglyphs on the wall. It was the most important place of worship in Egypt during the Theban period. It was called something that means 'The Most Perfect of Places.'"

We all waited for Caron to pronounce judgment. I, of course, would have her mummified and entombed in the Valley of the Drama Queens if she turned truculent. Finally, she sat back and sighed. "Yeah, that's okay, as long as we get to shop."

Mahmoud finished his lemonade and rose. He shook Peter's hand, then nodded to us and said, "Please call Bakr and tell him your plans. He will make sure to find out the location of the very best shops. Do not worry about letting him wait for you. He's on salary, so he will be content to sit in the car and read one of his tasteless paperback books. He will have an ample supply of bottled water and snacks for you in the car. If you will be so kind as to excuse me, I will hurry home. My son is participating in a concert at his school this evening, and Aisha is firm that I must go sit on a folding chair and pretend to enjoy the music. I have heard my son practicing his violin, so I know it will be abysmal, like the screeching of ravens in a field. I hope to see all of you soon. Good day." He went down to the curb and got into the back-seat of a black car. Seconds later the car slipped into the traffic and was lost from view.

"Can we go to the shops on the hotel grounds?" asked Caron. "I want to try on those sandals."

Peter opened his wallet and handed her several bills. "I'm sure you and Inez can find a few things that fit. We'll wait here." Once they'd left, he loosened his tie and unbuttoned his shirt collar. "How's the Presidential Suite, *Sitt* Malloy?"

"Stately," I said. "Where have you been staying since you got here?"

"Part of the time at the New Winter Palace and in a generic hotel in Cairo. I've been to Aswan, Port Said, Alexandria, and Ras Gharib, too. Mahmoud and a security specialist from the American Embassy have had me in meetings or on the road since the day I arrived. I'm as exhausted as you are. That's not to imply I'm going to sleep all day tomorrow. I have other ideas as well."

"I should hope so."

We were exchanging wicked smiles when a young man appeared at the table.

"Be ever so kind as to forgive me if I'm intruding," he said in an exaggerated British drawl. He had dark hair and wore a freshly ironed shirt with an ascot, and white trousers. His face was lightly tanned and smooth, as though he spent his days playing tennis or croquet with vapid young women from only the best families. I couldn't help comparing him to my image of Bertie Wooster, the amiable ne'er-do-well in the Wodehouse novels. "My father and I are sitting at a table over there. He's convinced that you must be Claire Malloy, and insisted that I make inquiries. I'm Alexander Bledrock, by the way. Shall I return to our table and tell him that he's a meddlesome old man?"

Peter looked up, annoyed. "Why does your father care?"

Alexander flopped down in the chair recently abandoned by Caron. He took out a thin gold case and selected a dark cigarette, tapped it against the case, and lit it. "I wouldn't go so far as to say he cares," he said, exhaling a plume of smoke. "He's curious, as are all the members of his little coterie. They come here every fall at the beginning of the season to ascertain if there are any promising excavations in progress. Most of them remain until the worst of the winter weather in England has passed, then go home and brag about descending into pits and surviving the lack of televised cricket matches."

I looked across the terrace at a portly man in a gray suit. He had a fringe of white hair, bushy white eyebrows that contrasted with his ruddy complexion, and a small, fussy mouth almost lost under an equally bushy white mustache. He wiggled his fingers at me as if he were a flirtatious walrus. "That's your father?" I asked, doing a bit of arithmetic in my head.

"His first wife died in a riding accident, and the second ran off with a bishop, or so the gossip goes. My mother was his third wife. He was thirty years older than she, but she was more interested in his title and his money than in a titillating relationship. She died when I was ten, probably out of boredom. Being mistress of a vast estate may sound glamorous, but she discovered that having to live there was monotonous at best."

I tried to control myself, but I couldn't. "Title?"

"The old boy's the Baron of Rochland," Alexander said, grinning at me. "Impressed?"

Peter was not. "Why is he curious about my wife? She only arrived yesterday."

Alexander beckoned to a waiter and ordered a brandy and soda. "You have to understand that the expatriate community here is small. The same people come year after year, and will continue to do so until they take their last barge ride to the netherworld. A few of them have villas in the outskirts of town, but most stay at the Winter Palace from October until March or April. Every now and then someone arranges an outing to a museum or an excavation site. They dutifully attend lectures about mummification or controversial interpretations of depictions of water lilies during the twenty-first dynasty. Once or twice during the season, the British ambassador invites them for tea in Cairo. Other than that, all they do is play bridge, congratulate themselves for avoiding the weather back home, complain about the service, and drink themselves silly at cocktail parties. Therefore, they're always madly curious about newcomers."

"But why me?" I asked.

"It began several weeks ago, when Ahmed—the toady hotel manager—went into a tizzy about your arrival. The poor chap was dreadfully distraught because he didn't know if he was to address you as *Sitt* Rosen or *Sitt* Malloy. He was scandalized at the thought you might not be properly married, and terrified that you might report him if he made the wrong assumption and offended either of you. He begged us for guidance. This led to highly spirited debates over gin rickeys and cucumber sandwiches, at times resulting in emphatic incoherency. I thought it was quite jolly. Then Miriam McHaver, who's here as a companion to her great-aunt, took the initiative and searched for your name on the Internet. The fact that you've been mentioned in conjunction with murder investigations kept us entertained for another week. Some of the ladies are absolutely giddy with speculation, as is my father. So there you have it, Mrs. Malloy, or Mrs. Rosen if you prefer. Your reputation has preceded you."

"And exceeded me," I said. "I am here on my honeymoon. My daughter and a friend came along, since I knew my husband would be occupied with business concerns part of the time."

Alexander eyed me for a moment, then turned to Peter. "Mr. Rosen, please don't be aggrieved because you've been neglected by the busybodies. What sort of business are you in?"

"Development," said Peter.

"How fascinating. Not a ski lodge, one assumes."

"I represent a company in the States that's considering building a resort a few miles south of Luxor. I'm exploring the legal aspects."

Alexander raised his eyebrows. "So you're a solicitor—no, I suppose the proper word is 'attorney.' 'Soliciting' has a negative connotation in America, doesn't it? Well, do forgive me and accept my father's invitation for a cocktail party tomorrow evening in his suite. It will be quite the fcather in his cap if he is the one to introduce the mysterious Claire Malloy to his compatriots. Shall we say six o'clock or thereabouts?"

I was surprised when Peter agreed, since I could think of nothing less agreeable than chatting with rich, bored Brits (with or without titles). Lord Bledrock, as I supposed he was called, was the stereotypic aristocrat. I could envision him sputtering at the butler when the eggs were not properly coddled. Lord Bledrock would pay his staff a pittance and throw away a hefty sum on a horse race.

"My father will be elated." Alexander finished his drink and stood up. "I'll pop by your suite and escort you. Mrs. Malloy, your presence will do much to liven things up, especially if you stumble across a fresh corpse. We're more accustomed to withered old mummies around here. In fact, you'll be introduced to some tomorrow evening." He ambled away and joined his father, whose eyes were bulging with excitement. With only a minor costume change, he could have been plucked from a Hogarth engraving set in an eighteenth-century house of ill repute.

"I hope you don't mind," Peter said to me. "It's . . . ah, business."

I kept my mouth shut while I reminded myself that Peter was not only my adoring husband and the object of my lustful passion, but also working with the nameless intelligence agencies. He had a reason for accepting the invitation, and we'd agreed that I would remain uninformed.

Caron and Inez came back to the table, each carrying a

plastic bag. Caron looked at our glasses, then said, "Do we have to drink tea? I'd rather have something cold. Do they have Coke or Pepsi?"

"There are some sodas in the mini-bar," I said, "and we can order a bucket of ice from room service. Shall we retreat upstairs?"

As we headed for the entrance, I noticed that I was being studied by various other patrons on the patio. Slitted eyes peered at me over the tops of newspapers and magazines. Conversations halted. I felt as though I had an unseemly stain on the seat of my slacks. Lord Bledrock was openly staring from beneath his bushy eyebrows as he sipped a glass of what appeared to be whiskey. Ahmed approached us as we went through the lobby, but Peter waved him off and clung to my arm until we reached the elevator.

Once we were safely in the suite, Caron and Inez retreated to their bedroom to gloat over their purchases. Peter and I went out to the balcony and sat down.

"Why," I said in a level voice, "did Ahmed go into a tizzy about how to address me?"

"I suppose because someone from the American Embassy made the reservation and specified this particular suite. Ahmed must have presumed that one of us is a high-level government dignitary. Presidents, prime ministers, celebrities, and royals have always stayed at the Winter Palace. Protocol must be observed. It's unfortunate that Ahmed made an issue of it. We're supposed to be ordinary tourists—a businessman, his wife, and their teenaged daughter and her friend."

"We're your cover?"

"Something like that," Peter admitted.

"Are we in any danger? I'd like to be warned so that I can carry a parasol to fend off attackers. In college, one of my physical ed electives was fencing. I wonder if I can find one with a metal blade in the shaft."

Peter considered this, then said, "You'll have to ask Bakr if he knows of a shop that sells that kind of thing. I doubt you can take it through security on the way home, though."

"You didn't answer my question."

"No, you're not in any danger. There is a rumor, unconfirmed and sketchy, that suggests that a militant Islamist organization is planning something that will have a major negative impact on the tourism industry and lead to a political crisis. Mahmoud has had very poor luck with infiltrating the organization, and his usual informers are too frightened to cooperate. However, if anything is going to happen, it will be early next year."

"If Mahmoud knows so little, then how can he know that nothing's going to happen tomorrow?"

Peter sighed. "He and others in the internal security agencies do have sources. They've intercepted e-mails and decoded encrypted messages on otherwise innocuous Web sites. They watch the ports for incoming shipments that might contain weapons or explosives, and they keep track of certain individuals' whereabouts."

"This sounds like the plot of one of those six-hundred-page thrillers," I said, unamused. "I'd much prefer a romance novel, with a moonlit beach and the distant sound of sentimental music. The only sounds I've heard so far are the prerecorded calls to prayer from the minarets. You'd think they'd go off at the same time, but no one seems to agree on the precise time."

"The muezzins aren't obsessed with Greenwich mean time. I'll fix drinks and we can sit here and watch the sunset over the Nile. That's romantic, isn't it?"

"It's not bad," I said, "as long as there's a second act."

Caron and Inez had already left for their outing to Karnak when I emerged from the master bedroom the following morning. Peter was asleep and showed no signs of stirring any time soon. I ordered coffee and rolls from room service, then went out to the balcony. On the terrace below I saw Sittermann in his white suit, drinking coffee and reading a newspaper. It must have been an old newspaper, since he was not too engrossed to watch other patrons as they settled at other tables and ordered from the hovering waiters. If he was lurking in hopes of finding other Americans, I wished him luck—and wished them my condolences. I've never considered myself to be a designated soul mate of any of my fellow 300 million Americans (Inez would know the exact figure) simply because we were in a foreign country. I am not the sort of tourist who stays in the dull familiarity of a Hilton, eats at the local McDonald's, and behaves rudely to the natives who don't speak English. This is not to imply that if I were visiting Mongolia, I would rent a yurt and subsist on curdled yak milk. I do have my minimum level of creature comforts.

I watched the triangular-sailed boats (feluccas, according to my guidebook) until I heard a gentle tap on the door. I admitted Abdullah, who beamed at me as he carried in a laden tray and put it on the coffee table.

"I trust madam is rested," he murmured as he began to arrange things. "I saw the young misses as they left through the lobby earlier. They are enjoying Luxor?" Without being asked, he carried the coffee carafe, cups, and saucers out to the table on the balcony, then returned for the milk pitcher, basket of rolls, and silverware wrapped in linen napkins. "Madam is enjoying Luxor, too?"

"Yes, thank you." I obediently returned to the balcony, where he had tacitly decreed I was to have my breakfast. "Now that my husband has arrived, I look forward to admiring all the temples and tombs."

"Madam will be careful, yes?"

"I've been told there's very little street crime. I know to drink bottled water and avoid fresh fruits and vegetables unless they have been peeled. I don't think I'll find myself in danger of being trampled by a camel, if that's what you mean. Or a dromedary, for that matter."

"The danger comes from those who will attempt to deceive you."

"What kind of danger?" I said, startled. "Who are you talking about, Abdullah?"

He gazed at the mountains across the Nile, his expression unfathomable. "I am an old man whose mind wanders. Please call room service when you are finished and I will come back for the tray. Will you be wishing to have your rooms cleaned?"

"Just the bedroom and bath on that side," I said, indicating Caron and Inez's quarters. "I believe there's a separate door to the corridor."

Abdullah bowed slightly. "As madam wishes."

After he was gone, I sat down and poured a cup of coffee. His obscure warning, coupled with Peter's remarks about a terrorist organization, disturbed me. The thought of sending Caron and Inez off for the day had seemed like a lovely idea, but now I wanted them to burst into the parlor with rustling plastic bags and smears of ice cream on their chins. I reminded myself that Bakr's references came from Chief Inspector Mahmoud el-Habachi. It was foolish to be alarmed by a houseman who could be well on his way to senility, or took malicious pleasure in alarming guests. I trusted Peter, and he trusted Mahmoud.

I went into the girls' room and found Inez's copy of *The Savage Sheik* on her bedside table. I took it back to the balcony, buttered a roll, then settled back. As ludicrous as it was, it proved to be engrossing.

The minarets were blaring when Peter finally came out of the bedroom. Although he lacked the sheik's supercilious sneer, he did look complacent. "Did you sleep well?" he asked as he sat down.

"Very well, thank you," I said. "Would you like me to order fresh coffee?"

"I thought we might go have lunch at a restaurant across the road. For some reason, I'm ravenous. Must be because of all that exercise last night. I hope the girls couldn't hear us when we were in the bathtub. I must say, *Sitt* Malloy, you are quite a talented mermaid."

Modesty prevented me from agreeing with him. "The girls were exhausted. Inez almost fell asleep at dinner, and I doubt Caron had any idea what she was eating. I heard them leaving at about nine this morning. I'm a little nervous about them going off with this driver."

Peter put his arms around me. "Bakr is a police officer. Mahmoud introduced him to me at the department. He's around thirty years old and lives with his parents. He may never rise very high in the ranks, but he's solid and methodical. He also knows that if you or the girls have a complaint, he'll be bumped down to traffic control. If that happens, his fiancée's parents will end the relationship and poor Bakr will be stuck at home with his old-fashioned father and mother, and three whiny sisters."

"In that case, I'm more nervous about him. Caron can be tyrannical when she senses she has the upper hand."

We took the elevator to the lobby and paused to admire the marble staircase. Ahmed materialized beside us, clasping his hands together. "Ah, Mr. Rosen and *Sitt* . . . Malloy-Rosen, I hope you are enjoying the amenities of your suite. If there's anything I can do, please do not hesitate to tell me. It will be an honor for me to serve you personally."

"It's adequate," Peter said gravely, "but the flowers are beginning to wilt. The young ladies are particularly fond of tangerines. I do hope there will be fresh ones every day. *Sitt* Malloy enjoys reading a newspaper with her morning coffee. *The Times,* and perhaps the *International Herald Tribune.*"

"Yes, of course," Ahmed said, backing away like a rabbit confronted by a coyote. "Fresh tangerines and flowers, and newspapers. I blame myself for not seeing to this already. Do accept my most humble apologies."

Peter and I continued to the porch and down one of the curved staircases. I waited until we reached the sidewalk alongside the corniche before I giggled. "The King of Prussia and his consort must have flowers, tangerines, and the news. I'm surprised you didn't order the man to lick the dust off your shoes."

Peter clutched my elbow and we darted across the first

lane to the median. "I might have, if I weren't wearing sandals. I don't want his tongue on my toes."

I fell silent, blushing as I recalled some of the activities the previous night. We made it safely to the pier, then went down a flight of stairs to a row of shops and restaurants along one side of a pedestrian walkway. On the other side was the Nile, a silky expanse of light chocolate-hued water, rippling from the wakes of crowded ferries and private runabouts. The cruise ships were dingier at this distance, the white paint chipped and stained, the windows smeared. It was hard to think of them as elegant and festive, despite the looped strings of party lights.

Peter found a table with an umbrella outside the door of a café. A young man in an apron brought us menus. We decided to sample the local beer with our sandwiches, and I was about to try a sip when I saw a figure striding in our direction.

"Oh, drat," I muttered, wishing I still had the menu so I could hide behind it. "It's that man who dumped himself on us at the breakfast buffet yesterday."

Peter glanced over his shoulder. "The man in the white suit with all the cameras and paraphernalia hanging around his neck? He looks like a member of the paparazzi. Maybe he thought you were a celebrity."

Sittermann stopped abruptly and used binoculars to scan the river. Something on the opposite bank held his attention for a long moment. He finally lowered the binoculars, turned around, and hurried back toward the steps that led up to the pier.

I released my breath. "I guess he didn't see us."

"Well, he saw something," Peter said, frowning as he looked in the same direction that Sittermann had. "There are a couple of houseboats moored near the pier the ferries use, but I don't see any activity on them. The feluccas are scenic, but hardly that enthralling."

"Maybe a fisherman caught an eel or something. He's a jerk from Texas who wants to build a theme park. You're

off-duty today, Lieutenant Rosen. I have some photos of
our wedding that Luanne gave me while she was driving us
to the airport. Would you like to see them?"

We ate lunch while we looked through the photos taken
in the Jorgesons' backyard. I had eschewed lace and satin
and worn a pale green summer frock, which I must admit
went well with my red hair. Luanne had tried to persuade
me to wear a broad-brimmed hat with a ribbon, but I'd resisted. Peter had backed down on his threat to wear a tuxedo
and looked remarkably handsome in a light suit and silk tie.
Caron stood stiffly behind us, pretty in pink and no doubt
sorry she'd opted to wear panty hose in the September heat.
Jorgeson, the best man, glowed as if he were personally responsible that Peter and I had finally made it down the garden path, so to speak. After the necessary formalities, the
few guests we'd invited toasted us with champagne, then
settled down to munch their way through the catered spread
while Peter and I escaped to an inn for an all too brief night
together.

It had lacked the drama of a reality show wedding, but it
had suited us perfectly.

After lunch, we dallied in the shops, then went back to
the hotel and snuck in through the New Winter Palace entrance. In our absence, all the rooms had been cleaned and
the breakfast items removed. The flowers were definitely
fresh, and a large bowl of tangerines was centered on the
coffee table. The folded copy of the *Herald Tribune* was
three days old, but Ahmed had tried. When Peter went into
the bedroom to make calls, I took a chilled bottle of water
out of the mini-bar and settled down on the balcony to read
more lurid prose.

At five thirty, we changed into more respectable attire.
After I'd applied a bit of makeup and checked my appearance, I sat down on the sofa and graciously accepted a martini. I was relating the saga of the proper English lady and
the untamed sheik with the smoldering eyes when we heard
a knock on the door.

"Oh, Mrs. Malloy, you look absolutely stunning,"

Alexander said as he came into the parlor. "After I had a few drinks last night, I couldn't prevent myself from wondering why you two agreed to this ghastly ordeal. It's not too late to claim ptomaine poisoning, you know. It would be less painful."

Peter was less than amused by Alexander's wit. "We're looking forward to meeting your father and his friends. Perhaps it will alleviate their fascination with my wife."

"Perhaps," Alexander said as he offered his arm to me. "May I escort the lady down the hall?"

"I'll risk it on my own," I said perversely, having never enjoyed being addressed in the third person. I gulped down the last of the martini and swept out the door.

The Baron of Rochland's rooms were at the far end of the hallway. As we went inside, I realized that his sitting room was decorated with the same decor as the Presidential Suite, suggesting there had been a deep discount on the fabric. I would have commented on it had Lord Bledrock not swooped down on me and squeezed my hand so tightly that I nearly yelped.

"Mrs. Malloy," he burbled with excitement. "My dear, dear woman! This is such an honor. I feel as though I'm meeting Dame Agatha. Please, allow Alexander to fix you up with a drink while I introduce you to my friends. You, too, Rosen." I was whisked over to a settee, where a corpulent lady with wispy gray hair was peering at me over the frames of her half-moon spectacles. Her double chin and high forehead distorted her face, and her heavily rouged cheeks glowed with neon intensity. "Rose, allow me to introduce Claire Malloy, the amateur detective who solves murders. Claire—do you mind if I address you with such informality?—is American. It's a very violent country, or so I've noticed from watching their television shows. They shoot each other with very little provocation. This, my dear, is Mrs. Rose McHaver. Her great-grandfather started a distillery in Glasgow in the middle of the nineteenth century. In its heyday, McHaver's was one of the best double-blend malt whiskies in the country. When Rose could no longer tolerate the weather, she moved to Cumbria. Quite as chilly, if you ask me."

Mrs. McHaver studied me as if I were carrying a concealed weapon. "How delightful to meet you, Mrs. Malloy," she said with a tight nod, then looked across the room. "Miriam! Do stop gawking at Alexander and come over here. I need a fresh drink."

Miriam came scuttling over. She was wearing a shapeless gray dress, exposing arms and legs so painfully thin that they looked as though they might snap. Her brown hair was pulled back into a tenuous bun. Thick glasses with heavy frames dominated her face, magnifying pale blue eyes and sparse eyelashes. Although the room was cool, she was damp with perspiration. "How do you do?" she said to me, extending a hand. "I'm Miriam McHaver, if you haven't already deduced that. I understand you're terribly clever."

"How nice to meet you." I forced myself to shake her hand. "This is Peter Rosen, my husband."

"Fetch me a martini, Miriam," Mrs. McHaver said before Peter could reply. "And this time, do try to remember to put in three olives. They're essential to the digestive process."

"Come along, Mrs. Malloy," said Lord Bledrock, steering me toward a blond woman and a tall, stooped man near the door to the balcony. In a low voice that surely carried across the room and into the next, he said, "In case you're perplexed, Mrs. McHaver resumed her family name after her husband, Cecil, wandered off in the jungles of Malaysia thirty years ago. A decent enough chap, but always was a bit vague." He gazed at the ceiling as if his mind had wandered off as well, then cleared his throat. "Mrs. McHaver tends to bully poor Miriam. The girl hardly ever makes a peep, which is just as well. Barely passed her A levels at a second-rate college, and teaches nursery school. Knows absolutely nothing about Egyptology." He put his hand on the small of my back and propelled me forward. "Claire, this is Dr. Shannon King, head of the archeology department at some little college in the States. Can't recall which one, but she can tell you. Shannon, this is our sleuth, Claire Malloy."

I noticed Peter had fallen out of formation and was standing by the bar, talking to Alexander. "How nice to meet you," I said to Dr. King, who appeared too young to be head of anything except a high school cheerleading squad, or in her case, perhaps the chess or Latin club. Her blond hair was sensibly short, her makeup deftly applied, her posture impeccable. She wore khaki pants and a white blouse that was unbuttoned far enough to allow a glimpse of a lacy bra, but her expression was steely. I suspected she would be as equally competent running a marathon as a departmental meeting.

She managed a polite smile. "You, too. I'm chairman of the archeology department at MacLeod College in Maine. Well, acting chairman. The dean has to observe academic protocol, which means advertising the position and reviewing applications. I expect formal notification by the end of the year." She bit her lip for a brief moment, as if holding back some sort of emotional outburst, then said, "This is Wallace Laxenby, the photographer for our current project."

"Wallace may not have the latest technology," Lord Bledrock said heartily, "but he certainly has experience. How long have you been at this, Wallace?"

"Decades," the man said, bobbling his head with such enthusiasm that I was afraid it might topple off and roll out to the balcony. His face was as wrinkled and weathered as Abdullah's, and his sport coat was frayed. His smile was much warmer than that of his companion, who now was glaring out the window at some unseen impediment to her academic promotion. "I first came out here more than forty years ago," Wallace continued. "We were all so young back then, and determined to make discoveries that would undermine the quintessence of the Egyptological doctrine of that time. Oskar was a graduate student. My wife and I introduced him to Magritta, and I stood as his best man when they married. We couldn't afford to stay in a hotel like this, so we lived in what amounted to a boardinghouse on the West Bank. No hot water, and often no electricity. Not that I can afford to stay here these days. MacLeod College barely gives us adequate funding to pay the workers." His shoulders heaved as he let out a morose sigh. "Poor Oskar, I do miss him." He pulled a soiled handkerchief out of his pocket and blew his nose. "Our first concession was—"

"I'm sure it was," Lord Bledrock said. "Come along, Claire. I must introduce you to the others."

Dr. King caught his arm. "I would like to continue the discussion we had earlier in the week. I need your decision as soon as possible."

"You will have my decision when I've had time to consider all the factors," he said, removing her hand as if it might leave an unsightly smudge on his sleeve. "You must excuse us. Others are waiting to meet Mrs. Malloy."

I was once again propelled into action. This time we stopped in front of a sofa, where two blue-haired ladies were eying me like greedy pigeons. They were both small and wiry, like underfed children, although such children hardly wore glittery rings and pearls. One wore lavender, the other lilac. Their consanguinity was obvious.

Lord Bledrock's mustache trembled with disapproval at the number of empty martini glasses on the coffee table in front of them, but he merely said, "Miss Cordelia, Miss Portia, this is Claire Malloy. She's the American sleuth."

They both twittered. One of them (and I had no idea which) said, "And you've come all this way to solve a mystery! How fascinating. I personally think it was Rose McHaver, in the ballroom, with the candlestick—unless, of course, it was Alexander, in the conservatory, with the rope. What do you think, Mrs. Malloy?"

The other tilted her head to stare at me. "We must first test her detective prowess, Cordelia. We must ask the perfect question."

I was, as Caron would say, clueless. I was hoping Lord Bledrock would rescue me, but he was proving himself to be worthless. We made quite a pair.

"Oh, I have it!" said Miss Portia, gleefully clapping her hands. "Mrs. Malloy, how do you titillate an ocelot?"

"Excuse me?" I said.

"You oscillate his tit a lot!" Miss Cordelia shrieked. She collapsed against her sister as they both laughed uncontrollably. "You . . . oscillate his . . . tit a lot!"

I looked over my shoulder. Peter was still standing near Alexander, but I could tell from his ill-controlled expression that he was as amused as the duo on the sofa. "I'll keep that in mind," I said. "I do believe I'd like a martini, Lord Bledrock. Nice meeting you, Miss Cordelia, Miss Portia."

They flapped their hands at me, still cackling with laughter between gasps.

I fled across the room and grabbed Peter's lapel. "Can we please leave?"

"Now, Claire," Alexander said, "you must ignore them, as we all do. The old girls are pickled to the gills. You have now heard the entirety of their repertoire of off-color jokes."

Peter gently removed my hand, kissed it, and gave me a martini. "A few more minutes, and then we'll go. Alexander has been telling me about the active concessions in the Valley of the Kings. I thought we might take the girls and go over there tomorrow. There's a bridge not too far from here. Bakr will drive us, so we won't have to risk one of the ferries dumping us in the Nile. I've heard rumors of crocodiles."

"I say," Alexander cut in, "would you mind if I tagged along?"

I had a vision of being packed into a van with all the people I'd met thus far. Rose McHaver would be barking at Miriam, while the two blue-haired women retold their joke numerous times, Wallace recited his personal history, and Lord Bledrock pontificated. Dr. King would be thumping the dashboard with her fist and futilely attempting to call the meeting to order. Before I could come up with a tactful remark, Peter said, "We'd be pleased. Shall we meet in the lobby after breakfast?"

Alexander read my mind better than my husband. "Only me, Mrs. Malloy. The others are attending a luncheon at Lady Emerson's villa, followed by a long afternoon of bridge and gin. I was going to spend the day reading and catching up on my correspondence. I'd much prefer to see if anyone's found a mummy."

"You're welcome to join us," I said, albeit ungraciously.

"I know a delightful little restaurant near the Ramesseum. It has a shady patio, and the food isn't too dreadful."

I saw Lord Bledrock heading toward us with the determination of a missile. To my relief, he paused as the door opened.

"Howdy," boomed a familiar voice. "Is this the shindig? I sure am tickled pink to be invited."

"Save me," I whispered to Peter. "I feel a headache coming on. Can we please leave *now*?"

Sittermann's white suit was slightly grimy, but his face was infused with joviality. He caught Lord Bledrock's hand and shook it with undue enthusiasm. "How's it going, old boy? What you got to drink? I sure could stand something stiffer than beer that tastes like horse piss. I can almost feel the hair on my chest sagging like a bull's balls on a busy day. How about a shot of whiskey with a splash of branch water?"

Even Peter, who was usually unflappable, shuddered.

CHAPTER 3

Peter and I had dinner at the swanky restaurant in the hotel, then went up to our suite. We'd changed into more comfortable attire and were sitting on the balcony when Caron and Inez arrived. My daughter had several bulging bags; Inez had limited herself to one. They dumped their trophies in their bedroom, then joined us.

"How was your day?" I asked.

"It was great," Caron said. "I could really get into having a chauffeur. Every time we got somewhere, he jumped out of the car and opened our doors. Inez tried to give him a tip when he brought us back here, but he wouldn't take it. Maybe he thinks he'll get a real one before we leave."

"I offered him ten pounds," Inez said, offended.

"Like he's going to fall over dead for two dollars? That works out to about twenty cents an hour."

"It was a polite gesture," I said. "Did you enjoy your guided tour of Karnak?"

Caron grinned. "We were afraid we'd get stuck with a boring old geezer, but we had a really neat guide. Her name is Salima. She told us about all the seriously wicked stuff that went on in the rooms at the back. And she's a master shopper. I felt like an amateur. She bargained with all the shop owners, but whatever she said must have been funny because they fell all over her."

"It was so cool," Inez added. "We were invited to sit

down and have mint tea right there in the stores. It was like we were nobility, or at least movie stars. All these tourists were staring at us through the window."

"She invited us to go to her house on Saturday," said Caron. "It's on the other side of the Nile, but she says she'll meet us in the lobby and take us over and back on a ferry."

I glanced at Peter. "Is this woman on Mahmoud's payroll?"

"I'll find out." He went into our bedroom and closed the door.

Inez regarded me soberly. "It would be very educational to learn how a middle-class family lives. Salima said it's not a big deal, just a birthday party for her younger brother. A lot of aunts and uncles and cousins will be there."

"We'll talk about it later," I said, then attempted to divert them with our plans to go to the West Bank the following day.

"Can Salima be our guide the next time you're trying to be ever so subtle about getting rid of us?" asked Caron, who is not easily diverted unless her physical comfort is at stake. "She knows everything about all these old temples and tombs. She went to Cambridge to study Egyptology. Her specialty is mummified animals."

"Animals?" I tried to envision a sarcophagus large enough to accommodate a camel, a cow, or even a donkey. A crocodile would be less challenging, if it wasn't too long. Hippopotami were out of the question.

Inez nodded. "When the pharaoh or one of his favorite wives died, they'd mummify some pets to put in the tomb. I don't guess PETA was around back then."

"Salima's going to take us to the Mummification Museum here," Caron said. "She knows all about how they cut open the corpse to remove the internal organs and pulled the brains out through the nose with a—"

Peter returned, sparing me from the graphic details. "I spoke to Mahmoud," he said. "Salima el-Musafira's father is a professor at the university in Cairo, is noted for his books on hieroglyphs, and lectures at universities in Europe. Her mother is a doctor. The family is well respected. They have a house in Gurna across the Nile and an apartment in Cairo. Salima has published in Egyptology journals, and currently has a small grant from the university to document preservation efforts in some of the excavations in the area. She supplements her income by giving tours. She's fluent in a dozen languages, and the embassies often engage her when there are dignitaries in town. Mahmoud was telling me how charming she is when Aisha started making caustic remarks in the background."

"See?" Caron said, as if rebutting an argument not yet on the table. "I told you she was okay. Can we go to the birthday party on Saturday?"

I reminded myself that the girls were seventeen, well beyond the age of requiring a babysitter. On the other hand, we were in a country where they did not speak the language and were unfamiliar with the cultural traditions. "I don't know. We'll have to talk about it."

Peter did not help. "You and I have been invited to go on a sunset cruise and have dinner on a *dahabiyya* that evening. Local bigwigs, attachés from the American and British embassies, and a few others. The girls were going to be stuck in the hotel. Mahmoud assured me that Salima is reliable."

"How old is she?" I asked.

Caron and Inez exchanged furtive looks. Caron at last shrugged and said, "I didn't ask to see her driver's license, Mother. I suppose she's in her early twenties, but she grew up here and she knows how to use the ferries and—"

I held up my hand in defeat. "All right, then, as long as we agree what time you'll be back. You'll need to dress conservatively, and find out if you're expected to bring a birthday present."

The girls retreated to their bedroom before I could continue. In two years they would be away at college, I thought, and free to make all of their own decisions. I wouldn't be there to demand that Caron tell me where she was going and with whom, and when she would be home. At the same time, this did not seem to be the place to start loosening the apron strings (as if I'd ever worn, much less owned, one).

Peter pulled his chair closer to mine. "They'll be fine."

"Maybe Bakr could go with them," I whimpered.

"They won't need a bodyguard." He gazed at the sky, trying not to meet my suddenly wary stare. "A chauffeur, I meant to say. It's just a family party, an opportunity to learn how other cultures celebrate."

I did my best to remain gloomy and unconvinced, but before too long I was distracted by Peter's delightfully ticklish assault on my neck and we retired for the night.

We received more than our fair share of stares when we went to the patio for the breakfast buffet. Peter was wearing slacks and a cotton shirt, and Caron and I both wore shorts and short-sleeved tops. Inez, in contrast, had been swept into the mystique of archeology—and not with a whisk broom. She had emerged from their bedroom in full khaki, with knee-length shorts, a belted field jacket with well-stocked pockets, a pair of binoculars and a camera hanging on straps around her neck, and a broad-brimmed cloth hat with a dangling chin strap. Her sturdy shoes and thick socks would serve her well if she found the need to climb a mountain or descend into a rough-hewn pit. A water bottle, compass, flashlight, and first-aid kit were clipped to her belt. I had no doubt she had a week's worth of rations and a Swiss Army knife somewhere on her body.

None of us had the courage to comment as we chose a table and sat down. The employees in their red fezzes watched us, their expressions admirably restrained. Caron's face was pink, but I suspected it wasn't due to their outing the previous day. Peter's lips were clamped together as if he'd used superglue when he brushed his teeth, and he expressed a sudden need to detour to the newsstand and buy a paper. His shoulders were quivering as he hurried toward the lobby.

Alexander arrived while we were eating. He dragged

over a chair from a nearby table, sat down with a pained
sigh, and ordered coffee from a waiter. After a guarded
glance at Inez, he said, "You're lucky to have made your escape when you did last night. That abysmal man—I've forgotten his name—would not shut up. He's building a theme
park out by the pyramids in Giza. Tut-O-Rama, or some
grotesque thing. I was literally driven to drink. Shannon
King was glowering like the embers in a *sheesa*. Lord and
Lady Fitzwillie showed up with Lady Emerson, who has
vehement views on the sanctity of the historical sites and
expressed them at length. My father was blustering, and
Wallace looked as though he was on the verge of a stroke.
The argument became so heated that I was certain Ahmed
would come knocking discreetly on the door."

"We had dinner reservations," I said mendaciously, then
introduced him to the girls. They gaped at him in response,
although I wasn't sure if they were awed by his father's title,
his accent, or his undeniably handsome demeanor. His stu-
diously casual attire had not come off the racks but off the
pages of glossy men's fashion magazines. Even my impec-
cably dressed husband looked a bit shabby in comparison.
"Please finish your breakfast," I said to the girls, hoping to
break their transfixed stares. "Bakr is meeting us outside in
fifteen minutes."

Alexander grinned at Inez. "I see you're well prepared for
all contingencies."

"I have extra sunscreen if you need some," she said, flus-
tered.

Caron carefully put down her fork. "I'm going to the
ladies' room. Inez, are you coming?"

The two fled like gawky fillies, their knees wobbling so
wildly I was afraid they were going to crash into a waiter—
or into Mrs. McHaver, who was poised in the doorway.
Miriam hovered behind her, peering over her aunt's broad
shoulder.

"God save us all," Alexander murmured as he lit a cigarette. "I suppose in this case I should be imploring Allah, but

my Arabic is shaky before noon. I say, shall we have a round of Bloody Marys before we go?"

Peter and I declined. Mrs. McHaver acknowledged us with a slight nod as she swept by and sat down at a table in the corner. Miriam paused at our table.

"Good morning," she said. Her tentative smile was aimed at all of us, but it was obvious that she was speaking to Alexander. Her eyelids quivered spasmodically as she attempted to give him a sultry gaze. "Are you off on an outing? I was so hoping you might come to Lady Emerson's this afternoon. I don't play bridge, and the others are always so engrossed that I feel as if I'm not there. I usually end up out in the garden, sketching. It's dreadfully dull. You could help me with irregular verbs. They're such a bother, but my aunt insists that I become fluent in Arabic, as well as French and German."

"So sorry, old girl, but I have a previous engagement," Alexander said, sending a cloud of smoke at her. "Luckily, you'll be there to make sure Mrs. McHaver's martinis have the proper number of olives. Essential to the digestive process, I understand. One simply cannot rely on the local servants to attend to such matters of magnitude."

Miriam's eyes narrowed. "If there's no persuading you, I do hope you enjoy your outing. Good day."

Alexander ground out his cigarette in a saucer. "Pitiful creature, isn't she? It would never occur to her to simply refuse to trail after her great-aunt like some sort of lapdog."

"She looks almost ashen in the sunlight," Peter said. "Is she ill?"

"I believe she's recovering from a prolonged bout of a mysterious fever." Alexander beckoned to a waiter and ordered more coffee. "I wasn't really paying much attention when her case was discussed. Last spring she was obliged to take a medical leave from her teaching position. Mrs. McHaver brought her to Luxor because the weather in Cumbria can be brutal in the autumn and winter. The girl didn't have the spirit to refuse, although she's not at all interested in archeology. She'd much prefer to be in her flat watching the telly and drinking watery tea."

"Her first trip out here?" I asked.

"She's come in the past, but just for holiday between terms. Miriam's parents died when she was quite young. Mrs. McHaver took her in and saw to her upbringing. I do feel sympathy for the girl, growing up in a remote house on the moors. No money of her own, forced to accept her great-aunt's charity. Given grudgingly, one would suppose. Mrs. McHaver doesn't pinch pences—she squeezes them until they scream for mercy."

I was sorry Caron wasn't at the table, since her concept of deprivation was defined by her lack of cell phone and credit cards.

"This is hardly a modest bed-and-breakfast," Peter pointed out.

"She does have to keep up appearances, doesn't she?" Alexander lit another cigarette. "I wouldn't be surprised if she's not paying the same room rate that her father used to pay fifty years ago. You'll notice that she herself does not entertain, but never declines an invitation. Don't let her fool you, though. She may seem like a stereotypic Scot, but there's more to her than you may suspect."

"And Miriam?" I asked.

"That I doubt, but who knows? One night she may snap and plunge a fish fork into her great-aunt's neck. Would you mind if I take a look at your newspaper?"

After a few minutes, we finished our coffee and met the girls in the lobby. Bakr was waiting for us in a small van at the curb. His shirt was already wrinkled and damp beneath his armpits, and his wisp of a mustache twitched like a convulsed caterpillar. He looked so alarmed by our approach that I wanted to clasp his arm and assure him that we harbored no cannibalistic notions. Alexander insisted that Inez sit in the front seat where she would have the best view, then took Caron's hand and coerced her into the back row with him. Peter and I took the middle seats. Bakr slid the

door closed, then hoisted himself into the driver's seat and
looked back at us.

"Mr. Rosen and Mrs. Malloy," he said, "Chief Inspector
Mahmoud el-Habachi sends his regards and wishes all of
you a pleasant day. There are bottles of water in the seat
pockets, so you must please to help yourselves. Behind the
last row is a box with fruit, potato chips, and—"

"Let's go," Alexander said cheerfully.

As we drove south, the corniche gave way to a typical
city street of stores, hotels, and restaurants. Some of the men
on the sidewalks wore long robes, others Western attire. The
women had scarves on their heads and drab, ankle-length
skirts, but some had cell phones plastered to their ears.
Groups of girls giggled as they window-shopped. Horse-
drawn carriages impeded traffic, eliciting shouts and blaring
horns. In a vacant lot, a donkey pulled a cart piled to a pre-
carious height with some sort of fresh produce, while men
squatted in the shade, smoking brown cigarettes. There was
a sense of modest prosperity; poverty was well concealed
from the tourists.

Eventually we left the congested traffic and drove past
fields, unadorned buildings, and houses ringed by palm trees
and dusty yards. I relaxed and sat back, aware for the first
time that Caron and Alexander were having a quiet conversation. Before I could turn around, Peter opened a bottle of
water and gave it to me.

"First impression?" he asked.

I thought for a moment. "It's unlike anything I've expe-
rienced, yet not overwhelming. Trucks and cars whizzing
past donkey carts that must have been using this route for
thousands of years. Satellite dishes on the roofs of houses
built out of mud bricks. The greenery here, with the contrast
of the barren mountains just beyond—two diametrically
different ecosystems." I leaned forward and tapped Inez's
shoulder. "Seen any camels?"

"Two so far. I'm going to keep a tally. Do you think a
baby camel should get a full mark or just a half?"

Bakr glanced at me in the rearview mirror. "The young

miss will see a few camels, but they are not so useful for farming. To the west is the sand and the oases, where there are many camels. Mrs. Malloy is comfortable? Should I turn up the air conditioner? Would you like to listen to music? Something to eat?"

"I think not," Peter said. "Mrs. Malloy is much tougher than she looks, Bakr. She can be as formidable as a falcon, as sly as a jackal, as dangerous as a cobra. In an earlier life, she was the wife of a powerful pharaoh, but on his death she seized the throne and ruled the land with an iron fist."

"Why, thank you," I said. "Did I decorate my tomb with taste and charm?"

"It was featured on the cover of *Better Homes and Burial Chambers.*"

I ignored the snickers from behind me. We drove across the bridge spanning the Nile, and then alongside flat green fields. White egrets circled above, looking for promising picnic spots. Children stood at the edge of the road or rode on donkeys. Laundry flapped on lines around houses without doors or windows, while goats and chickens wandered nearby. Bakr managed to navigate the rough streets through a small town, where men sat in front of cafés, their eyes tracking our progress. The garages had piles of discarded tires, and rusty metal signs written in Arabic that probably advertised soft drinks. It had the same ambiance as rural towns back home.

When we'd reached the far edge of town, Bakr pulled over. "We stop now at the *taftish* to purchase tickets. Will you be wanting to visit the Ramesseum and Medinet Habu?"

"The Ramesseum was built by Ramses II," Inez announced. "He was nineteenth dynasty, and lived to be ninety-six years old. He had over two hundred wives and concubines, including Nefertari. One colossus of Ramses bears a cartouche of his royal name, which was translated as Ozymandias and inspired the poem by Shelley. Nearby are the Osiris pillars and a hypostyle—"

"Next," Caron said from behind us.

"Medinet Habu was built by Ramses III. It's a mortuary

temple linked to the Theban necropolis. Ramses III was considered the last great pharaoh. He was murdered by his wives."

"Does it have a hypostyle hall, too?" demanded Caron. "I spent hours and hours looking at pillars yesterday. Frankly, when you've seen one pillar, you've seen them all. I thought we were going to—"

Peter held up his hand. "Enough. Thank you for the very informative synopsis, Inez. We'll save those sites for another day. Let's go on to the Valley of the Kings, Bakr."

"Yes, very good, sir." Bakr swung the van back into the trickle of traffic.

Inez was staring straight ahead, rigid with indignation. Behind us, Alexander muttered something to Caron that elicited a giggle. The last thing I needed was for Caron and Inez to squabble for the next two and a half weeks. Alexander was likely to be the incendiary spark, although I couldn't blame him for his sophisticated charm. I decided that I needed to have a word with him, if only to remind him that he was entirely too old to flirt with seventeen-year-old girls. If he ignored me, I would have no option except to tell Peter to thrash him soundly for his impertinence (or however the Brits phrase it).

Peter leaned toward me. "They'll work it out," he said softly. "Remember when you were that age and some handsome older guy flattered you?"

"I do. That's the problem."

"Care to elaborate?"

I took a guidebook out of my bag and opened it to the chapter on the Valley of the Kings. Although reading in a car often makes me queasy, I was not at all inclined to continue a discussion about episodes in my past. Some of them were worthy of interment in a tomb that rivaled King Tut's.

Bakr found a space in a parking lot clogged with tour buses and cars. After I'd made sure we were all equipped with sunglasses, sunblock, hats, and water bottles, we walked up a road to a strip of open-air shops selling sunglasses, sunblock, hats, water bottles—and an endless ar-

ray of souvenirs. Local craftsmen had been driven away by
purveyors of T-shirts, camera film, postcards, flimsy clothing, amateurish paintings, and colorful plastic figurines of
ancient Egyptian gods and goddesses.

I was fingering a carpet of dubious origin when Caron
grabbed my arm and dragged me aside.

"Why didn't you tell me that guy—Alexander—was
coming with us?" she whispered hotly.

"I didn't think about it," I admitted. "Last night at the
cocktail party he asked if he might accompany us."

"Look at me! My shorts are baggy and my shirt looks
like it came from a yard sale. I didn't even bother to dry my
hair this morning, since we were going to be out in the sun
all day. And Inez might as well be a shill at a sideshow at-
traction at some stupid county fair, trying to lure people inside to see a two-headed snake! I am so humiliated I Could
Die."

"Then we're at the right place."

"You are So Not Funny!" she snapped, then stomped
away.

I caught up with Peter, who was defending himself from
an eager merchant with a rack of glittery jewelry. Peter and I
exchanged amused looks, then headed for a kiosk to buy
tickets to enter the Valley of the Kings. Caron, I noticed, had
retreated to the shade of an awning to apply lip gloss, while
Alexander and Inez chatted nearby.

We rode in a faux trolley car up the hill to a concrete-
block building. Soldiers stood in the shade, impassively
watching mundane tourists and openly leering at scantily
clad women. I studied the valley, no more than fifty to sixty
feet across and defined by steep mountainsides lined with
what I supposed were goat paths. It was hard to believe that
over the millennia flash floods had carved this foreboding
reddish brown canyon in the limestone. Wadis branched
out on both sides; the map in the guidebook resembled a
pinnated leaf. Boulders and chunks of rocky rubble contin-
ually tumbled down the cliffs, altering the landscape. The
mutability, as well as the remoteness, had made a perfect

hideaway for the priests to bury their pharaohs in hopes the
tombs (and treasures within) would remain undisturbed.
Now the valley was protected by the soldiers at the entrance
and a few guards in a tiny building perched on the top of
one of the cliffs.

Inez was well prepared. "There are sixty-three excavated
tombs. The first, down that path on the right, belongs to
Ramses VII, and has been open to tourists since Greek and
Roman times. Ramses IV is next, and it has graffiti on the
walls dating back to 278 B.C. Farther up and on our left is
the tomb of at least six of the fifty sons of Ramses II. This
tomb has one hundred and twenty-one chambers and corridors, making it larger and more complex than any other
tombs that have been found to date in all of Egypt. On the
right is the tomb of Ramses II, who was the son of Seti I.
He and his father both had sarcophagi made of alabaster."
She paused for a breath. "The farthest tomb is that of Tuth-
mosis III at the end of the—"

"That's Tut," Alexander said, gesturing toward a long line
of tourists waiting in front of an entrance with a barred gate,
"or Tutankhamun, if you prefer. It's officially known as
KV62. Only one other tomb has been found since 1922, and
that was in 2006. There was great hope that KV63 would
also be filled with gold, jewelry, and of course a mummy or
two. The media and the Egyptologists were breathless with
anticipation."

"And . . . ?" said Caron. She'd managed to nudge Inez
away, and now was gazing at him with something closely
akin to adulation.

"Although it contained seven coffins, none had a
mummy," Inez said before Alexander could respond. "The
stone jars and the coffins held fragments of pots, fabric,
and natron, a form of carbonate salt used for cleansing and
cosmetic purposes as well as mummification. The style of
the lintel above the door is similar to the one at Tut's tomb,
leading to speculation that it might have served as a storage
area for another tomb built for Tut's wife, Ankhsenamon.

Their two known daughters were stillborn, their mummies found in Tut's tomb."

"Fascinating," Caron said as she gazed at the cloudless sky.

Alexander may have been the dilettante son of a baron, but he was not oblivious of the tension. "I say, Inez, you're better informed than I. Shall we all go have a look inside it?"

"Before we do that," Peter said, "why don't we have a look at the excavation in progress?"

"We met Dr. King last night," I said to the girls. "Her college in Maine is funding the project."

Alexander snorted. "In theory. Only colleges and foundations with established programs in Egyptology are granted concessions to excavate. They in turn allow individuals to raise money and do the actual labor. Howard Carter had Lord Carnarvon as his patron. These days, archeologists rely on private donations made through the college. My father, among others, has given a goodly sum to this project." He paused to light a cigarette. "It allows him free access to the site, which is off-limits to the tourists. It also allows me the same privilege, and all of you as my guests."

A group of Asians swarmed by us, camcorders readied. A much livelier group of Germans, the women dressed in tank tops and the men bare chested, brayed at some private joke. An older woman sat on a low wall, fanning herself with an open guidebook. A few determined parents ignored their whining offspring as they trudged up the winding road. Babies in strollers fidgeted and fussed.

The site we were seeking was only a couple of hundred feet past King Tut's entrance. It was ringed with yellow rope tied to rods, and a large truck was parked within a short distance. I'm not sure what I expected, but this appeared to be little more than a good-sized hole, maybe ten feet across, situated between the road and a steep incline. People milled about the rim, talking and gesturing. A tarp had been rigged on poles to provide a small patch of shade. The only activity seemed to come from the native workmen, who were going in and out of the hole with baskets made of what looked like sections of old tires.

Dr. King was the first to notice us. She pulled off her cloth hat and fluffed her blond hair with her fingertips. Tucking her sunglasses in her shirt pocket, she chirped, "Alexander, what a lovely surprise. I was hoping your father might come out today, but perhaps I can catch him later. All of you are welcome to duck under the rope and join us. Can we offer you some tea? Nabil, Hasham, get chairs out of the truck."

"Don't let us disrupt the work," Alexander murmured.

"No, it's no bother. We're always pleased to see you." She stared at Inez but, like the rest of us, could think of nothing to say. Her attention shifted to Peter. "We didn't have the opportunity to be introduced last evening, Mr. Rosen. I do hope we'll have a chance to get to know each other better. In a sense, we're both detectives, although my clues are found in antiquity. I'd love to hear about your more spectacular cases, perhaps over drinks in the hotel bar some evening?"

Although I did my best not to bristle, Peter sensed my displeasure. "I believe you met my wife, Claire Malloy. This is her daughter, Caron, and Inez Thornton."

"Yes, the fabled Mrs. Malloy," Shannon murmured, appraising me as if I were an unsuitable candidate for her program. "You look as though you're about to collapse from the heat and exertion. Please, do sit down in the shade. We have some water, although I'm afraid it's tepid."

"I'm fine, but thank you for your solicitude," I said. "Is this all there is to the excavation? I anticipated something more dramatic."

"Most people do. There's a great deal more complexity to archeology than what one picks up watching simple-minded cable shows. A doctoral degree requires a vigorous regimen of academic studies, as well as field experience. My parents swear I could read hieroglyphs before I learned the alphabet." She rested her hand on Alexander's shoulder. "I'm sure you could, too, since you grew up surrounded by

your father's marvelous collection. Isn't it quaint how so
many Americans think the word 'dynasty' refers to a TV
soap opera?"

It was obvious that Dr. Shannon King and I were not
destined to become close friends. I didn't know if her arrogance came from her advanced degree, academic status, or
blond hair, but I was less than impressed. Before I could
voice any of this, Peter once again came to my rescue.

"I understand the excavator is a German woman?"

Shannon was so engrossed in sending provocative
glances at Alexander that she was startled. "Why, yes. Let
me introduce you to Magritta and her staff." She beckoned
to a young man standing over two workmen who were siev-
ing rubble on a wide frame. "This is Jess Delmont, one of
my grad students. He's spending the semester here."

Jess Delmont lacked the panache of Howard Carter, or
even Inez. He was short and dumpy, with frizzy brown hair
in a ponytail and a sour expression. He managed a shrug.
"Hey, yeah, pleased to meet you."

"Our department requires a semester of fieldwork,"
Shannon continued. "Jess was hoping for an assignment in
Mesopotamia, but with the political situation, it just wasn't
feasible. Such a shame."

"Such a shame," he said, mocking her sugary tone. He
returned to his previous spot and looked down at the workmen, his arms crossed.

"Well, yes," Shannon said, disconcerted. "Let me fetch
Magritta."

Caron and Inez sat down on the chairs under the tarp,
neither of them acknowledging the other's proximity. I
sighed, then cautiously approached the rim of the hole.
Peter's arm around my waist was comforting. In that I am
not a spiteful person, I did not glance up to see if Shannon
noticed, and I took no satisfaction in her faint frown as she
descended a series of square steps ringed with rocks.

"Workmen's huts," Alexander commented. "They lived
in villages several hours away on foot. They would stay here

for ten days at a time, then go home for a few days. When the heat grew intolerable in the summer and the Nile flooded, they would stay home to plant crops."

"But those so-called huts are only a few feet square," I said. "They couldn't live in them."

"They stored their tools and whatever personal belongings they'd brought."

I bent forward. At the bottom of the hole were several people. I recognized Wallace Laxenby, the garrulous photographer I'd met at Lord Bledrock's cocktail party. Shannon, having lost her audience, had replaced her hat. A few minutes later, she reemerged, followed by a stout woman with cropped gray hair, leathery skin, and a square jaw. She regarded us with the beady stare of a snapping turtle.

"This is Magritta Vonderlochen," Shannon said. "Alexander has brought Claire Malloy and Peter Rosen out to visit."

"I see that."

"Magritta and her late husband, Oskar, have been working in Egypt for more than forty years. It used to be quite easy for archeologists to get concessions to excavate, but these days they need approved sponsorship. MacLeod College is honored to oversee this particular project."

Magritta's lip curled in response to Shannon's pointed remark. "This is true, but we still revere the glorious days of Borchardt, Brugsch, Lepsius, and Sethe. They did not have to beg for funds to pay the workmen, feed and house the staff, take menial jobs during the off-season in order to pay their own transportation. Nor did they have to answer to a personage such as Dr. King, who will take credit for whatever we find. The view from the podium is much nicer than that from the bottom of the pit."

"There's no need for this," Shannon said coldly. "You're lucky that MacLeod is allowing you to continue working the concession without Oskar. You'd best hope you make a significant discovery this season. The two of you have been at it for four years, and all you've found so far is a handful of shards. There are plenty of other excavators interested in this particular concession."

"Success requires diligence and perseverance. Oskar was convinced that we would find something of significance in this immediate area. When we open the tomb, it will be his final triumph. His life's work will be validated."

"If there is a tomb."

Magritta scowled. "You know nothing except what you have read in books by pompous scholars who have never dirtied their hands or endured the suffocating heat and dust. You stay in that fancy hotel where you have every luxury, and then fly back to your insignificant college to prattle about the hardship. Look at your hands. Are they scarred and calloused?"

"I am not a common laborer," Shannon retorted. "My objective is to evaluate your progress—which has been minimal, I might add. MacLeod College is losing enthusiasm for your so-called expertise. Oskar refused to write proper reports or even publish updates in the Egyptology journals. If you don't do better, you'll be reduced to digging holes in a sandbox in your own backyard."

"How dare you speak of Oskar with such impudence!"

Wallace Laxenby's face appeared from below. "What's all this?" he sputtered. "Shannon, I won't allow you to upset Magritta like this. If Oskar were alive, he would bound up the steps and turn you over his knee to paddle your well-padded backside until you shrieked for mercy."

In the ensuing silence, everyone covertly assessed Wallace's description of Shannon's anatomy. I decided, although with only the faintest flicker of smugness, that Wallace had not been entirely inaccurate.

"How—how dare you!" she gasped.

Alexander cleared his throat. "I do think a glass of tea sounds like a jolly good idea. Claire, Peter, will you join me under the canopy?"

"Nabil, fetch tea," said Magritta. "Jess, grab a brush and come back down with me. I need to get a better look at a shard before we extract it from the wall. Hasham, Hany, close your mouths and get to work. We only have a few hours left today."

Shannon realized that a half-dozen tourists who'd paused on the opposite side of the yellow rope had overheard the distasteful conversation. Her face was flushed as she turned her back on them and began to scribble on her clipboard. After a moment, she went over to the truck and got into the cab.

"Perhaps we should leave," I said as Peter and I sat down with the girls.

"Because of that spat?" Alexander chuckled maliciously. "It happens almost every day, and would in the evenings as well if Magritta were staying at the Winter Palace. She has a long-standing agreement with an Egyptian landlord to let a flat for six or seven months each year. I've never been invited there, but I expect it's lacking in amenities. My father offered to put her up in an adequate hotel. He has a sense of noblesse when it comes to his employees. The butler was given a week's leave to attend his mother's funeral in Cardiff, and one of the upstairs maids was not sacked after she had complications from an emergency appendectomy and was bedridden for several weeks during the hunting season."

"A true humanitarian," Peter said.

I took a sip of the hot, sweet tea, then put down the glass. "I'd really prefer to go now. There's really not much to see here. We can come back another day and go into some of the tombs."

Caron and Inez avoided looking at each other as we all rose. Alexander stopped at the edge of the hole and called down that we were leaving. The heat from the sun overhead was noticeable as we walked down the road to the entrance. When we reached the van, Bakr seemed to realize that we were not inclined to chatter and mutely opened the doors for us. Alexander got in the front seat, relegating the girls to the seat in the back. I found a handkerchief in my purse and did what I could to wipe the dusty perspiration off my face.

After we were back on the highway, Alexander suggested that we stop for lunch at the restaurant he'd mentioned earlier. No one objected. The parking lot in front of the squatty building was almost empty, but it was well into the afternoon and the tour buses had already rounded up their inmates and headed onward.

We walked down a sidewalk alongside the restaurant and found a large table under an arbor. Alexander offered to order for all of us and dealt briskly with a waiter in a reasonably clean apron. Beers and sodas were brought to the table. I was beginning to find the silence more oppressive than the heat, but no one seemed willing to offer so much as an idle observation.

I was about to blurt out some inane comment when Alexander said, "I guess you're wondering about Oskar."

I hadn't been, but the topic was more promising than the weather. "He's deceased, I gather."

"Yes, he died about four months ago—at the excavation site. The local police investigated and deemed it an accident. I think he was murdered."

CHAPTER 4

"No, sir, you are wrong," said Bakr, having reluctantly joined us at my insistence. "It was not murder. Chief Inspector el-Habachi was in charge of the investigation. He is a very smart man, and thorough. I myself accompanied him when he interrogated the guards on duty, who were most certain that Oskar Vonder–something, I cannot recall his exact name, was alone that night. His wife said he had been drinking, and this was confirmed during the autopsy. Chief Inspector el-Habachi examined all the evidence before he wrote the final report. The American Embassy was satisfied."

I glanced at Peter, who was more interested in the label on the beer bottle. "I thought he was German," I said.

Alexander shrugged. "A logical assumption. He was of German ancestry, but he and Magritta were both born in the States. He taught history at a community college during the summer terms. Magritta owns a small travel agency that specializes in educational tours of Egypt—the sort that ropes in groups of would-be scholars and lectures them incessantly while they're dragged to every site from Alexandria to the border of Sudan. I feel quite pale when I envision the horror of it. You'll see them in the lobby of the hotel, their sunburned faces drooping with exhaustion as they huddle next to a great pyramid of luggage. Those who survive should be awarded medals."

"And you think this guy was murdered by a disgruntled tourist?" asked Caron. "Give me a break."

I kicked her under the table. "Why do you think Oskar's death was not an accident?" I said.

"Chief Inspector el-Habachi was most thorough," insisted Bakr. He clearly was prepared to defend his boss at any cost. "Most very, very thorough."

Peter had yet to show any inclination to enter the conversation. I considered kicking him, then decided it was inappropriate to physically assault him on our honeymoon. "Well?" I prompted Alexander. "Surely you have a reason."

His eyes met mine. "I wish I did."

The waiter appeared, juggling plates of roasted chicken, grilled eggplant, and potatoes stewed with tomatoes and green beans. I discovered I had little appetite, although the food was agreeable. Caron kept her face lowered while she ate. Inez had pulled a notebook out of one of her pockets and was jotting down notes between bites. Peter, Alexander, and Bakr discussed Egypt's chances in a soccer match against some obscure rival.

After we'd all declined coffee, Peter settled the bill and we rode in silence back to the hotel. As we entered the lobby, Sittermann emerged from behind a potted plant. It seemed likely that he'd been lying in wait for us. There was very little entertainment to be had in the lobby, except watching jet-lagged tourists stagger in, panting from the climb up the staircase in front.

"Well, look who's here!" he said, clad in baggy white shorts and an egregiously floral shirt that must have come from a clearance sale rack at a cheap Hawaiian souvenir store. "I was hoping I might bump into you folks. How 'bout we go have a drink in the bar?"

"Thank you," I said, "but I think we'd prefer to retreat upstairs. Perhaps another time."

Sittermann clutched my arm. "Nonsense, Mrs. Malloy. I didn't have a chance to meet Mr. Rosen here at the little soiree last night. I heard he's looking into property hereabouts, same as me." He flung his free arm around Alexander's shoulder. "Your dad's a regular guy. That was my first time hanging around with the peers of the realm, and I sure did enjoy it. Those sweet grannies dressed in purple— well, I ain't ever heard such language. They laughed so hard I reckoned they was going to pee their panties!"

Caron and Inez had made it to the elevator and were holding the door. They both had the expression of bullfrogs caught in a blinding beam.

I removed Sittermann's hand and edged away from him. "I'm going up to the suite. Peter?"

He'd been acting so oddly that I wouldn't have been surprised if he'd agreed to have a drink with the insufferable Sittermann. Instead, he said, "No, I have a meeting in a few minutes. I'll be back in time for dinner." He sauntered back through the lobby entrance and down the stairs. I wondered if it was too late for an annulment.

Alexander hastily joined us in the elevator. "Another time, Mr. Sittermann. I must escort the ladies in Mr. Rosen's absence. Give my father a call on the house phone. He may be back by now."

When the elevator doors slid closed, we let out a collective sigh. Caron and Inez huddled in one corner, covertly watching Alexander. No one spoke until we reached the sanctity of the Presidential Suite. The girls fled into their bedroom. Alexander turned to leave, but I realized I had a fortuitous opportunity and suggested that he stay for a drink.

"Martinis on the balcony?" he asked, lifting an eyebrow, surely something all young men of his class were taught to do by their nannies. Advanced training would include insolent grins and ill-disguised disdain.

Once we were settled across the table from each other, I said, "Tell me about Oskar Vonderlochen's death."

"Does this mean you didn't lure me up here in order to seduce me?"

"Yes, it does, and while we're on the subject—"

"I know," he interrupted with a grin. "They're seventeen

and I'm a dirty old man of twenty-nine." He held up his palm. "I swear I have no intentions on their innocence. It will do them good to be exposed to rogues like me, and learn how to avoid being manipulated. I fear there are a lot of us out there. You're lucky, since I won't shatter their self-esteem or take advantage of their naïveté."

"If you do, I will track you down to the darkest corner on the planet," I said, "and do what's anatomically necessary to put an end to the Bledrock dynasty."

He took a sip of gin and gazed at the Nile. "Now, about Oskar. It was late last spring. The excavations close down about then, because of the heat. Oskar and Magritta had made little progress during the season. Shannon was making all manner of threats about giving the concession to someone else. Wallace had lapsed into drinking heavily and mumbling to himself. The two graduate students were on the verge of a mutiny. Some of the Brits had departed, but my father, Mrs. McHaver, and a few of the others were lingering. Miriam, I think, and maybe Portia and Cordelia. Lady Emerson had closed her villa and gone to Rome. Penelope and Paunchy were still here, but in the throes of a marital scandal involving the entire Danish archeology team, male and female. I'd flown in to help my father pack up his clothes and personal possessions, and arrange for his purchases to be shipped back to the estate in Kent."

"You don't stay the entire season?" I asked.

"Good lord, no," he said. "I'd go out of my mind. I have a job in the City, investment banking and that sort of drab thing, and I do have to pop into the office every now and then to water my potted plants and flirt with the secretaries."

"It doesn't sound like a demanding job."

"If you must know, I mainly handle the family trusts and those of a few other friends of the family. The firm can't afford to let me go. I really do work, Mrs. Malloy, but I also indulge myself. What's the point of being filthy rich if you don't enjoy it?" His grin was disarming, but his eyes were calculating, as though he was debating how much of his posturing I would buy. "So you have an idea of what was going on. The cocktail parties were gloomy. Tempers flared at every imagined slight or cross word. Bridge tables turned into battlefields. My father was especially irritable because he'd had little luck making acquisitions for his collection, and because his financial backing was coming to naught. Then something happened." He stopped and waited for me to demand that he continue.

I crossed my arms. "Oh, really?"

"Nabil, one of the workmen, showed up at the hotel late one afternoon to show us something. He claimed that after everyone had left for the day, he'd gone back into the pit to look for a missing brush. He was more likely looking for any coins that had fallen out of someone's pocket, but that doesn't matter. He found a piece of an amulet. My father was quite certain it was eighteenth dynasty, which meant it was of the same era as King Tut. Fitzwillie confirmed this. Shannon was stunned. Eventually, she sent a boy to fetch Oskar, Magritta, and Wallace. All of them sat around the table and stared at this little bit of gold. One would have assumed they'd found the Holy Grail."

"A broken amulet?"

"But with features reminiscent of those found in Tut's tomb. Amulets suggest mummies. Without going into the gruesome steps of mummification, as entertaining as they may be, amulets were wrapped between layers of linen for protection. This might lead one to think that some sort of burial chamber was very close at hand. The amulet could have been dropped when tomb robbers escaped with whatever treasures might be sold on the black market."

"So the tomb had already been robbed?" I asked, frowning. "Recently, I suppose, if this amulet was lying there."

Alexander shook his head. "Almost every tomb was robbed at some time during the last couple of thousand years, but that doesn't mean the robbers looted all the chambers. As for the bit of amulet, it may well have been covered up centuries earlier. Excavations are painfully slow and tedious. Each inch of rubble has to be examined."

"I still don't understand why the tomb hasn't been

opened after four years. The hole didn't look all that deep, even if progress is only a few inches a day."

"A reasonable observation," he said, swatting at a cloud of gnats. "The problem lies in the fact that at the end of every season, all the rubble is put back into the hole to prevent theft. Oskar, like his fellow excavators, was a modern-day Sisyphus, who was condemned to an eternity of hard labor in which he rolled a boulder to the top of a hill, then watched it roll all the way back down. It's rather a miracle that any tombs get opened these days."

"But there are guards," I pointed out.

"A couple of them in the hut at the top of a mountain and one or two at the entrance. It's a boring, thankless job, and they're paid a pittance. It's also possible the tomb robbers are friends or relatives. Corruption is a way of life here, from the most petty bureaucrats to those in high positions. It's no better or worse in our countries. The poor want to take care of their families, and the rich simply want to get richer. The black market in stolen antiquities is lucrative, and the collectors can be ruthless."

"Your point is that the guards can be bought, then."

"Persuaded to look the other way, or to ignore covert activity. Sometimes it's nothing more than settling down to listen to a football match on the radio or falling asleep. The Valley of the Kings is not impenetrable. One could enter from a wadi and stay in the shadows."

I considered this for a moment. "Let's get back to Oskar's death. A workman found an amulet, and everybody was thrilled. Then what?"

"Oskar couldn't wait until morning to get back to his precious site. According to Magritta's statement, he left their flat shortly before midnight, armed with a torch and a spade. He never returned, and his body was found in the pit early the next morning. One of the guards at the entrance admitted to accepting a few pounds to allow Oskar inside. It was not the first time Oskar had returned at night to ponder his lack of progress. The guard swore that he neither saw anyone else enter nor heard anything suspicious."

"He must have noticed that Oskar did not reappear."

Alexander went into the parlor to the mini-bar. "He said that he did check out all the tomb areas and eventually concluded Oskar had left without his noticing. He admitted that he didn't shine a torch into the pit."

"Not a conscientious sort, I gather," I said.

"After the investigation, he was transferred to a station on the Sudanese border." Alexander sat down. "Chief Inspector el-Habachi could find no evidence that anyone else had been there. Oskar had suffered several bruises and head injuries that could be explained as a result of his fall. There was a lot of loose gravel at the edge of the pit, and scuff marks that might have come from Oskar's futile attempt to regain his balance. His blood alcohol level was high."

"Well, then," I murmured, "why do you think he was murdered?"

"The timing, for one thing. Had nothing been found at the site to suggest a burial tomb, Shannon might well have taken away the concession. Oskar was too slow and methodical for her; she needed results both to impress her dean and to raise money to continue any projects the college might sponsor. The benefactors were losing enthusiasm as the years passed without any significant discoveries. The fragment of the amulet was a veritable shot of adrenaline to start off this new season."

"So you believe it was planted there for that reason?"

He nodded. "It could have been."

"By Oskar and Magritta?"

"Or Wallace, who knows he'll never be asked to work on another project. What is optimistically referred to as KV64 will be his last hurrah. The discovery was enough to ensure another season or two." Alexander picked up his glass and swirled its contents. "There are others with an interest in ensuring another season, as well."

"Shannon King, you mean?" I asked. "I'm familiar with the publish-or-perish policy of academia. Is this the archeological version of it?"

"It'll give her the opportunity to write it up for some of

the more prestigious journals, and if something of major significance is found, give interviews to the media. The opening of KV63 received worldwide attention from newspapers and cable television."

I sat back and studied him. "So you're basing your belief that Oskar was murdered solely on the coincidence of the timing? One of those you mentioned, or some mysterious party, killed Oskar so that the excavation would resume this year? Doesn't it make just as much sense to accept the official report that Oskar was excited about the discovery and went to poke around in the rubble? Could someone have anticipated that he would go to the Valley of the Kings in the middle of the night—which implies that someone was either watching his hotel or waiting near the site?"

"Well, if you want to get picky . . . ," muttered Alexander. "I thought you'd be intrigued."

"I'm on my honeymoon, Alexander. I left my magnifying glass and fingerprint kit at home."

"But not your reputation, Miss Marple."

I was about to offer a rather uncouth rebuttal when Caron, Inez, and a young woman came out to the balcony.

The woman thrust out her hand. "I am so excited to meet you, Mrs. Malloy! In fact, I am honored! I am Salima el-Musafira, your most humble servant and devoted fan." She spun around to Caron. "Dear girl, you must introduce me properly. Quickly, before I am rendered speechless and make an utter fool of myself."

"Pleased to meet you," I said cautiously.

"No, I am pleased to meet you, Mrs. Malloy." Shoving dark, curly hair out of her face, she perched on the balcony rail, seemingly oblivious to the peril of a three-story fall. "Caron and Inez, my dearest confidantes, I should like a martini." She glanced at Alexander, then turned her large brown eyes on me. Feigning a scowl of horrified embarrassment, she said, "Am I interrupting? My father says I am a dreadful pest at times. I cannot imagine why."

Alexander stood up. "Allow me to make you a martini, Miss el-Musafira."

"How charming!" She waited until he left, then smiled at me. "My mother says I must allow you to have a look at me so that you might permit the girls to come to my family's house on Saturday. She can be hopelessly old-fashioned at times, despite the fact she's a surgeon and clinic administrator as well."

Salima was most certainly not old-fashioned, I thought. Her face was heart shaped and defined by precise, elegant features, and her British accent almost as pronounced as Alexander's. She did not drawl, however. Everything she said shimmered with an almost manic enthusiasm, her hands fluttering and her expression reflecting a myriad of emotions. Although I was marginally old enough to be her mother, I felt more like a weary grandmother. I regretted not making Alexander entertain himself for a few minutes while I showered and changed into fresh clothes.

Caron and Inez dragged chairs from the parlor out to the balcony and mutely sat down, watching me. Alexander returned and offered Salima a glass.

"As Your Highness requested," he said with a grin.

Salima laughed. "I can assure you that the only blue blood in my veins came several generations ago from an Abyssinian princess. You're Lord Bledrock's son, aren't you? You must have forgotten the last time we encountered each other. I was in the midst of that terrible preadolescent stage and you were a despicable boor. You looked down your aristocratic nose and declared me to be a spoiled brat."

"Were you?" said Alexander.

She waggled a finger at him. "That's hardly the point, is it?" Dismissing him, she turned back to me. "Did you enjoy your outing to the Valley of the Kings?"

"It was very interesting," I said.

"I do hope you'll allow me to join you another time. There are several tombs barely mentioned in the guidebooks that are much more intriguing than that of the much-regaled Tutankhamun. Carnarvon and his cohorts made off with souvenirs, but the Egyptians managed to keep most of the contents of the tomb. Have you been to the Egyptian Museum in Cairo? It's vast, dusty, and disorganized, but they do have the solid gold death mask and coffin, and the incredible jewelry."

"We're hoping to have some time in Cairo during our stay."

"We haven't even seen the pyramids," Caron said. "I mean, who goes to Egypt and Doesn't See The Pyramids?"

Salima shook her head in sympathy, although her eyes were glittering. "Well, Mrs. Malloy, will you permit the girls to come to my little family gathering on Saturday? It will be boring, I fear. The older relatives don't speak English, and the younger ones tend to be overly excited in the presence of sweets and festivities. I solemnly promise to bring the girls back to the hotel by eleven o'clock."

Even Alexander was waiting for my reply. I realized I'd been ambushed and had no graceful retreat. "If you're sure they won't intrude . . . ," I began reluctantly. "After all, it is a family party and—"

"Good heavens no," Salima said. "It's settled, then. Caron, Inez, I'll be in the lobby at seven. Some of my aunts are priggish, so I suggest you dress conservatively. You might want to bring a box of candy or dried fruit for my mother, and a little something for Jamil." She gulped down the martini, hopped off the rail, and paused to touch my shoulder. "I'll take very good care of them, Mrs. Malloy. Have a lovely time at the dinner party on the *dahabiyya*. Mr. Bledrock, it's been ever so lovely seeing you again. We must get together in another ten years, unless, of course, you're occupied pulling wings off flies. *Ma'asalama,* everyone."

"Isn't she fantastic?" Caron demanded after the parlor door had closed. "She knows everybody in Luxor."

"I'd be surprised if she doesn't know everyone in Egypt," Alexander said. "She's hardly a shy sort."

"Hardly," I murmured.

Inez picked up the copy of *The Savage Sheik* that I'd left on a corner table. "I've been looking for this."

The three of them looked at me. It occurred to me that it was time to shower and change clothes, and I excused myself rather hastily. As I fled into the bedroom, giggles and snorts were audible from the balcony.

Peter returned as the sun was setting behind the mountains across the Nile. He went into the bathroom and emerged after half an hour, damp but clean and dressed decorously. I glanced up from my book (a civilized British mystery) as he came out to the balcony. "How was your meeting? I noticed that you didn't mention it until we ran into that lout in the lobby."

"Sorry about all that, but I knew you were capable of fending him off. Lovely evening, isn't it? Did you ever imagine you'd be gazing at the Nile as the moon rose?"

I allowed him to nuzzle my neck for a moment, and even went so far as to reciprocate in a seemly fashion. After a few minutes, he sat down across from me and sighed. "Bad news, I'm afraid. I have to fly to Cairo in the morning to meet with"—he hesitated—"some people. You and the girls can come along if you like, but I'll be tied up most of the time. I'll be back Saturday in time for us to have dinner on the *dahabiyya*."

There was no point in protesting. I reminded myself that I'd been warned this would happen—not that said warnings made it more palatable. I told him what Alexander had said about Oskar's death, and when he failed to offer speculation, I continued with Salima's whirlwind appearance. "I guess Caron and Inez will be safe with her," I added.

"Bakr can tag along if it'll make you feel better."

I shook my head. "The idea appeals, but the girls would be furious. It's not as if they've been sheltered all these years. Their track record is impressive. They've talked themselves out of more nasty situations than any politician ever has."

"Very few politicians have been taken into custody by an animal control officer," Peter murmured, grinning, "or stolen frozen frogs from the high school biology lab. Let's just hope they don't decide to steal the Sphinx."

On that note, we gathered up the would-be felons and went to dinner.

Lord Bledrock swept down on us at breakfast, his mustache trembling with anticipation. "Dear Claire, how delightful to find you here. I understand Rosen has gone to Cairo for a few days. I hope you'll allow us to entertain you and the young ladies in his absence."

Caron and Inez busied themselves with their waffles. I put down my coffee cup and said, "How did you happen to hear about Peter?"

"You must realize this is a tight little community. Ahmed noticed Rosen's departure and mentioned it to Alexander, who had been out taking an early-morning stroll with Miss Portia and Miss Cordelia. One of them told Miriam, who reported it to Mrs. McHaver, who called me to inquire if there was any hint of marital discord."

I started to protest, but he ignored me.

"However, Alexander suspected it was due to Rosen's meeting yesterday with Chief Inspector el-Habachi, who asserted that the trip was a business matter involving the Minister of Economic Development. You see, I can be quite the Hercule Poirot myself, when need be."

"Shall I assume you are also aware that I sneezed twice this morning while taking a shower?" I said.

He stepped back. "Now you mustn't think we were gossiping about you, Claire. It's our obligation to look after any young woman of our acquaintance who has been abandoned in such a fashion, if only for a few days. Several of us are attending a lecture this morning at the Mummification Museum on the floral motifs on the coffins of the twenty-first dynasty. Some Swedish chap who's written a book. I've met him, and his accent is impenetrable, but he has slides. I do hope you will join us."

I ignored the intakes of breath across the table. "Thank you for the invitation, Lord Bledrock, but we have other plans for the day." I looked at my watch. "Our driver will be picking us up soon, so we must go. I hope you enjoy the lecture."

Caron, Inez, and I hurried up the stairwell to the suite. Once I'd collapsed in a chair and caught my breath, I said, "Think of something."

"We could go to Luxor Temple," Inez suggested timidly. "It's next to the hotel."

"If we leave on foot, Ahmed will rat us out," said Caron. "But if we stay here, then the maid will say something and we'll end up on the local news."

"True." I leaned back, feeling empathy for a fox in a burrow on the day of the hunt. The hounds were baying in their kennel down the hall, eager to catch a whiff of us should we venture forth. "What a bunch of busybodies. Lord Bledrock is probably speculating about our outing, as well as my sneezes. I wouldn't be all that surprised if he were telling Ahmed to locate an allergist who makes house calls."

"What if," Inez said, "we have Bakr pick us up and drive around for a while, then drop us off at the Luxor Temple? They'll all be at the museum by then."

"Lame, but workable," Caron said, shrugging disdainfully since it was not her idea and was therefore second-rate at best. "Just promise me that we don't have to gaze soulfully at every hieroglyph while Japanese tourists take our pictures."

I called Bakr, and after fifteen minutes we crept down the stairs and out through the lobby of the New Winter Palace to the van waiting at the curb. Bakr took us to an area with narrow streets, crowded shops, and tourists burdened with dauntingly large backpacks and maps in hand. We bought a few native crafts to take home, then had tea and biscuits. An hour later, we decided it was safe to proceed to Luxor Temple.

Bakr dropped us off at the ticket office on the corniche, which was well away from the entrances to the Old and New Winter Palaces. Once inside, we headed down a stone walkway toward the imposing facade of the temple.

"That's the avenue of sphinxes," Inez said as she gestured to a long path flanked with smaller versions of the more famous Great Sphinx at Giza. "It used to go all the way to Karnak, which is three kilometers to the north. The temple is an expansion by Amenhotep III during the New Kingdom on the site of a sanctuary built by Hatshepsut. Over there by the entrance are the colossi of Ramses II and a pink granite obelisk. There were two obelisks, but the second is in the Place de la Concorde in Paris. The wall is twenty-four meters tall and—"

"Howdy!" boomed Sittermann, stepping out from behind one of the colossi. "Fancy meeting you here!"

I was almost glad to see him. "Good morning."

"Ain't this a dandy coincidence," he continued, oblivious to the chill in my voice. "I got some folks I want you to meet. Americans, just like us. I met 'em out at the Kharga Oasis."

Nudging and jostling, he hustled us inside the temple as if we were wayward calves. I tried to pause long enough to gape at the towering pillars and lucid blue sky above them, but Sittermann was relentless. We went through several rooms, edging our way past tour groups, until we were allowed to stop. A couple stood near a scaffold, talking to a mason above them.

"I was wondering where you two ran off," said Sittermann. "I want you to meet a real good friend of mine, Claire Malloy. She's over here with her husband, who's in development, same as me. Mrs. Malloy, this is Samuel. I don't rightly recollect his last name."

The young man turned around. His scruffy beard, stained T-shirt, cutoff jeans, and sandals were appropriate collegiate wear. A frayed canvas bag hung on a strap on his shoulder and an elaborate camera from another strap. His dark hair hung in his eyes in the style of punk celebrities. His shirtsleeve partly obscured an amateurish tattoo. "Hey," he said, squinting at me. "Samuel Berry, from Richmond. Pleased to meet you, ma'am."

His companion looked over her shoulder at me, then more closely at Caron and Inez. "Me, too," she said in a squeaky voice. "I'm Buffy Franz, from Marin County, across the bay from San Francisco." There was nothing scruffy about her appearance. Her ash blond hair was shoulder length and artfully flipped, her makeup adequate for a presidential reception, and her blouse and skirt discreetly adorned with designer labels. If she'd come from an oasis, she'd found a manicurist and a pedicurist in a mud hut next to a hair salon.

"How do you do?" I said. I was aware of Caron and Inez breathing on my neck, but neither spoke.

"Isn't this just fantastic?" demanded Buffy. "All these really big columns and statues and stuff? I just shudder when I think how old it is!"

"Me, too," Caron said softly. "Shudder, that is."

I stepped on her toe, but only hard enough to illicit a small gasp. "Yes, it is fascinating. Please don't let us interrupt you. There's so much more to see, I've been told. The . . . ah, hypostyle hall and so forth."

Sittermann deftly blocked my path. "Samuel and Buffy are staying at the Old Winter Palace. What say we have a look around here, then go back to the bar and cool off?"

"I'd rather eat spiders," Caron muttered in my ear.

Samuel frowned for a moment, then said, "Sure thing, Sittermann. The columned hall is this way, Mrs. Malloy. There are some great frescoes from the Roman period."

Buffy fell into step next to me. "This is my first time in Egypt. I'm not supposed to be here. My parents think I'm in Rome doing the junior year abroad thing, but it was really boring after the first few weeks. We had to go to classes and listen to these funny little Italian professors drone on and on about history and architecture. It was all I could do to sneak away for a few hours to shop. It was maddening. There I was, sitting on the Spanish Steps listening to a lecture about some dumb Bernini fountain, when Armani, Gucci, Versace, Valentino, Hermès, and Prada were all within a block. I thought I was going to throw up!"

"Brutal," Inez said ever so innocently.

Buffy sighed. "It was awful. So one night some of us went to a bar, and Sammy came in with a couple of guys he'd met at a youth hostel, and one thing led to another. Isn't it amazing? Even though the shopping here is positively dismal, I've always wanted to see the pyramids. They were built by aliens, you know. There's like no way those stones could have been piled up like that without the help of extraterrestrial technology. When we go back to Cairo, I'm going to bribe somebody to let me spend the night in the room at the bottom of the pyramid. Supposedly, if you have a crystal, it gets all kind of mystical power and you can use it to cure cancer and promote worldwide peace."

"Those are admirable goals," I said.

Samuel stopped until we caught up. "Buffy, lay off the crap about the aliens and crystals, okay? The pyramids were built by Egyptian laborers, who had nothing better to do during the season when the Nile flooded their fields. They had a system of ramps to move the stone blocks up the pyramid. Construction engineers figured it out a long time ago."

"I thought they were slaves," Buffy said, pouting.

"Don't rely on Hollywood for historical accuracy."

Sittermann, who'd been uncharacteristically quiet, swung around, nearly toppling an unwary tourist with a camcorder. "What are you, Samuel—a historian or an engineer?"

"An architect. I finished my degree in May, and I'm taking a year off before I settle down at a firm. I'm a big fan of the Graeco-Roman period. I'd been in Rome for a couple of months when I met Buffy. When I told her I was heading here, she begged to come along. She makes a cozy tent mate."

Buffy rolled her eyes. "As if I'd be caught dead in a tent. That hotel at the oasis was the nastiest place I've ever slept in. The sheets felt like old towels and the bathrooms were your worst nightmare."

"What were you doing out there?" I asked Samuel.

"There's a good museum of antiquities, a couple of temples, a necropolis, and the Monastery of Al-Kashef, which overlooks what was once the most significant crossroad in the Western Desert."

"Caravans and camels?" Inez asked, perking up. Behind her glasses, her eyes were bright.

Samuel grimaced. "It was the major route for the slave trade from Darfur to Asyut in the Nile Valley. Untold numbers of poor souls died of starvation and thirst along the route. The Brits finally put a stop to it, but not until the end of the nineteenth century. These days it's all Humvees and ATVs. Not very romantic."

"Why were you there?" I asked Sittermann. "It's a little desolate for a theme park. I guess you could have a giant sandbox and shovels."

"Now, now, Mrs. Malloy. I'm as curious as the next fellow. I have to admit I was hoping to see sheiks and exotic dancing girls instead of backpackers and ruins. Little Buffy here was the prettiest thing out there."

We remained silent as we resumed walking, although Buffy was wiggling her bottom and tossing coy glances at Samuel as if she were in contention for "Miss Sand Dune." Samuel gave us a detailed talk on the faintly visible fragments of Roman frescoes. Caron and Inez retreated to a pillar and perched on the base, whispering and sending dark looks at me. Buffy did her limited best to appear interested, then gave up and wandered into a shady corner to file her fingernails.

Samuel at last ran out of minutiae. Sittermann slapped him on the back, then took my arm in a proprietary way that set my teeth on edge. "I do believe we've earned that drink, Mrs. Malloy, and I'm not going allow you to beg off. Your husband's in Cairo. You're not one of those meek wives who are scared to be seen in public with a man other than their husband, are you? I'd be mighty disappointed in you. It ain't like you have to go to your room and iron his shirts."

"I drink with whomever I choose," I said as I removed his hand. "Thank you for the invitation. The girls and I have a car waiting for us, and an engagement for a late lunch. Perhaps we'll join you another time."

"Good thing you've got sweet young chaperones to protect your reputation."

I clamped down on my lip for a moment. "Samuel,

Buffy, I enjoyed meeting you. I hope you have a lovely time in Luxor."

I spun around and walked toward the front of the temple, confident that Caron and Inez were following me. We kept a brisk pace until we arrived outside the ticket office. I allowed myself to exhale. "That contemptible man!"

"We have an engagement for a late lunch?" Caron blotted her face with a tissue, then dug a lipstick out of her purse and pinkened her lips. "Thanks for mentioning it."

"I think she made it up," Inez volunteered.

Caron snorted. "The end justifies the means? How come you always jump down my throat when I tell one tiny fib?"

For a moment, I felt like the Savage Sheik facing a pair of whiny English ladies. They were saved only by the arrival of our car. Bakr leaped out and opened the back door for me.

"Did you enjoy your outing?" he asked. "Luxor Temple is very, very magnificent, is it not?"

I glared at him. "Just drive, okay?"

CHAPTER 5

We opted to have lunch at the Hilton, where we were safe from the unwanted attentions of Sittermann and the British contingent. Once we'd savored final bites of ice cream, we strolled around the pool and then found Bakr near the car, chatting with other drivers. "I'd like to have another look at the bookstore," I said to Caron and Inez. "What would you like to do?"

"Go back to Luxor Temple," Inez admitted. "I didn't have a chance to see Amenhotep III's birth room scenes and the barque shrine rebuilt by Alexander the Great. He's depicted as a pharaoh in the reliefs, although I don't see how he could—"

"I'd rather shop," Caron said. "I want to get souvenirs for Emily and Ashley. I can go with you, Mother."

Her tone, interjected with martyred sighs, suggested that I was begging for company on the way to the guillotine, but I merely nodded. Since we'd all be within easy walking of the Winter Palace, Bakr dropped Inez at the ticket office and then took Caron and me down to the quirky little mall. I told him that I would let him know about our plans for the next day as soon as we had any, then sent him home or to the police department or wherever he went when not hauling us around. From his expression, I inferred that he'd be much happier sitting in the car with his paperback and a can of soda.

Caron announced that she'd find me in an hour or so.

She had already disappeared into a swarm of tourists as I went into the bookstore. Sneezing occasionally, I poked through books with photographs of Egypt during its days under British rule. The text was dry and vaguely disapproving of the local culture. I moved on to botanical books, most of them written in German. Even when indecipherable, the written word has a certain glory. The invention of the wheel led to mobility (and the tainted gene pool that included SUVs), but the alphabet gave us the ability to communicate with humanity and our posterity. If one read German, anyway.

I bought a battered novel by an obscure English novelist who'd been disregarded due to her flagrant inclusion of plot, then realized almost two hours had elapsed since I'd parted ways with my daughter. I went out to the walkway and peered in the direction she'd taken. It was less crowded, as many of the tourists had faded away to their hotels for afternoon naps. The idea of a cold drink on the hotel terrace appealed, but I was reluctant to abandon Caron. Pop music blared from some of the shops as I walked by them, peering inside for a flash of red hair. Shopkeepers came to their doorways and held out linens for my inspection. A shoeshine boy approached with a glint in his eyes. *"La, la, shukran,"* I said in what was quite likely to be an excruciatingly bad accent. He looked down at my sandals, shrugged, and went after other prey.

I wasn't overly anxious, but I wasn't happy, either. Caron would not have gone back to the hotel without telling me. On the other hand, everyone seemed content to go about their business. She could not have been tricked into leaving with someone; nor could she be forcibly hauled away without making her displeasure loudly known. Loudly enough to be heard in Cairo.

I glanced at a shop with a dusty window and a display of antique jewelry and trinkets on the sill. It might be a place to find something for Luanne. I was about to go inside when I saw Lord Bledrock by the counter, conversing with a fashionably dressed Arab gentleman likely to be the proprietor.

I stepped back, bumping into a hovering shopkeeper with a selection of long robes draped over his arm.

"Hello, lady," he said. "You like these? I make you a special deal."

I shook my head, keeping an eye on the antiques shop door. "No, thank you. I'm not interested."

"American? I have a cousin who lives in America, in the city of Toledo. His name is Hany Husseini. Maybe you know him?"

"I've never been to Toledo," I said without turning my head. "But if I ever go there, I'll be sure to look him up."

He stuck a robe in front of my face. "This is very pretty with your eyes, *Sitt*. You try it on, yes?"

"No," I said. "I don't want to buy a robe. Please, if you don't mind, I'd—"

"A scarf, then. I have many fine scarves. I will give you a very good price because you are a nice lady."

"Nothing." I eased forward and ascertained that Lord Bledrock was still inside the antiques shop. If I ventured inside, the shopkeeper would attach himself to me with the tenacity of a leech. I risked looking back at him with a steely frown. "I am not going to purchase anything today, okay? Not a robe, a scarf, or anything else you intend to offer me. I may decide to come back another time and let you show me everything you have to sell. I may buy enough robes for the Mormon Tabernacle Choir." I held up a finger. "But only if you leave me alone today."

Crestfallen, he went into his shop. I risked another peek inside the antiques shop. Lord Bledrock was no longer visible. There were no white-haired walruses among those moving in the direction of the corniche. I'd turned away for only a few seconds, and Lord Bledrock was hardly nimble enough to vanish into the crowd. Odd, I thought, as I moved in front of the window and studied the jewelry.

"I have better pieces inside."

I looked up at the man in the doorway. He had short gray hair, wire-rimmed glasses, and a precise goatee. Like many of the educated Egyptians I'd met, he had a pronounced British accent. I nodded and followed him into the shop. The floor-to-ceiling shelves were jammed with books, magazines, and haphazard stacks of photographs. Jewelry and small articles made of gold and silver were sprinkled about the room on rickety end tables. What sunlight had found its way through the windows offered little illumination. It was hard to imagine the shop as a profitable business.

"I am Dr. Butros Guindi. Please allow me to offer you a glass of mint tea," he murmured, gesturing at a round table and three mismatched, uncomfortable-looking chairs. As I sat down, he went to the curtained doorway behind the counter and barked at someone in terse Arabic. "Make yourself comfortable," he said as he returned. "Girgis will bring us tea in a moment. Are you looking for anything in particular? A necklace or a bracelet? Perfume bottles?"

"I don't really know," I said. "A gift for a friend."

He scratched his chin, then plucked several items from their niches and put them on the table in front of me. "This bracelet was made in the forties for an English lady. The stones are semiprecious, but the craftsmanship is excellent. The filigree is very delicate, and required great skill." He paused as a boy appeared with two small glasses of tea and set them on the table. "The necklace comes from the Delta region. The amethysts are of good quality. I have these simple chains, too."

I admired them as we sipped the fragrant sweet tea. "Very nice," I finally said, "but I'm not sure what it is I'm looking for."

"That is often a problem."

"Not a serious one, though."

"Sometimes it is better not to look for anything."

"Anything?" I said, frowning.

"If you are not careful, you may not like what you find."

I had the unnerving feeling that we were not discussing jewelry. I realized he was staring at me with undue intensity, and hastily picked up an ornate gold box. "This is pretty."

"If one likes that sort of thing. It is a replica of a small jewelry case found in the tomb of a lesser pharaoh's wife. It was made thirty to forty years ago."

"Oh." I put it down and took another sip of tea. "I saw an acquaintance in here a few minutes ago. Does he collect antique jewelry?"

Dr. Guindi gave me a blank look. "A few minutes ago? You are mistaken, dear lady. At noon I had to close the shop and rush home to deal with a plumbing crisis. You are the first person to come in here since I returned."

"I saw him standing right over there by the counter, talking to you," I persisted. "Elderly, white hair, ruddy complexion."

"There was no one here. You saw a reflection in the glass. This gentleman you describe must have been across the walkway in another shop. If you will excuse me, I am expecting an international call." He took the glass from my hand and stood up. "Please come back another day. Perhaps by then you'll know what it is you're seeking."

He was trying to ease me out the door, but I wasn't ready to be summarily dismissed. "I must thank Girgis for the tea." Before Dr. Guindi could protest, I detoured behind the counter and pulled aside the curtain. The back room was small and crowded with cardboard boxes and wooden crates. A worktable was cluttered with small tools and brushes. Another table had a hot plate and the accouterments for making tea. Despite the shadows, I could see that no one was lurking there.

"Girgis has gone to run an errand for me," the proprietor said as he took my elbow and steered me to the entrance. "I will pass along your regards, Mrs. Malloy."

I found myself on the cobbled walkway, blinking in the sunlight. I spun around, but a "Closed" sign hung on the door and the owner had vanished. I had taken a few shaky steps when I realized he'd addressed me by name. I mentally replayed our conversation. He'd mentioned his name, but I most decidedly had not offered mine. I was pondering this when Caron stumbled into me.

Clutching my arm, she said, "I saw him again!"

"Saw who, dear?"

"That man who was following Inez and me the other day. The one with the mustache and the scar. He was wearing the same suit and everything!"

"He was shopping."

"He was following me!"

I glanced around but saw no one that fit his description. "Why do you think he was following you? This is the most convenient shopping area near the hotel. Have you and Inez been staying up half the night reading about that sheik?"

"I am not imagining this," she said, her forehead lowered ominously. Her eyes were glittering as brightly as the amethysts in the necklace that I'd been shown minutes earlier. "Just forget it, okay? Don't let my kidnapping or murder spoil your honeymoon. I'm going to the hotel, if you don't mind. Why don't you stay and find a T-shirt with camels on it for Peter? He can wear it to my funeral."

She stomped back toward the corniche. I trailed her at a prudent distance, keeping an eye out for Lord Bledrock and any stray shoppers with mustaches and scars. We continued in silence to the entrance of the Winter Palace and up the curved marble staircase to the lobby. If Ahmed was lurking around, he had enough sense not to attempt to divert either of us. The elevator ride was chilly. Once in the suite, Caron disappeared into her bedroom and slammed the door.

I freshened up and was reading on the balcony when Inez came into the suite, accompanied by Alexander. Blushing, she said, "I ran into him in the elevator, Mrs. Malloy."

"Literally," Alexander said with a grin. "She had her nose in a guidebook and nearly ran me down. Rather than file an assault charge, I negotiated for a vodka and tonic. If that's all right with you, of course . . ."

"Help yourself," I said to him. "There's ice in the bucket."

Inez scuttled into her bedroom as Alexander busied himself at the mini-bar. He was still grinning when he joined me. "She's quite a passionate student of all things Egyptian, isn't she?" he said.

"Unlike my daughter, who'd rather support the local economy." I paused for a moment, contemplating how to phrase my next remark. "Did you attend the lecture at the museum earlier today?"

"Unfortunately, I did, and it went on interminably. We just now got back to the hotel."

"Did everybody go?"

"With the exception of Mrs. McHaver, who is suffering from gout. She prides herself on having only the most aristocratic maladies. Poor Miriam was sent to take notes and report anything that might be considered controversial. However, since no one could understand a word the Swedish chap said, it was impossible to dispute his premises. Miss Portia and Miss Cordelia fluttered around like lavender moths. Lady Emerson and Lewis Ferncliff got into a terrible row over some scrap of papyrus. Wallace kept nipping from a flask and glowering at anyone who came within ten feet of him. Shannon tried to talk to my father, but he was in his typical dyspeptic mood. She finally slunk away in tears."

"Your father was there the entire time?"

Alexander eyed me over the rim of his glass. "He dozed off during the lecture. I jabbed him whenever he began to snore. Are you regretting that you missed the show? I can promise there'll be many repeat performances during the season."

"I thought I saw your father earlier this afternoon," I said.

"He may have been dreaming that he was elsewhere, but he was in the back row with me. You must have seen someone who resembled him."

"I suppose so," I said, still unconvinced. After a moment, I continued, "Why is Shannon so determined to talk to your father? Is she hoping for more financial support for the dig?"

"What she's hoping for is the position of department head at her cozy little college. Although I have no idea why, she seems to think the position is significant and will enhance her prestige with her colleagues in the field. Academia is an ugly battlefield in every country. British dons have resorted to murder over committee chairmanships and obscure awards. Scandinavian universities are rife with scandals involving plagiarism. The French prefer accusations of *mauvaise conduite sexuelle*."

"American academics resort to all of those," I admitted. "So what does Shannon want from your father, if not money?"

"He has an extensive collection of Egyptian antiquities at the house in Kent, the majority of it unavailable to scholars. Shannon wants him to endow a wing at her college and donate some of them to a permanent collection. He prefers to gloat over them in private. He's turned down every request, including those of the Metropolitan in New York and the British Museum. He sneered when someone asked him if he'd seen the traveling King Tut exhibition. Only Amun-Ra knows what he has locked away on the second floor."

"You don't?"

"Good heavens, no. When I was much younger, I used to try to pick the locks with my mother's hairpins, but I invariably set off the security alarms and was banished to the nursery in disgrace. I finally decided to let the old man wallow in his precious treasures, and dedicated myself to carousing and chasing women." He gazed at me. "I don't understand how you've been able to resist me."

"I seem to be the only woman who has," I said drily.

"Thus far."

When he'd finished his drink, I sent him away. At sunset, Caron and Inez came out to the balcony and we watched the feluccas gliding on the Nile.

Over breakfast even Caron agreed that we needed to get serious about the must-see sites. With Bakr providing transportation, we returned to the West Bank to admire the two massive statues known as the Colossi of Memnon, all that remained of a temple complex built by Amenhotep III, unfortunately without regard to its position in the floodplain.

When several tour buses parked in the lot, we continued on to the Ramesseum, where Inez chattered happily about Ramses II and I recited "Ozymandias" to an unappreciative audience. We returned to the Valley of the Kings to dutifully visit King Tut's tomb and a few others, and I sat in the shade of the visitor's center while Inez scrambled to the top of a hill to view the Temple of Hatshepsut. Caron was noticeably less fervent as she tagged along.

The following day Salima arrived in the van with Bakr, and we toured the half-dozen tombs in the Valley of the Queens. Salima had arranged special passes for us to visit the tomb of Nefertari, often closed to visitors. The spectacular wall paintings of the pharaoh's wife and a pantheon of gods and goddesses overwhelmed us. Salima provided the standard tourist spiel, but in a soft, lilting tone. Inez was speechless, and periodically pulled off her glasses to wipe her eyes. It was a pleasant respite from her incessant recitation of names and dates.

Afterward, we returned to the van to swill water from Bakr's stash of bottles and gaze at the valley, wider than that of the kings and less popular with the tourists. "Shall we call it a day?" I asked.

"I am drenched in perspiration," Caron said. "If I don't have a shower soon, my pores will literally shut down."

Inez, still resolutely dressed in her increasingly sweat-stained khakis, glanced up from one of her guidebooks and nodded.

I looked at Salima. "Can we drop you off somewhere?"

"Well, if you don't mind terribly, I thought I'd go back to the hotel with you. I'm having dinner at seven with the group from the University of Chicago, but I don't want to arrive early. I'll end up having a frightful row with someone. We don't always agree on restoration and preservation issues, and some of them"—she rolled her eyes—"are appallingly opinionated."

"Then why are you going?" I asked as Bakr started the van.

"There are times when one needs to have a frightful row

to invigorate oneself. I suspect that's the best reason for getting married."

"Perhaps," I murmured, thinking of some of the disagreements I'd had with Peter in the past. I would never describe them as "frightful rows," but he had been known to become rather testy when he felt as though I was interfering in an official police investigation. He never seemed to grasp that I was merely doing my civic duty to assist the authorities in their pursuit of justice. Now that I had married him, I would retire to a less stressful life of selling books and flipping through decorator magazines. In two years, Caron would be in college, preferably one that was not within easy driving distance. I looked out the window at the bleak lunar landscape, devoid of any trace of vitality or passion.

Caron poked Salima's arm. "Are you sure you're not hoping Alexander might drop by the suite for a cocktail?"

"Alexander?" she said. "Oh, you mean the cheeky bastard from London? I should say not. I ran into too many of his kind at Cambridge. There is a reason behind the cliché about the ne'er-do-well offspring of the peers of the realm. Vapid, spoiled, and insufferably smug. The only calluses on their hands come from wielding a cricket bat."

"Methinks the lady doth protest too much," Inez said without looking up.

"Don't be such a child," Salima retorted sulkily.

I agreed with Inez, but I wisely remained silent as we drove back across the bridge and through the crowded streets of Luxor. Bakr dropped us off at the hotel entrance. To my dismay, Sittermann waylaid us as soon as we entered the lobby.

"Well, isn't this a coincidence!" he boomed. "I was just about to leave a message for you, but here you are right in front of me. Who's this most fetching young lady? Not another one of your fillies, surely."

I could see Ahmed hovering behind a pillar, wringing his hands. I had no idea why he was agitated, unless he had tipped off Sittermann about the likely time of our return. If he had, I thought grimly, he would need Osiris's intervention to save himself. "This is Mr. Sittermann, from Texas," I said through clenched teeth. "Salima el-Musafira, a noted Egyptologist."

"I'm tickled pink to meet you, honey," Sittermann said. "Why don't you all join us out on the terrace for a drink?"

"I think we'd prefer to go upstairs," I said quickly.

He beamed at me. "Yeah, that would be a sight nicer, wouldn't it? I'll just get my group together and we'll be on your heels. In fact, I'll have the restaurant send up some platters of finger food and we can have ourselves a proper party. You don't have to do a thing, Mrs. Malloy. I'll take care of ice, glasses, and whiskey. See you in ten minutes, give or take."

He was gone before I could protest. Ahmed had managed to fade into the decor and, if he had any sense, would continue to stay there for a few days. For his sake, I hoped he'd pocketed a goodly sum.

"It seems that we're having a party," I said as we rode the elevator to the second floor.

"Maybe you are," Caron said. "I'm going to exfoliate my pores. It will take hours."

Inez took off her canvas hat and tucked it in a pocket. "The hotel has an Internet connection, and I promised my parents that I'd e-mail them once a week. I don't know how much it costs, but—"

"By all means," I said as the elevator door opened. "Salima, don't even think about it. You've already mentioned that your invitation is for seven o'clock."

Her eyes glittered. "No, I shall be Sekmet, the lioness goddess of vengeance and destruction, or better yet, Taweret. She's the hippopotamus goddess who scares away evil forces and protects women."

"Need a quick shot of gin?"

"Several."

We went into the suite, and the girls promptly disappeared into their room. I put on a clean shirt and ran a comb through my hair. When I came into the parlor, I wasn't surprised to find Salima on the sofa with a glass in her hand.

"Couldn't wait for ice?" I asked.

"I spent five years at Cambridge. The only ice I ever saw was on the sidewalks. It was highly entertaining to watch the fellows step on a slick spot and kersplat on their bums like giant bats dropping out of the sky."

I was visualizing the scene with some amusement when the parlor door opened and in came, in no particular order, Sittermann, Lord Bledrock, Miriam and Rose McHaver, Shannon King, Alexander, Samuel Berry, Buffy Franz, Wallace Laxenby, the Misses Portia and Cordelia, Lord and Lady Fitzwillie, and a couple of unknowns. They were all babbling with boundless vivacity, bumping into one another, and clearly expecting a well-laid bar and a grand spread of food.

"Hello," I said weakly.

Abdullah and several uniformed waiters wheeled in linen-draped tables and began to set up a bar and a buffet. Sittermann took charge and drawled orders in Arabic, while my purported guests rearranged furniture. Chairs were fetched from the balcony, my bedroom, and Caron and Inez's bedroom (despite the muffled shrieks).

"How do you do," said a formidable woman with jet-black hair. "I am Lady Amanda Peabody Emerson. You must be this Malloy woman of whom I've heard so much these last few weeks. Fancy yourself to be a detective, do you?"

"Give her a break, Mandy," Sittermann said as he sat down on the arm of the sofa and winked at me.

"She seems ill equipped," Lady Emerson pronounced firmly, then headed for the bar.

Alexander managed to squeeze himself between Salima and me. "I think you're very well equipped, my dear Claire. The old girl's jealous. She made a fortune off some deceased relative's fanciful memoirs of murder and intrigue a hundred years ago. Rumor has it she still collects royalties. Lady Emerson herself would never be caught dead within spitting distance of a camel."

"Nor would I," I said. I unwedged myself and went to circulate, making sure everyone had a drink. Samuel and Buffy seemed delighted to see me and gushed over the decor and view. Rose McHaver sat in one of the more comfortable chairs, thumping a lethal-looking walking stick as she waited for Miriam to fetch her a drink. Queen Victoria could not have looked more imperious. Wallace had retreated to a corner, martinis in both hands. Shannon was doing her best to interrupt Lord Bledrock's conversation with a pasty woman drooping under the weight of her diamonds. Miss Portia and Miss Cordelia were out on the balcony, lobbing ice cubes at unwary pedestrians crossing the terrace. Abdullah watched me with a faint grimace of reproof.

"Hope you've been having a good time," Sittermann said, clutching my elbow. "Been out exploring the West Bank, I hear."

"From whom do you hear this? I hardly consider myself a worthy topic of conversation."

"Word gets around."

"I have no idea what that word might be."

"Let's just say I'm concerned about you, Mrs. Malloy. A woman like yourself could find herself stumbling into trouble, especially if she pokes around the wrong places and asks too many questions."

"I beg your pardon!" I tried to remove his hand, but he tightened his grip. "The question in my mind at this moment has to do with why I shouldn't stomp down on your foot hard enough to turn your toes into bloody pulp."

"Spirited little thing, ain't you?"

"Who the hell do you think you are?" I said, struggling to keep my voice low.

He released my arm and stepped back. "Just someone who thinks you need to be warned against snooping around while your so-called husband is off in Cairo."

"How dare you—" I began, then stopped as he went out to the balcony. I forced myself to breathe evenly until my body stopped quivering with outrage. To my dismay, Samuel and Buffy joined me.

"Are you okay?" asked Buffy. "You look awfully pale,

like one of those albino fish that live in caves. They are so creepy."

Samuel nudged her aside. "Are you and Sittermann close friends?"

His question startled me. "Hardly," I said. "Why would you think we were?"

He flushed. "He acts pretty interested in you, that's all. I had the impression that you and he . . . well, I don't know. I mean, your husband's away and . . ."

"You men are all alike," Buffy said with the arrogant wisdom of youth. "If I hadn't been like totally bored in Rome, I would never have come with you. I could have gone skiing, you know, or taken off for a Greek island with fabulous beaches and hunky fishermen who know how to utilize their manly talents. All you do is take photographs of ruins in the blistering sun and hang out half the night with illiterate camel drivers. You told me we were going to see the pyramids, but all we've seen so far are pitiful villages in the middle of nowhere. I'm absolutely covered in flea bites. If I get lice, I'll track you down to the last sand dune in this filthy country and make you sorry."

"You invited yourself to come along with me," he muttered.

"That has nothing to do with it. Mrs. Malloy knows what I'm talking about."

They both glared at me. I licked my lips, but no glib responses came to mind. I realized that Wallace and Shannon had overheard Buffy's harangue on the indignities and were waiting for me to make a ruling. I wondered wildly if they represented the prosecution or the defense.

"Well," I said carefully, "it does seem as if you two might have discussed this back in Rome."

"All we did in Rome was have sex," Buffy said. "Then he said I should come to Egypt with him, and I asked if there were decent shops in Cairo, and he said yeah. He just forgot to mention that we weren't *going* to Cairo. Do you have any idea what they sell in local markets? Carcasses of dead animals, onions, and turnips, that's what. Brands of clothing that Wal-Mart wouldn't touch."

Samuel shook his head. "Some people enjoy learning about other cultures."

"In an air-conditioned classroom, maybe," she said, "but not in a stinky market with flies and cripples and screaming babies. And who cares about some culture in which the women hide their faces behind veils and stay home, while the men go to cafés and the mosques? I've had a really swell time reading an old issue of *People* for the hundredth time while Samuel hangs out with his buddies. One night they started shooting off guns like little boys with fireworks. I thought I'd never get to sleep."

"Making friends with the locals is the best way to find out about lesser-known Greek and Roman sites," Samuel said to me. "There are plenty of them that don't warrant mention in the guidebooks. Alexander liberated Egypt from the Persians three hundred years before the Christian era. He and his successor, Ptolemy, established a Graeco-Egyptian pantheon and built temples all over the country. The Romans came along next. The pharaonic sites get all the attention, but—"

"Samuel's just fascinated with broken columns and a few stone blocks," Buffy interrupted, sneering. "As long as they're in the middle of some forsaken expanse of rocks and sand. At least the Colosseum is surrounded by cafés and shops."

They were exchanging heated remarks as I eased away from them. I was contemplating locking myself in my bathroom until they left when Lord Bledrock shoved a martini glass in my hand.

"I hear you were allowed in Nefertari's tomb earlier today," he said. "You're really quite lucky. The Supreme Council of Antiquities rarely opens it to anyone. The humidity has a deleterious effect on the delicate paintings. The human body is quite soggy, as well as a source of bacteria and carbon dioxide. The only way to truly preserve the paintings is to keep them in a closed room with controlled humidity and temperature. I've often thought children should be reared in a similar environment, released only for brief appearances at holiday gatherings until they're old enough to be packed off to school."

"Why bother having them in the first place?"

His eyes widened in disbelief at my question. "One must have heirs."

I was not completely sure he wasn't serious. "What about daughters?"

"One marries them off to the heirs of other estates. What with all the taxes and onerous death duties, one must protect the family title. The first Baron of Rochland was an ally of Charles II. The Merry Monarch, as he was called, had fourteen illegitimate children by a string of mistresses. There are rumors that the baroness was one of them, although the history is vague. A delightful thought, eh?"

"You must be very proud."

He glanced at those who might have been within earshot, then drew me to a vacant corner. "Alexander mentioned that you were curious about the lecture. If the Swedish chap is staying in the hotel, I'm sure I could arrange an introduction. I found him to be tedious, but you might enjoy him."

"I'm surprised you stayed all afternoon," I said.

"Courtesy demanded as much. Can't just toddle off when the chap is talking about his life's work. I strongly believe one has to make sacrifices to maintain one's position in the community. Wouldn't you agree, Claire?"

"I would never argue the point with a baron."

"I say, you are the droll one, aren't you? I like that in a woman. Now, you must tell me what you think of the all the marvelous temples and tombs in the area. When I gaze at the tourists trudging up the hill to the Valley of the Kings, I envision a procession of mortuary priests dressed in their finest white robes, their shaved heads glittering in the sunlight, leading workmen bearing the treasures to be buried with their pharaoh in order to enure his safe passage into the next world. What a shame it is that these masterpieces of gold, silver, and precious jewels were intended to never be seen again by mortal eyes." He licked his lips in a disturbingly predatory way. "No living person had laid eyes on Tutankhamun's golden death mask for three thousand years when Carter opened the tomb. Although the curse was nothing more than a bit of journalistic sensationalism, it's easy to imagine why it became so popular. Do you believe in curses?"

"Should I?" I said.

"Yes, indeed. It can be very dangerous when one ventures into an unknown situation. It is often more prudent to mind one's own business."

"Is that a warning?"

"It is whatever you choose to make of it, Claire." He gazed at me for a moment, then said, "Have you tried the *baba ghanoug*? It's quite tasty."

CHAPTER 6

Salima slipped away shortly before seven, and the rest departed after a final round of drinks. Caron came out of her bedroom, and she and I pondered the wreckage while Abdullah supervised the cleanup crew. At his suggestion, we loaded plates with food before they wheeled out the serving tables. When at last everyone was gone, Caron and I flopped down in chairs on the balcony.

"What a nasty group," I said. "I hate to think what they're like at the end of the season. The hotel staff must be adept at removing bloodstains."

Caron inspected her fingernails. "The price of popularity—or notoriety, in your case."

"Did Inez have luck with the hotel Internet?"

"You'll have to ask her when she gets back. She probably heard how loud the party had become as soon as she stepped off the elevator, and went down to the lobby. I considered doing the same."

"That bad?"

"Along the lines of a street riot," she said. "So what are we doing tomorrow? More temples, tombs, and hieroglyphs?"

"Peter should be back by noon, so I thought I'd stick around here. You and Inez need to buy presents for the party at Salima's house, if you haven't changed your minds." I mentally crossed my fingers and tried once again.

"Spending the evening with all those children and elderly relatives doesn't sound exciting. It might turn out to be more tedious than this last gathering, but in Arabic."

"Nothing could be More Tedious, trust me. That awful man from Texas barged into our room and started asking me all sorts of really dumb questions. I kept telling him I needed to wash my hair, but he would not leave. I was ready to sling something at him when Alexander came in and dragged him away."

"What was your weapon of choice? A bottle of fingernail polish?"

"Inez's book about the sheik, of course." She shifted her attention to the new freckles on her arms. "Salima says there are still guys like him out in the desert. They don't kidnap English ladies or do that kind of overblown, theatrical stuff, but they do attack caravans and convoys to steal guns. They're extremist Muslims who think Egypt ought to be controlled by clerics. There's one group with an Arab name, El Asad or something, that means 'Lion of God.' "

"Salima told you that?"

"I'm a little old for Ali Baba. Anyway, Inez read about it in one of her books and asked. Bakr was driving us at the time, and he kept trying to shush Salima. He would have had more luck damming up a river with chicken wire."

I resolved to have a talk with Peter as soon as he returned, and one with Salima as well. I wasn't worried that Caron would obsess on rogue sheiks, but I was less sure about Inez. As a distraction for both of us, I asked Caron if she'd had any ideas about presents to take to the party. We were idly discussing possibilities when Inez skittered into the parlor and locked the door.

"I saw him," she said breathlessly.

"Lawrence of Arabia?" I asked.

"That sinister man who was following us earlier in the week, with the mustache and the scar. This time he was wearing a lime green suit and a bow tie. The scar looked—

I don't know—different somehow, sort of shorter. I'm sure it was him, though."

Caron shot me a smug look. "I saw him a couple of days ago in that little mall, but Certain People didn't believe me."

"I believed you saw him," I said. "I just found it hard to believe he was following you. What was he doing when you saw him, Inez?"

"Buying cigarettes in a shop in the hotel—or pretending to, anyway. He must have seen me coming and ducked inside."

"He could be a spy," Caron contributed, "and was passing a message to his organization via the shopkeeper. Maybe he works for that lion group."

Inez's eyes rounded. "El Asad li-allah? It's more of a cult, but very dangerous, Ms. Malloy. They have international links to organizations all over the Middle East and cells in other countries. The police don't even know who's the head of it because everybody's too scared to talk, even the snitches. They've infiltrated the government and the military, and—"

"That man . . ." Caron gripped the armrests of the chair as she leaned forward. "He could be plotting to kidnap us and demand a ransom. They have to think we're rich because of this suite and our driver and stuff. They need money to fund their terrorist attack on the present political regime. We could be held hostage in some filthy oasis, and tortured—or worse!"

"Wait a minute, girls," I said evenly. "Before you make any wild accusations, at least entertain the possibility that he's just a traveler who's staying in the hotel, smokes, and needs gifts to take home to his wife and children. The hotel has nearly a hundred rooms, and that means a lot of guests. Most of them stay at least several days. I saw a few familiar faces at Luxor Temple and at the Valley of the Kings. Tables on the terrace are staked out by the same people every afternoon. Half the people at breakfast nod at us every morning.

If you weren't obsessed with this poor man, you wouldn't even notice him. He may think you're following him. He may have taken refuge in the tobacco shop because you alarmed him, Inez."

"I'll bet he has a gun in a shoulder holster," Caron continued. "That's why his jackets are so frumpy."

Considering the situations they'd been in over the last few years, their paranoia wasn't surprising. Few teenagers, with the exception of Nancy Drew and the Hardy Boys, have found themselves involved in so many bizarre investigations. Only two months earlier we'd been in the midst of lords and ladies, as well as knights, a duke, a duchess, and a baron, but of the faux Renaissance variety and all behaving quite perniciously. And that was merely the latest escapade. Caron and Inez had teethed on misdemeanors and flirted with felonies. Only my diligence and Peter's influence at the police department had saved them from a rap sheet long enough to stretch across the Nile.

They exchanged looks. When neither deigned to argue with me, I went into the bedroom I shared with my so-called husband, found my robe and nightgown, and retreated to the bathroom to fill the expansive bathtub and exfoliate my pores until they begged for mercy.

Peter arrived in time for lunch. The girls had taken themselves off to the hotel pool for the afternoon, so I suggested that we go out to a restaurant and then do a bit of shopping for Luanne, the Jorgesons, and Peter's mother. Rather than call Bakr, we opted to explore the narrow streets behind the hotel.

Once we'd found a suitably quaint restaurant and ordered, I told Peter about the party I'd been coerced into hosting.

"Sounds worse than my meeting in Cairo," he said, dutifully smiling with husbandly sympathy. "Mahmoud came along. One would think he's accustomed to bureaucratic blathering, but he almost lost his temper a couple of times. He's not interested in the international intrigue—he wants to make sure his jurisdiction is safe."

"Is it?" I instinctively glanced out the window to make sure no one was covertly watching us from across the street.

"In general, yes, but like any city, there are neighborhoods where it's not safe for anyone to wander around late at night. Occasionally a backpacker is mugged, usually because of an overindulgence in beer and a lack of common sense." He stopped as a waiter put down our plates and hovered until we nodded. "Let's not talk about it. What have you and the girls been doing?"

I obliged with a recap of the sites we'd visited, then hesitated to collect my thoughts before I told him what had happened when Caron and I had gone shopping in the mall. "I was so sure it was Lord Bledrock in that antiques shop, but Alexander was adamant that they'd been at the lecture all afternoon. What's more, the proprietor implied that I was crazy."

Peter leaned across the table and squeezed my hand. "You've been awfully nervous about the girls going to this party tonight."

"I did not say I saw mummies lurking about in the garden at midnight," I said as I withdrew my hand. I was too mature and reasonable to react with Caron's petulance, so I settled for a haughty stare. The waiter, who was approaching with the check, turned around and went back into the kitchen. "It's remotely plausible that I saw someone with a strong resemblance to Lord Bledrock, but it was definitely not a reflection in the glass."

"And whoever it was left while you were distracted by the merchant next door. That's reasonable."

Peter had that faintly skeptical expression that never failed to annoy me. Had it not been for the faces peering at us through the beaded doorway of the kitchen, I might have mentioned as much. "Don't patronize me," I said in a steely voice.

"I'm not patronizing you, Claire. I believe you, but I don't know what I'm supposed to do about it. You could have seen Lord Bledrock, although I don't know why Alexander and the others would lie about it. Maybe it's nothing more than a misunderstanding. Alexander didn't mention that his father had taken off for a few minutes when they returned to the hotel. They all could have parted ways in the lobby to buy newspapers and magazines or gripe at the concierge's desk. He didn't know you were interested in the details."

"What about the proprietor?" I asked. "Dr. Guindi, I think he said. Why did he lie?"

"He had his own reasons," Peter said, beginning to sound a wee bit exasperated. "He might have thought you were some kind of cat burglar who would sneak into Lord Bledrock's suite and steal whatever silver and gold pieces you could find. Lord Bledrock may be a long-standing client with a propensity for expensive jewelry. The proprietor was being discreet."

"He used my name."

"Or said 'ma'asalama,' which is Arabic for good-bye. You misunderstood. It's a common neurological response to interpret foreign phrases into something the brain can process."

I leaned back, my arms crossed. My glower was sharp enough to etch a few new wrinkles in his roguish face. "Is that what you learned at spy camp? Do you use this technique when interrogating suspected terrorists, or do you prefer electrodes and water torture? I think it's time to change the subject. What shall we get your mother? A tasteful T-shirt with a depiction of a smirking camel jockey? A hand-woven flying carpet? A coffee mug with Tut's face?"

He had enough sense to make no further references to what he surely considered to be an episode provoked by an overly active imagination coupled with maternal wariness. We wandered in and out of shops, purchasing a goodly number of gifts, and returned to the hotel late in the afternoon. When we stepped out of the elevator on the third floor, Abdullah was in the hallway with a cleaning cart. He gave me a piercing stare, then offered to fetch us a bucket of ice.

I was trying to fathom his hostility, if that's what it was, as we went into the suite. The cocktail party had

been loud and messy, but surely it had been no worse than
Lord Bledrock's frequent gatherings. I'd seen Sittermann
slip Abdullah a healthy tip. It seemed likely that he did
not approve of women entertaining without a proper host.

The shower was running in the girls' bathroom; I hoped
that no one else in the hotel expected hot water in the immediate future. I left Peter to wait for the ice and went into
our bathroom to freshen up and gaze at my sunburned
face. He and the girls were sitting on the balcony when I
emerged, companionably listening to the incessant blare of
horns and reverberating boom boxes.

"Guess where we're all going Monday!" Caron demanded before I could sit down. "This is so cool."

"I don't suppose it's to a psychiatric facility for over-
wrought tourists," I said. I accepted a drink from Peter to let
him know he was on the road to forgiveness, but hardly at
his destination.

"To the Nubian Sea," Inez said excitedly. "It's called
Lake Nasser in the guidebooks, but that's not as classy. It
extends to the Sudan border. The British constructed Aswan
Dam at the turn of the nineteenth century in order to increase the amount of cultivated land. At the beginning of
the twentieth century it was rebuilt and—"

"What's odd," Caron said, "is that it's called the Upper
Nile, although if you look at a map, it's at the bottom. I
think it should be the Lower Nile."

Inez shook her head. "I already explained that. It origi-
nates in Burundi, and the Blue and White Niles converge at
Khartoum and empty into the Mediterranean. At a little
more than four thousand miles, it's the longest river in the
world. The Amazon carries a greater volume of water because of its tributaries."

"Here's a fig," Caron said as she proffered a bowl. "Why
don't you stuff it in your mouth?"

I looked at Peter, who said, "While you were in the
other room, I called Mahmoud and confirmed it. He's
arranged two first-class cabins with private balconies on a
luxury cruise ship for three nights. We board at Aswan in

the afternoon. Bakr will drive us there, and we'll fly back here on Thursday." He gave me a dose of the boyish charm, replete with a dimple and the full impact of his molasses brown eyes. "If that's all right with you."

"How can we possibly be ready to go on such short notice?" I said, thinking of all my clothes scattered in the bedroom. The chaos in the girls' room no doubt resembled the aftermath of a tornado that had touched down during a hurricane. "All that packing, and trying to figure out what to do with everything we've bought, and—"

"We won't vacate the suite," he said soothingly. "It's ours for three weeks, whether or not we're in residence. All we need to do is take enough for a few days. Dress is casual."

"Abu Simbel at dawn," Inez said dreamily. "As the sun rises above the mountains, the first rays catch the four colossi of Ramses II as they stand guard should any boats dare to encroach upon the pharaoh's land from the south."

"It sounds lovely," I said. Even lovelier, it would be miles away from Lord Bledrock and his cronies, including Sittermann. Abdullah might recover from his current displeasure with me as well. Ideally, Peter would not be beckoned to Cairo or wherever it was he actually went. We could have a few days of bona fide honeymoon moments, including sunrise at Abu Simbel.

Caron, who was astute if not versed in the art of mind reading, rolled her eyes and poked Inez. Sniggering, they went into their room to dress for the party. Peter told me that we would be departing for the dinner party on the *dahabiyya* within a few minutes. I returned to our room, changed into a dress, and grabbed a sweater. The girls decided to wait for Salima in the lobby, so we took the elevator together. They were, I think, less pleased with their decision when we all spotted Mrs. McHaver, Miriam, and Lord Bledrock sitting around one of the low tables.

"Where are you off to?" asked Lord Bledrock, standing up as we approached. "A fancy restaurant, I'd wager. Rosen, you'd better keep a close eye on this wife of yours. She's liable to catch the fancy of a Saudi prince and be whisked away to a vast marble palace, where she'll be draped in diamonds and rubies and lead a life of decadent luxury." His eyebrows wiggled as he attempted to pat my derrière, but I deftly avoided his hand.

"Neville has such naive fantasies," said Mrs. McHaver. "I suspect it's due to harsh toilet training in the nursery. Don't you agree, Miriam?" When she had no response, she thumped her cane on the wood floor. "Miriam!"

Miriam looked up, startled. "I couldn't say, Aunt Rose." She was wearing her standard attire of drab brown, but she had make an attempt to lessen her pallor with pale lipstick and a trace of blush. She still looked as if she could be sent flying across the lobby with the flick of a finger.

Mrs. McHaver sniffed. "We're waiting for Lady Emerson's car. She's arranged a small dinner party for a group of trustees from a university in the States. Mary and William is the name of the institution, I believe. Americans have such an odd way with names, and their spelling is atrocious."

"You'll have to excuse us," Peter said, keeping an eye on Lord Bledrock, who was once again maneuvering to get near me. "We, too, have a dinner party to attend. Caron, Inez, it might be more polite of you to wait for Salima on the terrace."

"Salima?" Mrs. McHaver heaved her ample chest like a startled pigeon. "I presume you're speaking of the gal who was in your suite yesterday evening. I've met her father, Dr. el-Musafira. I was not at all impressed with his knowledge of the syntactic structure of the early Coptic manuscripts. One would think someone of his international repute has more than fleeting familiarity with such fields." She pointed her finger at the girls. "Is she taking you to bars and nightclubs? I hope you do not intend to take advantage of the laxity in alcoholic beverages being served to teenagers. Many a young girl has seen her career expectations brought to a halt as the result of a single night's indiscretion."

Caron returned her stare. "I already have twins, Beth

and Macbeth. They're at home, being toilet trained by their nanny."

She spun around and stomped toward the exit. Peter murmured something indistinguishable, as he, Inez, and I fled out the door. Caron was already at the bottom of the staircase, her expression as immutable as the faces carved on the colossi.

"Beth and Macbeth?" I said.

"I was going to add that the nanny's name was Mary Poppins, but I let it go," she said without smiling. "Who does she think she is? No wonder Miriam quivers every time the old witch pokes her with that horrible, gnarly finger!"

"I doubt Mrs. McHaver will give you any more advice," Peter said drily. "Salima should be here shortly. If you have any problems, call Bakr and he'll come pick you up. We'll see you at eleven."

Before I could launch into the short lecture I'd been rehearsing in my mind all day, Peter caught my arm and firmly escorted me to the sidewalk and across the corniche. My objections, which I was voicing stridently, were drowned out by arrival of a dozen drummers, a horn player, cheering spectators, and a bride in a white dress with voluminous stiff petticoats. Old women in long black skirts began to ululate. Flower petals were flung into the air. The decibel level was alarming.

I was looking back over my shoulder as we went down steps to the pier. A servant in a white jacket gestured at a narrow plank that led to a motorboat. My previous indignation at Peter's high-handed behavior vanished as I assessed my chances of surviving the short but perilous trip wearing high heels. There were no crocodiles in the Nile, I reminded myself, or piranhas. On the other hand, debris floated in the water, and the redolence was not appealing.

"Shall I carry you?" Peter asked.

"Don't be absurd." I took off each shoe, said a silent prayer to Taweret, the hippopotamus goddess (it seemed appropriate), and teetered across the plank. My breathing may have been shallow for the five-minute ride to the *dahabiyya*, but I was quite capable of smiling graciously as we were helped on board and introduced to an assortment of British, American, and Egyptian dignitaries, none of whom seemed likely to have an affiliation with Mary and William.

A short flight of metal steps led to the upper deck, open and with ample seating on benches and around a long table. At the front (or the bow, for the nautically minded) were boxes of produce, a stove, a grill, and counter space. Several Egyptian men in white jackets were stirring large pots and chopping vegetables.

I accepted a glass of wine and sat by the railing, watching fishermen pull in their nets as the sun began to sink. The houses set back from the bank were likely to be the homes of those with decent incomes. Children and dogs cavorted in the yards, while goats watched us incuriously. A heron wading in a pool failed to notice us. Lights began to glitter on the sloping mountainsides. We glided past dark cruise boats moored three across at piers. The muezzins in distant minarets beckoned the pious to prayer. On the lower deck, one of the crew members unfurled a prayer rug and knelt.

Peter sat down next to me and put his arm around my shoulder. As the sun disappeared behind the mountains, the sky rippled with rosy hues. A flock of birds were silhouetted as they flew downstream in an unsteady formation. We remained on the bench for a few more minutes, then reluctantly turned around to be sociable.

I had been dreading a long, convoluted conversation about policies and economics, but such subjects were avoided. The next few hours passed pleasantly, with discussion about travel misfortunes and worthy destinations. We were served an array of beef, chicken, and vegetables, along with plentiful wine, followed by coffee and dessert. I realized we'd turned back toward Luxor and were approaching the location where the *dahabiyya* had been anchored. Peter and several other of the male guests went downstairs, supposedly to examine the cabin facilities. I was not at all annoyed to be spared any high-level networking or whatever they were up to. The rest of us finished our coffee, then began to gather our things and thank the hostess, who smiled bravely and no doubt was quite ready for us to disembark.

The motorboat made several trips to the pier before it was our turn. Our fellow passengers, one an attaché from the American Embassy and the other his counterpart from the British Embassy, had drunk enough to be as daunted by the plank as I was (although for other reasons). Peter kept a firm grip on my shoulder as he steered me to the concrete pier. We all went up to the corniche. The two diplomats invited us to go to a nightclub with them, but we declined and waited until they'd found a taxi and departed.

"What time is it?" I asked Peter.

"The girls won't be back for an hour, if that's what you're wondering. Why don't we sit on the terrace? We can drink coffee and smoke *sheesa*."

"That sounds illegal."

"It's a water pipe, very traditional. You pick a flavor of tobacco, and the waiter puts it in a special cup over an ember. It's milder than you might think it would be."

"Is this a ruse so that you can seduce me later?"

"Absolutely."

The terrace was moderately busy. A few of the patrons were the hotel guests I'd mentioned to Caron and Inez; others were businessmen with loosened ties and weary faces. A young Arab woman in conservative dress sat down near us and ordered coffee and a water pipe. I nudged Peter to watch as she pulled out a cell phone and conducted a conversation between puffs.

Since neither of us smoked, we decided to pass on the *sheesa* and settled for coffee, brandy, and a platter of dried fruit. The wall surrounding the hotel muffled the sounds of the taxis and clopping feet of the carriage horses.

"Did you and your colleagues on the *dahabiyya* solve the world's problems?" I asked idly.

"Only if the world's problems involve leaky plumbing behind mahogany paneling. The boat was built eighty years ago and refurbished twenty years ago by an American tour facilitator. I wasn't able to provide any useful suggestions."

"The Rosen boys didn't play pirates on the family yacht?"

"No, we played lawyers in the attic. We had a courtroom, a library, and an old dining room table we used for negotiating mergers and hostile takeovers by foreign investors. They always made me be Taiwan."

"With Monopoly money?"

"No money ever exchanged hands. It was all about stock certificates and proxies."

"Am I ever going to meet these other Rosen boys—and their mother?"

"One of these days." He popped a date in his mouth and looked away, adding something under his breath that suggested hell might be expecting a blizzard.

The young woman put away her cell phone, took out some pound notes to pay her bill, demurely tugged her scarf into place, and wafted away. I realized that other patrons had begun leaving, as well. Our waiter came to the table and inquired if we might like more coffee. He did not seem enthusiastic about the proposition.

"What time is it?" I asked Peter.

"About eleven. Maybe the girls came in through the New Winter Palace entrance, just in case Mrs. McHaver was still lurking in the lobby. You wait here and I'll go upstairs to check."

An iron clamp squeezed my stomach. I regretted having nibbled so many dates and apricots and drunk so much bitter coffee. "Salima promised to have them here at eleven."

"And they probably are here, wondering where we are. I'll be back in five minutes."

"We should have called the suite on the house phone when we got here," I said, trying to sound confident despite the waver in my voice. "It was a child's birthday party, after all. How late could it last?"

"It won't take me any longer to go upstairs than it would to call. You wait here in case they come straggling back with an assortment of lame excuses."

I resolved to remain outwardly calm as I kept a careful eye on the walkway from the corniche to the hotel entrance. Caron and Inez were likely to be watching TV or reading that cursed book. Salima's family was reputable (despite her father's woeful lack of expertise in the syntactic structure of early Coptic manuscripts). Mahmoud had spoken highly of her. She would not have been hired to escort dignitaries around the archeological sites if she wasn't reliable. She had a grant to do research.

And if she had appeared at that moment, I would have grabbed her by the back of her neck and flung her into the Nile.

It took Peter a long while to return, or so it seemed. "They aren't there," he said as he sat down. "It didn't look as though anyone has been in the suite except for the maid who turned down the beds and left fresh towels in the bathrooms. None of the staff in the lobby has seen them since we left."

"Did you call Mahmoud?"

"I think we should wait a few more minutes. It's not eleven thirty yet, and I hate to disturb him at home. Caron and Inez are seventeen years old, not seven."

"Then call Salima's house," I said.

"Everyone there is likely to have gone to bed by now. Salima and the girls may be waiting for a ferry or crossing the Nile right now. Luxor isn't like Cairo, Claire. There's very little crime, and Salima knows how to avoid potentially troublesome areas. She grew up here, remember?"

"You're the one who mentioned muggings," I pointed out acerbically. "Three young women, on their own, late at night. I'd be surprised if that town has streetlights. There certainly aren't any crowds of tourists at this hour."

Peter waved over the waiter and ordered two brandies. "Fifteen minutes, okay? If they haven't shown up by then, I'll call Mahmoud and ask him to call Salima's father."

"While they're being held in some vacant alley by a bunch of thugs. They could have been drugged . . . or molested." I shivered as gruesome images flashed across my mind. "What about that man they claimed was following them? He could be a murderer or a terrorist and—"

"What man?" Peter said, startled.

I tried to explain, but I could hear myself garbling the words and getting shriller by the second. "A scar—he has a scar," I continued, unable to stop. "Inez saw him last evening. He might have grabbed them in the elevator or a hallway and dragged them into his room! If he's staying here, I mean. We don't really know if he's a guest or not. Go find Ahmed and make him let you into all the rooms. No, we'll need a team for every floor. And the New Winter Palace, too. He could be staying there. What if he's already checked out?"

Peter closed his eyes and waited until I began to whimper incoherently. "I don't think we can demand that Ahmed start barging into rooms at this hour. This mysterious man is apt to be nothing more than what you surmised—a businessman. Young women are not abducted off the streets and sold into white slavery these days. At least not American women in Egypt."

"Okay," I said, gulping. "But we have to do something. What about Bakr? He could have gone to pick them up in New Gurna or whatever it's called."

"He lives with his parents and sisters. A call at this hour might not be appreciated."

"Do you think I care?"

Peter grimaced. "All right, I'll go back upstairs and check again. If they're not there, I'll call Mahmoud and see what he thinks. Do you want to come with me or stay here?"

"Here, I suppose. I realize I'm being ridiculous, Peter, but this isn't Farberville and the girls aren't practiced travelers. Neither of them has ever been out of the country.

They don't speak the language." I held up my hand. "Yes, I know they've squirmed out of a lot of bad situations, but sometimes they needed help, and I can't do anything because they could be . . ." Unable to voice my fears, I wiped my eyes with a napkin. "Promise you'll call Mahmoud."

He hugged me, then went into the hotel. I plucked at the napkin (had it been paper, I would have shredded it). The only customers left were three young men, all blond and tanned, in T-shirts and sport jackets, looking as though they had just come in from a lacrosse match. Their table was littered with beer bottles and their high spirits were obvious. They were so carefree and boisterous that I wanted to march over and lecture them about responsibility. It would not be well received, I suspected.

I was considering hurling dates and figs at them when Alexander sat down across from me. I dropped the potential missile and said, "What are you doing here?"

"Well, for one thing, I'm staying in the hotel, and the restaurant is closed," he said. "I thought I'd have a drop of brandy before I retired. Also, I ran into your husband on the third floor, and he told me what's going on. I came down to wait with you until he comes back."

"Wait someplace else," I growled.

"You needn't be so worried about the girls. Salima will have them here any minute. She may seem rather giddy, but she's savvy and she knows how to avoid sticky situations."

"How do you know?"

"I made inquiries," he said, shrugging. "I am by nature an inquisitive sort, although hardly of your caliber."

"I am not inquisitive." I picked up a dried fig, then put it down before I was overcome by the impulse to test my aim. "I prefer to mind my own business, and I wish you'd do the same. Why don't you trot back upstairs and raid your father's suite for brandy?"

"I tried, but the door's locked. He knows me well enough to have made sure I don't have access. One weekend when he and Mumsy were in Bath, I came home from Eton with a few friends and we decimated the ancestral wine cellar. He almost swallowed his tongue."

"Surely he's back by now," I said. "He and the McHavers were going to a dinner party at Lady Emerson's villa."

"Lady Emerson's villa? They told you that?"

"We spoke to them in the lobby just before seven o'clock. It sounded as though it would be very dry and proper. Mrs. McHaver doesn't seem the type to whoop it up until midnight with lowly college dignitaries from the U.S."

"You might be surprised." Alexander gestured to the waiter, whose smile was increasingly forced. "A touch more brandy, Claire?"

I stared at the sidewalk. A few tourists were still wandering in from what I surmised may have been nightclubs. I was surprised to see Jess Delmont, the grad student from MacLeod College, slinking toward the hotel entrance. Although Shannon King was a guest, I'd assumed the other members of her team, like Magritta, were in cheaper accommodations.

Alexander sucked in a breath. "I wonder what he's doing here. It's late for a social call, not that I'd consider him convivial in any case. Every year MacLeod College sends a couple of them. They arrive with glowing faces, convinced they'll be opening a tomb that rivals King Tut's. Then they discover that they'll be at the site at seven in the morning, sorting through dusty rubble in the hot sun, and back at their horrid hotel rooms at four o'clock to collapse on lumpy beds and watch cockroaches race across the ceiling. To add to the insult, they pay for the privilege. At least Nabil and the other workmen get paid. It's much more glamorous in the cinema."

"I'm sure it is," I said distractedly. Two figures were shuffling up the sidewalk, dressed in ponderous black robes and scarves that had been wound around their heads to cover everything but their eyes. I was about to dismiss them as hotel guests when I saw a flash of a hot pink sandal beneath one of the robes.

"Just a minute!" I said, standing up with such impetuosity that my chair tipped over.

A pair of green eyes flickered in my direction.

CHAPTER 7

"This had better be good," I said as I sat on the edge of the sofa. Caron and Inez, who resembled escapees from a third-rate harem, stood in the middle of the room. They'd removed the scarves and pushed back their sweaty hair, but the faded black robes were shabby and frayed. Their feet were dusty. Peter had gone into our bedroom to call Mahmoud back and assure him that the girls were safe. He had seemed nothing more than relieved. I, on the other hand, was in the throes of maternal fury.

"Can we change first?" asked Caron. "These things are hot."

"You have one minute, starting right now."

"I sort of need to use the bathroom," Inez said timidly. "Badly."

"The clock is ticking."

As they dashed into their room, I took a bottle of water from the mini-bar, splashed a few drops in my palm, and patted my cheeks. Spontaneous combustion was a real threat, I decided as I forced myself to breathe more deeply. When they returned, dressed in T-shirts and shorts, I pointed at two chairs. "Don't even think about lying. I'm in no mood for elaborate fabrication. Do you realize it's after midnight? Peter called Mahmoud, who sent the police to bang on doors in that village—all because you couldn't bother to get back here on time. And when you finally showed up, you were in disguise and tried to sneak past me!

Didn't it occur to you that I was worried sick? This isn't Farberville, for pity's sake."

Caron rolled her eyes. "Are you going to lecture us all night, or would you prefer to hear what happened?"

"It was really scary," Inez added.

Peter came in and sat down next to me. "Mahmoud's calling off the cavalry. I apologized, but he sounded chilly."

"He'll understand when his children turn into teenagers," I said, sounding rather chilly myself. "All right, girls, from the beginning."

Caron settled back in the chair as if preparing to offer an amusing anecdote. "Salima came shortly after you left. We took a ferry to a pier on the West Bank, then walked to her parents' house. She was telling us all about Cambridge and how they really do go punting on the Thames—which they call Isis for some crazy reason. She lived in a musty little room in an ancient building, and had to share the bathroom with a bunch of other students. They toasted crumpets in their fireplaces late at night. Whenever they could, they took the train to London to go to nightclubs and wine bars. Of course she had to hang out at the British Museum, because—"

"You walked to Salima's parents' house. Then what?"

"There were at least two dozen people, about half children. We were introduced to her mother and father—"

"Her *mamma* and *babba*," Inez said. "There were *tantes* and *oncles,* her *grandmère,* and cousins. Salima's brother seemed to like the colored pencils and sketchbook we gave him, although he was a lot more excited about the Game Boy. They served a regular birthday cake, along with meat and cheese sandwiches, pickled vegetables and dips, and *ta'amiyya* in pita pockets. It's made of mashed fava beans, with olive oil, and fried in little patties. It's also known as felafel."

"So the party was uneventful," I said before Inez launched into the recipe, which I had no doubt she could, given any encouragement whatsoever.

"It was okay," Caron conceded, "although it would have

been more fun with a piñata or something. The party broke up at nine, and we were walking to the pier when one of Salima's cousins rushed up, bawling and blubbering. Her name's Nevine. Major boyfriend crisis. They had an argument earlier in the week, and she thought they'd made up, but he was at a nightclub in a hotel with another girl, blah, blah, blah. Salima tried to calm her down, then agreed to go with her and try to help them sort it out. She wanted to put us on a ferry first, but we said we'd go with them, since it was still early. I mean, we've never even been to a nightclub back home, and it sounded interesting."

"Educational, too," chirped Inez.

I narrowed my eyes. "The reason you've never been to a nightclub is because you're not old enough, remember?"

Caron shrugged. "It wasn't like they were going to check our IDs at the door, Mother. We just wanted to see what it was like. We weren't going to drink beer. Besides, we haven't met anybody remotely our age since we arrived. Even the ones who aren't fossilized are all out of college and have jobs. Alexander is nearly thirty."

I heard an odd noise from Peter that might have been a suppressed laugh, obliging me to elbow him in a discreet but emphatic manner. This was not the time for the good cop–bad cop routine. I would have much preferred that we were sitting at a scarred table in a claustrophobic pea green interrogation room, with a lightbulb dangling nakedly above our heads. I briefly considered calling the concierge to see if a laundry room in the basement might be available, then dismissed the idea.

"That's not quite true," I said, "but you have a point. Not a very good one, but you may continue."

"We went up some narrow streets to this nightclub on the ground floor of a little hotel. The name was in Arabic, but it had a neon sign with a blue camel. It wasn't very big and it was absolutely packed with people, mostly Egyptians and a few scraggly tourists. A lot of them were smoking cigarettes and cigars. It was hot and dark, and the music was really loud. Salima got us sodas and Nevine found us a place to sit with some girls she knew, and then they left to go deal with the boyfriend. For a second, I thought I saw Samuel, that guy from Virginia or wherever with the brainless girlfriend, but then people got in the way and I didn't see him after that. Nevine's friends didn't speak any English and were jabbering away in Arabic. The smoke and the noise got to be awful. We finally decided to go look for Salima and tell her that we'd find the way to the ferry on our own. They'd gone toward the back, so we started trying to squeeze through all the dancers and sweaty bodies." She paused for maximum effect. "That's when we saw Him."

"Nevine's boyfriend?" asked Peter.

"No, the man who's been following us. The one with the scar."

Inez blinked soberly. "And a mustache. He was wearing jeans and a turtleneck. It was so dark we could barely see across the room, but he was wearing sunglasses. It was unbelievably suspicious. I thought I was going to throw up on somebody's foot. Caron finally shoved me, and we made it to a back exit."

"Where," Caron said, regaining center stage, "we ducked around a corner and crouched behind some garbage bags. That's when we heard the same door open and footsteps coming in our direction. We were totally paralyzed, but I realized we had to get out of there before the guy got to the corner. We ran along the street, then started turning down alleys. We had to dodge around boxes and piles of concrete bags and rubble. Dogs were barking at us. An old lady yelled at us from an upstairs window. Some men came out of a café and tried to block us. One of them grabbed Inez, and she whacked him."

"Not really," Inez said, turning pink. "I just sort of swung at him. He started laughing so hard he let go of me." She made a fist and looked at it. "No wonder."

"Was this man with the scar chasing you?" asked Peter.

Caron shrugged. "Somebody was. We caught glimpses of him whenever we looked back. Finally, we got to the edge of town. The only place to go was up a path, so we did. It was a nightmare. We were tripping and sliding on the loose rocks, and it was too dark to see where we were going. Inez was wheezing so raggedly I thought she was going to pass out. There was nowhere to hide, even though it was so dark we couldn't see much of anything. It was like we were on a different planet, pursued by a carnivorous beast. Sweat was literally streaming down my face, and my leg muscles were screaming in agony."

I couldn't be sure how much she was embellishing the story, since she was more than adept at exaggeration when it served her purpose. "Was it wise to leave the town? Why didn't you just stop and ask someone for help?"

"As if they all speak English? It's not a trendy tourist destination, Mother. It's a grubby little town that probably didn't have electricity until a year ago and still lacks plumbing. The businesses were closed and the shutters drawn on the ground-level apartments. There were goats in the streets,—Egyptian goats, bleating in Arabic."

Peter leaned forward, his elbows resting on his knees. If he had the same doubts that I did, he was masking them. "Then what happened?"

"We stayed on the path until we came to a dirt road. We crossed it and dived behind some big rocks to catch our breath. The footsteps stopped, so we knew the man was nearby, listening for us. I bit down on my lip so hard I thought it would start bleeding. I'm sure it will be all swollen tomorrow and I'll look like a boxer. Inez started hiccuping, but luckily he didn't seem to hear it. All I could think of was how idiotic it would be if we were murdered because of Inez's pathetic little spasms."

The door of the parlor flew open and Salima burst into the room. She was gabbling so loudly and rapidly that it was impossible to understand much of what she was saying. She flung herself around Inez's neck and then around Caron's, hugging them so fiercely their eyes bulged. "You're safe, my darlings!" she shrieked. "I was so worried about you! I've been searching everywhere for the last hour. You cannot believe how utterly distraught I've been!"

She flung herself onto a chair and wiped her eyes with her shirt cuff. "A drink! I must have a drink or I shall expire from sheer anxiety!" She lapsed into gasps and mutters, some of which seemed to be expressing gratitude to the entire pantheon for the girls' safe return to the hotel.

While the rest of us stared at her, Peter made a martini and put it in her hand. "How nice of you to drop by at this hour, Miss el-Musafira."

"Oh, dear," Salima moaned, "you're furious at me. You should be. It was all my fault, Mrs. Malloy. Well, technically, it was ninety percent Nevine's fault, since she was the one who caused the crisis." She took a sip and fell back. "If you want to throw me off the balcony—and I wouldn't blame you—please let me finish the martini first. I've had a dreadful time this evening."

"You're not the only one," I said coldly.

Salima hastily set down the glass. "Permit me to explain my inexcusable behavior. I assume Caron and Inez have told you why we went to the Sapphire Camel. Once they were safely settled, Nevine and I went to find her boyfriend, who was in the back with some silly slut. A shouting match erupted. Nevine bolted out the back door, and Gamil went after her. So I, naturally, went after them, as did several of the aggrieved's friends and relatives, some of whom are my relatives as well, although I am loath to admit it. The verbal assaults escalated into a scuffle. One of Nevine's more emotional brothers threw a punch, and Gamil stumbled and cut his forehead. Blood, hysterics, invectives, and that sort of thing ensued. Nosy neighbors came outside to cheer. The police arrived. Everybody was tripping all over everybody else to get away. Nevine and I managed to pull Gamil up and hustle him away to the emergency clinic. Although the damage was minimal, he was covered with blood. It took forever for the nurse to stitch him up. They were clinging to each other like thistles and declaring eternal devotion when I slipped away and went back to the Camel to look for the girls." She shrugged, then reached for her martini. "After I discovered they'd vanished, I went to the pier and ascertained that they had not taken a ferry. I made sure they weren't at my parents' house, then ran up and down every street, my heart beating so hard I was nearly blind. On my third or fourth trip to the pier, someone finally said they'd caught a ride on a felucca. I would have called, but I lost my cell phone along the way. I came here as soon as I could."

"You must be exhausted," I said, unimpressed.

"I am indeed," Salima said. "But all that matters is that they are safe now."

"No thanks to you," Caron said. "We were almost murdered, if you must know. We were stalked by a psychotic, and nearly kidnapped."

"And then ravaged," added Inez, settling her glasses more squarely on her nose so she could stare at Salima. "In a tent in a remote oasis."

"In Gurna?" Salima raised her eyebrows. "It's hardly a remote oasis."

"He would have taken us to one," Inez said firmly.

"Who?" asked Salima, bewildered.

"The man who's stalking us," Caron said. "We spotted him after you abandoned us in that nightclub."

"I abandoned you? Please, darlings, I left you at a table with Nevine's girlfriends."

"Enough!" I barked. "I don't want to hear any more fanciful tales or excuses from any of you."

Peter seemed overwhelmed by the presence of unhappy females. "We still haven't heard the rest of the story," he said with a slightly daunted smile.

Caron cleared her throat. "So there we were, hiding behind the rocks. Inez's hiccups finally stopped; otherwise he surely would have found us and plunged his dagger into our hearts. It was so quiet you could have heard a cobra slithering by. We waited for a long time, then decided it was safer to follow the road back to the town than to risk bumping into the man, who might have been somewhere on the path. Just as we were about to stand up, we heard voices."

"And a curious squeaky noise," Inez said.

"Which," Caron continued seamlessly, "I recognized as the sound of a wooden wheel rubbing against the side of a cart. I peeked over the rocks and saw the cart coming along the road from the mountainside. As it came closer, we could see that it was being pulled by a donkey. There were six or seven men walking alongside it, talking in low voices. At least three of them were carrying rifles. It didn't seem prudent to ask if we could hitch a ride. When they got within about ten feet of us, they stopped. One of them trotted down the road, while the rest lit cigarettes and waited."

Salima opened her mouth, but I cut her off. "Could you see what was in the cart?" I asked.

Inez shook her head. "There was a tarp tied over it. It must have been heavy, because the poor donkey was puffing."

"And then?" I prompted them.

"One of the wheels fell off the cart," Caron said, "I guess because the men were leaning against it. Whatever was under the tarp slid against the side with an awful thump. They got all upset and started hissing and spitting at each other. I don't know what they were saying, but it probably wasn't very nice. Finally, some of them lifted the cart and the others got the wheel back in place. The man who'd gone ahead came back, and then they all went down the road."

"How very peculiar," said Salima, who'd managed to obtain a tangerine during the narrative and was peeling it with a pensive frown. "That road—if I'm thinking of the correct one—goes around the far edge of town and then north alongside the river for a mile or so. There's nothing that way except for a few houses."

I wasn't as interested in the cart's destination as I was in my daughter and Inez's. "Please continue, Caron."

"We waited for a long time after they were gone, in case that man was across the road. Finally we decided that we couldn't crouch there forever, so we stayed on the far side of the road as long as we could, then ducked across it and into the backyard of a house. The robes and scarves were on a clothesline. We pulled them over our clothes and made our way to the pier, staying in the shadows as much as we could. Rather than wait half an hour for the ferry, we gave some guy a hundred pounds to take us across the Nile on his felucca. He seemed to think it was very funny."

Peter did not. "Was there a chance the cart might have been conveying weapons?"

Inez bent over, coughing convulsively. Caron, who was not renowned for her Florence Nightingale impulses, jumped up and began to thump Inez's back. Salima went to the mini-bar and grabbed a bottle of water. Peter raised his eyebrows at me, but all I could do was shake my head.

When at last Inez regained control, she sat up, her face red and shiny. "No, just a lot of things like pots and jars. There was enough moonlight for us to see broken pieces scattered in the road. We thought maybe they were made by village craftsmen to be sold at the tourist shops."

"Why would they be transported at night?" I asked. "Pots and jars, no matter how beautifully crafted, don't necessitate an armed escort." I looked at Peter. "Could they have been filled with illegal drugs?"

"It's possible. I'll talk to Mahmoud in the morning. If jars broke when the cart tipped, there should be some evidence in the road. Caron and Inez, he may want you two to help him find the precise spot."

"It was dark and we were lost," Caron protested. "Besides, we have to pack for the cruise. Salima knows which road it was. She can show Mahmoud."

"Not tomorrow," Salima said. "My father and I are going to Cairo to attend a lecture given by one of his old friends from Zurich. We're taking an early morning flight. I'll draw a map of the road I believe the girls were on, and they can show it to Chief Inspector el-Habachi."

"Besides," I said, "the girls need the opportunity to find the owner of the robes and scarves that they stole and return them, as well as offer a generous payment in apology for any inconvenience they might have caused. The money will come out of their shopping allowance."

"I'd rather attend the lecture by the guy from Zurich," Caron said glumly as she reached for a tangerine. "Even if it's in Swiss."

CHAPTER 8

Caron and Inez dragged in just as Peter and I were finishing lunch on the balcony. Inez went into the bedroom, but Caron opted to allow us to appreciate the cataclysmic depth of her indignation.

"That was a waste of time," she began sourly. "I mean, how could it not be? Chief Inspector el-Habachi kept making us try to reconstruct the way we went after we went out the back door of the hotel. Last night we were too terrified to stand around and read stupid street signs in Arabic—as if we could anyway. The fronts of the buildings look the same. All of the alleys are narrow and cluttered with garbage bags and piles of junk. There are more vicious dogs over there than . . . I don't know, puckers of cellulite on Rhonda Maguire's thighs."

"Did you return the clothing?"

"Yes, Mother. We apologized, and Bakr translated for us. The lady was kind of annoyed until we gave her fifty pounds. Then she was all friendly and wanted to sell us the robes for another twenty. Like I can see us walking to class in them." She picked up the remaining french fries on my plate and crammed them in her mouth. "Can we order lunch?"

"Did you locate the road?" asked Peter, trying not to wince as she went after his fries as well.

"I think so," she said indistinctly. "There were cart marks in the dirt, anyway. Of course they could have been there for days, or maybe dynasties, but there was one place where it looked as if a lot of men had been scuffling around. There were footprints behind the rocks on the side of the road. Wow, like actual footprints. I had to restrain myself from whooping in delight."

I put down my wineglass. "Did the police find any evidence of whatever might have been in the cart?"

Her eyes flickered for an instant, and she hesitated. Finding a sudden fascination with the hazy clouds, she said, "Not bullets or packages of heroin, if that's what you're implying. There were a few slivers of pottery in the dust. The men must have come back later with flashlights and picked up as much as they could. The chief inspector was pissed off, as if it was our fault. He made us stand there for almost an hour while his men crawled around like gimpy field mice, then had Bakr drive us back here. We only had time for a roll at breakfast." Her hand fluttered to her forehead. "I'm beginning to feel faint, from either the sun or low blood sugar. Or then again, maybe from the thrill-a-minute experience of being dragged down every stinky alley in that dumb town."

"I'm sure it must be one of those," Peter said, although it was obvious from Caron's expression that he had failed miserably in his feeble attempt at sympathy. "Room service will take at least half an hour. You'll do better if you go to the restaurant." He put down his napkin and pushed back his chair. "I think I'll go to the police station and talk to Mahmoud. He's likely to be frustrated."

"It's Not My Fault," Caron said as she spun around. "Inez and I both kept telling him that we weren't sure where we went. A psychotic stalker can be a distraction, you know."

"Which wouldn't have happened if you hadn't gone to the nightclub," I pointed out.

"Not necessarily. You keep insisting he's just some ordinary businessman. Don't you think it's kind of a coincidence that he was there?"

Peter studied her for a moment. "I agree that it's not likely to have been a coincidence. Mahmoud will question the staff and track down some of the patrons. Other people must have noticed him, too, especially if he was dressed the way Inez described." Before Caron could express further outrage, he bent down to give me a swift kiss. "I'll be back in time to finish packing. Perhaps we might enjoy the illumination at Luxor Temple tonight. It's hokey but very dramatic, with booming voices, flashing lights, and all that."

"Oh, please, spare me." Caron went to the doorway of the bedroom she shared with Inez. "Let's eat, darling," she said loudly, imitating Salima. "Your camel awaits you in the hall."

"Then shriek for the sheik to join us," Inez trilled. "The sheik, *très chic*!"

There is a reason why newlyweds should go on their honeymoons before they have children. Or teenagers.

I'd finished packing my things and Peter's, and was reading a mystery novel on the balcony when Abdullah materialized at my side. Had I been a giddy heroine, I would have swooned, or at least let out a blood-chilling screech.

"Begging the *sitt*'s pardon," he murmured. "The door was ajar, and I was alarmed. The Winter Palace is very safe, but thieves have been able to slip in through the basement and take the service elevators."

I found my breath. "Thank you for your vigilance, Abdullah. I will call if I encounter any thieves in the suite."

"I will take extra care while you, Mr. Rosen, and the young misses are away."

"How do you know we'll be away?" I demanded.

"One hears things."

"Did you hear what happened to the young misses last night?"

Abdullah began to brush crumbs off the chair cushions. "It must have been alarming for the *sitt*. Visitors are much safer in Luxor after dark."

"Especially snoopy ones who ask too many questions?"

"That is not for me to say. Will you be wanting to have tea here later?"

His expression was as imperturbable as that of the Sphinx. If the lower floors of the hotel were on fire, with raging flames threatening to destroy the entire structure, I could picture him in the doorway of the suite, gravely saying, "*Sitt* Malloy, if I may be so bold as to disturb you . . ."

"I'm not sure," I said. "My husband and the girls are out at the moment. We'll call room service unless we decide to have tea on the terrace." I glanced at my watch, suddenly annoyed. The girls, having sworn they would not leave the hotel grounds, had gone downstairs for lunch almost two hours earlier.

"The young misses are using the computer in the lower lobby," Abdullah said. He hesitated, then looked out at the Nile. "It is very nice weather for a cruise, *Sitt* Malloy. I do hope you enjoy yourselves."

He turned to leave. As he reached the door to the hall, Alexander breezed past him and came out to the balcony.

"Is this a tag team event?" I asked, wishing I could get back to my novel.

"You should appreciate my restraint." He sat down and propped his feet on the rail of the balcony. "I'm dreadfully eager to hear what happened last night. Did Caron and Inez have a decent excuse for coming in late? At school, we had an antiquated curfew, strictly enforced by caning and endless hours of supervised study in a cramped, stuffy room where so much as a cough was forbidden. To avoid such brutal punishment, I became quite adept at shinnying up the drainpipe to the roof, then skittering from chimney to chimney until I was above my bedroom window. I came very close to breaking my neck on innumerable occasions. The reckless abandon of youth."

"Maybe you should have run away and joined a circus."

"That's a peculiar American tradition," he said. "Shall we drink to it while you tell me what tale the girls concocted to avoid your wrath?"

"I suppose so." My response was perfunctory, since he was already headed for the mini-bar. When he returned, I merely told him that the girls had gotten separated from

Salima and lost in the alleys of Gurna. His look of incredulousness provoked me into adding that they'd taken the robes and scarves to avoid being noticed, and therefore harassed, by the local males.

"I wish my headmaster had been as gullible as you, Mrs. Malloy." He took a noisy sip of his martini, then said, "My father and his cohorts are having cocktails this evening in his suite. He hopes you and Mr. Rosen will join us. Magritta will be there with her weekly report, which one has to suffer through with feigned interest. We can count on Shannon to make rude remarks about the lack of progress, followed by Wallace's blustery defense. Mrs. McHaver will interrupt with caustic comments, while Miriam twitches as if she's infected with some sort of exotic rash. Unless a miracle occurs, Miss Portia and Miss Cordelia will get totally potted and sing bawdy songs from the war era. Given enough gin, Lady Emerson may bash someone with her parasol. I'm hoping it will be Sittermann."

"It sounds delightful, Alexander, but we have some last-minute packing to do before we leave in the morning."

"Ah, yes, the cruise on the Nubian Sea. The ship is rumored to be terribly posh. Have you ever seen the film version of Agatha Christie's *Death on the Nile*? I doubt the cabins will be as spacious, but the lounge is done in an elegant Victorian decor. Don't take any midnight strolls on the deck, and you should be fine."

"Are you implying we'll be in danger?"

"Prudence is a virtue. If you'll excuse me, I must convey your regrets to my father. He'll be distraught. He's enamored of you, Mrs. Malloy. If you weren't happily married, you could have been the next Lady Bledrock. What a delightful stepmother you would have been, and I the envy of every chap in the county."

I returned my attention to the mysterious affair at Whitbread Crossing, where the local squire had been found bludgeoned in a ditch, much to the dismay of the bumbling constable. After an hour, I began to think that crumpets and tea sounded like an excellent idea. Rather than call room service, I decided to go downstairs and drag Caron and Inez away from the computer before they ran up a bill comparable to the gross national product of an obscure South Pacific kingdom.

I carefully locked the door that led to the hall, then took the elevator to the lobby. A bellman directed me to the grimy, claustrophobic computer room. Caron and Inez were hunched in front of the monitor.

"Still sending e-mail?" I asked, trying to catch a glimpse over their shoulders.

Inez hit a key and the screen went dark. "Hi, Ms. Malloy," she said in a strangled voice. "I was—well, I was looking up Abu Simbel on the Internet." She yanked off her glasses and began to clean them on the hem of her shirt. "Did you know that it would have been covered by Lake Nasser, so an international effort was made to raise money so that it could be moved two hundred and ten meters away? It took the UNESCO team four years, and it's considered—"

"Fascinating, and so forth," Caron said. "Is Peter back yet?"

"No," I said, bemused by their flushed faces. "I came down to see if you wanted to have tea with me on the terrace."

They looked at each other as if I'd suggested something preposterous and potentially fatal. Caron at last said, "We need to go up to the suite and pack. I don't know what we're supposed to wear. Are we sitting at the captain's table? That'd be cool."

"Don't count on it," I said. "Take one nice outfit, just in case people do dress for dinner on the final night. Other than that, T-shirts, shorts, and walking shoes."

Inez shut down the computer with a few deft clicks. They edged around me and scurried toward the elevators. I was heading for the desk when Ahmed caught me.

"Is there something I can do for you, *Sitt* Malloy-Rosen? I do hope Abdullah is seeing to your needs. He is very old, you know, and not as quick as he used to be. I would fire him, but his father and his grandfather also worked here. His father served drinks to Howard Carter and Lord Carnarvon in our bar. It looks much the same now as it did then. We are very proud of it."

His smirk reminded me of a gargoyle on a cathedral. "Abdullah is quite competent," I said evenly. "If my husband comes through the lobby within the next hour, please let him know I'll be on the terrace."

"Of course, *Sitt* Malloy-Rosen, and do have a pleasant cruise. The ship is very nice, I hear, very nice indeed."

I nodded, then continued out to the terrace. To my relief, Lord Bledrock was not at his usual table, nor was Mrs. McHaver. I found a shady table and ordered tea and cakes. Weary tourists staggered up the marble stairs from their day trips, laden with shopping bags filled with items bought on a whim, to be gazed at with bafflement when they returned home. Carriages lined the curb of the corniche, their drivers eternally optimistic. Two Saudi men in long white *thobes,* their heads covered with red-and-white-checkered *ghutras* held in place with black cords, walked by, intent on their conversation. Following them were two women in black burqas. Their attire reminded me of the clothes taken by Caron and Inez. Peter and I had discussed their story after we'd retired for the night, but had finally agreed that it was impossible to separate the truth from the hyperbole. They might have been chased through the alleys. On the other hand, they might have panicked when a nightclub employee opened the back door to set out a crate of empty bottles. From that point, any footstep would have been misconstrued. The cart on the road could well have been transporting inexpensive pottery, and the men armed with nothing more lethal than walking sticks.

My thoughts were going nowhere when Samuel Berry and Buffy Franz asked if they could join me. Having no plausible reason to say no, I gestured at the empty chairs. Samuel ordered drinks from the waiter, then rocked back and closed his eyes. He'd trimmed his beard, I noticed, but he was still scruffy enough to earn a few curious glances from other customers.

"I am so glad we spotted you," Buffy said, who was a paragon of perfection from her moussed blond hair to her designer sandals, "because I just don't know what to do. We're going on this same cruise tomorrow, just so Sammie can prowl around a bunch of old ruins. I have no idea what to take. I've been on cruise ships where you have to look sensational every night at dinner, and I've been on the ones where people wear robes over bathing suits. I just hate not being dressed appropriately, don't you?"

"Oh yes," I said. "I lie awake nights worrying about it. I was told this was casual. I'm taking a dress and a sweater, along with clothes for the excursions."

"I don't have any of my good jewelry. The few pieces Daddy let me bring are in Rome with the rest of my luggage. It never occurred to me I might go on a cruise."

"Then don't," Samuel said, his eyes still closed.

She swatted at him. "And do what—sit around the hotel? Hey, maybe there's a hot bingo game somewhere in town. Now that'd be exciting . . ."

He grinned. "Sittermann will be delighted to escort you."

"I hadn't thought of that." Her lips pursed as she toyed with her napkin. "He's creepy, but he's rich. And Alexander Bledrock—one day he'll be a baron. That is so cool. Maybe I'll persuade one of them to take me to Cairo to see the pyramids in the moonlight. Daddy must know somebody who knows somebody at the American Embassy. We might just drop in for dinner."

"Sounds like a blast."

She gave him a dark look. "And then I'll fly back to Rome. You can go by yourself to all those litter boxes that you call oases."

I thought it sounded like an excellent idea, and I expected Samuel to concur. Therefore, I was surprised when he reached across the table to stroke her cheek and said, "Aw, baby, I was teasing. I don't want you to leave. The oases may have been crude, but we certainly managed to have some fun in the sleeping bag, didn't we? Remember that night when we went out into the desert and . . ." He glanced at me, then gazed intently at her. "Please don't go back to Rome. You'll have a great time on the cruise, especially since you'll have people to hang out with. You and Mrs. Malloy can lie on the top deck all day, while a waiter brings you fancy drinks. Maybe there'll be a hot tub. We'll sneak up there at midnight and lie naked in the steamy water. Antony and Cleopatra, under a sparkling canopy of stars. That ought to make a good story when you get back home."

Buffy ate one of the cakes while she pondered all this. To my dismay, instead of opting for the Cairo-Rome scenario, she said, "Well, I do like cruises."

Had she but known.

We drove to Aswan in a military convoy, which I found unnerving. As Caron pointed out numerous times, it was a peculiar way to protect tourists, since we made a convenient, economical target, should anyone be inclined to plant a few roadside bombs or land mines. As we drove through uniformly brown, dusty towns, the soldiers began to peel away in their jeeps and trucks, until we were under the protection of two camo-clad youngsters who might have been recruited that morning.

We boarded the *Nubian Queen* at a dock near the dam. Peter and I had a nondescript cabin down the hall from the admittedly spectacular lounge, replete with a dozen sitting areas, columns, large windows, and a curved mahogany bar beneath a stained-glass window. I could not help thinking about Alexander's remarks as Peter and I unpacked, then went to the lounge.

The cruise director, a pleasant Egyptian gentleman with impeccable English, came by to apologize for the suite having already been booked. We assured him that our cabin was satisfactory. Some of the other eighty or so passengers nodded politely as they found seats and ordered drinks.

From remarks I could overhear, I concluded that they were primarily German and British, with a sprinkling of Americans. The only Arabs I saw were wearing stiff white jackets and fetching drinks from the bar for the infidels. After a few minutes, Caron and Inez joined us. We were sipping a bon voyage toast when Samuel and Buffy sat down.

"Very impressive engineering," Samuel commented as the ship began to move away from the dock, giving us a view of the dam. "When Nasser decided to have it built, it resulted in an international uproar involving the Suez Canal. The UN had to intervene. It took thirty-five thousand workers to build it, and over four hundred and fifty of them died during the construction. Not, I suppose, that Nasser and the financiers noticed. The deaths of working-class people scarcely matter when unemployment is high and labor is cheap."

"Our cabin is itsy-bitsy," Buffy said, "and I don't see how two people can fit on the balcony." She looked at Caron and Inez, both of whom were attempting to disguise themselves as brocade armchairs. "There's absolutely no shelf space in the bathroom for hair and skin products, is there? I don't know how I'm going to survive."

Inez made an attempt to divert her by reeling off the number of cubic meters of concrete required to construct Aswan Dam, but Buffy refused to fall for it.

"Did you see the prices in the gift shop?" She allowed Samuel to hand her a glass of champagne. "They claim it's all Nubian craftsmanship, but I bet there are 'made in China' labels in the wastebasket. What about entertainment on board? No casino, no stage—and no hot tub on the top deck. I asked. What are we supposed to do at night?"

"On two nights, native musicians and dancers come on board," Peter said. "You'll be tired after visiting the tombs and temples. They require stairs and a lot of walking."

Buffy's brow creased. "I don't know about that. I need to do some serious work on my tan lines. Do you think there are decent deck chairs somewhere?"

"You bet your well-shaped fanny there are!" boomed a familiar voice that made my stomach churn.

I gazed with dismay as Sittermann dragged over a chair and sat down. "I didn't realize you were coming," I managed to say. Beside me, Peter sighed. Caron and Inez looked as if they were about to verbalize their displeasure, so I quickly added, "We didn't see you in the convoy."

He propped his feet on the edge of the table, giving all of us an unwanted view of his hairy legs and knobby ankles. "No, I flew down to Aswan this morning. Who's ready for another drink?" He held up a hand and snapped his fingers. "That drive must have left you all drier than a bleached skull of a steer that wandered off from the herd. Back home, I've got a collection of them nailed up on the rec room walls. Some of my guests say they feel like they're being watched. Ain't that a hoot and a holler!"

"Definitely," Peter said.

"And so tasteful," I murmured.

Caron rolled her eyes. "Like we give a hoot."

"You folks going ashore after lunch to visit Kalabsha Temple?" Sittermann went on, clearly oblivious to anything short of a volcanic eruption. "I hear tell it's nothing as fancy as Karnak, just another jumble of rocks. I was thinking I might skip it and see if I can get up a little poker game. Anybody in the mood for five-card stud?"

Samuel stiffened. "The Temple of Kalabsha was built by Augustus Caesar between 30 B.C. and A.D. 14 and dedicated to a composite of Nubian and Egyptian gods. The Rock Temple of Beit al-Wali has several fine reliefs detailing the pharaoh's gory victory over the Nubians. The Temple of Kertassi is Graeco-Roman and has two impressive Hathor-headed columns, as well as some prehistoric carvings and paintings."

"Samuel, have you met Inez?" asked Caron. "You two must have been joined at the hippocampus in a previous life."

"Is that supposed to be funny?" Inez demanded.

Samuel mumbled something and headed for the staircase that led to the upper deck. After a moment, the girls announced that they wanted some fresh air and went outside to the narrow walkway along the side of the ship.

I grabbed Peter's wrist before he could follow them, thereby abandoning me to the company of Buffy and Sittermann. Sitting in the bottom of Magritta's excavation would have been preferable—or in a portable toilet on a busy street or even in a dentist's deceptively benign recliner. "Oh, dear," I said to Peter, quivering delicately, "I do believe that the drive has left me a little queasy. Would you mind if we go to our cabin so I can lie down for a few minutes?"

"Not at all," my husband said with alacrity. "You're looking pale." He stood up and yanked me to my feet. "You must excuse my wife. You wouldn't think someone who's seen more corpses than a coroner would be quite so frail, but she is. I've tried to keep her away from the martinis while we're here, but she gulps them down every time I leave her alone for more than a few minutes. She's been in rehab so many times that they've named a detox ward after her, and—"

"Thank you so very much for your candor," I said icily. "I'm going to our cabin. Please feel free to stay here for another hour or two and share more of your concerns with all these lovely people in the lounge. You do seem to have engaged their curiosity."

He caught up with me as I stomped down the corridor. "I was trying to help. This way, you have an excuse to go hide whenever Sittermann gets too close."

"Rehab? Detox?"

"I had to make it sound convincing, didn't I?"

"No." I did not look back at him.

In the cabin, we agreed to a tentative truce. I decided to pass up both lunch and the outing. Peter said he'd find the girls and accompany them, allowing me to savor a much-deserved afternoon of solitude on the balcony. An hour later I watched the launches as they moved toward shore, noting

without much interest that although Samuel was among the
disembarking passengers, Buffy and Sittermann were not.
The latter struck me as a card shark, but I had a feeling the
former knew when to hold 'em.

After a buffet dinner on the upper deck, Peter and I returned
to our cabin. He'd arranged for a bottle of wine to be delivered. We went out to the balcony, which was no longer than
six feet and only a few feet wide, and sat down on metal
chairs to ponder the darkly silhouetted mountains rising
from the placid water. No lights twinkled along the distant
shore. The engines of the ship hummed, and voices from
the upper deck mingled with music from the lounge.

I slipped my hand in Peter's. "Is there any hope you'll
tell me what's going on?"

"We had an agreement," he began, then stopped to take a
deep breath and exhale in a frustrated whoosh. "No, there
isn't any hope because we don't really know what's going
on, if anything. We have no concrete evidence. There's a
vague ambiance of unease in Luxor. Mahmoud's usual
sources have either refused to talk or abruptly disappeared.
The people in Cairo have been hearing rumors about activity
involving El Asad li-allah." He squeezed my hand before I
could interrupt. "No, nothing suggesting that they're going
to attack tourists or bomb hotels. El Asad himself is purported to be in the Luxor area, but that's speculation at best."

"Himself? It couldn't be a woman?"

"Not in an extremist Muslim cult. These are the guys
who think women should stay home and obey the males in
the family, and believe their mission is to replace secularism with their interpretation of the Koran. Like the radical
faction of any religion, they're easily swayed by charis-
matic leaders who are adept at editing and citing out of
context. This particular group has neither the funds nor the
membership to act in the immediate future."

I thought about this for a moment. "The uneasiness must
be contagious. I certainly have been getting a lot of veiled

warnings not to meddle. I don't understand why anybody thinks I would. It's not as though I've been asking everybody about his politics or depth of religious fervor. Perhaps I should be flattered that I have such an international reputation for intuitive brilliance."

He chuckled in a dismissive, and therefore annoying, way. "This time it's not about you, Claire. Not everyone believes I'm a businessman looking at a potential real estate investment. I'm sure my trips to the police department have been noted by interested parties. You're merely my wife."

"Merely your wife?" I sputtered. My hand shook as I refilled my wineglass. A month ago, reciting marriage vows in Jorgeson's backyard, I'd had hopes that Peter would finally begin to appreciate my keen observational prowess and attention to detail, no matter how trifling. At that moment, I would have happily aligned myself with Nekhbet, the vulture goddess of the Upper Nile. "Would you prefer that I hand over my dowry and learn to crochet? As soon as we get home, I'll invite your captain's wife over for lunch and we'll start planning the Christmas party at the PD. Jorgeson will make an excellent Santa. After that, I can join the arts center ladies' auxiliary and help with the spring fashion show at the country club. That is what wives do, isn't it?"

"And learn to cook a decent rice pilaf."

"Your mother doesn't know how to boil water. If she wants to serve rice pilaf, she hires Uncle Ben to come over and cook it himself."

"He's retired."

I stood up. "I believe I'll retire as well, at least for the night."

Peter cut me off at the door. After he'd made his mute apologies on the balcony and in the cabin on the bed, utilizing the full range of his amazing amatory talents, we agreed that it might be nice to go to the lounge and have brandy while we enjoyed the Nubian musicians.

Later, when Peter and I were in bed and he was asleep, I realized that I'd learned almost nothing from our earlier conversation. Marriage had not changed his resistance to sharing information. Nor had it dampened my inclination to investigate.

By the following day, Buffy seemed to have forgotten her vision of spending the cruise on a deck chair. After an unspeakably early breakfast, passengers were ferried in launches to a rough stone pier. At one end was a steep path lined with rocks. It looked as though pitons might be useful. Although Inez might have had some in one of her pockets, I was as ill equipped as the rest of the passengers.

Caron and Inez had escaped with an earlier group, but Buffy, Samuel, and Sittermann lingered with Peter and me until we had no choice but to go together in the last launch. After some scrambling and muted curses, we arrived at the top of the hill. There were no vendors, no cafés, no tour buses, no restroom facilities. It was the first time that we'd seen sand. As we walked up a slope, I discovered quickly that it was not my preferred surface.

"This is the unfinished Temple of Maharakka," the cruise director said, "and dates from the Roman period. Beyond it is the Temple of Dakka, built between the second century B.C. and the first century A.D. You can climb steps cut into the wall to the roof for a view. It's about a kilometer away from here. Should you still be in the mood, the walk to Wadi es Sebua is difficult but worthwhile. It has an alley of lion-headed sphinxes and a colossal statue of Ramses II. The launches will be waiting whenever you wish to return to the ship, but please keep in mind that we sail at noon." He gave us a small salute and fled back to the pier.

Some of our fellow passengers were heading for the second site, while others sat in the shade, red faced and already miserable. My sympathies lay with them, but Peter slipped his arm around my waist and said, "We don't want to embarrass the girls, do we?"

Sittermann put his hands on his hips and squinted at the ruins of the temple. "I reckon I'm game if you all are, but I have to admit all these Ramses and Amons and Tuts are beginning to sound like the refrain of a country ballad, the country being Egypt in this case. There's no pizzazz in blocks of granite and eroded statues. In terms of marketability, I'd say what they need is—"

"Why don't you go back to the ship?" I suggested nicely.

He took out his camera. "How about you all stand in a group so I can get a good shot? I promised the boys at the Rotary Club back home that I'd do a slide show at our luncheon meeting next month. That ain't to say all of the members will stay awake. Some of those ol' boys were born about the time Ramses-the-whatever was canoodling with Nefertari."

We did not oblige him with a photo op, but instead trudged dutifully to the temple. Samuel darted about, talking excitedly about the inscriptions. Buffy stayed near him, sneaking peeks at her watch and no doubt calculating the approach of prime tanning time. Inez, I noticed, was lecturing a group of passengers about the influence of Augustus and Tiberius.

When she at last lost her audience, she joined Peter and me in the shade of a wall. Caron appeared from wherever she'd been cowering, and we headed for the Temple of Dakka. Sittermann was taking photographs as if he was on commission for *National Geographic,* although his subject seemed to be backsides of increasingly stressed tourists. Buffy and Samuel were hissing at each other. Other passengers were falling by the wayside, until we numbered no more than a dozen or so. Although I was in top physical condition for a bookseller who can rip into boxes of books without raising a sweat, I was beginning to feel a certain discomfort in my calves as the sand squished underfoot.

I was more than ready to retreat to the ship after we'd climbed the steps at Dakka and obligingly admired the view of sand, rocks, and the Nubian Sea. I could almost hear the tinkle of ice cubes in my very tall, very cold drink as I sat in the lounge.

"Don't be such a wimp," Caron said, correctly interpreting the blissful look on my face. "If Buffy can do it . . ."

"The next temple has a most delectable juxtaposition of Ramses II offering flowers to Saint Peter," Samuel inserted. "The original reliefs were plastered over when the building was converted into a church. Some of the plaster deteriorated."

"Poor Ramses," Inez said. She took a tissue from one of her numerous pockets and dabbed the corner of her eye. "He would have been mortified."

I was not swayed by Inez's bizarre emotional display, but I was surprised to see that Buffy had gone ahead of us and was no longer visible. "All right," I said ungraciously. "Let's go weep for Ramses."

My thighs were howling, albeit silently, as we came up the last hundred feet and gazed at a rather unimpressive structure. I was more concerned about the long walk back to the pier than the mortification of Ramses II, who seemed to have exalted himself on the majority of temples in the Nile Valley and deserved a little bit of humility. Peter was having a quiet conversation with Samuel about the Roman era, while Sittermann continued his maniacal obsession with his camera and Inez steeled herself for the upcoming ordeal.

Buffy was now within our sight—as were two men on horseback. She was standing next to a glistening black horse, speaking with some vehemence to its rider, a young Arab with a tattered rag tied around his head. He was ill shaven, with a hooked nose, heavy eyebrows, stained teeth—and a rifle slung across his back. It was peculiar, to put it mildly. I stopped abruptly, as did my companions.

"What's she doing?" asked Caron.

"She can't know them," Inez volunteered in a thin voice.

From behind me, I heard Sittermann's camera clicking, as well as others. Peter clutched my elbow and said, "I don't like this. Something's wrong."

Samuel began to head toward the odd group, his mouth tight. I agreed that some sort of action was required, but I had no idea what it might be. The few remaining passengers from the ship were gawking.

I had every intention of saying something when the rider

leaned down, grabbed Buffy by the arm, and dragged her across the saddle in front of him. He banged his ankles against the horse's belly and it took off at a gallop. The second horseman followed at an equally furious pace. I could see Buffy struggling, but the rider had a tight clutch on the back of her shirt. The second rider fired a shot into the sky.

Seconds later, they disappeared behind a hill.

"What the hell . . . ?" Sittermann said.

CHAPTER 9

We stood there like a cluster of hypostyle columns, too stunned to so much as twitch. There was no sound, no cloud of dust, no distant shrieks. The sky was lucid, unmarred by even a wispy cloud. The sunlight no longer danced on the sand; it sank without a sparkle.

Samuel was frozen in mid-step. His foot finally came down and he reeled around. "What just happened?" he demanded hoarsely.

"I don't know," Peter said, as bewildered as the rest of us.

"Was she abducted?" asked a thin blond woman from the ship.

Samuel began to run in the direction the riders had taken, a gallant but futile effort on his part. Peter nudged me. "Let's get in the shade," he said, "and decide what we ought to do. Maybe someone has a cell phone."

"There's no reception here," Sittermann said, "but I agree there's not much point in getting a sunstroke. Come along, little dogies. There's a nice patch of shade next to that wall."

"Can we kill him?" Caron whispered to me as we headed for the temple.

"It's okay with me, "I said, "but there are a lot of witnesses."

"Do you think anybody will testify against me?"

"Good point."

No one seemed to have anything to say. After a few

minutes, Samuel joined us, panting and soaked with sweat. "I couldn't even see which way they went," he said as he leaned against a rock and gulped down some water. "They've vanished. This is unreal. I feel like I must be dreaming."

"Reckon not," Sittermann said.

Samuel shook his head. "That's what you'd say in my dream. Maybe Osiris will show up next and point me in the right direction. I'll make my way to a fabulous temple, where Buffy will be seated on a golden throne, playing with an asp."

"As much as we'd love to hear the details, we can't just sit here," I said. "Anyone have any bright ideas?"

"We need to go back to the ship," one of the passengers said, mopping his face with a handkerchief. "The captain will call the police, and they can deal with it."

Peter stood up. "Everybody stay together and let's go as quickly as we can. If you feel faint, say so and we'll stop for a minute. Agreed?"

Sittermann reached over as if he intended to help me to my feet. I got up with amazing agility, gestured at the girls, and looked back at the spot we'd last seen Buffy. It looked eerily normal, merely sand and rocks. In another situation, I might have found it romantic, in the same way I imagined the moors would be if populated by dyspeptic heroes and raven-haired virgins with heaving bosoms.

"Seventy thousand square kilometers of desert," Samuel said as he fell into step beside me. "The size of—I hate to say this—Texas."

"Well, they haven't had time to ride from Amarillo to El Paso," I said. "The police will know where to find them."

"Yeah, sure," he muttered.

I caught up with Peter. His jaw was tight, his eyes slitted. I doubted that he was in the mood for speculation. We trudged slowly but steadily in the direction of the sea. When we reached Dakka, we mutely sought shade and took deep swills from our water bottles. Samuel continued to mutter under his breath; no one seemed willing to attempt to comfort him. The final stretch to Maharakka was excruciatingly painful. Every grain of the sand was now my enemy. Conversation was reduced to grunts and wheezes. Even Caron and Inez were pink faced as we scrambled down the slope to the primitive pier and onto the launches.

As soon as we were on board the *Nubian Queen,* Peter and Samuel headed for the lower deck to find the captain. Since I had nothing to contribute, I went to the cabin and sponged off the accumulated grit and perspiration. Feeling much better in a clean shirt and sandals, I went to the lounge for a much-needed cold drink.

Two American men I'd met at dinner the previous evening waved for me to join them. One was a gray-haired, loquacious Egyptologist, the other a much quieter connoisseur of architecture and art. The older man, who'd introduced himself as "Dennis from North Carolina, ma'am," demanded to know what was being done.

"You know as much as I do," I admitted. "I suppose the police have been notified. The horseman can't have taken Buffy too far."

"There could be a Bedouin camp in the area," Joel, the younger one, said. "The men thought she was flirting with them, and snatched her as a prank. They must be regretting it by now."

Dennis had been taking almost as many photographs as Sittermann. He pulled out his camera and began clicking a button on the back of it. "Digital," he said for my benefit. "You can see all the pictures I took this morning. Although I was trying to get a decent shot of Wadi es Sebua, I may have caught a few of the horsemen as well. Here's one of you, Mrs. Malloy."

He held the camera so that I could see a tiny rectangle that reflected my grimace as I navigated the uneven path. It was not my most flattering demeanor. He continued clicking for a few moments, then said, "I thought so. You can't see much of the men's faces, but the police can enlarge it."

Buffy, her hands on her hips, appeared to be speaking to the Arabs. Bewildered, I waited as the man clicked to the next photograph. In this one, her head was tilted as if she understood what they were saying. I found it hard to believe that they spoke English or that she spoke Arabic. Of course, I thought, they might have been proffering an unseen object and attempting to haggle over its price. It was likely that Buffy was capable of shopping in any language, be it Arabic, Urdu, or an obscure Chinese dialect. I toyed with the idea, which made a lot more sense. She'd managed to offend them during the negotiations, and they'd grabbed her in a fit of anger.

"What are you looking at, Mother?" Caron said as she and Inez sat down.

"Digital photos," Dennis said, saving me from a minor display of ignorance of the wizardry of technology. "It can hold six hundred shots on one memory card. Look, here's your friend haranguing our fellow cruise mates. The blonde looks like she's half-asleep."

"I was not haranguing them," Inez said stiffly. "I was answering their questions."

Joel grinned at her. "I didn't hear them asking any."

Peter entered the lounge before Inez could come up with a retort, although, to be candid, I was looking forward to hearing it. He stopped by the piano to address the entire room. "The captain has contacted the authorities. At the moment, we're in the middle of nowhere. There are some soldiers in Abu Simbel, and more in Aswan. They'll join up to cover this area and all the way to Kharga Oasis to the west, if necessary. If any of you were close enough to see or hear what happened with Buffy and the horseback riders, please let me know." He waited for a moment, then shrugged. "That's really about all. Lunch is being served on the upper deck, and we'll be sailing shortly."

When Peter joined us, he studied the photos of Buffy and her abductors. "Interesting," he murmured, noticing the same thing that I found curious. "Turn over the memory card to the police in Abu Simbel. They can send the images via the Internet. Take very good care of it until then."

"Give them the memory card?" the man sputtered. "Unthinkable, utterly unthinkable. I have some very dramatic shots of the reliefs at Beit al-Wali. I intend to use them for an article I'm writing for a prestigious Egyptology periodical. The juxtaposition of light and shadows brings out the intricate details of—"

"The police will be fascinated," Peter said, "and will let you tell them all about it from your cell. A woman has been kidnapped. It's serious."

Caron leaned forward. "Do you think they'll hold her for ransom?"

"Why her?" asked Inez. "She was wearing regular clothes and no jewelry except for little earrings. She told me she couldn't wear her watch because of the danger of a tan line." She lowered her voice. "If they wanted a ransom, that blond woman over there is fabulously rich. She has a private jet and vacation houses all over the world. She invited me to visit her in Costa Rica this summer."

"She *what*?" Caron said with a gasp. "You didn't tell me!"

Inez took off her cloth hat and ran her fingers through her limp brown hair. "She collects characters, she said. She was very impressed with my khaki outfit. It seems I have a certain *je ne sais quoi*."

"You look like a refugee from a Foreign Legion surplus store."

"I'll be wearing a bikini in Costa Rica," Inez said smugly. "Shall I bring you back a parrot?"

"It's preferable to a case of malaria."

Peter held up his hands. "That's enough. If you two don't cut it out, you can have lunch in your cabin—and stay there the rest of the afternoon."

Caron stared at him, then at me. "He can't say that to me, Mother."

"He just did," I said. "Shall we go up for lunch, everybody?"

I was hungry, but I couldn't eat more than a few bites of salad. I kept looking back at the receding view of Maharakka as the ship continued south. We were scheduled for a visit to the temples of Amada and Derr, but I wasn't in the mood for more sand and yet another jumble of rocks. When our waiter brought coffee, I said as much to Peter, who admitted he preferred to wait on board in case there was information about Buffy. I was reluctant to allow Caron and Inez to go ashore, but Dennis and Joel agreed to stay near them and keep an eye out for suspicious men on horseback.

After a while, Peter and I were alone on the deck. The staff had been reluctant to abandon us, but Peter had slipped the more persistent ones a few pounds to purchase our privacy.

"Did you talk to Mahmoud?" I asked.

"I told him what happened. He was surprised. In general, Egyptians are very friendly and courteous to tourists. They may expect baksheesh, but even Cairo is safer than most large cities. The Bedouins are peaceful, and mostly settled in government housing instead of tents."

"What about this terrorist group?"

"We've already discussed that, Claire. They're not into small-time crime. The last thing a covert organization wants is to have its members arrested for shoplifting or brawling. As Inez pointed out, Buffy doesn't dress as though she's from a wealthy family willing to cough up big bucks for her return."

"Would you cough up big bucks for my return?" I asked sweetly. Admittedly, it was a silly thing to say, but we were on our honeymoon.

"The sun and moon," he said with a properly amorous leer. "You are my jewel of the Nile, my sultry Cleopatra, my diamond in the vast sands of the Sahara."

"Not bad," I said. "Shall we go check with the captain?"

As we went down to the lounge, I noticed that quite a few of the other passengers seemed to share my lack of enthusiasm for another temple. Abu Simbel would be less worrisome, since it was near the water and would be crowded with tour groups and eager guides. We continued down the curved staircase to the lower deck and followed a corridor to the pilot room.

The captain and the cruise director were in the middle of an unhappy discussion that focused, I surmised, on Buffy. Neither of them looked especially pleased to see us.

"Have you heard anything?" asked Peter.

"I presume you are asking about the girl," the cruise director said, plucking invisible lint off his sleeve. "The answer to that is no. If you're asking about my future with the company, then the answer is no less palatable. When the *Nubian Queen* returns to Aswan, my replacement will be waiting."

"It wasn't your fault," I said.

"I suppose not, but someone must be punished for the company's embarrassment. In the old days, the sultan would have arranged a public execution. My head would have ended up on a pike at the pier, and my entrails fed to the vultures." He sighed loudly. "As it is, I will go back to Cairo and try to find work as a doorman, all because of that girl."

I bristled. "It wasn't her fault, either. None of us were warned about the potential danger of being abducted by militant rebels."

"Ah, yes, you've been reading that nonsensical book," he said with a sneer. "There are no savage sheiks these days, Mrs. Malloy, any more than there were eighty years ago. With a few exceptions, the few tourist fatalities come from reckless behavior, such as driving off the paved roads into the desert or scuba diving in the Red Sea without adequate training."

"The exceptions being the attacks at the Temple of Hatshepsut and the Red Sea?" I said, staring at him. "The tour bus outside the Cairo Museum?"

"How many Arabs have died because of American aggression?" he countered.

Peter intervened. "Let's go, dear. The captain will let me know if he receives any information."

I was hustled back along the corridor, fuming silently. Sittermann was waiting at the top of the stairs, dressed in baggy shorts and another outlandish print shirt. All he lacked was a plastic lei and flip-flops.

"Well, there you two are," he said. "I was just about to go down to the pilot room, but I reckon that's where you were. Have they heard anything?"

"No," Peter said. "Now, if you'll excuse us—"

Sittermann blocked our way to the corridor that led to our cabin. "Why don't you all come along to my room for a drink and a chat? I have some new information that might prove kind of interesting."

"You?" I said, arching my eyebrows.

"About Buffy."

Peter and I exchanged looks as Sittermann led us to the upper deck and around a corner to a door. He unlocked it and gestured for us to precede him. His cabin, and I use the term loosely, was a vast sitting room with a bar, wicker furniture, and sliding glass doors to a sizable balcony. An open door on one side gave me a glimpse of a bedroom with a king-sized bed and a pile of silk pillows. It was not as large as the Presidential Suite at the Old Winter Palace, but our cabin on the ship could have been tucked in a corner.

"Wine?" Sittermann said as he went behind the bar. "Martinis? You name it, I got it. In fact, Mrs. Malloy, if you'd like to slip away while your husband and I talk business, there's a Jacuzzi in the bathroom. You can stretch out and look at the mountains while all them bubbles soothe your aching muscles."

"How did you get this?" I demanded.

"The owner of the cruise company owed me a little favor."

Peter sat down on the sofa and distractedly picked up a dried apricot from the platter of pastries and fruit on the table. After a moment, he replaced it. His expression was blank, but I could almost hear him thinking furiously.

"Not in the mood for a bath, Mrs. Malloy?" Sittermann went on. "I seem to recollect you're a scotch drinker. I'll call for some ice."

"I'd prefer lemonade," I said mendaciously, then joined Peter. We both watched Sittermann as he picked up the telephone and ordered ice and lemonade. "This is crazy," I whispered.

"So it is," Sittermann said, sitting down on a nearby chair and propping his ankle on his knee. "By all rights, you two should have gotten this little bit of heaven for yourselves, it being your honeymoon and all. Guess I got lucky." He leaned forward and took a honey-coated piece of baklava. "Maybe I should get to the point. I managed to make a few calls while everybody was having lunch."

"To whom?" Peter asked, coming out of his trance.

"Business associates back home." He ate the baklava, then licked his glistening fingers with the complacency of a well-fed cat. "It turns out there's something fishy about this girl calling herself Buffy. Her passport identifies her as Eleanor Franz from Sausalito, but her home address is bogus and her parents don't exist in the system."

"Maybe they're in the witness protection program," I said, having had some recent experience with such things. "Or her mother remarried and uses her husband's name."

Sittermann gazed at me. "And they all live together in a BMW dealership?"

"What about the college group in Rome?" I persisted.

"Hundreds of colleges and universities have programs in Rome, but none of them claimed her."

"Maybe these business associates of yours haven't been able to get in touch with every last program."

"You'd be surprised at how efficient they are," he said with a smirk.

Peter stood up and glowered at Sittermann. "How did you find out all this? Who are you? Who are these so-called 'associates' that can dig up that kind of information in a matter of hours?"

"I am a concerned fellow American," Sittermann said solemnly. "I shiver to think about that poor little thing in the clutches of wild-eyed tribesmen, who might at this very moment be ravishing her. It may take a passel of them to subdue her, I admit, 'cause the girl does have spunk. I've always admired spunk."

Peter looked as if he was on the verge of leaping at Sittermann's throat. Although I could hardly fault him, I doubted it would produce more than brief satisfaction. I caught his hand and tugged at it until he sank down beside me.

"Why are you telling us?" I asked.

"I'm beginning to think Mr. Rosen is more than a simple businessman like myself, and you, Mrs. Malloy, have quite a reputation."

"I think you'd better explain," Peter said, his face flushed.

Sittermann did not respond but instead went to the bar and began to uncork a bottle of wine. I could hear Peter's breathing as he struggled to regain control of his temper. His outburst had surprised me, since he tended to display increasing iciness when he was upset with me. He also had the unfortunate tendency to lapse into passive-aggressive retaliation, such as having my car impounded or assigning a police officer to dog me.

Sittermann brought us each a glass of wine. "I thought you might be interested, that's all. Samuel Berry seems to have taken a dislike to me for some reason, and he wouldn't spit on me if I was on fire. Why don't you toss a few questions in his direction and see if he has any answers?" A telephone rang in the bedroom. "Dadgummit, as much as I hate to end this little party, I got to take that call. I sure have enjoyed talking with you. Take the wine with you. It's a Cabernet Sauvignon from Château Margaux. Got a nice twang to it."

Peter and I carried our glasses out to the deck where lunch had been served. Neither of us spoke for well over five minutes, but sipped wine and tried to digest the peculiar encounter with Sittermann.

"Expensive taste for a Texan," Peter said at last.

"It does have a nice twang."

"I don't know if we should believe a word he says," Peter went on, looking at the mountains that jutted out of the water. "I don't trust him."

"What would be the purpose in telling us all that about Buffy if it's a fabrication? Why bother?"

"So we'll question Samuel, I suppose."

"Samuel didn't come up here for lunch," I said. "He wasn't in the lounge afterward, either. Do you think he went to the temple with the others? That would be rather callous, considering how upset he was about Buffy."

Peter finished his wine and put down his glass. "I'm going to find out if the captain has heard anything more from the military or the local police."

"And call Mahmoud to tell him what Sittermann said?"

"The American Embassy. If the girl's not found soon, it may set off an international incident. There's nothing the press loves more than a pretty American girl who's disappeared under mysterious circumstances. Stories about war, famine, and genocide are buried on the back pages these days. Even terrorism is getting boring. I won't be surprised to find BBC and CNN at Abu Simbel tomorrow, cameras whirring and microphones being waved like batons." He gave me a perfunctory kiss on the cheek. "I'll meet you later in the lounge. I doubt they stock wine from Château Margaux, but I'll ask."

I listened to his footsteps as he went downstairs, then leaned back and replayed my few encounters with Buffy. She was very much the vapid stereotype of a pampered California princess. She'd gone to Rome for a semester of shopping. Samuel seemed to be her sole motivation for coming to Egypt. But why would she have a fake passport? I had no idea how one acquired such a thing. Any concept she had of the black market would involve designer rip-offs and counterfeit purses.

I decided to have a word with Samuel, if he was on board. I would have preferred to search Sittermann's suite, but he was likely to still be there. Unless, I corrected myself, he had a private elevator along with his well-stocked bar and personal communication center.

The cabin roster was posted behind the reception desk

on the lower deck. The cabin shared by Buffy and Samuel was farther down our corridor. I squeezed past cleaning carts and smiled vaguely at stewards laden with fresh towels. Once I reached the door, I stopped for a moment to decide how best to proceed, then gave up and knocked. After two or three minutes, Samuel opened the door.

"Mrs. Malloy," he said flatly.

"May I come in?"

"Uh, yeah, sure," he said, stepping back. His hair was damp and he'd changed into clean clothes. How he'd found clean clothes qualified as a small mystery. The cabin looked as if it had been flipped over and shaken. Clothes were draped over the chairs and bed and piled on the floor. The surface of the dresser was cluttered with Buffy's hair products and makeup, much of it overturned. An open drawer filled with her underwear (unless Samuel had a well-hidden passion for lingerie) was a jumble of lace and silk. "Sorry about the mess," he added as he swept clothes off the bed. "Buffy brought enough for a monthlong cruise. She kept insisting that she be prepared for every imaginable level of dress."

"So I see." I sat down and turned on the sympathy. "You must be really worried about her. What a dreadful, shocking thing for her to be grabbed like that."

"No kidding. I kept expecting a director to yell 'Cut!' any second, and the movie crew to emerge from behind rocks. She's just a kid, you know. Sure, she can be annoying with all her prattle, but she's not malicious. She just came along with me because she was bored in Rome. I shouldn't have let her come. This is all my fault."

"I don't agree." I hoped he would sit down, but he went over to the window and looked out. "Samuel, do you think you ought to get in touch with Buffy's parents?"

"When there's something to tell them. Right now, they don't even know she's in Egypt, so there's no point in sending them into hysterics. She's probably in some dumpy neighborhood in Aswan, trying to call the police, or in Abu Simbel at a bar. She'll have everybody in the place fighting to buy her drinks. Anyway, the captain promised that he'd send for me as soon as he heard something."

"You two met at a bar in Rome?"

"A couple of weeks ago. I was hanging out, and she came in with some girlfriends. She glided right over to my table, and ten minutes later she was sitting in my lap. When I told her I was leaving for Egypt, she decided that she wanted to come along. I tried to talk her out of it, but she went back to her apartment, packed, and showed up at the hostel. It was okay with me, but later I began to wish I'd made sure she understood that I wasn't going for the exotic nightclubs and luxury hotels. She kept looking around the airport for Peter O'Toole and Omar Sharif."

"Do you know the name of her college?"

"Some liberal arts college. She's not Stanford material. She majoring in a ridiculous field like children's recreation management so she can be a lacrosse coach."

"Oh," I murmured.

Samuel closed the window shade. "I'd better go find the captain. He might have forgotten to send up a message. Thanks for coming by, Mrs. Malloy."

It seemed as though nobody on the ship wanted my company, I thought as I got up. I'd been run off by pretty much everybody, including my husband. "Did Buffy bring her passport on the cruise?"

"How should I know? I haven't seen it lying around in here. She might have it in her bag, or she may have left it in her luggage at the hotel in Luxor. I told her she wouldn't need it."

"And obviously you couldn't find it," I said, gesturing at the clutter. "Or maybe you finally did. It's hard to tell."

"What's your point, Mrs. Malloy?

I tried to come up with a credible response. "The American Embassy might need the information," I said at last. "They could use the photograph to send flyers to the military and the local police stations. She would have to show it if she got a hotel room or used a credit card to get money at a bank. Assuming she's in Aswan or Abu Simbel . . ."

Samuel shrugged. "I'll tell the captain to let the authorities know I have a few photos that I took at the oases—should flyers become necessary." He opened the door for me. "I'll see you later, Mrs. Malloy."

As I headed for our cabin, I realized his parting comment had sounded like a threat.

CHAPTER 10

I failed to see the temples of Abu Simbel at sunrise, having sacrificed aesthetics for sleep. While we ate breakfast at a more civilized hour, Inez raved about the majesty of the moment, and would have carried on at length had I not shushed her. It was indeed spectacular, set into a mountainside and guarded by colossal statues of Ramses II, seated on either side of the entrance. Three of them, that is; a fourth had been toppled by an earthquake centuries ago and left in pieces as it had been when discovered in the early nineteenth century. The nearby Temple of Hathor, built by Ramses as a tribute to his wife, Nefertari, was also fronted by statues, although the old boy outnumbered his wife.

Peter left for the pilot room, no doubt to confer madly with the American Embassy and his covert comrades. He'd been up and down the stairs all night, and the few times he'd come into the cabin he had paced and mumbled in a most unromantic fashion. Buffy had not surfaced in any towns or oases; nor had anyone claimed to have seen her.

Inez finally left me to my coffee and went up to the small observation deck. I would have liked to find out what Sittermann might have heard from his "associates," but I hadn't seen him at dinner or afterward in the lounge, where we were entertained by Nubian musicians and dancers. Samuel had not appeared, either. I doubted the two had been consoling each other all night over a bottle of expensive wine.

Caron sat down across from me and stared gloomily at her laden plate. "This is so Not Fair."

"The sunshine?" I asked. "The breathtaking view of the temples? The freshly baked rolls and hand-squeezed orange juice? The fact that a waiter is hovering discreetly to make sure no insect dares invade your personal space?"

"Why should Buffy be the one to be kidnapped by a sheik? She's probably just pouting in some tent because she doesn't have her conditioner and her moisturizers. Never mind that she's wearing a silk robe and tons of jewelry. The servants are on their knees, begging her forgiveness because they don't have the most recent issue of *Entertainment Weekly*."

"You're annoyed because *you* weren't kidnapped?" I said, appalled. "Does reading that ridiculous book make you more qualified?"

"When she gets back, she'll be interviewed on every single talk show and have dinner in the White House, like she's the poster child for international kidnap victims. Somebody better show her a map of the world before she opens her mouth and says something really stupid. I'd bet my allowance she doesn't even know that Egypt is in Africa."

I pushed aside my coffee. "If Buffy's still alive, she's liable to be in a filthy little mud house, sleeping on a dirt floor and eating rancid meat. She may have been beaten and raped."

"Not her," Caron said, jabbing at a turkey sausage.

I waved off the waiter, who had an eye on my coffee cup. "Your naïveté is absurd, as well as petty and selfish, and I don't want any more of it. If you can't find any sympathy, then keep your mouth closed."

"Oh, right," she said. "Poor Buffy. I hope she's surviving without her curling iron." Ignoring my hiss, she took a bite of a roll and gazed at the temples. "I got up with Inez this morning to watch the sunrise. It was pretty cool until that rich woman wiggled her way to the railing between us and started asking Inez about Hathor and those people. After that, I might as well have been bird poop."

I was beginning to understand Caron's snit. "Listen, dear, fellow travelers can become very chummy, especially in a foreign country, but once they get home . . ."

"Mitzi invited Inez to fly with her to Cairo on her private jet, and then on to Greece for a Mediterranean cruise on her yacht."

"And?" I said, trying not to gulp so loudly the waiter felt obliged to thump me on the back.

"Inez said she didn't think she could, but her voice trembled. Mitzi must think Inez is some sort of biped encyclopedia just because she can spout off all that stuff about pharaohs and gods. Inez isn't going to impress anybody with her vast knowledge of ancient Greece. She nearly threw up when she had to be in a skit based on *Lysistrata* in Mrs. McLair's class, and she thinks the story about Leda and the swan is out of a bird-watchers' guidebook."

"You don't need to worry about Mitzi's invitation. Peter's arranged for our luggage to be taken ashore while we're at the temple, and we'll head from there to the airport. A private jet sounds nice, but we'll be on a commercial airline to Luxor. I'm not sure when we'll go to Cairo. The middle of next week, maybe."

Caron made a face. "I sounded pretty juvenile, didn't I? Is it too late to plead jet lag?"

"Much too late," I said sternly. "I'll allow you this one display of petulance. You're entitled to be a bit overwhelmed by everything that's happened in the last month, including the wedding. You don't have to think of Peter as your stepfather unless you want to. He can just be my husband."

"I haven't decided. I was pissed off yesterday when he acted like he had the right to send me to my cabin, even if I deserved it. Then again, I would have been pissed off at you, too. Maybe it's okay." She put down her napkin. "I'd better finish packing. Do you know where Inez is?"

I did, but I shrugged and watched Caron go down the steps. She and I had never sat down and discussed her feelings about Peter. She'd occasionally resented his presence

over the last several years, but she'd resented almost everything at one time or another, including the weather, her
class schedule, her lack of designer jeans, and my rare demands that she fill in for me at the Book Depot. I was so
accustomed to her outbursts that I seldom listened to the
nuances. I hoped I wasn't like the cheerful residents of
Pompeii, oblivious to Vesuvius when it began to spew a little smoke.

The waiter cracked under the strain and began to sweep
crumbs off the table. I returned to the cabin, made sure I
hadn't overlooked any of my or Peter's things, and went to
the lounge. The other passengers began to filter in for a final
cup of coffee or tea before boarding the launches. Most of
them were sailing back to Aswan, stopping at a few more
sites along the way. Although I am not at all claustrophobic,
I was eager to escape the tiny cabin and the forced cama-
raderie. Dennis, who'd given Peter the memory disc from
his camera (after requiring a signed note promising it would
be returned), and Joel stopped to wish me a pleasant flight
to Luxor, then went outside to jockey for seats in the first
launch. Eventually, the rest of my party joined me. When I
glanced inquiringly at Peter, he shook his head. Caron and
Inez were both silent as well. It did not bode well for a jolly
outing.

The launch deposited us on what was nothing more than
a ledge. For the first time, I could see the stairs that led all
the way to the top of the hillside. I eyed them unhappily.
My calves still ached from the interminable hike at Maharakka, Dakka, and Wadi es Sebua. This was worse.

"I don't suppose that's an escalator," I said to Peter as we
sidled along the ledge to a slightly wider patch of dirt and
loose rocks.

Grinning, he took my hand. "One step at a time."

The other passengers were progressing like a swarm of
ants. I took a deep breath, and we began the ascent. Someone had been thoughtful enough to design places to sit
along the way. I availed myself of them as necessary, then
glumly watched elderly passengers hurry past us, chatting

cheerfully as they went. Eventually we arrived at the top of what proved to be more than eighty torturous steps, then walked down a steep path to the facades of the two temples.

Several tour groups were already there, taking photos while their guides droned about the intricacies of the design. I found a rock of acceptable height and sat down to pull off my shoes and massage my feet. I declined Peter's invitation to go inside the temple, trying not to think about the walk back up the hill to the tourist center. When we got to Luxor, I vowed to spend countless hours in a hot, bubbly bath, sipping icy drinks and making peace with my legs and feet.

Eventually, Peter, Caron, and Inez emerged from the second temple and we trooped up the hill. The girls lagged behind us, whispering to each other. I was relieved that they were more amiable, since I had no enthusiasm for further bickering. When we arrived at the center, Peter and I found a shady café table while Caron and Inez shopped at the rows of stalls that undoubtedly had the exact same things as every other tourist destination in Egypt. There had to be a market for tacky T-shirts and amateurish replicas of tomb relics, but I had no theory about the demographics of the buyers.

A private car was waiting for us. The ride to the airport and the flight back to Luxor were unremarkable. No one seemed inclined to discuss Buffy, and what conversation there was concerned the amenities on the ship. Caron refrained from making snide remarks about Mitizi, and Inez kept her nose in one of her travel books. Bakr was waiting for us at the airport. He greeted us enthusiastically, loaded our luggage, and drove us to the Winter Palace.

As usual, Ahmed was lurking in the lobby. "Mr. Rosen and dear *Sitt* Malloy-Rosen," he gushed, grasping my hand in a moist clamp, "I hope you enjoyed the cruise. Egyptians are very proud of the dam at Aswan and the prosperity it has brought us. Were the accommodations on the ship to your liking? Have you had lunch? *Sitt* Malloy-Rosen, I have saved many newspapers for you. Abdullah will bring them up immediately. You have both received messages. If you will allow me a moment to find them, I will—"

"Send them to the suite," Peter said. He led me to the elevator and pushed the button. "If you don't mind, I'm going to Mahmoud's office. We need prints of the photos of Buffy and the horsemen to distribute to the military. Why don't you and the girls order room service?"

Before I could respond, I found myself staring at his back as he hurried toward the lobby. The elevator doors opened. "Do you want to wait for room service?" I asked Caron and Inez.

"I think I'll check e-mail first," Inez said, blinking at me like an owlet.

"We'll eat at the restaurant," Caron added. "See you later."

I rode the elevator in solitude, annoyed at being so handily dismissed. A cleaning cart in the hall was the only suggestion of life on the third floor. I let myself into the Presidential Suite and went out to the balcony. It felt very much like home, although my apartment in Farberville was hardly as posh. Peter and I had not had time to look at houses, since he'd been off learning how to be a spook before and after the wedding. I was gazing at my ring to assure myself that we were indeed married when Abdullah appeared at my side.

"Your newspaper and messages, *Sitt* Malloy," he said gravely. "I also brought a bucket of ice and some fresh fruit. Will you be ordering room service?"

"Did you miss me, Abdullah?"

"Yes, *Sitt*, as did Lord Bledrock and his group. You will find an invitation for a cocktail party among the messages. I believe they have heard rumors about the young American lady who has gone missing."

"What have you heard?" I asked him.

"Nothing more than gossip at the cafés and shops. There are more police officers on the street and at the tourist sites. I myself was asked to provide identification when I came to work this morning. Hotel security has placed a metal detector at the service entrance, which made many of us late to our work."

I tried to read his expression, but I might have had more luck with a newspaper in Arabic. "So what do you make of it, Abdullah? Was Miss Franz snatched by a couple of brash young men, or is there something more sinister going on?"

"That is not for me to say, *Sitt*. Please let me know if you require anything else." He glided across the living room and out the front door.

I hadn't really expected him to confide in me. I sat down and glanced through the messages. The majority of them were for Peter and came from the embassy as well as purported international investment firms that might as well announce themselves as "Spies 'R' Us." I paused as I found a message asking me to call Luanne Bradshaw. It was curious—and alarming. Luanne was not the sort to expect an update on my honeymoon, especially when it involved the machinations of an international call. I squinted at the lengthy string of digits necessary to call her back. Peter probably knew how to call London, Paris, CIA headquarters, and the North Pole, but I didn't want to wait for him to come back from the police station.

I was dithering when Alexander breezed into the suite, bearing a tray with covered dishes. He set it down on the table. "I ran into the girls downstairs, and they said you haven't eaten since breakfast on the ship. I brought you a salad, an omelet, and a selection of pastries. How about a drink?"

"Do you have a key?" I asked with an unfriendly look.

"No. Abdullah saw me struggling and unlocked the door for me. I think he suspects we're engaging in a bit of hanky-panky. I think the idea is delightful. Is there a chance . . . ?"

"There's ice by the mini-bar," I said.

I tucked the messages in my pocket while he availed himself of my less than gracious hospitality, and picked at the salad when he joined me. Feeling guilty, I said, "Thank you for bringing me lunch, Alexander. I understand rumors have been flying up and down the staid corridors of the hotel. What's the current theory?"

He poked his finger in his drink to stir it. "Ransom. The girl's father will pay a small fortune for her return. The Arabs who took her will be more than willing to give her back for Hummers, which are a lot more useful than spoiled California princesses. They've already realized that they can't get more than a hundred camels for her. Mrs. McHaver is quite certain that the girl's virtue has been tarnished beyond redemption, but she's an anomaly from the Victorian era. My father, in contrast, is concerned about potential international repercussions."

"He's a politician? I thought he was more into riding to the hounds, shooting pheasants, and pinching parlor maids."

"He has no interest in politics, I assure you, and hardly ever bothers to show up at the House of Lords. He's worried that enhanced security at the docks will make it more challenging to slip antiquities out of Egypt. It could be awkward if the contents of some of his crates were subjected to proper documentation."

"The Baron of Rochland deals in black-market antiquities?" I said, almost choking on a bite of tomato. I set down my fork and stared at him.

"I did mention his private collection, if I recall. Not all of it would stand up to scrutiny. Are you quite sure you wouldn't like a glass of wine with your lunch? There's a decent selection in the cabinet."

"No," I said distractedly, picturing Lord Bledrock creeping around a freighter in the middle of the night, dressed in black, his white hair tucked under a knitted cap. The image came straight out of a 1940s movie, complete with heavy fog and the raspy reverberation of the ship's horn. Miriam McHaver in the shadows, tears welling in her eyes. Sittermann in a trench coat, prowling like a feral cat.

Alexander finished his drink. "If all you're going to do is gape at the lovely lunch that I brought you, I shall be on my way. Perhaps you'll be more sociable at the little party this evening. You and your husband must come. There's been a curious increase in activity at the excavation site. Farewell, my lovely Mrs. Malloy."

I gave up on my noir fantasy and ate enough to tide me over until tea. After I'd replaced the covers on the plates, I went into the parlor and sat down by the telephone. Rather than tackling the innumerable numbers required to call Luanne, I punched the button for the concierge's desk and asked him to put through the call. A minute later, Luanne answered the phone with her typical Yankee briskness.

"Hey," I said. "What happened?"

She ignored my question and asked about the flight, the hotel, and so on. I obliged with somewhat terse answers, aware that the meter was running, then brought the conversation back to her message to call me.

"Strangest thing," she said slowly. "I went by your apartment last night to water that pathetic weed you call a houseplant. I'm not sure, but I got the impression that someone had searched your apartment. It wasn't obvious. Superficially, no one would have even noticed. The contents of your drawers and cabinets were almost too neat, as if someone had moved them and then very carefully replaced them. The stack of books by your bed was too precisely aligned. The patina of dust on the furniture was gone. What really caught me was that whoever was there was so overwhelmed with pity for your houseplant that he couldn't stop himself from watering it. I have to admit it was turning yellow and dropping leaves, but I thought it was pining for you."

"You called me because the apartment was tidy and you forgot when you last watered my plant?" I said.

"I watered it four or five days ago. There's no way the soil would still be moist. Somebody was there, and he was methodical as well as neat. Nothing seemed to be missing, but I don't know where you keep your crown jewels and stock certificates."

"At Windsor Castle." I went on to describe the Baron of Rochland, his eligible son, Lady Emerson's lethal parasol, and the other odd characters, then ended the call without going into the current crisis. I felt as bewildered as Alice

must have when she imprudently stepped through a looking glass. Rather than trying to sort it out, I retreated to the
bathroom.

I'd had a most satisfactory soak and was wrapped in the
hotel's luxurious robe when Peter returned. After he called
room service for tea and sandwiches, we went out on the
balcony.

"What about Buffy?" I asked.

"Still missing," he said, "and it's been twenty-four hours.
It doesn't look good. And before you ask, I checked with
the American Embassy and they haven't been able to locate her parents or her group in Rome."

"Maybe you were talking to the wrong people. Sittermann seems to know everything about her, right down to
her home address. Has he been questioned?"

"He's disappeared. He had his luggage taken ashore at
Abu Simbel, but he didn't take a flight from the airport. If
he arranged for a car and driver, he avoided the obligatory
military escort back to Luxor. According to Mahmoud,
that's not uncommon. A native driver knows how to go
around the checkpoints, and bribery works well. Nobody at
the embassy has ever heard of him."

"What do your colleagues think?"

"I made a call from a safe phone, but I'll have to wait for
a reply."

"You call them from 'a safe phone'?" I tried not to giggle. "Is that why we're sitting out here? Is a bird going to
land on the rail with a note tied around its leg? Do you have
a decoder ring?"

"I've had a decoder ring since I was in second grade, but
it's in a box in the attic in Newport. Shall we discuss something else?"

Abdullah arrived with tea, smiled, and left. I told Peter
about Luanne's assertion that my apartment had been
searched. Neither of us was impressed with her self-
proclaimed keen power of observation. When I mentioned
Lord Bledrock's invitation, Peter muttered something unpleasant and went into our bedroom to take a nap.

I was reading the amazingly lurid prose in *The Savage Sheik,* trying with no success to picture Buffy describing her captor as "a lustful brute with a devilish twinkle in his steely blue eyes," when I heard a soft tap on the door. Since everyone else seemed to stroll into the room, I was puzzled as I opened the door.

"Miriam?" I said, then stepped back. "Please come in."

"Thank you, Mrs. Malloy," she said in a low voice. She glanced over her shoulder, then ducked inside. "I'm so sorry to interrupt you like this. I saw your daughter and her friend in the lobby, and realized you were back. I won't take very much of your time. I hope you don't mind dreadfully."

"No, not at all," I said. "Come out to the balcony. My husband's in our room, resting."

"Thank you," she murmured, glancing about nervously as we went through the sitting room. "I do so love this view. All the noise and activity below us, and the serenity of the mountains across the Nile. Such a fascinating contrast of modern and ancient, don't you think? Those barely visible lines along the mountains are paths still used by goat herders today, as they were in the time of the pharaohs three thousand years ago." She gripped the rail and bent over. "Look, there's Lord Bledrock and my aunt, having drinks on the terrace. I don't suppose you have a flowerpot I could chuck at them, do you?" She spun around and put her hand to her mouth, but her eyes were bright. "Oh, dear, I shouldn't have said that. Aunt Rose was kind enough to take me in when I was orphaned at a young age. She paid for my basic needs and schooling. I have only the warmest regard for her."

I made sure my chair was well away from the railing and that I could make it inside in a step. "I'm sure you do, Miriam. The tea is tepid by now. May I offer you a drink?"

"No, thank you. I need your advice, Mrs. Malloy. You appear to be quite friendly with Alexander. I've discovered . . . well, that I might be growing just the tiniest bit fond of him, even though he acts as though I'm not worthy of his attention. I haven't had much experience with men. I went to a girls' school and was much too shy to mingle with the boys brought in for dances. I always found a way to serve punch so that I could avoid conversation. I devoted myself to my studies at the university, and spent the holidays with my aunt. She has provided me with wonderful opportunities to travel, but I rarely have any free time. She can be so very demanding, as you must have seen."

Miriam had uttered more words in the last five minutes than I'd heard from her since we were introduced at Lord Bledrock's party. Sadly, I was at a loss to come up with any of my own. There had been a tinge of resentment in her voice when she mentioned my purported friendship with Alexander, as if I'd made an effort to enamor him with my womanly wiles.

"Alexander likes to hide out from his father," I finally said.

She sat down across from me, her hands folded in her lap and her legs crossed at the ankles. "How can I persuade him to notice me, Mrs. Malloy? Should I have any hope? I realize I'm not beautiful or clever, but I am capable of intelligent conversation. What do you and he discuss? Temples and tombs? Hieroglyphs? More contemporary subjects such as politics? Art and literature? If only I knew, I could prepare myself."

"We don't really talk about much of anything," I admitted. "He told me a little bit about his family and his youthful escapades. Idle chatter, mostly. I'm afraid he finds his father, Mrs. McHaver, the Misses Portia and Cordelia, and the rest of the group tedious." I winced as I realized what I'd said. "Not you, of course, but the cocktail parties, bridge games, and lectures."

"He does seem to go off on his own quite a lot," Miriam said thoughtfully. "Do you have any idea where he goes?"

"I don't keep track of his activities. He went with us to the Valley of the Kings one day. My husband invited him." This wasn't exactly true, but I wanted to remind her that I was happily married and had no designs on Alexander.

"Other than that, I have no idea what he does when he's on his own, as you put it."

She leaned forward, her expression intent. "He's friendly with your husband?"

"I suppose so." I was getting increasingly uncomfortable. The balcony had never seemed spacious, but it was shrinking rapidly. I would have squirmed if it had not been unbecoming. "Not drinking buddies or anything like that," I added. "Alexander has been in Luxor before and was kind enough to offer his expertise, that's all."

"Is your husband still looking into real estate opportunities? I've noticed that he's gone quite often."

"He has obligations to his colleagues. I knew before we came that he would be gone some of the time, which is partly why I brought along the girls." I'd stumbled onto a safer topic and grasped at it. "You said that you saw them downstairs. What were they doing?"

Miriam smiled wryly. "E-mailing their boyfriends, I suspect. They were in the computer room, sitting so close to each other that no one could catch a glimpse of the monitor. When I was that age, I used to wonder what it would be like to have a boyfriend. The other girls shared their secrets with each other, but no one ever bothered to ask my advice. Why would they? The only date I ever had was dictated by the matron, who arranged for me to attend the school Christmas dance with a boy from Saint Cutthroat's. He was a big, horrid pig with bad breath and stained teeth. I was miserable the entire time."

"Hmmm," I said, wishing that either Peter would rouse himself or the girls would return to the suite.

"What do you know about this young woman named Salima?"

"She studied at Cambridge. Her father is a professor in Cairo and her family lives across the river. She can be overly enthusiastic and opinionated, but that's not uncommon at her age." It occurred to me that she and Miriam were likely to be the same age. "That doesn't excuse her behavior," I added. "She took Caron and Inez to a birthday party at her parents' house and then to a nightclub, where she lost track of them. Peter and I were frantic until they came back to the hotel."

"I'm sure you were. The nightclubs in Gurna have a terrible reputation for excessive drinking and drugs. The police don't interfere unless there's a brawl that spills out into the streets. The girls must have been terrified to be abandoned like that, without a single familiar face in the crowd."

I bit my lip to stop myself from blurting out the rest of the story. "Well, they were introduced to some local girls, and they thought they saw Samuel Berry. You've heard about Buffy?"

"That sort of thing could only happen to someone like her," Miriam said. "It's so melodramatic and juvenile. I wouldn't be surprised if she arranged it beforehand, just to get attention and sympathy. Late last week I heard her and Samuel arguing about the cruise in the restaurant. They were so loud it was impossible not to overhear what was said. He insisted that he couldn't afford to go, but she was adamant. I lingered over coffee, expecting her to jab him with a fork if she didn't get her way. It was crass."

"I'm sure it was," I said, straining to hear indications that Peter was moving about in the bedroom. I heard snoring.

"So the girls saw Samuel in Gurna on Saturday night," Miriam went on, as if interviewing me for an article in the society column. "Did they see anyone else they recognized?"

"Not really. I've enjoyed talking with you, Miriam, but I need to finish unpacking and send out our dirty laundry. Everything gets so dusty here."

"But we will see you and your husband tonight, won't we? Alexander will be there, and—well, I'm hoping you can encourage him to notice me. I'll be ever so grateful, Mrs. Malloy. Do promise that you'll come."

I would have promised her anything short of a dive off the balcony to see her leave. "Yes, we'll try our best."

After I'd seen her out into the hallway, I locked the door

and collapsed on the sofa. I was glaring at the door as Caron and Inez came in. They glanced at me, exchanged looks, and fled to their bedroom.

Peter and I arrived at Lord Bledrock's suite to find the party well under way and the cocktails flowing. Alexander had taken refuge behind the bar, which made me think of Miriam's sad tale of being a social misfit. He, in contrast, was chatting with Lady Emerson as he poured her a drink. We joined him before Lord Bledrock could get his clutches on me.

Lady Emerson gave us a bleary smile and wafted back into the crowd to pounce on the Fitzwillies. Alexander looked at Peter. "Any news about the girl?"

"No. I spoke to the embassy and the local police officials, who are in constant communication with the military. They've searched the villages at the oases, but . . ."

"It's a vast area with wadis and valleys," Alexander said as he handed me a scotch and water. "This will be the second night they have her."

They continued their muted conversation. I listened with minimal attention as I scanned the room. Mrs. McHaver had staked out her roost on the sofa, her lips drawn in disapproval as though she were presiding over a rowdy session of Parliament. Miriam hovered, as usual. Shannon King and Wallace Laxenby were in their spot near the door to the balcony. Lord Bledrock was seated in a chair near Miss Portia and Miss Cordelia, who were regaling him with one of their jokes. The redness of his complexion implied that the joke was less than decorous. I was surprised to see Jess Delmont, the surly grad student assigned to the dig, standing in a corner, wolfing down canapés. He dressed in a long-sleeved shirt and tie, but he still had an untamed look about him. He reminded me of the physics majors who roamed the campus and were in constant danger of stepping into traffic. Other members of Lord Bledrock's coterie were present, including the scandalous couple, Penelope and Paunchy. The din of voices and laughter was daunting.

I sucked in a breath as Lord Bledrock spotted me and leaped to his feet. I was trying to edge behind Peter when the door of the suite flew open. Nabil, the head workman at the excavation, stood in the doorway, flapping his hands and shouting in Arabic. Conversations halted as we all turned to stare at him.

At which moment, he fell facedown on the carpet.

CHAPTER 11

"Good heavens!" said Lord Bledrock, gazing at the body sprawled at his feet. "What will these local workmen think of next? What shall we do? It doesn't seem proper to simply step over him."

Peter brushed past me, squatted next to Nabil, and felt his neck. "He's alive, but his breathing is unsteady and his pulse is erratic. Alexander, help me move him to a bed."

"Now see here, Rosen," Lord Bledrock began to bluster. "I'm sure he's a nice enough chap, but I can't have him sprawled across my bed. What if he were to die there? I wouldn't feel at all comfortable with that."

"Let Abdullah deal with it," Mrs. McHaver pronounced. "They're probably cousins or in-laws. There's no call to inconvenience Neville."

Magritta came in from the balcony and nearly trampled Shannon King in her haste to reach Nabil's body. She pushed Peter aside and jabbed Nabil's back with the ferocity of a woodpecker. When he failed to respond, she bent over his face and peered at it. "He needs a doctor," she announced. "He may have been poisoned."

"Or he's drunk," Miss Portia said, giggling. "Miss Cordelia once passed out at a luncheon given by Lady Maronmont. There she was, her face in the chicken salad, snuffling like a hound. Lady Maronmont was speechless for days afterward."

"Poisoned?" said Alexander. "With what?"

Magritta stood up. "I should know? Do I look like a toxicologist?"

"He's your employee," Shannon said accusingly, "and therefore your responsibility."

"I'll call for a doctor." Alexander went into an adjoining room.

Peter was silent, his face furrowed with indecision. I knew he was resisting the urge to take charge of the scene and thus risk his cover as a businessman. His jaw was clamped so tightly he was endangering his adorable molars. I slipped my hand in his and whispered, "Shouldn't you call Mahmoud?"

"No," he said in an undertone, his lips unmoving. He backed me into a corner and added, "Say that you need to look in on Caron and Inez, then go to the suite. Mahmoud's number is on a pad by the telephone in our bedroom. If you can't get through to him, call Bakr."

"Was Nabil poisoned?" I asked.

"Do I look like a toxicologist?"

"I have no idea, but you're in danger of looking like a person who'll be sleeping on the sofa tonight."

"The lab will run tests," he said. "Nabil's color isn't good, and he has some sort of respiratory difficulty. A heart attack could account for that. Poisoning seems far-fetched. Will you please make the call?"

Despite Lord Bledrock's assertion that they couldn't step over the body on the floor, everyone seemed to be finding ways to get to the bar to replenish drinks. Magritta resumed jabbing Nabil's back, which would be covered with small bruises if he survived. I slipped out the door and hurried down the corridor. I had no more confidence in my ability to make a local call than I did in my ability to make an international one, but Caron or Inez could assist me. I faltered as I remembered they had gone to the lobby for the evening to play cards with some American teenagers they'd met in the computer room. This was not a call I wanted to make through the concierge.

I was debating options when Samuel came out of the el-

evator. We were equally surprised to be staring at each
other underneath an inept painting of a sunset behind the
pyramids in Giza.

"Are you okay, Mrs. Malloy?" he asked. "You look awfully pale."

"What are you doing here?"

"Lord Bledrock's party. He invited me. It's not my idea
of a good time, but I wanted to ask your husband if he'd
heard anything more about Buffy. I don't have any contacts
at the embassy, and I can't get past the receptionist. I can't
stand not doing anything to find her." He sat down on the
bench provided for those guests who needed a few minutes
to recover from the arduous fifteen-second elevator ride
before they continued to their rooms. "Has he?"

"Has he what?" I said distractedly.

"Heard anything more about Buffy? Do you need me to
help you to your suite, Mrs. Malloy?"

"No, he hasn't, and I don't need any help. When did you
get back from Abu Simbel?"

Samuel gave me a puzzled look. "Earlier today. The
captain arranged for me to be taken ashore before breakfast, and I went directly to the airport. I had this crazy idea
that Buffy would be in the hotel, gloating over all the fuss
about her abduction."

"You think she arranged it?" I asked.

He looked down at the carpet. "Why would she? The
idea's insane. It's more likely that the horsemen came to
their senses and dumped her somewhere. Instead of telling
anyone, she decided to take advantage of her temporary
celebrity status as a victim. When she broke off a fingernail
at the oasis at Farafra I thought she was going to demand a
lavish funeral for it, with professional mourners and a gold
coffin."

"Well, there's been no word about her, and she certainly hasn't checked into any hotels in Luxor." I turned
toward the suite, then stopped. "When did Lord Bledrock
invite you?"

"This afternoon, at the excavation. There's been quite a

buzz out there the last few days. Magritta's crew uncovered a stone step. When I got there, there must have been two dozen people standing around the rim of the pit, watching and offering advice. Wallace was photographing every pebble. Magritta got so fed up with Shannon that she began shrieking at her in German. I don't know what she said, but I'll bet it wasn't flattering."

"A stone step? When we were there last week, we saw steps leading down along the edge of the hut foundations. Lots of them."

Samuel gave me a condescending smile, thus earning my animosity in all future encounters. "This particular step dates back to the original construction, and suggests there may be a tomb. Considering its proximity to Tut's tomb, it may be of the same era. The excavation has been blocked from view from the path with canvas screens, and the Supreme Council of Antiquities was notified. Shannon King alerted the media, of course. If something of significance is found, she's a lock for the department chairmanship."

"How thrilling for her," I said. My first husband had thrown himself into the petty viciousness of departmental politics. Plotting in the faculty lounge was no more than an entertaining pastime. They were satisfied to cause dissension on a daily basis and gloat at wine and cheese affairs on the weekends.

Samuel stood up. "If you don't need help, I guess I'll go on to Lord Bledrock's party. Please don't repeat what I said about Buffy. I'm truly worried about her."

"Run along," I said. "I need to check on Caron and Inez."

"They're downstairs, playing poker with some kids. Your daughter looked annoyed, but her friend was raking in the pound notes." Samuel remained where he stood, clearly worried about me. "I saw them not more than five minutes ago, and they're fine. Ahmed is keeping an eye on the group. No alcoholic beverages or anything like that."

"Wonderful." I spun around and continued to the suite, hoping he wouldn't follow me. Once inside, I locked the door and went into the bedroom to find Mahmoud's telephone number. I punched the appropriate number for an outside line, then punched the remainder of the numbers and hoped for the best. Whoever answered at the police department did not speak English. I bleated Mahmoud's name several times and at last was connected to someone else. It was not Mahmoud, but I conveyed the message and replaced the receiver, feeling as though I'd done my duty.

Instead of racing back to Lord Bledrock's suite, I sat down on the bed and tried to sort things out. Nabil had been poised to make some sort of dramatic announcement but had fallen on his face instead. A step had been uncovered at the excavation site that aspired to be known as KV64. Buffy was in the clutches of twenty-first-century desert tribesmen. Samuel was back, but Sittermann was not. My apartment had been searched. Inez knew how to play poker. Everything deserved to be qualified with "maybe."

I was contemplating the wisdom of a couple of aspirin when Salima came into the parlor and said, "Hello? Anybody here? I do so need a martini."

"I locked the door," I said as I came out of the bedroom. "How is it that nobody even notices?"

Salima was wearing very tight jeans, a silk blouse, and high heels. Her hair was artfully tousled and her makeup deftly applied, as if she'd flown in from Paris or Rome. "Caron and Inez didn't lock their door. Did I mention I need a martini? I've been invited to Lord Bledrock's soiree, but I cannot face those people when I'm sober. Shall I make one for you?"

It was a moot issue, in that she was already taking out glasses and a bottle of gin from the shelf next to the mini-bar. "Yes, thank you," I said as I sat down. "How was Cairo?"

"Tedious. I hear there was some excitement on the cruise." She set down a martini in front of me and draped herself across a chair, her high heels dangling from her toes. "I have a vague memory of the American girl. Not the brightest jewel on the tiara, if I recall. Her boyfriend isn't unattractive, but he's shady. He has the look of someone who'd rob a tomb." She laughed, then gulped down her drink. "Based on no more than a few minutes of conversation, mind you. He was undoubtedly the president of some college honor society and an inspiration to family and friends. After all, his field of expertise is Graeco-Roman architecture. Mine is mummified pussycats."

"Why did you come here instead of the party at the other end of the corridor?"

"Because I want to hear the dirt. Was the girl grabbed by a sheik in a voluminous white robe, with a dagger clutched between his teeth, mounted on a stallion?"

"A couple of scruffy guys," I admitted. "You might pretend to be worried about her. The rest of us are."

Salima stopped smiling. "I am worried about her, Mrs. Malloy. This could cause an international situation. My father and I went to a reception at the American Embassy to meet a flock of scholars from a university. There was a palpable tension, simply because we're Arabs. I don't want to be harangued on the street when I'm in New York, or heckled while giving a lecture in D.C. I already get enough dirty looks in airports. What happened at Wadi es Sebua?"

I told her what I'd seen, which wasn't much, and after a second martini told her what Sittermann had said. "I have no theory how he could have found that out," I continued. "My husband's . . . connections didn't have that information."

"But now they do," she said succinctly, not bothering to make the obvious comment. "Did she have her passport in the cabin?"

"Samuel didn't know. He mentioned that she left the majority of her luggage here at the hotel, maybe in a storage room in the basement."

Salima sat up. "I've always dreamed of exploring a tomb at the bottom of a stairwell. Howard Carter stayed here. He might have left mummies propped against the wall and scarabs scattered on the floor. I think we should have a look."

It was a terrible idea, and I said as much as we took the elevator to the lobby. Ahmed was behind the desk, snap-

ping at his underlings. In some unseen corner, I heard Inez
chortle as she no doubt dragged in another pot. Bellmen in
white coats and red felt fezzes eyed us indifferently.

"Now what?" I said as Salima and I huddled behind a
pillar.

"You're the next best thing to a master criminal, Mrs.
Malloy. You tell me," Salima whispered.

"I saw a door marked "Staff Only" past the computer
room. It might lead to the lower levels." I stopped and
frowned at her. "I am unfamiliar with the strategies of a master criminal, Salima. The most heinous crime I've committed involved overdue library books." Technically speaking,
this wasn't true, but I saw no reason to accept responsibility
for her rash scheme.

We strolled across the lobby, ever so casually, and went
down a few steps to the computer room. No one was there
or at the counter where I supposed one arranged to run up
an enormous bill. The door beyond it was ajar. As I clutched
Salima's elbow, we found ourselves in a dim, grubby hallway. Cleaning carts were lined against the wall. Machines
clunked. Desperate moths fluttered around low-wattage
bare bulbs. My shoes squeaked as we walked on the sticky
floor past a freight elevator and a laundry room.

"Any more bright ideas?" I asked.

Salima opened a door, then quickly closed it. "Cleaning
supplies. Your turn."

I discovered a boiler not unlike the paleolithic one at my
bookstore a million miles away in Farberville. "Your turn."

We continued down the hallway in this fashion until I
found a room crowded with suitcases and trunks. An open
padlock hung from a bolt. I fumbled until I found the light
switch, then dragged Salima inside. "My goodness," I said,
awed. "Most of these are tagged from the UK. The Brits are
well equipped for the entire season."

"Lord Bledrock brought six cases of gin, and Mrs.
McHaver stockpiled enough scotch to keep the staff inebri-
ated for a year," Salima said from behind a stack of crates.
"Neither of them would notice if I were to . . ."

"Don't even think about it." I began to peer at suitcases haphazardly piled in a corner. Some were battered from travel and covered with decals, others merely bruised. "Over here. If we're going to do this, we're going to share the blame."

She joined me and we regarded three suitcases, all labeled with the name Franz. "Louis Vuitton," Salima said, "and locked."

"Your idea—and your call."

"I think we should go up to the bar in the lobby and think about it over a martini."

"If we have another martini, we won't be able to find this room again."

Salima sat down on a steamer trunk and rubbed her forehead. "Do you know how to pick locks?"

I sat down on a nearby trunk that appeared to have been in use since the Crimean War. "Only from what I've read in mystery novels, and they don't include instructions. I've never had any luck with hairpins. Not that I have a hairpin."

"Me, neither," she said.

It was unlikely that we could remain in the room for much longer without being discovered by an employee. It would be challenging to explain our presence to hotel security, as well as to Ahmed and whoever else appeared on the scene. Such as Peter, who was surely aware of my absence by now. It had been over half an hour since I'd left Lord Bledrock's party to make one simple phone call.

We both caught our breath as we heard a cart rumbling down the hall. Wordlessly we moved to a corner and crouched down behind a metal shelving unit for smaller suitcases and flimsy cardboard boxes held together with string and tape. The cart stopped by the door, and the padlock clicked. The sound was disheartening, at the very least. The cart continued on its way until we could not longer hear it.

"We seem to have a problem," I said as we came out of hiding.

"But we don't have to worry about dehydration. How unfortunate we don't have proper glasses."

"We need to work on an explanation for being here," I said. "Our only crime so far is being in an unauthorized location, possibly with the intent to steal valuables. Let's not compound the misdemeanor by drinking Mrs. McHaver's cache."

"It's excellent scotch. Lord Bledrock has a bottle behind his bar, and I tried a wee drop. She wouldn't begrudge us a few sips."

"Will you please cut that out and pay attention? We can't stay here all night. Peter's already wondering why I'm not back at the party. Once he finds out I'm not in our suite or in the lobby, he'll assume something dire happened to me. Mahmoud, the chief inspector, is on his way to the hotel."

"Is he psychic?"

I told her about Nabil. "His arrival might have something to do with the excitement at the excavation. Have you heard about the portentous step?"

"There was a small twitter at the university yesterday," she said. "Archeologists are always finding something or other that's going to shatter all the prevailing theories. A step, a lintel, a shard with a partial hieroglyph, a bead—none of monumental significance. They act just as hysterically when they come across a scrap of bone from a goat that died five years ago."

"Didn't something like this happen last spring?"

"You're referring to Oskar Vonderlochen?" Salima began to prowl among the pillars of crates and luggage. "Yes, they found a scarab, and it was authenticated as being of the era of Tutankhamun. That doesn't mean his concubines are stashed inside a tomb, their coffins neatly arranged on tiers. Oskar was desperate, because he was afraid he'd lose the concession. He overreacted, but he had Shannon King breathing down his neck to produce something before the end of the season. Lord Bledrock was beginning to voice misgivings about future financial support. It was silly of Oskar to go out there alone, especially when he was drunk."

"Why didn't Magritta go with him?"

"She claimed she was asleep. Gossip has it that she wasn't in her own bed." Salima staggered into view, carrying a metal box. "Tools," she said, panting. "We might as well look inside Buffy's luggage while we're here." She took out a hammer.

"Wait! Monsieur Vuitton will never forgive us if we smash the locks. Find a little screwdriver."

She found several, and in ten minutes we mastered the art of springing the locks with minimal damage. I opened the smallest bag and pawed through the contents. "Hair products, moisturizers, and that sort of thing," I said. "Postcards from New York and San Francisco, unsigned, with banal messages. A letter from someone named Bunnikins, describing what they did"—I stopped reading and folded up the letter—"in a hotel room in Paris. It's . . . ah, explicit."

Salima opened another bag. "This is peculiar. The clothes are cheap and ratty. I can't picture Buffy wearing them." She held up a polyester blouse. "It's missing a button, and the seam in the armpit is torn." She dropped it and continued digging. "These pants would never fit her—much too large. This dress is stained, and has a faint smell of fish."

I moved on to the third bag. The clothes were as unfashionable, as well as wrinkled and in varying stages of disrepair. "Why on earth would she bring these things? I've never seen her wear anything without a label that howled of money. Why would she even own them?"

Salima examined the clothes more carefully. "A lot of them seem to have been bought in Italy, possibly at a flea market. Very lower class, mostly used."

"She didn't bring them from home," I said slowly. "She bought them after she arrived in Rome. Maybe she fell madly in love with an Italian bricklayer, and was going to run away with him and lead the life of a plump housewife in some obscure village."

"Buffy?"

"Just a thought." I closed the suitcase and put it with the others. "In any case, she must have taken her passport on

the cruise. Sittermann probably found it in her cabin and
sent the information to his mysterious associates. They used
the Internet to attempt to verify the personal data. Why Sittermann bothered is the question. He met Samuel and Buffy
a week ago at an oasis. He's not a dear old family friend
or an inconsolable lover. The Egyptian authorities and the
American Embassy would have gotten the passport information from customs in Cairo in the event Buffy wasn't
found safe and well within a few days."

Salima rose and brushed the dust off her derrière.
"You'll have to ask him, if we ever get out of here. The situation doesn't look promising. It's one thing to open a suitcase lock when it's here in front of us. The padlock is on
the other side of the door. Tomorrow morning some unsus-
pecting bellman will come in to leave or fetch luggage, and
find us passed out on the floor amidst empty bottles of
McHaver's finest scotch whiskey. What's more, I was planning to dine on canapés in Lord Bledrock's suite. I wonder
if any of these aristocrats sent boxes with tins of caviar and
smoked oysters."

"Call room service," I said dispiritedly. "Order me a
sandwich and a bottle of water while you're at it."

She blinked at me, then took a cell phone out of her
pocket. "I forgot I had this. Do you have a menu?"

"You might have remembered this earlier."

"Don't be petty. I am a law-abiding citizen, and I was
overwhelmed by the audacity of our crime."

"And I'm Nefertari, for 'whose sake the sun doth rise,'
according to the travel guide."

"Any clever ideas whom I should call? My father will
be displeased. I can't trust my relatives to stay quiet about
this, and my friends are either in Cairo or off at digs. I can
call information and get the number of the hotel. Surely the
manager won't file charges, since he'd have to admit to
sloppy security in the most venerated hotel on the Nile."

I grabbed the phone away from her. "You are not going
to call Ahmed. He'll be in Lord Bledrock's suite, ratting us

out, before you can hang up. He seems to think Peter is the U.S. Secretary of State in disguise."

"Is he?" asked Salima.

I went to the door and rattled it on the off chance the padlock was not fully engaged. "Of course not," I said firmly. "He's in real estate and development."

"Like Sittermann."

"Yes." I mentally cursed the hapless employee who'd clicked the padlock, as well as his or her family, camels, goats, and satellite dish. The lightbulb flickered above my head. I spun around. "Did you see any packs of lightbulbs on a shelf? This one has a limited life expectancy."

"Should I call housekeeping?"

Sighing, I sat back down. The only thing worse than having Peter catch me in the act was the specter of sitting in the dark all night. Although the room had no windows, it had vents, cracks, and numerous other potential entrances for bewhiskered visitors. "All right," I said, "call the hotel desk and explain the problem. We'll have a few minutes to concoct some transparently false reason for being here. At least I'll have a honeymoon to remember after the divorce."

"I could ask for Bledrock's suite and hope Alexander answers," she said. "He already thinks I'm an insipid brat, so I don't have anything to lose. He can tell Abdullah that his father wants another bottle of gin and wheedle the key out of him. You can hide, and after Alexander lets me out, I'll make sure the padlock is left open. You can sneak out once we're gone."

"You'll have to tell Alexander something."

She blushed. "I'll distract him with expressions of my undying gratitude. It worked wonderfully with my tutor, who was a doddery old man with hair poking out of his ears and a distasteful habit of whistling through his teeth. He spoke Hungarian with a lisp. I don't know how I survived."

I considered her scheme. "What will you do if a police officer answers the phone?"

"Hang up and think of something else."

To our mutual dismay, the lightbulb made a small popping sound and went dark. The only thing visible was a narrow strip of light under the door. It was much like being in a cave, or quite possibly in the most distant chamber of a burial tomb. The air had a stale, oppressive odor that I hadn't noticed earlier. I felt sure the walls were closing in, although I couldn't actually see them. Something rustled behind me.

Salima's disembodied voice said, "This may slow me down."

"Well, don't be all night about it."

"Afraid we're in the sequel to the sequel of that inane movie about the mummy? No one in Hollywood looked at a photograph of a mummy. They weren't wrapped for optimum mobility, you know. By the time they're discovered, they're really just a desiccated, pathetic bundle of brown bones."

"I don't want to be dragged out of here by hotel security," I said, not elaborating on my anxiety regarding mice, rats, bats—and snakes, for all I knew. "Go ahead and try to get Alexander."

She got busy on her cell phone, chattering in Arabic. I would have taken the opportunity to have a more careful look at the contents of Buffy's suitcases, had I been able to see beyond the tip of my nose. As it was, I had to settle for imagining Peter's expression as he realized I'd been gone far too long. He'd had time to go to the suite, where he would find nothing more telltale than two glasses on the coffee table.

"It's ringing," Salima said. "Any suggestions about what I should say to Alexander?"

"Make him promise not to say anything, then tell him where we are and what he needs to do. Don't try to explain. I can't think of a plausible lie, but maybe we can come up with something before he gets here."

Someone else answered the phone. Salima giggled nervously, then asked to speak to Alexander, as if she were an adolescent girl who had chanced upon the telephone number of her idol. It seemed to work. A minute later, she resumed her normal voice, cautioned him not to speak,

described our location, and told him to come as quickly as
he could. The light on her cell phone blinked out as she
turned it off.

"Now all we can do is wait," she said. "It's a good thing
you're here. He wouldn't come dashing to my rescue. He
was such a horrid boy, all smirky and superior because he
went to some antiquated prep school. I wasn't fond of his
parents, either. Lord Bledrock used to give me pennies, and
his stepmother always patted me on the head as if I were a
lapdog. I dreaded their visits, but my father felt obliged to
entertain them."

"Alexander has mellowed, and you've grown up."

"Maybe," she said sulkily.

I heard a noise outside the door. "That was quick," I said
in a low voice. "Too quick, actually. Even if Alexander left
the suite immediately, he'd just now be reaching the lobby.
I'd suggest we hide if we weren't in danger of breaking an
arm or leg in the process."

The padlock fell open with a clunk and the door opened.
The light from the corridor blinded me as my eyes struggled to adjust. A figure stood silhouetted in the doorway.

"Alexander?" I said without much hope.

"Hardly, ma'am. Sittermann at your service. Why don't
you two fine ladies come out of that nasty room before a
cockroach runs up your pant leg? I saw some by the pier
that were bigger than newborn pups." He looked over his
shoulder. "The coast is clear, if that's worrying you. I don't
recommend you push your luck, though. The employees
bring the dirty towels to the laundry room after they finish
turning down beds for the evening."

I muttered an unseemly expletive as Salima and I went
out to the hallway. Sittermann was beaming at us; I did
not reciprocate. "How did you know we were here?" I demanded. "How did you undo the padlock?"

"You want to stand here all night?" He clasped my elbow
with one hand and Salima's with his other. "I reckon we can
discuss your questions elsewhere. Right offhand, I'd suggest the bar in the lobby. That way you can call your hus-

band and tell him where you are. Salima, you might want to keep an eye out for young Bledrock. He's likely to come storming the castle any second now. He's a mite upset."

I submitted to being hustled out of the hallway and into the lobby, all the while thinking furiously. By the time we reached a table in the bar, I had more questions. I suspected I would not receive answers. Salima gasped as she spotted Alexander heading for the front desk and hurried over to catch him.

"Well, Sittermann?" I said.

"Scotch and water, right? I'm surprised you and the little Egyptian gal didn't swipe a bottle of McHaver's finest. I'm a bourbon drinker myself. Ain't classy, I know, but that doesn't worry me." He barked the order to the bartender, then sat back and grinned at me. "Found yourself in a real pickle, didn't you? There was one time back when I was in college, some of my fraternity brothers and I decided we was going to sneak into the Alpha Theta Eta house, so we shinnied up—"

"Don't even bother," I said. "I wouldn't believe you if you told me what time it is. How did you know where we were?"

His grin widened. "What a thing to say, Mrs. Malloy. I have been nothing but honest with you since the day we met. Don't you think you ought to call your husband? You can tell him you came down here to make sure your girls weren't up to anything naughty. There's a house phone on the concierge's desk."

I stalked across the lobby, ignoring the startled look from Caron as I went past the card game, and picked up the receiver. Lord Bledrock answered with a bleat. I made polite noises while he described the chaos in the suite—his suite, mind you—and finally persuaded him to allow me to speak to Peter.

"Hello, dear. Is Mahmoud there yet?" I asked.

"Where are you?"

"In the lobby, calling from the concierge's phone. What about Nabil?"

"The doctor thinks he had a heart attack. As soon as an ambulance arrives, he'll supervise Nabil's evacuation via the service elevator. Ahmed is terrified that the hotel guests will be scandalized if they discover a local workman had the audacity to behave so crudely within the sacred confines." Peter paused. "Why are you in the lobby? Is there a crisis involving Caron and Inez? Are they in trouble?"

"No, they're fine." I stared at a potted palm while I tried to come up with something that was not precisely a lie. One should never lie to one's beloved spouse, at least not for the first few months. "Salima showed up after I called the police department. We came down here, and subsequently bumped into Sittermann. It was quite unexpected, considering the circumstances." I realized I was babbling myself into deeper trouble. "Because I didn't know he was back in Luxor, I mean. He didn't take a launch to Abu Simbel this morning, and I assumed he was still on the ship. Same thing with Samuel. Is he there now? Did he mention we met by the elevator?"

"Samuel's here," Peter said slowly. "Alexander's not, however. He received a call a few minutes ago, then left without a word. Do you know anything about that, Claire?"

"He's here, talking to Salima. They make a handsome couple. It's unfortunate that they can't seem to have a civilized conversation. Now that you know I'm fine, you can get back to pretending you're not a cop. It must be a terrible strain." I hung up before he noticed the gaps in my story, some of them large enough to drive a camel through.

Salima and Alexander joined me. Salima's lips were clamped together, and her eyes were simmering. Alexander looked no less furious. If they inadvertently bumped shoulders, the lobby might be consumed by a fireball.

"What is this about, Mrs. Malloy?" he said icily. "All I'm hearing from Miss el-Musafira is rubbish, interspersed with gibberish. Not that I'm surprised. She's as arrogant and insufferable now as she was as a child. Please be kind enough to explain this nonsense about a room in the basement."

"It's complicated," I conceded, "but I'll try. Right now, I'd like to ask Sittermann some questions."

Alexander surveyed the lobby. "And just how are you going to do that, if I may be so bold?"

Sittermann was gone.

CHAPTER 12

Salima and Alexander ignored me when I suggested that we go back upstairs, and were glowering at each other as I left. The door to Lord Bledrock's suite was open. Nabil was no longer supine on the floor. Peter was behind the bar, morosely watching the others, who were huddled around the low table in front of the sofa. Mrs. McHaver had taken a seat between Miss Portia and Miss Cordelia, and the three were staring raptly at something on the table. Lady Emerson, the Fitzwillies, Wallace, and Jess nudged one another for the best position. Lord Bledrock was on tiptoe, peering over Miriam's shoulder. Paunchy, living up to his name, presented a bulky barrier. I couldn't see anything because of the wall of bodies, but I presumed they had not laid out Nabil in order to perform an autopsy.

"What happened?" I asked Peter.

"Mahmoud went on to the hospital. Nabil was still alive when they left, although the doctor is worried." He paused as a shriek came from the group across the room, then he continued, "I've seen symptoms like his after an overdose of a methamphetamine—dilated pupils, intense sweating, erratic heartbeat. Illegal drugs are available, but Mahmoud said that this kind isn't common among the older Egyptians. They prefer to smoke hashish or opium."

"And Nabil was coming here," I said. "Hardly the time to get high."

The shrieks were getting louder. Magritta yanked Jess

away from the group and dragged him out to the balcony for an inaudible but emphatic conversation. Shannon was cackling with glee. Wallace stood up and moved away, looking worried. Mrs. McHaver thumped her cane, in her case possibly an extravagant display of pleasure. Lady Emerson whacked Lord Bledrock on the back, as if they were comrades in a trench on the front line.

"What's all that about?" I asked Peter.

"Some artifact Nabil had in his pocket, wrapped in a rag. I didn't get a good look at it. Miriam spotted it when she knelt next to him to wipe his face with a washcloth. As soon as she picked it up, the rest of them swooped in like vultures and snatched it from her. Mahmoud and the doctor arrived seconds later, followed by medics with a gurney. I was going to mention it to Mahmoud, but then Ahmed arrived and began squawking about the hotel's reputation. Lord Bledrock took offense at the implication that it was his fault, and pretty soon they were all offering opinions and outlandish theories. Mahmoud was not inclined to linger once Nabil was ready to be transported to the hospital."

Although my beloved had the courage of a rogue elephant, he seemed content to observe the Egyptologists from a safe distance. Having forsaken my last shred of dignity in a dark room in the basement, I went over to Miriam. "Why is everybody so excited?"

"I was wondering where you were, Mrs. Malloy. I do hope you're not ill." She plucked a tendril of a dusty cobweb off my shoulder. "Wherever have you been?"

I stepped out of plucking range. "You found something in Nabil's pocket?"

"It may prove to be of the greatest importance," she said. "It will have to be verified, of course, but if it's authentic . . ." Overwhelmed by well-disguised emotion, she took a sip of sherry. "It's known as a *shabti* or *shawabti,* a small servant statue buried with a deceased person of importance. It's in the shape of a *mummiform* coffin, with the arms folded over the chest, and made of a paste called faience that's glazed and fired. This one is missing the head, but the cartouches on the front appear to bear the nomen and prenomen of Ramses VIII. His tomb has never been discovered."

"You know a lot about Egyptology," I said.

"My aunt made sure of that. There were days in my childhood when I was not allowed out of my room until I deciphered pages and pages of hieroglyphs. I kept a packet of biscuits in my wardrobe to tide me over." Her short laugh held such bitterness that I flinched. "None of us has a perfect childhood, but enough of that. We Scots are a sturdy, uncomplaining lot. Would you like to see the *shabti*?"

"Yes," I said, unnerved by her rapid transitions.

I followed her to the group still huddled around the coffee table. The object of their attention, placed reverently on a pristine handkerchief, was about four inches long. A few patches of color beneath the grime indicated it had been blue. It was chipped and worn, and headless. Lady Emerson accepted a magnifying glass from Lord Bledrock and leaned forward, her mouth tight with concentration.

"Yes, Neville," she murmured. "Definitely Akhenamon's name in the cartouche. This must be from the tomb of Ramses VIII. His prenomen is unique."

Shannon grabbed the magnifying glass. "My lovely *shabti*," she cooed. "This little man, this treasure, will bring us all the financial backing we'll ever need to continue the excavation. My articles will be the lead story in all the prestigious journals, and I'll be in demand to do presentations at conferences worldwide."

"Your lovely *shabti*?" Magritta said from behind Lord Bledrock's chair. "The Egyptian authorities may disagree. It won't end up in your college's collection."

Shannon sneered at her. "I wasn't planning to steal it, Magritta. I, for one, have a reputation to uphold."

"And I don't?"

"Well," murmured Shannon, feigning tactfulness, "you know how important it is to maintain a daily log and document the progress. Your reports are, shall we say, sporadic and uninformative. MacLeod College has a lot at stake here. I believe it's time for me to take charge of the concession. You'll still handle the daily, manual aspects of the excavation, naturally. Wallace can continue to take photographs in the old-fashioned manner, but newspapers and journals require digital photographs these days. Jess will handle that."

"As you wish," Wallace said, his face sagging. "I'm too old to learn how to use these newfangled gizmos. Can't figure out all those buttons. You and I are dinosaurs, Magritta, a species on the edge of extinction. Just as well Oskar's not here to share our fate."

Magritta stomped to the bar. After a moment, Wallace went out to the balcony, where I dearly hoped he was not considering an unobtrusive descent. Those remaining around the coffee table resumed fighting for the magnifying glass. Mrs. McHaver ordered Miriam to fetch a book from their room. Lord Bledrock started to pick up the *shabti*, but Lady Emerson rapped his knuckles. There was definitely a squabble brewing, and it had potential to escalate into a brawl.

I returned to the bar and poured myself a glass of water. "Where's Samuel?" I asked Peter. "I saw him coming here earlier."

"He stayed for a few minutes, then left. He had the right idea. I think I'd better go to the hospital. The doctor seemed to think Nabil will survive, although he may not regain consciousness immediately. The blood work will show if he has amphetamines in his system. As you said, it's peculiar that he would take something on his way here."

"Nabil would never take drugs," Magritta inserted coldly. "Oskar hired him when we first came out here, and promoted him to head of the crew twenty years ago. We had meals at his home and attended his daughters' weddings. Over the years, Nabil has dismissed workers for even the smallest infractions. Excavations are dangerous sites. Sloppiness can result in bad falls or dislodge stones on those in the bottom of the pit. There is no workmen's compensation in this country. If these men are unable to work, they cannot support their families."

I felt as though I'd been accused of failing to provide health care and fair labor practices. "Yes, I can understand the importance of keeping a clear head on the job. May I ask you about this step that was uncovered in the last few days? I was told it might suggest a link to King Tut's tomb."

"Ah, that," she said, refilling her glass with gin and taking a gulp. "There are some similarities, but it's far from conclusive. I have seen steps like this before, and they have led to nothing more than a room filled with debris. It is typical even at construction sites in this day for the builders to dispose of the waste near the primary site. The *shabti* is a different matter. It would never have been discarded."

"And it's from a royal tomb," said Peter, who clearly had been doing more than observing the scene. I felt a wave of wifely pride at his ability to eavesdrop and quite possibly read lips in such an unobtrusive manner. If that sort of thing was taught at spy camp, I was sure he must have earned the highest grade in the class.

"They were put in the tombs," Magritta said, as though speaking to a class of first-grade children, "often dozens of them, to aid the pharaoh in the next life."

My pride was replaced with annoyance at her tone. I held back a sudden urge to shake her and point out that although she and the others might be well versed in ancient Egyptian funerary rituals, none of them could decipher an ISBN number or track down an out-of-print book for a valued customer. Peter could interpret blood splatters with his eyes closed. They would be lost if confronted with a corpse that had not been dead for less than three thousand years.

Peter grimaced at me as he left. I stuck a piece of pita in my mouth and chewed it intently. Magritta took the opportunity to slosh more gin in her glass. "What puzzles me," she went on, as though she still had an enthralled audience, "is . . . well, it's hard to say. Even with the rubble, the workmen have keen eyesight. This afternoon was chaotic, though.

The people in this room, colleagues from nearby sites, and
an underling from the Supreme Council of Antiquities—in
and out of the pit to observe the step. We must have served
tea to three dozen people. That horrid Sittermann stomped
around, making ignorant remarks. Miss Cordelia had too
much sun and had to be carried back to the guardhouse
amidst great flutter. Lady Emerson claimed the step was
meaningless, that she'd seen countless of them over the
years. The workmen had to squirm past an endless stream of
gawkers to get up to the top with their carriers."

"You're wondering why nobody saw the *shabti*?"

"We're lucky nobody stepped on it. The obvious explanation is that Nabil found it after we quit work this afternoon. He often lingers in order to tidy up the day's progress
and make sure that the equipment is stored safely. Some of
the workmen are too eager to leave and forget to put away
their tools. The canvas barriers are meant only to keep back
tourists during the day. Some of them have been known to
come right up to the edge of the pit to take photographs, endangering themselves as well as those of us below."

"If Nabil did a last-minute inspection, he must have uncovered the *shabti* and raced here to show it to you. He was
so excited that his blood pressure shot up. By the time he
reached this suite, he was probably already having a heart
attack."

She was still frowning. "Yes, that makes sense. It would
take him some time to walk to the main road and catch a
bus to the pier. The ferries are crowded late in the afternoon, and Nabil is too courteous to push others aside. He
also might have had trouble when he finally arrived at the
hotel. He would not have been allowed to go through the
lobby and take the elevator. He must have been beside himself by the time he found the service entrance and made it
up here to the third floor. All that while he had the *shabti* in
his pocket, glowing like an ember." She brushed away a
tear. "Such a devoted friend, so fierce and loyal."

"How did he know you were here?" I asked.

"This afternoon Lord Bledrock invited all of us, and I

didn't feel as though I could decline. He and Mrs. McHaver have provided most of the financing for the last several years. One doesn't bite the proverbial hand."

"Mrs. McHaver? I thought she was . . . less than wealthy."

Magritta glanced over my shoulder. "She pretends to have a limited income, but a lot of antiquities leave the country in crates that arrived full of bottles of scotch. Expensive baubles, some with proper papers and others without."

"From the black market?" I said, flabbergasted. "That prim Scottish lady? I can picture her striding across the moors or having a row with the vicar about the sinful ways of the village youth, but . . ." I forced myself not to turn around and stare at Mrs. McHaver as if she'd been exposed as a serial killer. "She's an avid collector, like Lord Bledrock?"

"No," Magritta said. "She's a dealer with an international reputation—in certain circles, that is. Nabil has told me that she is very generous with workmen at many excavations, giving them regular payments to keep her informed. Sometimes smaller artifacts have vanished from these very sites before they were cataloged. I do my best to stay next to her when she comes to my site, and Nabil has instructions to keep my crew away from her."

"Does Shannon know this?"

"I suspect she's heard rumors, but Mrs. McHaver donates a goodly amount of money every year. Without private funding, most colleges would have to give up their concessions. The Egyptian government doesn't have the financial resources to protect all the present and future sites, much less the current inventory. Most of what is sent to the Cairo Museum ends up in warehouses, which are systematically looted by thieves. Who knows what would have happened to the Rosetta Stone had it not been sent to the British Museum? The Egyptians are still irate over the matter. I am not entirely unsympathetic to either side's position."

I was hoping I was not doomed to argue the merits of

colonialism when an obstreperous argument broke out around the table. It seemed to concern whether the *shabti* should technically be called a *ushabati* or a *shawabti*. I nodded at Magritta and slipped out the door.

When I arrived at the Presidential Suite, I made sure the door from the girls' bedroom to the hallway was locked. I glumly noted the clothes strewn on the floor and the half-emptied suitcases. Dresser drawers were open, their contents jumbled. Plastic shopping bags were piled on the dresser and on chairs, along with books, magazines, water bottles, and empty candy boxes. Inez's stack of books was daunting, but I found *The Savage Sheik* next to the bed and took it with me. It had not been in good condition when Inez had chanced across it in a used-book store, and the yellowed pages were likely to come loose from the binding before we'd all finished reading it. I smiled as I imagined countless repressed English ladies gasping as they savored every word of it, then hiding it in a cupboard whenever proper company arrived.

I was curled on the sofa, engrossed in the sheik's sardonic smirk as he recaptured his victim at an oasis for the third or fourth time, when Caron and Inez returned. Inez took immediate refuge in their bedroom.

"I have never been so humiliated in my life!" Caron said, staring at me. "When's the next flight home? I don't care if I have to wait all night at the airport. Tell Bakr I'll be packed and ready to leave in an hour."

"Because I was in the lobby earlier?" I said. "I didn't go there to check on you, dear. It's complicated, but—"

"You could have danced through the lobby with a flower in your navel, for all I care. That Is Not what I'm talking about."

"Would you care to tell me what you *are* talking about?"

"Just forget it—okay?" She flounced into the bedroom. Seconds later, the bathroom door slammed. Seventeen, going on seven.

Peter showed up just as I was ready to give up on him

and call room service. Neither Caron nor Inez voiced interest in dinner, so Peter and I went across the corniche to the row of cafés alongside the Nile.

Once we'd ordered, I asked him about Nabil.

"Still alive, but in intensive care," he said, "and his heart attack was brought on by an overdose of a methamphetamine. Mahmoud sent some of his officers to locate the other workmen on the crew and find out if that sort of thing has been going on behind Magritta's back. It's a hard job, loading the carriers and hauling up the rocks to be screened. Six days a week, for a meager salary. Most of them sleep in a makeshift camp outside Gurna and only go home to their villages when they have a couple of days off."

"Maybe the younger men use drugs, but it's hard to imagine someone like Nabil risking it, or even condoning it."

Peter waited as our food was served. "Have I eaten today? I don't remember."

"Not since breakfast on the boat," I said, watching him attack the chicken and couscous. I ate a few bites, then gazed at the feluccas as they glided by, their sails catching the last rays as the sun disappeared behind the mountains. The metal ships at the pier had not yet begun to glitter with party lights. The café patrons were muted, too weary from an arduous day of sightseeing to bestir themselves to make idle chatter. Since we were below street level, the noise from the traffic was less bothersome.

When Peter finished and sat back, I said, "Any news about Buffy?"

"Sittermann was right about the information on her passport. She had to show a birth certificate to get the passport, and she has a Social Security number, but her home address is bogus. By tomorrow, we'll know if she's ever been enrolled in any of the colleges or universities in California. None of the study-abroad programs in Rome have heard of her."

"There might be some clues in her suitcases in the hotel basement," I volunteered virtuously. "Like, say, postcards that had to have been sent to an address somewhere, and possibly a letter that refers to a hotel in Paris."

His expression iced over. "And you know this because . . . ?"

A reasonable question. "Shall we have coffee?" I said.

"You went through her suitcases in the basement of the hotel?"

"The ice cream is supposed to be quite good. Why don't you catch the waiter's eye? I'd like to see a dessert menu."

"When did you do this?" He looked away for a moment. "After you went to call Mahmoud. Now why would you think her suitcases were there?" He held up his hand before I could reply. To my relief, the waiter noticed and appeared at the table. He gathered up our dishes, then put menus on the table and waited.

"Pistachio mint," I said after a moment, "and coffee."

"Nothing," growled the love of my life. He looked so perturbed that I was afraid one of us might end up treading water shortly. "Did Samuel tell you this?"

"It was a logical deduction. When Salima showed up and asked about Buffy, I told her. She suggested that we go have a look, but I could have refused. I was only trying to be helpful, Peter. You had to stay in Lord Bledrock's suite to make sure they didn't heave the body off the balcony because it was inconveniently located. If we hadn't gotten locked in, I would have gone back up to the front desk and called you." And I would have, sooner or later, I thought, avoiding his cold stare.

"Locked in." It wasn't even a question.

"Not with evil intent. An employee walked by, saw the padlock, and snapped it closed."

"That must have been a challenge for the renowned Miss Marple of Farberville. Am I to expect a charge for damages to the door when we check out?"

I laughed gaily. "Heavens no. I may be more curious than the average citizen, but I am opposed to vandalism. There's no excuse for it, under any circumstances. Those who destroy private property deserved to be prosecuted and forced to make full reparations. Do you remember when some criminal sprayed an obscenity on the side of the Book Depot? I demanded a full investigation, but the officer—"

"How did you get out?"

His single-mindedness was beginning to exasperate me. However, after noting that his hands were throttling the arm-rests of the chair, I said, "Sittermann. He must have been following us. We all agreed it was prudent to go up to the lobby before more employees arrived, but while I was calling you, he vanished. I had no idea he was back in Luxor. There's something very screwy about him, Peter. He could be watching us through binoculars from his hotel room right this minute. I think you should have Mahmoud take him into custody and interrogate him."

"He's not staying at the Winter Palace," Peter said wryly, "nor was he before the cruise. Mahmoud has already queried all the hotels in and around Luxor. He must be holed up in a private residence."

"Or under a rock. There are a lot of rocks around here, in case you haven't noticed." I spooned up a bite of ice cream. "He behaved as if he were staying at the hotel. When he took it upon himself to throw the party in our suite, he arranged for the food and alcohol . . ." I watched the ice cream dribble back into the dish. "And it'll be on our bill. He didn't sign the tab in the bar earlier, either. What an arrogant toad he is."

"With access to the room where Buffy's suitcases are stored."

"He either has a key or knows how to pick locks," I said. "Not only an arrogant toad, but a sneaky one as well."

Peter pushed back his chair and put a thick stack of pound notes on the table. "You can order coffee when we get back to the suite. I need to have Mahmoud send someone to stand outside that door in the basement the rest of the night. You might have mentioned this earlier, Claire."

I followed him to the street. Rather than gallantly offer his arm to assist me, he left me on the curb and dodged cabs across the corniche. It was, I thought with a sigh, better than being left at the altar.

He was long gone before I emerged from the shower the next morning. He was still sulking, although I had told him in more detail what Salima and I had found in Buffy's suitcases. He did not appear to care that they were Louis Vuitton. Since he had worn designer diapers at birth, brand names did not impress him.

I left a note for Caron and Inez, who were asleep, and went to the terrace for breakfast. I was watching a small bird table-hopping like a starlet when I felt a poke in the back. Unamused, I glanced up.

"May Miriam and I join you?" asked Mrs. McHaver. "There are no vacant tables at the moment, and I'm having a bit of trouble with my knees. Arthritis is not unexpected at my age, I must admit, but I resent it all the same." She waited until Miriam pulled out a chair, then sat down. "I'm considering having one of those chairlift machines installed at my home. My ancestors will be howling from their graves, but I think it might be rather fun. Have you any experience with them, Mrs. Malloy?"

I shook my head, too startled to attempt to reply. Miriam sat down next to me and busied herself straightening the sugar packets.

"I used to ride a bicycle when I was a girl," Mrs. McHaver continued. "I would sail down the hills with gay abandon, letting my braids fly behind me. There was one time I shall never forget. I came around a corner and into a flock of sheep. They scattered, but not quickly enough, and I landed in a ditch. I must have looked a mess when I finally wheeled my broken bicycle home that day."

"Would madam care for coffee or tea?" asked a waiter.

She raised her eyebrows. "I cannot believe the staff has not yet learned my preference. Tea, you dolt, with milk, and be quick about it!"

"Shall I fetch your breakfast from the buffet?" Miriam asked.

"Yes," she said, flapping her hand. "Go, go."

"A nice morning," I managed to say as Miriam scurried inside.

"A bit chilly now, but it will warm up later by the time we arrive at the Valley of the Kings. You are coming, are you not? I understand you have a van and driver at your disposal. I intended to ride with Neville, but when I called his room to inquire about a time, Alexander said he'd left more than an hour ago. The discovery of the *shabti* has reduced him to schoolboy glee. If this excavation proves to be the tomb of Ramses VIII, the name Bledrock will rival that of Carnarvon in the annals of Egyptological discoveries. You are familiar with Lord Carnarvon, I presume."

"He financed Howard Carter's explorations," I said. I wanted to scurry away in the way Miriam had, although I might have scurried much farther and failed to return. "I saw the photographs in the bar."

"Some say there was a curse on anyone who disturbed King Tutankhamun's place of burial. Soon after the tomb was discovered, Carter's canary was killed by a cobra. Lord Carnarvon died the following year from an infected mosquito bite. At the moment of his death, his dog howled and then fell over dead. The lights in Cairo went out. More than two dozen archeologists who went into the tomb died during the nineteen-twenties. We can only hope there is not such a curse surrounding the tomb of Ramses VIII."

"You believe all that?"

She pursed her lips and stared at the flowers in the garden. "Do I believe that the Green Lady roams Skipness Castle, or that a ghostly piper appears before weddings at Culzean Castle? That Mary Queen of Scots haunts Borthwick Castle? Or that the Loch Ness monster is an aberration from the prehistoric era? Everything we think we know about ancient Egypt is based on speculation and interpretation. No one can disprove a negative, Mrs. Malloy. You cannot prove for certain that Robert Burns did not show up at my house one winter evening when I was alone. You may deem it highly improbable, but you cannot offer concrete proof that it never happened."

I was more in the mood for muesli than metaphysics for breakfast. I excused myself and went inside to the buffet. When I returned, Mrs. McHaver and Miriam were digging into plates of turkey sausages, omelets, and rolls.

After Mrs. McHaver savored the final bite and allowed Miriam to refill her teacup, she said, "It would be most kind of you to include us in your party when you go the Valley of the Kings this morning. We shall meet you in the lobby over here in precisely half an hour. Come along, Miriam; I need you to hand-wash some of my undergarments. The cost of the hotel laundry service is absurdly high, and the women have been known to pilfer whatever catches their fancy." She snapped her fingers at a waiter, who immediately pulled back her chair. Without a word, she swept by me and went inside.

Caron and Inez were still in bed when I reached the suite. I roused them long enough to ask if they wanted to go on the outing, then sighed as they both buried their heads under their pillows. Since I had no idea when Peter might bother to show up, I decided I might as well allow Bakr to drive me and my inimical breakfast companions to the excavation. I would stay for no more than an hour and be back in time for lunch should Peter make himself available. Odds were not good, but it was our honeymoon, after all.

I succeeded on my third attempt to call Bakr and asked him to pick me up. I hurriedly brushed my teeth, changed into sensible shoes, grabbed a bottle of water, and sprinted down the stairwell with at least forty seconds to spare. Even in the New Winter Palace's less regal lobby, Mrs. McHaver looked as though she was seated on a throne—or at the head of a tribunal. Miriam was juggling hats, water bottles, a fan, a bulging woven bag, two cameras, and a thermos. Mrs. McHaver was tapping her foot and staring pointedly at a clock above the entrance.

Alexander called my name. I skidded to a halt and waited.

"Are you heading for the Valley?" he asked as he came out of the short hallway that led to the terrace. "My father was in a dither earlier and left while I was shaving. I resigned myself to taking a ferry, but if you've booked your vehicle . . ."

"By all means." I grabbed his arm. "We'll make such a jolly group—you, Mrs. McHaver, Miriam, and I. Don't even think about calling shotgun."

"Shotgun? You're armed?"

"Never mind." I pushed him into a chair next to Miriam and went outside to look for Bakr's van. It was there, to my relief, so I announced as much and watched Mrs. McHaver thump her way across the lobby. I hadn't had time to ponder our conversation at breakfast, or even Magritta's accusations concerning her from the previous night. Placating Peter had taken all of my energy.

Mrs. McHaver made it clear she'd expected a more luxurious mode of transportation, but all I could do was shrug. After she'd been helped into the van, I scrambled into the front seat and we drove away from the hotel.

"Have you heard?" Bakr asked me in a low voice. "Chief Inspector el-Habachi is furious. All of the police officers who were supposed to be off-duty today have been called in and given assignments. Soldiers are already stationed along the road to inspect vehicles and identity papers. The police station is louder than a playground."

"What's that?" Mrs. McHaver demanded. "And speak up, young man. It's very difficult to hear you over all this traffic. Did you say something about soldiers at a playground? Haven't they anything better to do?" She rapped my shoulder with her cane. "What is he saying, Mrs. Malloy? It makes no sense, no sense at all."

Bakr cleared his throat. "There has been an accident in the Valley of the Kings. Chief Inspector el-Habachi and Mrs. Malloy's husband are there now. The head of the national security is on his way from Cairo."

"What kind of accident?" Alexander asked.

"I do not know. I am not of the rank to be given privileged

information." He pressed the horn as he veered around a carriage, then kept his eyes on the road.

Miriam laughed unconvincingly. "Surely it's an overturned tramcar or a gang of drunken Germans forcing their way into a tomb."

"At this hour?" Mrs. McHaver snorted. "The Oktoberfest is held in Munich, not Luxor. My late husband and I were hiking in Bavaria one year and didn't realize until too late that we had chosen an inopportune time. The disgraceful behavior, the drunkenness, the copulation in public places! We took the next train to Rome and never returned to Germany."

"How fortunate," Alexander drawled, ". . . for the Romans, that is."

Mrs. McHaver harrumphed and fell silent. We drove across the bridge and through Gurna to the road that led past the Ramesseum. As we neared the entrance to the Valley of the Kings, we began to see soldiers in jeeps parked along the edge of the road. In several instances, cars had been stopped and their occupants were being questioned.

"I have a special license plate," Bakr murmured, saving me the bother of asking. He parked by the gate and conversed in Arabic with a guard while we got out of the van. "Please stay with this man," Bakr said to us. "He will escort you where you wish to go."

The parking lot was nearly empty, I noticed, and no tour buses were idling along the back row. The soldiers at the entrance waved us by. I dropped behind Mrs. McHaver, who was making slow but relentless progress up the walkway, and gestured for Alexander to join me.

"Having one of those déjà vu moments?" I asked him.

"I wasn't here last spring, if you're referring to Oskar Vonderlochen's so-called accident. We can rule out overturned tramcars but not marauding Teutonic warriors bearing cell phones and beer."

"But all the excitement over that artifact last night, and now an accident. You believe it's just a coincidence?"

"I don't believe anything, Mrs. Malloy, including

Salima's ridiculous story about the two of you locking yourselves in a laundry room in the basement last night. She
may well be a pathological liar, but I must say I thought better of you."

"I never said we locked ourselves in a laundry room."

"Well, then?"

"Where's that little tram? If it's not operating, they
should have sent a jeep to fetch us. Mrs. McHaver is an elderly lady in need of assistance."

"Then I shall assist her," he said huffily, catching up with
her to offer his arm.

I did not harrumph, but only because I would have felt
silly. I watched their backs as we made our way to the guard
station, where several dozen soldiers and guards were smoking cigarettes and watching us.

Mrs. McHaver waved her cane at one of them. "See here,
you idle oaf, fetch a vehicle and be quick about it. I shall
wait in the shade until you do. Miriam, pour me a cup of
tea and open that packet of digestive biscuits. I am feeling
faint."

The soldiers melted away. Mrs. McHaver sat down on a
flat rock and took off her hat. Miriam poured tea from the
thermos into a cup, then sat down to search through her
knapsack. Alexander lit a cigarette and gazed at the mountains looming on either side of the valley. I found another
perch and opened my water bottle. If we were to be buried
under an avalanche of rocks, I needed to prepare myself as
best I could.

Within five minutes, a jeep pulled up. The driver grinned
nervously and pointed at the empty seats. Alexander helped
Mrs. McHaver into the seat next to the driver, then climbed
in the back, leaving the empty row for Miriam and me.

"This is worrisome," Miriam said, clinging to the back
of the seat as the jeep bounced up the road. "I have this horrid premonition. Everyone was excited about the *shabti*, and
a goodly amount of alcohol was consumed as the evening
went on. Shannon began taunting Magritta and Wallace.
Poor Wallace burst into tears, and Magritta counterattacked

with aspersions on Shannon's lack of field experience and shoddy credentials. That repulsive American graduate student tried to put his hand down the front of my dress. At one point, I feared that my aunt and Lady Emerson might engage in a duel with parasol and cane. Miss Portia offered to make book on the outcome. Ahmed came up several times to beg Lord Bledrock to restrain the party."

"So sorry I missed it," I said. "The *shabti* must be cursed."

Her lips twitched, but she did not reply. Official cars, jeeps, and an ambulance were parked in the road by the excavation site. The workmen sat on a wall, smoking brown cigarettes and watching the activity as though they had ringside seats at a mud-wrestling match. The canvas tarps had been removed. The men standing near the pit were primarily dressed in khaki, although I caught a glimpse of Peter in a particularly fetching bronze cotton pullover. Lord Bledrock's white hair bobbled into sight briefly. Other men in suits and ties were likely to be bureaucrats. Mahmoud was issuing orders to his uniformed officers.

I squirmed through the crowd and touched Peter's shoulder. "What's going on?"

"They're bringing up the body now," he said. "We need to move out of the way."

"Whose body?"

"Shannon King's. A guard found her this morning while he was making his rounds. He called to report, then closed the Valley before the tourists and buses arrived. There was quite a scene at the front gate when Mahmoud and I arrived. The Ministry of Tourism must be flooded with calls from angry tour directors, and probably a few embassies as well."

"Oh, dear," I said, shocked. "What happened?"

"Shannon?" said Alexander, who'd come up behind us. "My God, what happened to her? Is she dead?"

Magritta joined us. "Of course she's dead. Would these buffoons be moving so slowly if she wasn't?" Groaning, she gulped down water from a bottle. "I cannot believe the timing. The head of the Supreme Council of Antiquities will be here today to inspect the excavation and grant us permission to continue. Once something of significance has been uncovered, they take a keen interest in making sure that proper procedures are followed. They have the right to withdraw the concession if they're not satisfied."

"You're not concerned about Shannon?" I asked her.

"I'm very sorry, naturally, but if she wanted to do something reckless, I wish she had done it at the Winter Palace, not here. When I think of all the years Oskar and I devoted to finding a tomb . . ."

"Peter, my darling," I said, "would you help me find a seat in the shade? You know how fragile I am."

"About as fragile as a tank," he said under his breath as he escorted me to a low rock shaded by an overhang. "Mahmoud thinks Dr. King came out here at least an hour before sunrise. The guards who were on duty swear they never saw her, but they're not about to admit they accepted a bribe to look the other way. There are pieces of glass from a champagne bottle in the pit. Lord Bledrock said that she was inebriated when she left his suite, and mumbling about the need for better security at the site. He was worried about her, but not so much that he saw her safely to her room. They were all displeased by her verbal attacks on Magritta and Wallace. He went so far as to describe her as 'lacking grace.' That's the ultimate insult in his circle."

"How did she get here at that hour?"

"Most likely a taxi driver, who's now home asleep. If the taxi driver is a conscientious citizen, he'll contact the police later today, but it's possible he charged her an outrageous fare and will decide not to get involved."

I glanced at the pit, then looked away as several officers emerged with a body bag. "The modern-day version of a mummy, I suppose. She didn't have the *shabti* with her, did she?"

"It's in the safe in Lord Bledrock's suite. He put it there when things got rowdy. He said Shannon was in no condition to take proper care of it."

"It doesn't sound as though she was." I took a sip of

water and blotted my face with a tissue. "Has Mahmoud acknowledged the parallel with what happened to Oskar Vonderlochen last spring?"

"Oh yeah," Peter said. "I need to go back to Luxor and make some phone calls to, ah, interested parties. You might as well come, too. There's nothing to see. I assume Bakr drove you, so we can ride back together."

"Along with Mrs. McHaver, Miriam, and Alexander. I was waylaid at breakfast, and bullied into offering them a ride. If I'm a tank, Mrs. McHaver is a battalion. Her deceased husband's name was probably MacArthur. Quite a mouthful if she'd hyphenated."

"Gather them up and start for the parking lot. I'll catch up with you after I have a few words with Mahmoud and a certain Mr. Jones from the American Embassy."

"Taxi drivers may work from dusk till dawn, but a spy's work is never done," I said with a grin, then obediently followed his instructions.

CHAPTER 13

Caron and Inez were sitting on the balcony when I returned, Peter having kept the van so that Bakr could drive him to wherever clandestine calls were to be made. I had no idea what was going on in the basement; nor did I want to find out at the expense of marital bliss (which was in short supply).

I called a greeting, then went into our bedroom to freshen up and change into less sensible shoes. "Did you sleep late?" I asked as I joined them.

"Where have you been?" demanded Caron.

"In the Valley of the Kings. There was an accident at the excavation site. Did you two ever meet Shannon King, the blond woman from the college in Maine?"

"We saw her in the lobby a couple of times," Inez said. "Is she going to be okay?"

I shook my head. "Do you recall what Alexander said about Oskar Vonderlochen going out to the Valley late at night and tumbling into the pit? She seems to have done the same thing. A guard found her early this morning. From what I heard, she drank heavily last night and most likely took a taxi over there. She bribed a guard, then staggered up the hill and . . . fell."

"Alexander said he thought this Oskar person was murdered," Caron said, shivering. "It's like there's a curse. I don't think we ought to go there anymore. In fact, I don't think we ought to stay in Egypt. We're juniors, Mother. We have to protect our reputations."

"Everybody at school already thinks we're weird," Inez added gloomily.

"But not boring," I said with a bright smile.

Caron and Inez exchanged looks, which seemed to be their primary mode of communication for the last ten days. Before I pointed this out, Caron said, "By the way, our room was searched."

"Oh, really? How could you tell? I was in there yesterday, and it looked worse than the back room of a thrift store. Clothes everywhere, suitcases on the floor, towels on the backs of chairs, enough plastic shopping bags to build a squishy pyramid." I had doubted Luanne's assertion that my apartment had been searched because it was too tidy. I was even more reluctant to buy theirs. "I don't know how anyone can clean in there without a bulldozer. Is something missing?"

Caron hesitated. "Not really, but things have been disturbed. It may look like a mess to you, but it's actually very organized."

"In its own way," Inez said, nodding. "Do you think that man with the scar got in while we were on the cruise?"

"Why would he?" I asked.

"Why was he stalking us?" Caron countered. "Maybe he ordered his henchmen to kidnap us before we got to Abu Simbel. They grabbed Buffy by mistake. I'll bet they're sorry now."

I conceded defeat. "Peter's gone off again. Do you want to have lunch in one of the cafés in the neighborhood? There are some little shops with local crafts."

Inez blushed. "I sort of told this boy from Ohio that I'd meet him at the pool this afternoon. I promise I won't leave the hotel grounds, Mrs. Malloy. He and his parents are staying here. I have their room number if you want to call them."

I glanced at Caron, who was simmering dangerously. "That'll be fine, Inez. Caron and I will enjoy a chance to go shopping."

"Sure we will," said my darling daughter, her words enunciated with lethal precision. "I can't think of anything

I'd rather do than buy a camel made out of clay and a set of napkin rings. Inez, you'd better wear a lot of sunscreen. Your nose is liable to start peeling any minute now. It's already flaky."

"It is not."

"Like you stuck on onion skins. You should cover it with a Band-Aid."

Inez shoved back her hair. "You should cover your whole face with a Band-Aid."

"Go get ready," I said, unamused.

There was no conversation in the girls' bedroom, although I knew dirty looks were as abundant as dirty socks on the floor. I told Inez to meet us at four, and then Caron and I went down through the lobby to the corniche. We headed in the direction of Luxor Temple and walked up the side street into the neighborhood where Peter and I had eaten lunch the previous week.

Caron claimed to have no interest in where we ate, so I selected a café. Once we were seated, I said, "Why are you so sure your room was searched? It's not as if anyone would think you had expensive jewelry or camera equipment. When I asked you if anything was missing, you were evasive. Is something missing?"

"You should have seen Inez flirting with that boy last night. It was disgusting." She picked up a menu. "This is all in Arabic. How are we supposed to order? I'm not about to point at something and end up with a bowl of mushy potatoes and green beans. I loathe mushy potatoes and green beans. I loathe everything about this place and this trip. You should have just brought Inez and let me stay home with one of my friends. If I wanted to see boring old temples, I could have watched the Discovery Channel. At least I could have had a pizza while I was soaking up all that culture."

A waiter appeared, begged our pardon, and put down menus written in English. Caron crossed her arms. I ordered for both of us, then acknowledged the futility of attempting any sort of semicivilized conversation with her.

She relinquished her martyred pose only when the waiter brought us kebabs and rice, although she ignored my chatter as she ate.

"All right," I said when we went out to the street, "I give up. If you want to spend the next couple of hours feeling sorry for yourself, then you'll have to do so alone in the suite. Or you can go spy on Inez. I'm going to browse in some of these shops."

"I might as well stay with you."

"I'm not sure I want your company. Head that way, take the second left, and left again at the corniche. Do you have a room key?"

She took her time weighing the options. "Okay, I'm sorry, Mother," she said in a somewhat credible tone. "It's just that—well, it's not my fault that I never learned how to play poker. Inez's creepy little brother taught her. Everybody thought she was so clever because she knows all these different games. I sat there like a clump of mud on the sofa, totally confused. Whenever I did something stupid, they all snickered—even Inez."

"You'll have to get over it. Focus on what you do well, and don't try to compete in every arena."

"So now you're Confucius?"

"Let's look for jewelry," I said. "Maybe some earrings or a chain."

We drifted in and out of shops, unable to find anything that caught Caron's eye. Clay camels were in abundance, as well as scarves, slippers, and decorative boxes. Empty-handed, we eventually ended up on the corniche and turned toward the hotel. I hesitated as we came to the sandwich board at the entrance to the alley mall.

"There are some antique jewelry stores at the far end," I murmured.

"What about that man with the scar?" Caron said, sounding like a child being sent into the dark on Halloween night.

"We'll stick together," I said firmly. "If you see him, you can point him out and I'll confront him."

"Confucius with a stun gun?"

"Absolutely." I made sure she stayed next to me as we ran the gauntlet of shopkeepers with the finest wares at the cheapest prices in all of Luxor, only for us because we were such beautiful and gracious American ladies. I felt as if I had a tattoo of the flag on my forehead. We smiled and nodded but refused to be drawn inside. Eventually we came to the shops I'd mentioned.

Caron's trepidation that we might bump into her stalker was replaced by the calculating look of a seasoned shopper. We went inside several shops, where she examined jewelry with the assurance of a certified appraiser. Shopkeepers beamed with anticipation as they pulled out trays, then deflated with misery as she shook her head. Her skill had no genetic basis; I would have bought the first item that appeared remotely suitable and retired to the bookstore.

"That's nice," I said as she tried on yet another ring.

"It's close, but it won't do. I am not about to go back to the hotel and listen to Inez prattle about that boy unless I have something to flaunt under her nose. You might want something for yourself, Mother. You can tell Peter it was a gift from a mysterious suitor and he might stop disappearing every other hour. He was here for a couple of weeks before we arrived, you know. Maybe he was lonely and took up with a belly dancer. He could be meeting her."

"Ten more minutes."

"All right," she said. "I was just pointing out the obvious. If you're going to stick your head in the sand, this is the place to do it."

We reached the shop where I'd seen Lord Bledrock—or hadn't, according to pretty much everybody else. The proprietor was standing in the doorway, smoking a pipe.

"Mrs. Malloy," he said, "and your daughter. You are shopping, I see."

"Good afternoon. I'm afraid I don't recall your name."

"Dr. Butros Guindi, at your service. Come inside and we'll have a glass of tea." He took Caron's arm. "We must find a piece of jewelry to adorn this charming creature. Sil-

ver or gold? Gold is more expensive, but surely your stepfather can afford it. He is a wealthy man, is he not?"

"How do you know?" I said.

"Please make yourselves comfortable while I have a
word with Girgis. Miss Malloy, if you see anything you like,
feel free to try it on."

He went behind the curtain. I sat down while Caron
moved about the shop, picking up various objects to examine them in the dusty sunlight. The air was warm and held
a trace of incense. My eyelids were beginning to droop
when I heard a muffled gasp.

"What's wrong, dear?" I said as I sat upright.

Dr. Guindi emerged before she could reply. "Is there a
problem? It's impossible to keep the shop completely free
of spiders and insects, although Girgis does his best. Ah,
Miss Malloy, you have come across some of my most trea-
sured stock. Sit down and I'll bring the display case to you.
Your mother may be interested, too."

I certainly was. Caron would not have gasped if she'd
encountered a spider; she would have screeched. She was
pale as she sat down near me, her lower lip clamped under
her teeth. "What's wrong?" I whispered.

"Nothing."

Dr. Guindi set down a wooden box holding a half-dozen
figurines. They were eight to ten inches long, their heads intact. Their beards were elongated black rectangles; their eyes
were flat as they gazed into the eternal afterlife. "*Shabtis*,"
he said. "These are particularly fine ones. Would you care
to pick one up, Miss Malloy? I ask that you do so carefully.
They date back to the twenty-first dynasty. Those made at
a later date are more accurately described as funerary figurines, although modern Egyptologists use the terms more
loosely."

Caron was staring at them with a horrified expression.
"Are these really that old?"

"These are, yes," he said, "but there are many counter-
feits as well. Only highly trained experts can tell the difference. Many tourists have returned home to boast to their

friends about having smuggled a priceless artifact through customs, when in truth its value is negligible. Some of the better replicas from the nineteenth century are collectible as curiosities."

"Does Lord Bledrock have any in his private collection?" I asked.

"I wouldn't know," Dr. Guindi said with a shrug. "Let me see why Girgis is so slow." He picked up the box and went into the back room.

Caron gripped my wrist. "Let's go, Mother."

"That would be rude. Why don't you keep looking for a ring? They're scattered around all over the shop. Did you see the ones on the window ledge?"

"I'm about to get sick. That's rude, too, you know. It must be from lunch. The meat on the kebab smelled kind of funny, like it was spoiled. We have to leave right this minute." She started for the door.

I couldn't send her back to the hotel on her own, having vowed to defend her from her imaginary stalker. I called to Dr. Guindi that we were leaving, then caught up with her outside the shop. "There was nothing wrong with the kebab," I said as we made our way to the corniche.

"That's easy for you to say, since your insides aren't heaving."

I trailed her back to the hotel and up to the suite, where she immediately disappeared into the bathroom. I listened for sounds of retching, but whatever was happening was muted. The sight of the *shabti* had provoked her reaction, I thought as I settled on the balcony. I hadn't mentioned the one found at the excavation, and there was no way for the girls to have heard about it. Even if they had, I could see no reason that they would have cared.

Inez came back at four, squared her shoulders as best she could, and went into their bedroom. I expected a loud argument, but all I could hear was a low buzz of voices. Relieved, I decided to have a drink. I was calling room service for a bucket of ice when Alexander came into the suite.

"The door wasn't locked," he said, "and it is the cocktail

hour. My father and his cronies are sitting around his suite, swaddled in such gloom that I'm surprised no one has suffocated. My only hope of survival was to come here and bask in the glow of an invigorating companion. Your husband's not here, is he? I don't want the chap to get jealous."

"He has no reason to be jealous."

"Alas, he does not." Alexander set out glasses and bottles of gin, scotch, and vermouth, then went out to the balcony. After rearranging the furniture to his satisfaction, he sat back and crossed his legs. "Any thoughts about Shannon's purported accident in the early hours of the morning? Have you interviewed the suspects and gained keen insight into their whereabouts? Some of them have motives, and in a sense, all of them had opportunity. I must admit it's difficult to picture any of them finding his or her way across the Nile and up the road to the Valley. Then again, determination might win out over inebriation. Shannon made her way there, despite her wobbly legs and tendency to bump into furniture as the night went on."

Abdullah entered with a bucket of ice and a platter of sandwiches. "Good afternoon, *Sitt* Malloy. I thought you might enjoy something to eat."

I cut him off in the parlor, where I hoped Alexander wouldn't be able to hear me. "Abdullah, have you heard what happened to Dr. King?"

"Yes, a terrible thing. It is dangerous for women to go off by themselves in the night. Will there be anything else?"

"Do you know the name of the taxi driver who took her across the river?"

"I am familiar with his family. They live in a small house in the south part of the city."

I would have been surprised if Abdullah didn't know not only the driver, but also his relatives, pets, and friends. "Has he gone to the police yet? I know they want to question him."

"I cannot say, *Sitt*. This man, Sobny, drives his taxi at night and must sleep during the day. Is there anything else you might want?"

"Yes, I'd like to hear why you know all this. Were you here at the hotel at three o'clock in the morning—or is there a conspiracy among the staff to spy on the guests and keep track of all their activities?"

Abdullah looked pained at my accusation. "Nothing like that, *Sitt* Malloy. There was some gossip. Dr. King was barely able to walk when she arrived in the lobby very early this morning, but she insisted on taking a taxi. The night manager and a bellman helped her out to the curb, and then waited with her until Sobny drove up. They were worried about her. What gossip there is stays within the hotel. The Winter Palace has a reputation for discretion."

"And her accident?" I persisted.

"That was on the news. There is a small television set in the basement."

"Oh," I said, feeling foolish. "We won't be needing anything else, Abdullah. Thank you for the ice and sandwiches."

"I believe *Sitt* Malloy is familiar with the basement. Have a pleasurable evening." He glided out of the room.

"What on earth were you badgering him about?" Alexander asked from the doorway to the balcony. "The guy's at least twenty years older than my father. He probably earns less than a thousand pounds a week, and I mean Egyptian pounds, not Her Majesty's currency of the realm."

"Nothing," I muttered. "He's just so insufferably smug and omniscient, as if nothing that goes on around here escapes his notice. I'm sure he knows my shoe size and Peter's preference in reading material."

"You really do need a drink." Alexander busied himself at the mini-bar, then brought me a scotch and water.

We went back out to the balcony and sat in silence for a long while. I thought about calling Mahmoud with the taxi driver's name, but doing so would antagonize Peter, who'd assume I'd been grilling the hotel staff. Which, to a limited extent, I had. "So there's a meeting of the gloom-and-doom society in your father's suite? Will the excavation be closed down?"

"Nobody knows. Magritta's furious, naturally. The discovery of the *shabti* strongly suggests that she may have stumbled across the first really important find since Carter opened Tut's tomb. Last night she was overwhelmed with visions of fame, if not fortune. Her photo in the bar alongside of Carter and Carnarvon. Interviews with the media and articles in the prestigious journals. A book deal. The ultimate feather in her professional cap." He paused to take a sip of his martini and lick his lips. "Shannon would have given her some competition. Pretty young blondes make better talk show guests. It would have made for a most intriguing situation. Imagine the two of them in a studio, separated only by a scholarly moderator with a wispy goatee and bifocals."

"Well, that won't happen now," I said.

"True."

"And your father won't be pressured to display his collection at MacLeod College."

"He's relieved. Shannon cornered him around midnight and tore into him about it. The old boy's too much of a gentleman to raise his voice to a lady, but he was displeased. After she left, he blustered for half an hour about her impertinence. He compared her to a commoner daring to demand that Queen Victoria hang her undies on a clothesline at Buckingham Palace. Lady Emerson thought it was hysterically funny, and even Mrs. McHaver was amused."

"And Miriam?" I asked.

"She almost smiled, although it might have been the death of her. I've encountered more animation from a smoked salmon. Have you ever noticed how she sniffles?"

"No, I can't say that I have. Run along and console someone, Alexander."

He put down his glass, winked at me, and sauntered across the room to the door. "Perhaps later, Mrs. Malloy," he called as he left.

Caron and Inez emerged from their bedroom. There were no red scratches on either's face, to my relief.

"We're going to check e-mail," Caron called. "Back in an hour or so."

Once again I was alone. I heard a siren below and went to look over the balcony railing. An ambulance raced past, lights flashing. Peter would know how Nabil was faring in the ICU, I thought as I continued to stand at the railing. Perhaps Mahmoud had questioned the other workmen at the excavation to find out when and why Nabil had overdosed on a methamphetamine. Or perhaps Mahmoud had been too preoccupied by Shannon's accident to worry about a laborer.

On the terrace below, I noticed Samuel seated at a table. A waiter set down drinks and waited until Samuel had signed the tab. Moments later, Miriam came out of the lobby and sat down across from him. I could see that they were conversing, but their faces weren't visible from my vantage point. Miriam began to drum her fingers on the table. Samuel bent forward and spoke to her at some length. Peter might have been able to read their lips. As an amateur in basic surveillance skills, I would have settled on seeing their expressions.

I was debating whether or not to go to the lobby and then ever so casually join them when Sittermann, wearing his white suit and a hat, came up the walk from the corniche. I would have hurtled a glass at him had I not realized the danger to the other occupants on the terrace. I was about to hurtle an invective instead when he sat down with Samuel and Miriam. Whatever he said caused both of them to sit back.

Rather than passively watch any longer, I dashed through the sitting room, grabbing my purse, and raced to the elevator. Although I knew it was futile, I jabbed the button again and again until the car arrived and the doors slid open. Two sunburned tourists shrank into a corner, staring at me as I squirmed like an insect facing annihilation beneath a boot sole.

Ahmed tried to waylay me as I went through the lobby, but I ignored him. When I reached the terrace, I stopped. Miriam had vanished—and so had Sittermann. I bit back the urge to howl with frustration. Samuel glanced up as I grabbed his shoulder.

"Where's Sittermann?" I snapped.

"Who?"

"Don't give me that! Did he go into the hotel?"

"I'm not sure what you're talking about," he said, trying to pull himself free.

My grip tightened. "I saw him from my balcony less than five minutes ago. Where is he?"

"That guy from Texas? The really loud—"

"Which way did he go?" I lowered my voice, aware that I was attracting attention. "Just point, okay?"

Samuel gestured in the direction of Luxor Temple, visible above the trees in the garden. "Why don't you sit here and have something cool to drink, Mrs. Malloy? You're looking awfully upset."

I went to the corniche and looked to the right. A couple of taxi drivers were leaning against the temple wall, smoking cigarettes and waiting for weary tourists to emerge. Sittermann was nowhere in sight. On the far side of the corniche, a policeman was talking to a carriage driver. I stopped at the corner. To my right were all the narrow streets where Caron and I had been earlier. If he'd gone that way, I'd never find him.

The taxi drivers drew back as I approached the entrance to the temple. The man in the ticket kiosk was reading a magazine, but he set it aside when I cleared my throat.

"Did a man in a white suit come in here a few minutes ago?" I asked.

"Twenty pound."

"A man," I said slowly, "tall like this." I held my hand several inches above my head. "American, dressed in white." Since I was wearing green, I looked around, then touched the margin of his magazine. "White."

His eyes widened with confusion. He pushed the magazine under the grill and said, "*Kora. Ah* . . . football."

The cover of the magazine depicted a swarthy man in

shorts leaping into the air as a soccer ball rocketed off his head. "No, not football," I said. "A man, tall, dressed in white."

"Italian," the ticket seller said, pointing at the photo. "Very good football."

I was going to find myself with a date to the next match if I persisted. I took out a twenty-pound bill and handed it over. Two guards at a table opened my purse to make sure I wasn't armed and dangerous. I crossed my fingers and said, "Did a man in a white suit come in here?" One of them nodded. I went down the steps to the area in front of the temple complex. The avenue of sphinxes was on my left, the colossal statues of Ramses II on my right. Unless Sittermann was crouched behind one of the stone sphinxes, he'd gone into the temple.

Although we'd been there before, we'd been in a lot of temples since then and I couldn't remember the layout. I went into the courtyard. Most of the tour groups had departed, and the few remaining tourists were milling about with guidebooks and cameras. I made my way through the colonnade, watching for Sittermann. What he was doing was beyond speculation; he'd shown no great enthusiasm for the architecture or history. I was sure he could no more differentiate between Ramses II and Ramses IV than I could. He was a Tut man, at best.

I stopped in the next courtyard and sat on the base of a pillar. The last of the tourists, a tweedy man and his formidable female companion, gave me disapproving looks as they left in the direction of the entrance. Above the pillars, the sky was pale blue. Clouds tinged with dark edges moved ponderously toward the mountains east of the city. The sonorous atonal chant of the muezzins summoning the pious to prayer reverberated in the empty courtyard. Forced to rely on scenes from movies, I pictured myself as a royal princess, surrounded by kowtowing servants and stern, bearded priests in tall hats and white robes.

Therefore, I was startled when Sittermann's face appeared above me. I bit back a yelp as I stumbled to my feet.

"Why, if it ain't Mrs. Malloy," he said. "Darned if we don't keep bumping into each other in the most peculiar places. Fancying yourself as Cleopatra?"

"I want to talk to you."

"I suspected that might be why you followed me. I'm sorry about running out last night, but I had an urgent matter that I had to deal with before it bit me on the buttocks."

"Speaking of deals, what's yours?" I said, irritated by his benign smile. "And don't give me that nonsense about a theme park. I want answers, Mr. Sittermann."

He took a handkerchief from his back pocket and wiped his neck. Once he was finished, he returned it to his pocket. "Mrs. Malloy, I have no obligation to answer questions in order to satisfy your curiosity. You may believe whatever you choose."

"Your accent slipped," I pointed out politely.

"Yes, I suppose it did. Why don't you run along back to the hotel and watch the sunset from your balcony? Make a drink, put your feet up, and relax. Not everyone has the opportunity to watch the sun set over the Nile. You should take advantage of the opportunity while you're here."

I was growing alarmed by his abrupt transition from extroverted Texan mogul to . . . whatever. He and I were the only two people in this far area of the temple complex. The sun was still shining, but shadows encroached and the air was cooler. I was reasonably confident that my screams would be heard if he threatened me. There were more than enough columns to make for a spirited game of chase all the way back to the entrance of the temple complex. Once I was there, the security guards might be bewildered, but they would come to my assistance.

"I'm not going to behave in an ungentlemanly fashion," he said. "Just stroll out of here and go back to the hotel. I allowed you to follow me here so I could ask you to keep your nose out of this mess. That's all I can do, since you seem to have made up your mind to interfere."

"You *allowed* me to follow you?" I said, offended. "What made you so certain that I would? I could have stayed in the suite and read a book, or joined Samuel for a drink on the terrace."

"But here you are, Mrs. Malloy."

"What if I said I was coming here anyway, merely to enjoy the temple when it wasn't crowded?"

"I'd say I didn't believe you." He touched the brim of his hat. "I must be off now. I assume you can find your way out on your own. Give my regards to your husband and young Bledrock."

He went through a narrow doorway. I leaned against the column and muttered some colorful comments that were inappropriate in any religious setting, even one that had been decommissioned for nearly two millennia.

Two backpackers walked by, nervously glancing at me. I gave them a wan smile, then crept over to the doorway through which Sittermann had disappeared. Beyond it was a vast open yard with stacks of flat rocks and broken pottery. In a corner, native workmen were drinking tea from tin cups. Tools were aligned on a low rock wall. It was, I surmised, the restoration area, and off-limits to casual visitors. Not that there was anything casual about Sittermann, I thought as I turned around and started toward the entrance.

I froze as I saw a figure propped against a column in the colonnade. He wore a dark business suit and sunglasses, and a mustache dominated his features. Almost, that is.

The scar was quite visible.

CHAPTER 14

I was sorry I didn't actually have a stun gun; the most lethal object in my purse was the heavy brass key from the hotel. Confrontation was not necessarily my best option, I decided as I went through the doorway into the restoration area. I stepped over a yellow tape and made my way through the labyrinth of rocks and broken pillars. Sittermann had all of a thirty-second lead, but he had vanished.

I looked over my shoulder, then went to the far wall where the workmen were sitting. "Did any of you see which way that man in the white suit went?"

The workmen stared at me.

"Is there another exit?" I persisted.

Another round of stares.

"No, I didn't think so," I said. "I'd love to stay and chat some more, guys, but I need to figure out how to get back out to the corniche without bumping into the other man, the one with the mustache and scar. As much as I'd like to shove him into a corner and demand to know who he is and why he's been frightening my daughter and her friend, this just isn't the place. Any suggestions?"

"There's a gate over there," said a workman, pointing at a corner. "It'll put you on the backstreet where the carriages park when the horses need a break. You can ride back to your hotel in style."

It took me a minute to respond. "Thank you. I apologize if I sounded like an idiot. I certainly feel like one."

"I grew up in Toronto," he said, "and work as a stonemason for the restoration team. As for the man in the white suit, he cut across the yard in the direction of the entrance. Didn't see a second man. I'd offer to escort you, but we're about to knock off and I want to make sure everything's put away."

"The gate will be fine." I smiled weakly and left before I further embarrassed myself, if such a thing was possible. The Canadian and his crew hadn't seen the elusive stalker, and I wasn't entirely sure I had, either. Incipient sunstroke could have transformed an ordinary tourist into an ominous figure in the shadows. The carriage drivers watched me as I came out onto a rough sidewalk, but no one offered me a ride. Like a pedestrian wary of speeding buses, I looked both ways before I stepped off the curb and followed the exterior wall of the temple around the corner to the corniche. Late afternoon traffic was raucous as drivers blew their horns and outmaneuvered one another to get around buses and carriages.

Samuel was no longer on the terrace. I went into the lobby, but Ahmed caught me before I reached the elevator.

"*Sitt* Malloy-Rosen," he said breathlessly, "how fortunate that I saw you. I have a message from Mr. Rosen. He called the suite, he said, but no one answered. I told him I saw you earlier, going out to the terrace. I searched for you there, and then in the restaurant. I was beginning to despair when—"

"What is Mr. Rosen's message?"

Ahmed was disappointed that I didn't want to hear about his diligent search for me behind every potted plant and porcelain teapot. "Mr. Rosen said that he is sorry, but he has gone to Cairo for the weekend. He did not say why."

"His girlfriend, a belly dancer. Her name is Fatima and she has a ruby in her navel."

"On your honeymoon?" Ahmed said, gasping. "Surely not. He must have important business there—with businessmen and bureaucrats."

"Very important." I stepped back to escape the overpowering gust of breath mints. "Thank you for passing along

Mr. Rosen's message. I'll tell him that you told me at your first opportunity."

He closed in on me. "These belly dancers are prostitutes, *Sitt* Malloy-Rosen, and the clubs where they can be found are often dangerous, particularly in Cairo. I do hope Mr. Rosen is aware of this."

"Yes, I hope so as much as you." I punched the elevator button, struggling not to smile. Ahmed looked as though he wished to elaborate, but I held up my hand as I backed into the elevator. He was on the verge of tears as the doors closed. I was, too, but for a different reason.

After Caron, Inez, and I had a quiet dinner in the restaurant, we went to the lobby. The girls gravitated toward a card game in one corner. I watched curiously to see if I could pick out Inez's pool date, but no sparks were visible. I sat down at a table in the bar and ordered coffee. Another romantic night, I thought with a grimace. At least Peter and I had had some private interludes on the ship. My face and other areas of my anatomy began to turn warm, and I was disconcerted when the waiter intruded with my coffee.

"*Shukran*," I mumbled.

"You're looking awfully smug," Alexander said as he sat down and lit a cigarette.

"I wish I were. What are you up to tonight?"

"Hanging around a bar, hoping to meet a beautiful lady who's been abandoned by her lover. Our eyes will lock across the table in a gaze fraught with unspoken desires. The lights will dim and treacly violin music will fill the room. Two lonely souls, drawn together through fate."

"You need a Humphrey Bogart accent to pull this off."

Alexander laughed. "I'd sound like a bullfrog." He waved over the waiter and ordered two brandies. "My father and the others have gone to Lady Emerson's for dinner and cards. All but Miriam, who pleaded a headache. She's probably slitting her wrists in their room, but doing it over the washbasin to minimize the mess. She's very fastidious."

"Why are you so boorish about her?" I asked.

"I am many things," he said, "but never boorish. I prefer to think of myself as perceptive and articulate. Miriam annoys me. It's not as though she's an orphaned waif living on crusts of bread off Mrs. McHaver's kitchen floor. The only reason she's so ghastly pale is that she avoids the sun. She's not as frail as she'd like you to believe, either. You should have seen her wrestling Mrs. McHaver's luggage out of the trunk of a taxi when they arrived at the hotel. The bellmen were awed."

"If you say so."

"You should never question the son of a baron. It's not done."

I listened to the whoops and laughter from the card game. Caron appeared to be holding her own. I wondered if she'd sucked in her arrogance long enough to ask Inez for a few tips. At nearby tables, elderly couples carried on low conversations, occasionally touching hands. Other couples whispered intimate secrets. I felt very isolated. Alexander was not an adequate substitute for Peter. Neither was a long, hot bath and a good book, but it was the best I could do.

A rapping noise awoke me. Bewildered, I looked through the shuttered window at the embryonic morning light. The rapping, low and insistent, continued. I grimaced as I sat up. Had my husband been asleep beside me, I would have poked him and bade him do his manly duty. He was, however, AWOL for the remainder of the weekend. I realized the miscreant was at the door that led from the bedroom to the hallway.

Clad in a T-shirt and boxers, I forced myself out of bed and ran my fingers through my hair before opening the door.

"I am so sorry, Mrs. Malloy," Samuel said. "This is a gawd-awful hour to disturb you, but I couldn't wait any longer. As soon as it started getting light, I had to come. I hope you'll understand."

"This better be good," I said.

"It's—uh, well, kind of complicated. Can I come in?"

He had not changed clothes since I'd seen him on the

terrace. His cheeks were stubbly, his hair sticking out at angles, and his eyes bloodshot. I was afraid he might collapse at my feet and begin to sob at any moment. I did not want to be caught in the scene by some bushy-tailed tourist with a perverse desire to be the first in line at the breakfast buffet.

"Come through here," I said, "and go into the parlor. Call room service for coffee and whatever else you want. Keep your voice down; the girls are sleeping in the other bedroom. I'll be out in ten minutes."

"I knew you'd understand," he said with such intensity that I flinched.

"I can assure you, Samuel, that I do not."

I dressed as quickly as I could and did the minimum required in the bathroom to make myself remotely presentable. I went into the parlor. Samuel had pulled back the drapes and opened the doors to the balcony. His back was to me as he stared at the mountains to the west. He looked more like a construction worker than an architect, but I'd met librarians built like grizzly bears and truck drivers no sturdier than fashion models.

"Okay," I said. "Explain."

He stiffened, and his hands tightened on the railing. "Buffy called late last night, maybe a couple of hours after midnight. I could barely hear her voice. She said she was at the Kharga Oasis, locked in a windowless room in a hotel. I told her to call the police, but she wouldn't. She's terrified that if the police show up, her captors will kill her."

"And this room has a pay phone?"

"She said she managed to steal a cell phone from one of them. It went dead before she could say any more."

There was a more civilized tap on the door. I admitted Abdullah, who merely raised his eyebrows when he saw Samuel. He put the tray on the coffee table and gazed stonily at me.

"That will be all," I said. "Thank you for coming so promptly. If we need anything else, I'll call. Run along and gossip about me."

Once Abdullah was gone, I poured myself a cup of coffee and went out to the balcony. "Did you believe Buffy?"

"Why wouldn't I? I mean, we all saw those men grab her and gallop away. She must have been going through hell since then. They could have done"—he gulped—"anything to her. She was almost hysterical when she called. Why don't you believe her?"

"I didn't say that." I took a sip of coffee and waited for the caffeine to jolt some neurons into activity. It was not my best time of day for keen insights and ruthless analysis. "There's just been too much going on around here. Maybe aliens did build the pyramids. It'd make as much sense."

"I don't think so, Mrs. Malloy."

"And don't patronize me. You're the one who came bursting in here at five thirty in the morning with some wild story about Buffy in a hotel in an oasis."

"Does that mean you won't go with me?"

I nearly choked on a mouthful of coffee. I managed to put the cup on the table before it sloshed all over me. "Me? That's absurd. Chief Inspector el-Habachi will make an ideal companion. He can wear a burqa. Those things are voluminous. He could have an arsenal strapped to his body. Once he sees the situation, he can decide how to get Buffy out intact."

Samuel slumped back in the chair. "Regulations. He'll have to tell his superiors where's he going, and then the whole thing will escalate like a sandstorm. Buffy made it clear that the men'll kill her if they panic. I thought we could go get her, and then deal with the authorities."

"How are we going to do that? I'm not a commando, Samuel. I don't watch war movies, and I've never read a book about paramilitary raids. You need Tom Clancy, not Agatha Christie."

He began to pace within the confines of the balcony, which limited him to about four steps in any direction. "I've had a lot of time to think about it. We'll drive over and start nosing around like ordinary tourists. This hotel is

near the town center. Nobody will suspect us. That'll give
us a chance to have a closer look and see if we can figure
out which room Buffy's in."

"And waltz out with her. Don't you think that might attract a little attention?" I shook my head as I refilled my
coffee cup. "If these men are as desperate and trigger-happy
as she claims, what's to stop them from . . . stopping
us? I can't imagine them politely requesting that we mind
our own business."

"All I'm asking you to do is drive over to the oasis with
me, Mrs. Malloy. If I go alone, I'll stand out. Someone may
remember seeing Buffy and me there a couple of weeks
ago. They won't notice the two of us, if we're merely having lunch and buying postcards."

I considered ordering another pot of coffee. "Having
lunch and buying postcards does not equate with breaking
into a locked room in a hotel."

"So we drive over and assess the situation. If it looks impossible, we'll go to the police. It's only a hundred miles.
We'll be back here in time for tea." He squeezed my shoulder. "I know a place where I can rent a car. I'll meet you
outside in an hour." He left without waiting for my answer.

I wondered how many pots of coffee I could drink in an
hour. Two, even three, I concluded. And then I would go
downstairs and tell Samuel as nicely as possible that he was
out of his mind and that I had no intention of driving out to
a desert oasis in order to have my head blown off by maniacal kidnappers.

Not on my honeymoon, anyway.

The road twisted through the mountains and into the desert.
I'd expected gold-flecked dunes shifting in the winds, but
this desert lacked grandeur. Stretches of sand were marred by
jutting rock formations. The car was cramped and ancient;
the glove compartment was apt to contain the remains of
Napoléon's lunch (pâté de fois gras sandwiches). Wind whis-
tled through holes in the floorboard. The cracked upholstery

was held together with duct tape. Each pothole we hit sent both of us bouncing high enough to brush the interior roof. Rust had resulted in a jagged sunroof of sorts.

"I thought you said a hundred miles!" I yelled over the roar of the strained engine.

"I did!" He yanked the steering wheel but was too late to avoid a particularly treacherous pothole. The car landed with a whomp, as did I. "I'm afraid to drive any faster. The tires are already shot. A blowout will send us off the road."

"Then slow down!" I closed my eyes and asked myself for the hundredth time what I was doing. I'd tried to call Peter, but since I didn't know where he was staying, the best I could do was the American Embassy. It did not seem discreet to leave a message on the answering machine there. I could easily believe the CIA tapped every foreign embassy's telephone system in D.C. It was likely that other governments reciprocated in their own countries.

"Another hour and we should be there," Samuel said encouragingly.

"I can hardly wait to get myself shot." I resettled my sunglasses on my nose and tried to distract myself with the hostile landscape. Although I knew that deserts were home to rodents, snakes, and insects, we seemed to be the sole indications of life as far as I could see. Why all the invading armies over the millennia were bent on capturing the land was hard to understand. I would have handed it over without a quibble.

Kharga was not a picturesque village with waving palm trees and lush gardens. The rough streets were crowded with donkey carts, decrepit trucks, and dark storefronts. Many of the buildings were constructed of concrete blocks, the walls covered with Arabic graffiti. Tour vans were parked in the weeds of vacant lots.

"What's the name of the hotel?" I asked as I peered out the window.

"The Desert Inn. Not terribly original, I'm afraid. When Buffy and I were here, I was warned not to stay there. Small, airless rooms, communal bathrooms, brackish tap water. It wouldn't have bothered me, but—well, we found someplace a little bit better."

Traffic stopped as a herd of camels ambled into the street. A dozen Arab men in long robes and sandals gathered to shake their fists and berate one another. The camels ignored the minor uproar, but bystanders were entertained and egged on their factions.

"This could take forever," Samuel said as he turned onto a side street and parked. He put the car key under his seat, then twisted around and took a bottle of water from the backseat floor. After offering it to me, he took a deep drink. "If I remember, the hotel's three blocks away."

"How far is the police station?"

"If we tell the police, we'll be risking Buffy's life. You don't know these people as well as I do. They're excitable and passionate. Any small-town cop is going to go berserk at the opportunity to be a hero by rescuing the blond American girl. He and his fellow cops will snatch up weapons and storm the hotel, shooting everything that moves. The kidnappers will kill Buffy in retaliation. Tourists will get killed, as well as the hotel staff and kids in nearby houses." He clutched my knee. "Please, Mrs. Malloy. We've come all this way. Let's at least check out the situation before we do something rash."

I removed his hand. "All right, but I still don't understand what you think we can do. Presumably, Buffy is being held by heavily armed guards. They may be tired of her, but they're not going to unlock her door and stand back while we hustle her out of the hotel. They're more likely to shoot us, as well as her."

"Don't you care about her?" he said, his voice breaking.

"No," I said, "not especially. It would be a tragedy if she were killed—as it would be if any innocent party were. I'd feel bad about it. Then again, I'd feel worse if I were killed trying to rescue her." I looked at him. "I didn't realize the two of you had any emotional entanglement. I still don't understand why you brought her along with you to Egypt. Did you honestly believe there was a hardy, adventurous traveler buried under all that makeup? Weren't you just a bit worried when you saw her matching Louis Vuitton luggage that she might not be a backpack girl at heart?"

"She insisted," he said lamely. "I warned her that we wouldn't find four-star accommodations at these places. How do you know about her luggage?"

"I must have seen it somewhere." I got out of the car and breathed in the exhaust fumes from the traffic jam at the corner. "Let's go find the Desert Inn."

Instead of going back to the main street, we went down an alley that seemed to run parallel with it. As we stepped around garbage bags and construction debris, I thought about Caron and Inez's harrowing story in Gurna. They thought they'd seen Samuel in the hotel nightclub, along with their stalker.

"Do you ever go to Gurna in the evenings?" I asked him as we ducked under a clothesline.

He pulled me away before I stepped in a pile of a redolent reminder of the presence of dogs. "A couple of times. The bar at the Winter Palace is too refined for my taste. You know, I thought I saw your daughter and her friend about a week ago. The place was packed, and I wasn't sure since I'd only just met them. Buffy had a headache, she claimed, but she was upset because she'd gotten a pedicure that wasn't up to her standards. Instead of listening to her complain, I went out on my own."

His response had been quick and overly detailed, as though he'd rehearsed it. Or he was nervous, I thought, and blathering to hide it. We both had every right to be nervous, since we were walking into a potential disaster. We turned back toward the main street. Traffic was now backed up in both directions, and horns were blaring. Unhappy camels brayed loudly. It might have been the most exciting thing to happen in this remote town in a long time. I hoped we weren't about to instigate a much more memorable event.

The hotel was on the next corner. It was a two-story structure made of uninspired concrete blocks, and the sign was weathered almost to the point of illegibility. An old man squatted beside the doorway, glowering defiantly at anyone who approached.

"We may have a problem," Samuel murmured as we walked across the street and sat down at a table outside a café.

"You're just now realizing that? Have you forgotten you're the one who mentioned guns and people getting killed? That old man isn't the problem, for pity's sake. The worst thing he might do is pinch you when you walk by him, or spit on your shoe." I studied the building, feeling like a bank robber determining when the armored truck made its daily pickups. "We'll be conspicuous, though."

A waiter came out and put down a menu. After a moment, he shrugged and went back into the café. The cacophony from the traffic jam was getting louder. The old man across the street stood up and shaded his eyes. I willed him to go join in the fun, but he took only a few steps and stopped.

Samuel pushed back his chair. "We can't stay here all afternoon. I'm going to see if there's a back entrance into the hotel. Order coffee or something so the waiter doesn't shoo you away."

"The waiter will not shoo me away," I said, "unless I choose to be shooed. Go on and have a look." I opened my purse and took out a tissue to blot my damp face. It was much hotter than in Luxor. Deserts are like that.

Samuel made his way through the donkey carts and cars blocking the street. I settled back to watch and wait, although I doubted any armored trucks would drive up in the next decade or so. The closest thing to a bank guard was the old man. I checked my watch. Women with their heads wrapped in scarves peered out of the window in a house next to the hotel, curiosity overcoming modesty. The waiter and another man came out of the café and stood behind me, guffawing as a cart tipped and spilled hundreds of cabbages onto the street. The driver began to scream at the donkey, who took it stoically.

Samuel had not returned after thirty minutes. I was less concerned about him than I was about a certain sensation that required a ladies' room. The café did not appeal. If it had a rest room, it would be primitive and less than sanitary. After another five minutes, I realized that I had a perfect excuse to go inside the hotel.

The old man did not glance at me as I went across the street and entered the Desert Inn. The front room was dim and shabby. From behind a desk, a young woman gaped at me, bewildered. It struck me as peculiar, since an inn might expect to have an occasional tourist come in to inquire about a room. My head was bare, but I was dressed decorously. My face was grimy, but not so badly as to warrant her trepidation.

"Do you speak English?" I asked politely.

"A little." The woman backed away, as though I were holding a weapon of some sort. Behind her, a limp curtain covering a doorway twitched. I heard agitated whispers and stifled giggles. Children, I surmised, instead of fierce, gun-wielding thugs.

"Oh, good," I said, hoping for the best. "I wonder if you might allow me to use your facilities—your bathroom? I had quite a lot of coffee this morning, followed by a very bumpy ride." I illustrated this with a few hops. "Bumpy."

"You want the bathroom?" She was increasingly alarmed and seemed on the verge of dashing out of the room. She was liable to trip over the spies behind the curtain, who were giggling more loudly. "You are alone? This is not . . ."

I opted for an apologetic smile. "I'll just be a minute."

The woman opened a drawer and pulled out a loop of cord with a dozen keys. "Up there," she whispered, pointing at the stained ceiling. "At the end."

"Thank you." I took the keys from her trembling hand, nodded, and went up a short flight of stairs to a narrow corridor lined with closed doors. I realized that Buffy was likely to be in one of the rooms—and I had the keys. However, I had a more pressing problem, so I hurried toward the door the desk clerk had indicated. Halfway down the corridor, a door opened and two men stepped out, cutting me off. They were swarthy, with unshaven faces, deep-set dark eyes, and brown teeth. The cloths tied around their heads were stained with sweat, as were their pants and frayed shirts. One had a pistol tucked under his belt.

I gulped, then moistened my lips and said, "Good afternoon, gentlemen. I'm looking for the bathroom."

They spoke to each other in rapid Arabic, darting slitted looks at me and at the empty corridor behind me. From inside their room I heard the cheers of a thousand soccer fans. One of the men glanced over his shoulder at what I cleverly surmised was a TV set. He said something to his companion, who rolled his eyes and replied with what may have been a crude expression of displeasure.

"If you'll excuse me," I said, putting on a pinched smile and fidgeting, "I really need to be on my way. One of those imperatives of nature, you know. It's much more difficult for us ladies. We require some privacy, so we simply can't find an alley and . . . relieve ourselves. That's the only thing I envied about boys when I was growing up, you know. It didn't seem fair." I sensed they were weakening, and began to move toward them. "Who's playing today? Egypt? I do hope your team is doing well this year. The sport is catching on back home, but it's not nearly as popular as it is in other countries."

An announcer began to jabber excitedly from inside their room. There was a burst of thunderous applause as someone somewhere did something of note. I eased by the men, who were both halfway into the room watching the TV screen. When neither of them barked at me, I halted in front of the door and fumbled through the keys. They all had bits of masking tape with Arabic squiggles on them. Rather than trying to match the squiggle on the door, I began to try each key.

On my fourth attempt, the key slid into the lock and I opened the door. Having anticipated a primitive bathroom (sanitation was no longer an issue), I was startled to see nothing more than a narrow iron bed—and Buffy.

"Mrs. Malloy!" she gasped. "What the hell are you doing here?"

"You might pretend to be a little more pleased to see me."

"I . . . uh, I am glad to see you. It's just that . . . that I thought Samuel—where is he? Did he come with you?"

"He came with me, but he wandered off." I tried without success to decipher her horrified expression. "Would you prefer to wait for him so that you can swoon into his arms? It's up to you, Buffy. However, I do think it might be wiser for us to leave while we can."

She remained on the edge of the bed, her forehead puckered with irritation. "He wandered off? What does that mean? Where did he go?"

"I have no idea. I assume the two men in the room several doors away are responsible for your incarceration. At the moment, they're engrossed with a soccer match on TV. I suggest we tiptoe past their room and downstairs. The only person I saw was a young woman who looked incapable of letting out the tiniest yelp." I wrapped my hand around Buffy's wrist and yanked her to her feet. "Shall we?"

I had to drag her down the corridor. The floors creaked, but I heard no sounds other than the soccer announcer's voice and another round of cheers. The lobby was unoccupied. Buffy seemed reluctant to move quickly, although she did not appear weak with hunger or suffering from a physical assault. I resisted an impulse to shake her into more active cooperation. She was young and had been through an ordeal for the last forty-eight hours.

As soon as we reached the sidewalk, I propelled her down the side street. We turned again at the alley I was fairly confident would bring us to the car in only a few blocks. "Could you please cooperate?" I said to her, my annoyance growing as I clung to her wrist.

"What about Samuel?" she said mulishly.

"Samuel's a big boy. If we don't spot him before we get to the car, we'll leave him. He can take a bus back to Luxor, or hitch a ride with a caravan. The goal today is to get you—and me—out of here without being killed. It is not to reunite young lovers. You can deal with that at your convenience." I gave her wrist a more forceful yank, eliciting a

squeal of protest. "If your captor is a captivatingly handsome sheik, you can drop him a postcard. You can write him
a love letter in the sand, for that matter." I yanked again,
hoping I didn't dislocate her shoulder. It would be embarrassing if her only injury was caused by me. "There's the
car. Get in and duck."

She froze. I opened the door, shoved her in, and hurried
around to the driver's side. She was sprawled across both
seats, so I pushed her out of my way, slammed my door
closed, and felt for the key under the seat.

"Ow," she said from the floor of the car. "You didn't
have to do that, Mrs. Malloy."

"Stay there and be quiet!" I snapped. I found the key and
started the car. It had been several years since I'd driven a
stick shift, but I eventually ground the gears into reverse
and backed away from the curb. After some more exploration, I managed to convince the car to lurch forward.
"We'll have to stay away from the main street because of
the camel jam. We should be able to get back on it in two or
three blocks. It'll be easy to find the highway from there.
You stay where you are. I don't want anykne to notice your
blond hair."

"We have to find Samuel," she said, glaring at me.

"No, we don't. If you recall, you were the hostage. He's
merely another tourist—in his case, stranded. There are
plenty of tour vans in town. Somebody will give him a lift
to Luxor."

When she tried to get up, I firmly pushed her head down.
It became a bit of a game, since she stealthily assessed her
chances each time I was obliged to shift gears. Eventually, I
turned onto the main road as it headed out to the desert.
"You can get up now," I said, feeling most unfriendly.

"About time," she grumbled as she crawled into the seat.
"It's utterly gross and sticky down there. I'll have to get a
tetanus shot when we get back. If anybody in this country
knows what a tetanus shot is, anyway."

"Perhaps you should express a small degree of gratitude
for being rescued. I didn't have to risk my life for you, much

less a painfully swollen bladder and an ominous realization that there aren't any roadside rest areas between here and Luxor."

"You could pull over somewhere and go behind some rocks," she suggested, overlooking my pointed remark about gratitude. "It's not like this is a California freeway."

I shot her a chilly look. "Speaking of California, you're not from there. You don't live in Sausalito unless your daddy owns a car dealership with an apartment over the body shop."

She let her head flop back and closed her eyes. "Do you have any aspirin? My head is about to implode. I haven't had anything but bread for two days, and my blood sugar is careening. And water—I need water. They gave me a bottle last night, but none since then. I was locked in that room for—I don't know—at least a day and a half. No window, so I couldn't tell for sure if it was day or night. I had to guess from the nosie level of the traffic. It was so gruesome." She turned her face away and whimpered softly. "I thought I was going to die."

I gave up and turned my attention to avoiding potholes while making the best time I could. After a while, I was obliged to stop at the edge of the road. Buffy had not made a sound, but I took the ignition key with me when I carefully made my way behind one of the craggy rock formations.

CHAPTER 15

I parked in front of the Winter Palace, then nudged Buffy, who'd been dozing since my brief pit stop. I'd been imploring every deity I'd ever heard of not to let us run out of gas along the highway. One of them (the Almighty OPEC, perhaps) had allowed us to run on fumes the last few miles.

"Honey, we're home. You can get out of the car now," I said. "Never mind; you're welcome to stay here if you prefer. I myself am going in the hotel." Uninterested in her decision, I slammed the car door and climbed the curved staircase to the lobby. Ahmed stared at me as I put down the car key in front of him. "There's a really ugly car out front. Feel free to have it towed. Is my husband back?"

"No, *Sitt* Malloy-Rosen, he is not. Is this car yours? We have valet parking, if you would like us to—"

"I don't care what you do with it, although you should remove Miss Franz before you do anything drastic."

"Miss Franz who was kidnapped? She is with you? This is wonderful news." His voice dropped and he leaned forward. "Were liberties taken with her person? Should I send for a doctor?"

"You'll have to ask her. Is her luggage still in the basement storage room? I suspect she'd rather have her shampoo and moisturizers than a doctor."

He stood upright and cleared his throat. "About the storage room in the basement, *Sitt* Malloy-Rosen. The Winter

Palace prides itself on taking care of its guests' valued possessions. There have been rumors that you and a young lady, as yet to be identified, were seen—"

"There are always rumors, aren't there?" Smiling brightly, I went to the elevator and willed myself not to look back at him. Once I'd let myself into the suite, I flopped on the sofa and let weariness invade my every nerve and muscle. My back ached from the tension of driving the horrid car through a minefield of potholes and rocks. My neck was a mass of steel rods, and my fingers were numb. My tongue had mutated into thick sandpaper, but I couldn't muster the energy to stagger to the mini-bar and take out a bottle of chilled water.

I allowed myself a couple of minutes, then went into the bedroom. I dialed the number of the police station and repeated Mahmoud's name until I finally breached the protective barriers of bureaucracy and he came on the line. After I finished my terse recital, I listened to the sound of his measured breathing.

"Miss Buffy Franz is in a car parked in front of the Winter Palace?" he said at last.

"I don't know if she is now, but she was ten minutes ago."

"And you rescued her from a hotel room at the Kharga Oasis?"

"That's what I just told you, Mahmoud," I said, trying to be patient. "Her boyfriend, Samuel"—I floundered for a moment, but I'd been up since dawn—"Berry, that's his surname, may still be over there, or he could be on his way back to Luxor."

"And Peter is not aware of any of this?"

I switched the receiver to my other ear. "I don't know how to get in touch with Peter. He went to Cairo yesterday. I was hoping you might have some idea how to contact him."

"Yes, I will try," Mahmoud said. "You are unharmed, I trust. What about the girl?"

"We didn't discuss it, but she appears to be fine. She may have some scratches on her knees from the floorboard of the car. I thought it was better that she not be seen until we were well away from the town. It seemed like a good idea at the time. She may have felt differently about it."

He made a small noise. "I will do everything I can to reach Peter. Will you please stay where you are until I speak again to you? Not just in the hotel, but in the Presidential Suite with the doors locked. I need to assure him that you're safe."

I agreed and hung up. In that Caron and Inez had not appeared when I arrived, I surmised they were elsewhere. I'd left a scribbled note for them, saying only that I would be back in time for tea. It was four o'clock, according to the clock beside the telephone. Since tea was not among their daily rituals at home, they might not be attuned to the time. Disinclined to fret until they returned, I called the desk.

"Ahmed," I said briskly, "in that the Winter Palace prides itself on taking care of its guests' valued possessions and I am a guest, I'd like to report that I'm missing two of mine. They're females, seventeen years of age. Please have a bell-man track them down in the lobby of the New Winter Place, on the terrace, or by the pool, and tell them to get up here immediately. Thank you so much."

I went into the bathroom and took a shower, then wrapped my hair in a towel and slipped into the hotel bathrobe. Feeling much improved, I fetched a bottle of water from the mini-bar and went out to the balcony. I was torn between modest pride at my accomplishment and leeriness at Peter's reaction when he learned about it. Which he probably had by now. I wasn't sure if he would drop everything and fly back to Luxor in order to clasp me in his arms and shower me with admiring kisses—or start investigating the divorce procedure in Egypt. I'd read somewhere that Muslim law required the husband to do little more than utter the fateful sentence three times. Peter had learned enough Arabic at spy camp to handle it in a respectable accent.

I was feeling rather sorry for myself when Caron and Inez burst into the room. "Mother!" Caron shrieked. "You rescued her! Everybody in the hotel is going crazy! Ahmed is going to send you an enormous bouquet of roses. The bellmen all clapped when Inez and I went by them, like we were on the red carpet."

"It was really cool," Inez added, unable to match Caron's fervent pitch but doing her best. "Everybody's coming up to congratulate you." She noticed my attire. "You might want to get dressed."

"Everybody?" I echoed, appalled. "Shouldn't Buffy be getting all the hoopla?"

"That inspector friend of Peter's is in the lobby," Caron said. "As soon as Buffy cleans up, he's going to take her to the police station to get her statement. He told us to remind you to stay here until he can talk to you."

"Did he mention Peter?" I asked.

Caron poked my shoulder. "He didn't say. You've only got a few minutes, Mother. I'll be so humiliated if you don't put on some clothes and makeup. You look like boiled beef."

I was putting on shorts and a shirt when the partygoers arrived. I could hear Lord Bledrock issuing orders to employees about where to arrange the ice, glasses, and bottles. Mrs. McHaver's cane thumped as she swept around the room. Miss Cordelia and Miss Portia laughed shrilly at some remark. I couldn't hear Miriam's voice, but I would have been shocked if I had. Alexander requested orders for drinks. Lady Emerson commented peevishly about food. Furniture scraped as it was dragged in from the balcony. Magritta demanded a martini, easy on the vermouth.

I was considering my chances of slipping out the bedroom door to the hall and scampering downstairs when I heard Sittermann's drawling voice. I was so stunned by his audacity that I was unable to finish buttoning my shirt.

"I learned long before God made little green apples that you can never trust a skinny lawyer or a redheaded woman," he said. "I knew when I first set eyes on Mrs. Malloy that she was a spunky broad. She could grab ol' Satan by the tail and swing him around her head if she had a mind to. She reminds me of this gal I knew up in Amarillo, name of Pearly

Sue. She had a no-good husband what went every Saturday night to get drunk and find himself a cheap hooker. Well, Pearly Sue got mighty fed up, so she bought herself a dinky little chain saw and—"

"Sittermann," Lord Bledrock said sternly, "there are ladies present. You really must watch your language."

"But do continue," said Miss Portia.

I managed the last button and banged open the door to the sitting room. "My goodness," I said in a flat voice. "What a surprise to find all of you here."

Sittermann had the sense to close his mouth and move into a corner. Mrs. McHaver whacked her cane on the coffee table. "We must drink a toast to Mrs. Malloy for her courage and ingenuity. Not all of us would be so foolhardy as to rush into danger without regard to the consequences to ourselves and others."

"Jolly good job," said Lord Bledrock.

The others repeated the sentiment and downed their drinks while I stood and watched. Alexander came to my rescue with a scotch and water and kept his hand on my arm until I was seated in one of the upholstered chairs. Miriam brought me a plate of hors d'oeuvres and a napkin. "You must be exhausted," she whispered.

I was too hungry to answer. Lady Emerson gave me a few minutes to wolf down pastry triangles filled with cheese, grape leaves rolled around rice and minced lamb, and pickled vegetables. "Slow down, Mrs. Malloy," she said. "You're liable to end up with a tummy ache. We're dying to hear what happened at the Kharga Oasis. Buffy was able to tell us some of it in the lobby, before she left with the police inspector to give them a statement. You must have been terrified when the men attacked you in the hall outside her door. She said she nearly fainted when she heard shots."

"Forcing you to not only disarm them but knock them unconscious," said Miriam. "I wouldn't know how to start."

"How many were there?" Mrs. McHaver asked. "Buffy estimated at least six, and possibly more."

"Don't forget the woman in the lobby." Lord Bledrock thumped my shoulder. "She was armed as well. How did you manage to wrest the keys from her?"

I held up my hand. "It wasn't nearly that dramatic."

"Modesty becomes you, Mrs. Malloy," Sittermann said, giving me a sly smile. "Most women would leap at the chance to be heroines, but you just sit there looking all demure. Why, I do believe you're blushing. Ain't that the sweetest thing!"

My face was hot, but not from any feigned exhibition of modesty. Under different circumstances (as he well knew), I would have dashed the contents of my glass in his face, then requested a refill so I could do it again. I forced myself to look away. Caron and Inez were huddled in a corner, both of them more interested in watching than contributing to the blather. Alexander wiggled his eyebrows at me. I was not amused. Magritta and Wallace were in the doorway to the balcony. She nodded, but he was too far into his cups to react.

"You haven't explained, Mrs. Malloy," Mrs. McHaver said. "We're waiting."

"I think," I said, then paused and listened as they all inhaled in anticipation, "that I need another drink."

The next hour was surreal. Given an occasional nod or shrug from me, they formulated a story that would have sold to Hollywood in the twinkling of a producer's eye. Samuel, having received the cryptic message and allowed me to decipher it, had stolen a car and driven to the Kharga Oasis, where he was promptly beaten senseless by thugs and dragged out of the script. I'd stormed the lobby—no, I'd boldly marched into the lobby. Knocked the girl out and tied her up—impossible, too violent—intimidated her with a steely stare (much better). That, of course, wouldn't slow down the half-dozen maniacal bearded henchmen dressed in flowing robes, daggers between their teeth—all right, a shade too much. Uzis were downgraded to pistols. I'd knocked a man down, grabbed his weapon, and ordered all of them into one room. Shots were exchanged (Alexander pointed his finger at Caron and made explosive noises; she retaliated as she threw herself behind a chair) and curses rang through the hall. Buffy, chained to the bed frame— tied up, anyway—quivered with fear as the door flew open (Miriam produced a classy quiver). I fired at a man who'd dared to sneak up behind me—terrorists can be so sneaky—then unlocked, untied, Buffy and literally carried her limp body down the stairs (Inez flung herself into Caron's arms, but Caron wasn't prepared and they both went over with a thud). We dodged bullets (everybody with the exception of Mrs. McHaver and Wallace began firing their index fingers at me; I obligingly twitched) until we reached the stolen car. I flung Buffy's body in the backseat and sped down the narrow streets (lots of engines revved) until we reached the highway. Only then did Buffy regain consciousness and sob with gratitude.

It was time for a round of drinks.

I headed for Sittermann, who ducked behind Miss Portia and Miss Cordelia and joined Mrs. McHaver on the sofa. As long as the room was crowded, he could manage to stay on the far side from me. I conceded defeat for the moment and handed my glass to Alexander.

"Have you heard anything more about Shannon's accident?" I asked him.

"Nothing credible." He poured my drink and dropped in some ice. "You should have called me before you took off with Samuel. I would have gone with you."

"I would never disturb a baron's son before he's had his breakfast," I said. "It just isn't done."

"You could have gotten yourself killed."

"If you'd been along, I could have gotten both of us killed. It's funny, though. I was never in any danger. Despite the fanciful tale of my heroics, all I did was accept the key and go unlock Buffy's door. Nobody tried to stop me. No shots were fired. Buffy was grubby and ill-tempered, but she was okay. I spotted a plate of food and a can of soda under her bed. Maybe she was reluctant to leave because she hadn't finished her lunch."

"She didn't say anything about what happened after the horseman grabbed her and galloped away so dramatically?"

"She didn't say anything, period. No, that's not true. She kept insisting that we ought to wait for Samuel. I wasn't pleased to leave him behind, but he's capable of getting back here on his own. It's not as if we left him on a deserted island . . . and as far as I know, he wasn't mugged." I thought for a while as I sipped my drink. "He was gone for more than thirty minutes. It shouldn't have taken him more than five or ten minutes. The Desert Inn is not a sprawling resort with multiple swimming pools and a golf course."

Alexander shrugged. "The good inspector will find him. There's nothing you can do about it. Where's your friend Salima?"

"Why do you care?" I said. "According to you, she's a brat, isn't she?"

"Yes, I suppose she is. My father is glowering at me over an empty glass. If you'll excuse me, Mrs. Malloy . . ."

I glanced at Sittermann, but I could tell he was keeping an eye on me. I considered making my way toward him just to force him to move, then decided to have a word with Magritta instead. She'd propped Wallace in a corner by now and was drinking steadily, as though she aspired to reach his level of alcohol-induced stupor.

"Were you allowed to go back to work today?" I asked her.

"I wasted the day watching the underling from the antiquities department examine every shard we set aside in the last five years. It's just as well. Without Nabil, I'm going to have to reorganize the crew." She gave me a bleary look. "You may not have heard. Nabil died of heart failure last night. I'm short of funds, but I'll scrape together a small sum for his widow. Wallace is taking it badly, as you can see."

"What's it been, Maggie? Forty years?" he said, moaning. "Forty backbreaking years, and we haven't found a mummy. It wouldn't have to have been a royal. I would have been happy with a dentist or a priest." He hiccuped. "I would have been happy with a mummified cat. Forty years, and not even a damn cat." He hiccuped again, sliding perilously. Magritta caught him and repositioned him. "Not even a damn cat," he repeated as his eyes closed.

"But you might have found the tomb of Ramses VIII," I said to Magritta. "The *shabti* has his name on it, doesn't it?"

"Yes," she said drily, "in layman's terms, anyway."

"And Nabil discovered it at your excavation site."

"That seems to be the consensus."

She wasn't the type to clap her hands with glee, but she was showing no enthusiasm whatsoever. I tried again. "Don't you believe that's where Nabil found it?"

"I'm quite sure he found it there."

"As was Shannon King, right?"

Magritta stared at the bottom of her empty glass. "She believed that's where Nabil found it. That's why she went out there two nights ago. The funny thing is that I almost did, too. I don't buy into any of this supernatural nonsense, but I could hear Oskar forbidding me to go. If there are such things as souls, his is swirling about in the Valley of the Kings. Once he learns ancient Egyptian, he'll hear some fascinating stories from the pharaohs. I hope they're fascinating, anyway. Eternity is a very long time."

Wallace slithered to the floor. She stepped over his outstretched legs and went to the makeshift bar. Caron and Inez joined me.

"These people are obnoxious," Caron said in the scathing tone she used when adults did not behave properly. "Can we lock ourselves in our bedroom?"

"I don't see why not," I said, "as long as you promise not to leave. I have no clue what's going on, but I'm worried. We're going to stick together until Peter gets back from Cairo."

"Are you sure he's coming back?"

My jaw dropped. "Why wouldn't he?"

"He's gotten awfully perturbed in the past when you've meddled," Inez said helpfully.

I was going to point out that rescuing Buffy hardly qualified as mere meddling, but instead sighed and told them to stay in their bedroom until everyone was gone. To my regret, Wallace was the only one who was not having a lovely time. Magritta had perked up and was arguing with Lady Emerson. Miss Portia and Miss Cordelia had captured Sittermann, each of them clinging to an arm and staring up with an adoring smile. Mrs. McHaver was lecturing the room at large about the intolerable delays caused by official paperwork and general bungling. Alexander was in conversation with Miriam, who looked giddy, while Lord Bledrock flourished an unopened bottle of gin above his head as if it were a trophy. The Fitzwillies were nibbling at hors d'oeuvres like piranhas.

I caught my breath when the door opened. An unfamiliar couple came inside and stopped. "Hi," the woman gushed, seizing the nearest elbow, which happened to belong to Lord Bledrock. "We're the Adamses of Morning Glory, Maine. I'm Debbie, and this is Donnie. I believe our son Godfrey was playing cards in the lobby with your"—she looked at him—"granddaughter yesterday."

"How do you do," said Lord Bledrock helplessly.

She wiggled her fingers at Sittermann. "When Mr. Sittermann found out we live in Maine, he asked if we knew MacLeod College. I told him it was the funniest coincidence, because our oldest daughter went to MacLeod and graduated two years ago with a degree in musicology. We didn't know Dr. King, since she was in a different department, but Donnie and I feel awful just the same. Mr. Sittermann insisted that we come up here and share our fond memories with all of you."

"And have a drink," Donnie said. "I could use a drink."

"By all means," Lord Bledrock said, inching away from the woman. "Alexander is our bartender. He's my son."

Mrs. Adams realized she'd stuck her foot in something. She and Donnie went to the bar and waited in mute apprehension until Alexander came over to make them drinks. Minutes later, three teenaged boys peered into the room. Sittermann boomed at them to make themselves at home. I knocked on the door to Caron and Inez's room and suggested they come out to entertain their poker friends. Had the hallway been wide enough, I had no doubt Sittermann would have arranged for a tour bus to stop outside the suite and spew out its passengers.

I squeezed through the crowd and sat down next to Wallace. "You and me," I said, patting his knee, "alone at last."

"Not even a damn cat," he mumbled.

The party broke up only when Chief Inspector el-Habachi came into the room several hours later and announced that he needed the room to be vacated so he could question me. Mrs. Adams, who'd not figured out who Lord Bledrock was but had figured out how to replenish her drink, threw herself around the old boy's neck and hugged him until his eyes bulged. Purses were gathered up from the floor. Miss Portia and Miss Cordelia cackled as Sittermann offered to escort them to their room. Mrs. McHaver thumped out, trailed by Miriam. The girls wistfully said good-bye to the boys. Lord Bledrock gave the hotel employee a thick wad of notes and told him to clean up the room. Magritta was still arguing with Lady Emerson about an obscure site with a convoluted name as they staggered out the door.

The evacuation took ten minutes. I at last stood up and made sure Sittermann hadn't found a way to sneak back in and slither under the sofa. "Oh, Mahmoud," I said as I emerged from my hiding place, "I'm so glad to see you. They're insane, all of them. They talk so loudly while consuming an astonishing quantity of alcohol. Not one of them would have bothered to look at me if I screamed 'Fire!' Shall we put the chairs back on the balcony and sit out there while the room is cleaned?"

"An excellent idea." He picked up one chair and I dragged the other. Once we were seated, he said, "There's a man on the floor in the corner. Do you know him?"

"Wallace Laxenby, the photographer," I said. "I was using him for a backrest. I don't know what we ought to do with him. He's not staying at this hotel. Magritta left with Lady Emerson." I leaned back and peeked at the curled figure. "I suppose we can just leave him there. What do you think?"

Mahmoud shrugged. "It's your suite. Would you like a drink before room service takes away the ice?"

"Ice water would be nice," I admitted, "with a splash of scotch." I leaned back and gazed at the moon, obscured by clouds yet making its presence known. "Did you talk to Peter?"

Mahmoud returned to the balcony with my drink. "He will arrive back in Luxor tomorrow at five o'clock. I told him that Aisha was eager to meet you and hoped you might come for dinner, but he said that it would be better if you and he had some privacy. Caron and Inez are still invited. Unless they object, Bakr will be outside the hotel at five to drive them to my house and drive them back here at ten."

"Is he really pissed?"

"I'm not familiar with that word in that context, but if you're asking if he's angry, yes, very much so. He did not shout or curse, of course. He spoke quietly and politely. That may have been because he was in the ambassador's reception room."

"Ah well." I propped my feet on the rail, cradling my drink in my hands. "Magritta told me that Nabil didn't survive. Did you find out if he used methamphetamines?"

"His family and those he worked with all agreed that he would not knowingly use such drugs. His wife told me that he was reluctant to apply an herbal liniment when his muscles were sore. At your husband's suggestion, we sent the clothes Nabil was wearing to our lab. They found traces of loose tobacco in his pocket. He rarely smoked, but he would accept a cigarette if it was offered to him."

"The tobacco was laced with the drug?"

"So it seems. Someone gave him the cigarette, and he saved it for a later time. He was ecstatic when he found the *shabti* in the rubble in the pit. He wrapped it carefully and headed here as quickly as he could. Along the way, he smoked the cigarette to calm his nerves, although it had the opposite effect. He became increasingly excited as he imagined his entrance with this priceless treasure. His heart was pounding, and it's likely he was having difficulty breathing by the time he raced up the service stairs and along the hall to Lord Bledrock's suite."

"How did he know where it was?" I asked. "I don't imagine he was familiar with the hotel layout."

"An employee in the basement told him," Mahmoud said. "He shouldn't have, but Nabil was respected in working-class circles. He said Nabil was jabbering like a madman, waving his hands and unable to stand still."

"And when he finally opened the door of the suite, his heart crashed," I murmured. "He never got to present Magritta with the *shabti*. All those years they toiled together in the heat and dirt, praying to come upon something of significance. How very sad."

"His only brush with fame was a photo of him taken ten years ago at a dig at Saqqara and published in *KMT,* an Egyptology journal. It was framed and hung in a place of honor in his house. He was in the background with a dozen workmen, but his wife pointed him out."

"The question is who might haven given him the lethal cigarette, "I said.

Mahmoud shrugged. "The workmen said he was always fair about assigning tasks and did his share. No trouble with family members or neighbors. He was devout, but not to excess. This was not a crime of passion or personal vengeance. I think we have to conclude the motive lies with those involved in the excavation."

"All of the people who were here when you arrived were at the dig that afternoon," I said. "Not the couple from Maine, who were invited by the elusive Mr. Sittermann—which he did to annoy me."

Mahmoud rumbled under his breath. "Sittermann is elusive, as you said. There is no record of him entering the country, so we cannot verify any information from his passport. He has been to the Cairo offices of several ministries that oversee foreign development and tourism. They've met him, but no one has seen his credentials."

"Why didn't you take him into custody when you arrived here?" I demanded.

"For what reason? We have laws to protect the populace from police harassment and unlawful confinement, as you do in your country. Until he has broken a law, we can do nothing about him."

"Are you keeping him under surveillance?"

"With limited success, I am sorry to say. We have even assigned undercover agents to follow him into hotels and nightclubs. One night he waved them over and offered to buy them drinks. When he doesn't seem to care, my men have no problem sticking with him. When he wishes to be rid of them, he vanishes." Mahmoud rocked back in his chair and glanced at me. "Do you know of any laws he may have broken?"

I shook my head. "If I think of something, I'll let you know. Are you planning to question the Brits and Americans?"

"They'll be asked if they saw anyone give something to Nabil, but I have small hope anyone will say something of significance. You saw for yourself the babbling and confusion at the site. Many people were already in the Valley when we managed to have the entrance closed. Others"—he smiled at me—"bullied their way in. But yes, we will question all of them tomorrow. At the moment, I'm hiding out from my superiors, government representatives from Cairo, and the media. The young woman's abduction and daring rescue make a more compelling story than the death of a local workman."

"What did Buffy have to say about her ordeal? If she was traumatized, she disguised it well."

"Miss Franz explained at length how she was too exhausted to remember all the details. She was also upset about split ends, although she would not elaborate. Is that the same as loose ends?"

"No," I said, twirling a curl at him.

Mahmoud nodded thoughtfully. "Split ends. I must remember that. Anyway, her recitation was disjointed, which
is why I'm so late getting here. After she insisted on being
brought back to the hotel, I spread out all my notes and tried
to put them in a logical sequence." He pressed his fingertips
together and propped his chin on them, looking like a professor confronted with a paradox. "On the morning you were
at Wadi es Sebua, she decided to go ahead of your group in
order to find a place to sit in the shade and file a broken fingernail. The two horsemen rode up, and one of them made
some kind of remark in English. She described it as a
'smart-ass pickup line.' Whatever she said in response an-
gered them. One of them grabbed her arm and yanked her
across his saddle. She made it clear that this was extremely
uncomfortable and offered to show me bruises on her ab-
domen. I declined. After a long while of being jounced, she
was allowed to get down and have a drink of water. She
voiced her displeasure with such passion that her hands were
secured behind her and a cloth bag was put over her head."

I could almost hear Buffy describing the scene to Mahmoud, who must have been biting his lip. "Does she know
where they took her?"

"The first night they slept in a rocky recess in a mountain.
The second day they came to a road and a cluster of mud-
brick huts. Miss Franz was permitted a short amount of time
for personal concerns, then was tossed in the backseat of a
car. She remained bound with her head covered while they
drove to the Kharga Oasis. She was very vague about how
she ended up in the hotel room. She claims she passed out
from the heat and the tainted air in the bag. When she regained consciousness, she was lying on the bed. She didn't
see anyone until you unlocked the door."

"She has no idea who these men were?" I asked. "Did either of them speak English?"

"She says not. Her description could fit half the young
men in this country. The military has sent men along the
road south of Kharga to identify the place where she was
transferred to a car. I won't be surprised if the huts have

been abandoned for decades. They're used only by passing travelers who want to exercise or rest in the shade for a few minutes."

I did not say that I would have been thrilled beyond my wildest expectations had I seen similar huts on the highway coming back from Kharga. Mahmoud had spent enough time with Peter to share his disapproval of my more creative escapades. The relationship between husband and wife deserved discretion, but cops blabbed to one another like mouthy kindergartners. I wasn't about to mention my undignified moment behind a rock.

"No one saw her being carried inside?"

"There's a kitchen door that opens onto an alley. They could have transferred in a matter of seconds. The police over there went to the Desert Inn and searched the premises. The property is owned by an old man with cloudy eyes and a mind that no longer functions well. His daughter said the only guests were two men who arrived yesterday afternoon. She prepared food for them. The police found them in the room. They claimed to be itinerant laborers heading for Cairo to find work at a construction site. They were planning to take a bus north in the morning, and were unaware of an American girl in another room."

"Did they admit seeing me in the corridor?" I asked.

"They told the police they heard footsteps and went to look. They concluded that you were a crazy foreigner, German or French, possibly a prostitute. They were debating whether or not to tell the daughter when Kenya scored a goal. After that, they said they forgot the incident."

"Those jerks," I muttered. The ghastly drive across the desert to Kharga had played havoc with my hair, and I'd been too focused on rescuing Buffy to put on lipstick after our arrival. I had not been at my most becoming. By no means, however, had I resembled a prostitute of any nationality. I went inside the parlor, glowered at Wallace, and added a few drops of scotch to my watery drink.

"Buffy was lying," I said as I returned. "She called

Samuel on a cell phone. She had food and water. Someone came into the room."

"The daughter. She was afraid she'd get into trouble with the police if she admitted she knew Buffy was there. She swore she had no idea why the men put Buffy in the room and locked the door. As for the cell phone, she doesn't have one because of the expense. The police found one in the room the men were staying in, but the younger one claimed he found it in the street and didn't know how to make it work. One of the policemen verified that its battery was dead."

Neither Mahmoud nor I was satisfied with anyone's story, including Buffy's. We picked at the more glaring holes, then gave up for the night. Before he left, he made me promise to stay on the hotel premises and within arm's reach of Caron and Inez until Peter returned. When I asked if I should consider myself under house arrest, he merely chuckled.

Wallace was snoring in the corner. I propped a pillow under his head, went to Caron and Inez's room to warn them not to be alarmed if they heard peculiar noises during the night, and collapsed in bed.

It had been one long day.

CHAPTER 16

"This is stupid," Caron grumbled as we trudged downstairs for breakfast, less than thrilled at the opportunity to appreciate my company all day. "We were stuck here yesterday while you were off pretending to be Indiana Jones. Now we're stuck here today as well. I don't see why we can't go anywhere until Peter gets back. What if he decides to stay in Cairo another day or two?"

"Couldn't we at least go to Luxor Temple?" said Inez. "I didn't have a chance to take pictures of the barque shrine of Alexander the Great. There's a relief of him dressed like a pharaoh."

I herded them out to the patio. "We are not going to Luxor Temple or anyplace else. There's something going on that seems to involve the excavation in the Valley of the Kings. Two people have been murdered, three if you count Oskar Vonderlochen last spring."

"I thought his fall was determined to be an accident," Inez said, covertly checking the other tables to see if the boys were there. "Alexander may not have agreed, but he didn't give a reason."

"He was just trying to get Mother's attention," Caron said coolly. "Remember that new sophomore last year who told everybody she was an orphan and lived in a cardboard box in the woods? Everybody felt so sorry for her until one of the teachers heard the story and went to the principal. It turned

out she was mad at her parents because they wouldn't let her
get a learner's permit. How lame can you get?"

I ordered coffee from a waiter and sent the girls to the
buffet. I wasn't looking forward to spending the day with
them either, but I didn't want to risk anything that might
further corrode my relationship with Peter. Why he ever believed a wedding ring would transform me into a meek little
wife eluded me. We'd bumped heads so often in the past
that I knew the contours of his skull. I was reflecting on this
when I saw Salima's face appear between two flowerpots
set on the low wall. She scanned the terrace, then agilely
hopped over the wall and strolled over to the table.

"Had to make sure the waiters didn't see me," she said as
she sat down. "I refuse to pay the exorbitant price for breakfast. It costs as much as dinner in Cairo. Maybe Caron or
Inez will let me have a roll."

"Where have you been lately?" I asked.

"Here and there, but not risking my life to save a rather
vapid girl. You're quite the talk of Luxor. If you want to
hold a press conference, I'll be your interpreter. I did it once
for one of your senators. He was on a fact-finding mission,
he said, although I don't know what facts he thought he'd
find in a hotel room with his virile young aide."

"No press conference," I said.

She made a face, then beamed at the girls as they sat
down. "Good morning, my darlings. Would one of you mind
popping back inside to get me a glass of grapefruit juice and
a toasted muffin? I haven't had a bite to eat all day."

"It's nine o'clock," Inez said.

"But I've been up for hours and hours," Salima said.
"Butter and marmalade, and also a few turkey sausages."

Inez obligingly trooped back inside.

Caron went trolling for sympathy. "We have to stay at
the hotel all day," she said to Salima. "We can't even go
across the street and look at the shops there."

"You poor, deprived creature." Salima gave me a face-
tiously stern look. "Can't you see how her fingers are itching

to caress a price tag? What about the local economy? Think of all the shop owners' children who will go to bed tonight with growling bellies. What if all tourists felt this way?"

I tossed my napkin at her. "Your brow is beading with compassion and your nose beginning to run with pathos. Maybe this will help."

She laughed and tossed the napkin back to me. A waiter set a coffee cup in front of her and glided away. "He used to date my cousin," she said in a low voice. "He wouldn't dare report me to hotel security. I do think it's best for me to avoid the lobby for a while. That pompous twit of a manager has the preposterous idea that I was involved in a breach of security in the hotel's basement a few nights ago. Can you imagine such a ridiculous thing? I, renowned lecturer at Cairo University, noted expert on mummified animals, am not a master criminal."

"Why would you be in the basement?" Caron asked. She glanced at me. "You were both there, weren't you? I don't even want to know why."

"Probably not," I said.

Inez returned with a plate for Salima. I was about to fetch one for myself when Alexander leaned over my shoulder and refilled my coffee cup. "Good morning, ladies," he said. "You're all looking lovely. Mrs. Malloy, allow me to wait upon you. Rolls? A freshly made omelet with herbs and cheese? Something more typical of Egyptian breakfast fare? Whatever madam wishes, she shall have."

"Won't you join us?" I said. It was a formality, since he was already taking a chair from a nearby table. "Did everyone make it home safely last night?"

"A party?" Salima scowled ferociously. "How could there be a party if I was not invited?"

"No one was invited." I went into the buffet and gazed without interest at the spread. I took a croissant and a few spoonfuls of things, then went back to the table. "Did it occur to any of you that you waltzed off without Wallace?" I asked Alexander.

"Did we?" Alexander rubbed his forehead. "I don't re-call seeing the chap. Was he there?"

Caron gave him a disapproving look. "Until three in the morning, when he stumbled into our room and fell across the bed. Inez and I put him out in the hall. I guess Abdullah found him and did something with him."

"How curious," said Alexander. He tore my croissant in half and began to butter it. "Magritta usually keeps track of him, but she's been distracted since the discovery of the *shabti*. When we went to the Valley yesterday, she was in a foul mood because of the forced delay while the bureau-crats from Cairo pick through boxes of chips and slivers of pottery. That grad student—Jess, I think—didn't show up, although there really isn't anything he or the crew can do until they get official approval to continue."

"He wasn't in my suite last night," I said.

Alexander took the remainder of the croissant. "Magritta has to socialize with her financial backers, but Jess doesn't. I suspect he prefers the cheap restaurants and nightclubs, where he'll run into other American students if he's lucky. He doesn't seem to be terribly interested in the pharaonic era."

"Will he have to stay now?" asked Inez, looking as though she might apply for the position if it became avail-able. "Will MacLeod College continue to sponsor the con-cession without Dr. King?"

"I should think so," Salima said. "A week ago, maybe not. Shannon was clearly the driving force, badgering peo-ple such as my father and Mrs. McHaver for money, writ-ing journal reports about the progress. She reminded me of a rabid fan on the sidelines of a football match when her team was losing. Badly." She stopped to pour the last of the coffee into her cup. "The uncovering of the step was prom-ising, but there was no strong indication that there might be a tomb remaining to be found. The *shabti* is something al-together different. Quite a coincidence, appearing at a time when MacLeod might have been weighing the possibility of giving up its concession. I do believe we need more coffee if we're going to stay here."

"Well, I'm not," Alexander said, rising. "I look forward to seeing you lovely ladies in the future. Good day."

Salima banged down her cup. "What an egotistical cad he is! He didn't say one word to me. This chair could have been empty, for all he noticed." She slumped back and stuck out her lower lip. Her expression reminded me of a balky camel.

"Mother," Caron said, "there's something we have to tell you."

"In private," Inez added. "Upstairs would be better."

"In case you start yelling or something. You probably will."

"Fine," I said. I couldn't imagine what they could have done of such astonishing magnitude that I would explode. I hadn't been with them night and day, but I trusted them not to sneak out of the hotel at night. They weren't always as candid and straightforward as I would have liked. However, I wasn't exactly an exemplary role model.

"I adore secrets," Salima said. "If I can't come upstairs, I shall have no choice but to fling myself in the Nile to be mauled by crocodiles. Could you sleep at night knowing you were responsible? Didn't I take you to the most expensive shops and get you discounts? Didn't I make up all sorts of lurid stories about human sacrifices in the name of Ra and Osiris? Does my heartfelt affection mean nothing to you?"

"You can come," Caron said. "You'll probably yell at us, too."

Salima refused to go through the lobby to the elevator, so we climbed the stairs. Abdullah was in the suite, restocking the bar with bottles and cans of soda.

"Coffee or tea, *Sitt?*" he asked. When I shook my head, he left without strewing any pearls of wisdom.

I sat down on the sofa. "Well?"

Caron gave Inez a panicky look, then took a deep breath.

"It sort of goes back to when I told you our room was searched," she began.

"Ah!" Salima said. "That explains it. I think I'll call room service for champagne and orange juice. We must celebrate with a mimosa." The rest of us gaped at her. "Or not," she continued airily. "It was just a suggestion. Even I think it's too early for a martini, although I have been up for several hours and it must be the cocktail hour in Hong Kong by now."

"What's going on?" I pointed at Inez. "See if you can find a better place to start."

Inez took off her glasses and cleaned them on the hem of her T-shirt. "The night we went to Salima's house for the birthday party. We told you about the nightclub in the hotel and that man who was after us."

"He really was," Caron said, slathering on sincerity with such fervor that I knew the story was going to be ludicrous, "and we really were scared."

I turned back to Inez. "Continue."

"And all the stuff about how he chased us—"

"—down dark alleys, where rabid dogs snarled at us," said Caron, "and we had to fight to escape street thugs who would have dragged us into an empty building and tortured us until we passed out from the pain."

Inez frowned at her. "Or something like that. So we hid behind some rocks next to the road. It's just that after the donkey cart and those men stopped, then went on down the hill . . . we sort of didn't mention that we found something." She looked so miserable that I almost wanted to give her a hug, but I wasn't sure I might lose my resolve and strangle both her and Caron.

"A little blue Egyptian figurine?" chirped Salima.

"How do you know?" muttered Caron.

"A wild guess, darling. I have an uncanny knack for such things."

I was now in the mood to strangle all three of them and ask Abdullah to dispose of the bodies in a way that would not sully the hotel's reputation. "Could you please explain for my benefit?" I said coldly. "Without any interruptions? This is worse than a cable show with commercials every three minutes. That's not to imply we've had three minutes thus far. Salima, I will put you out in the hall and hold the door closed if necessary."

Salima flopped into a chair, opened her mouth, then thought better of it and began to inspect her fingernails.

"Yeah, a figurine," Caron said. "We thought it was just another trinket for tourists. They're for sale at all the shops and kiosks near the sites. It had some hieroglyphs on it that made it different. We kept trying to research them on the Internet, but we didn't get anywhere."

"Inez wasn't e-mailing her parents all that time?"

"I e-mailed them a few times," Inez said, gulping. "I told them what we did each day, but that was about it. I didn't mention the stalker because I knew my mother would get hysterical and call the American Embassy. My brother rents all these movies about terrorists trying to blow up New York City and Los Angeles."

"May I assume this figurine was a *shabti*?" I asked carefully.

"Yeah," Caron said. "The one we found was faded blue. The head had been broken off."

"Why didn't you mention it to Peter and me?"

"Or me?" chirped Salima.

"I don't know. It was kinda cool to have found it the way we did. We didn't think it was worth anything."

"A souvenir of that night," Inez said. "When we got back to school, we could tell the story and then show it as proof. It wasn't made out of plastic and it looked really old."

I stared at Salima. "Is this the *shabti* that was found at the excavation?"

"There is only one way to be sure of that." She stood up and gestured to the girls. "Let's knock up Lord Bledrock."

"What?" Caron gasped.

"I beg your pardon. That's Brit speak for tapping on his door to ascertain if he's awake. You Yanks have some very peculiar obsessions concerning sexual conduct. Come along. We don't want to miss him."

Caron, Inez, and I trailed her to the far end of the hall, then waited as she knocked him up (so to speak). He came to the door in a bathrobe, his hair damp and droplets of toothpaste foam dotting his mustache.

"Good morning," he said, his eyes darting from one to another of us. "I say, have I forgotten something? It's possible that last night we agreed upon a time to engage in some activity, but I must admit I have no memory of it. I wish I could say I've forgotten that uncouth woman who kept flinging herself on me while her husband slapped me on the back as if I were choking on a bit of gristle. I fear they shall haunt my dreams for years. Do tell me if they mentioned when they're leaving Luxor."

"Nothing like that, you silly old thing," Salima said, laughing. "Hmm, how nice and clean you smell, and you're all rosy from your bath. If we didn't have witnesses, I would be tempted to shove you into the room and tear off your robe."

He twinkled at her. "Miss el-Musafira, my dear girl. Shall I send them away?"

"Ask her what she wants," came Alexander's voice from inside the room. "Start with a shilling."

I nudged Salima out of the doorway and said, "I hope we're not disturbing you, Lord Bledrock. My daughter and her friend didn't have a chance to see the *shabti*. They're both terribly interested in Egyptian antiquities."

"Yeah," Caron said without enthusiasm. "Terribly interested."

Lord Bledrock made an effort to regain his composure. "Certainly. Bring them in. You can wait here with Alexander while I get dressed; then I'll open the safe. I'm always delighted when young people show an interest in Egyptology. My son doesn't even recall when he saw his first mummy. It was an insignificant pharaoh's wife, I admit, but all the same . . ." He went into the bedroom and closed the door.

Alexander opened a newspaper. "Making your round of morning calls? I don't believe we have a silver tray by the door, but you can leave your cards on the table."

"We came by to show the *shabti* to the girls," I said mildly.

"Of course you did." He turned to the next page.

"What's wrong with you?" demanded Salima. "Half an hour ago you were oozing charm like a cheap gigolo. Now you're all snooty, as if we've broken some unspoken rule of etiquette by daring to invade your personal space! Would you prefer that we wait in the hall? We'll leave it up to you to explain *that* to your father."

Worried that Caron and Inez might start applauding, I said, "Why don't you let your father know that we'll be down in my room until he's ready for company? Come along, girls."

"What, what?" Lord Bledrock said as he came out of the bedroom, now dressed in a suit and a pale blue tie. "Please, Claire, do sit here on the sofa. Would you care to have a cup of tea? Room service will be here any moment. Little Salima, how you've blossomed. Even when you were a child, you had striking dark eyes and delicate features. I knew you'd turn out to be a fine filly."

Salima gave Alexander a sly smile. "Lord Bledrock, you are too kind. Do you think we could have a peek at the *shabti*?"

"I took it out of the safe in my bedroom closet." He opened a small wooden box and drew back a piece of flannel. "Isn't it remarkable? Ramses VIII was the seventh pharaoh of the twentieth dynasty. Almost nothing is known about him, and his reign lasted no more that two years at the most. All we have is an inscription at Medinet Habu. But now it seems we may have found his tomb. Just imagine if no tomb robbers ever stumbled across it and it's as it was more than four thousand years ago. The sarcophagi, the jewelry, the coffin, the mask—and the mummy!" He thrust the box into Caron's hand and turned away, his shoulders heaving.

"Good heavens, Father," Alexander said reproachfully. "Don't make a spectacle of yourself in front of the ladies and Miss el-Musafira. When it comes down to it, a mummy's just a pile of old bones wrapped in rotting linen."

Caron and Inez were staring at the headless *shabti*. Caron looked up at me and nodded. Salima took the box from Caron and moved nearer the window to study it more closely. "Magnificent," Salima murmured. "The cartouche is well defined. The prenomen is Akhenamon, so it really must be from the tomb of Ramses VIII. I'm amazed the Supreme Council of Antiquities has allowed you to keep it in your possession. Has anyone arrived from the Cairo Museum?"

Lord Bledrock blew his nose. "They're descending like jackals, slobbering to get their hands on this precious treasure. Had so many not been aware of its discovery, it might have found a safer home. A much safer home."

"In a castle in Kent?" I suggested.

"Who can say?" He took the box from Salima and reverently replaced the flannel before closing the lid. "I must tuck him back in the safe. Only I know the combination, which I set myself, but if something were to happen to me, hotel security has a master code. The chaps from Cairo will be here this afternoon to take possession. I long for the good old days, when benefactors were rewarded for their investment."

Salima arched her eyebrows. "When benefactors carried off whatever they could stuff in their pockets? Lord Carnarvon and his friends looted King Tut's tomb. So many priceless pieces are now in foreign museums or in the lairs of private collectors, pieces that are key to the Egyptian heritage."

"Balderdash!" Lord Bledrock said. "You know as well as I that this may well end up in a cardboard box in the basement of the Cairo Museum. If people can't take proper care of their heritage, they don't deserve to have one!" He stomped into his bedroom and slammed the door.

"Now look what you've gone and done," chided

Alexander. "You could have cajoled him into making a nice donation to your little exhibit at the museum, perhaps enough to buy some glass cleaner to polish those smudgy display cases."

Salima hissed something at him in Arabic, and he replied. Aware that they were not exchanging compliments, I dragged Caron and Inez out of the room. "Your language book doesn't cover everything, does it?" I asked Inez.

"I don't think we need a translation," she said.

"I wish they'd stop behaving like adolescents," Caron said as I unlocked the door. "Now do you believe someone searched our room? If you'd listened to us the first time, instead of making rude remarks, I would have told you what was missing."

"I asked you at the time, and you said nothing," I pointed out. "You can't claim candor in retrospect."

She rolled her eyes and grimaced for my benefit. "So what are we going to do all day? Watch nature shows on TV? Play cards? Throw furniture off the balcony and bet on how high it bounces?"

I was still annoyed that they hadn't mentioned the *shabti* before we went on the cruise. Now they'd clearly decided on their excuse, fine-tuned it, and would stick to it no matter what I said. I couldn't ground them. I could send them to their room, but they probably would hang out there all afternoon in any case.

The best I could come up with was a petty display of maternal authority. "Go get your room picked up," I said. "Put away the clean clothes, make a pile of dirty clothes to be laundered, and organize what you've bought. I'm going to sit on the balcony and read. Don't even think about slipping out through your room to go down to the lobby. When the mood strikes, I'll be in to assess your progress."

Caron nodded. "Okay, and we're really sorry we didn't tell you and Peter about the *shabti*. We didn't think it was valuable, so we wrapped it in tissue paper and put it in a drawer with our other souvenirs."

"That's the truth, Mrs. Malloy," Inez said, her eyes blinking solemnly.

I gave each of them a kiss on the cheek. "If that was an apology, I accept it. Now get busy with your clothes."

I found a mystery novel and made myself comfortable on the balcony, but I was unable to concentrate on the tidy English village and the obliging suspects who dropped by for tea. I closed my eyes and envisioned *shabtis* on a chessboard, moving from square to square as I considered possibilities and combinations. There were too many hands rearranging the blue playing pieces, I thought glumly. I knew I was being manipulated as well. Sittermann seemed to be a grand master, but he was not the only one involved in what was an increasingly nasty situation.

Peter wouldn't be back until five. I considered calling Mahmoud, but it seemed likely that he had written me off as a reckless busybody with an overly active imagination. Which was not an unreasonable opinion, I admitted as I wandered into the girls' bedroom. There was a marginal improvement in the decor, although several crumpled pairs of shorts and filthy socks were in the middle of the floor. Inez was on the bed, reading *The Savage Sheik,* her toes curled and her expression glazed. Caron was peeling the price tag off the sole of a sandal.

"I'm going to call room service for coffee and rolls," I said. "Would you like anything?" Neither of them looked up. I went back into the sitting room and placed the order, adding some pastries. When Abdullah came into the suite, I asked him to carry the tray to the balcony.

"A very nice day, *Sitt*," he murmured.

"You're exuding disapproval," I said to him. "Is it because I appear to keep having parties while my husband is gone?"

"It is not for me to offer judgment. I do not always understand the way of American women. If this is the way they choose to behave, then they should do so. I have seen some of the television shows. America is very different from Egypt."

"I can't argue with that. Do you have daughters, Abdullah? Did they stay at home behind the shutters until you chose husbands for them?"

"Few families are that traditional these days, *Sitt* Malloy. One of my daughters is a nurse in Alexandria, and another does secretarial duties for Lady Emerson. The youngest is in Paris, studying art history and hoping to work at a museum when she completes her degree."

"I'm impressed that you were able to pay for their educations," I said.

"I have always been a frugal man. Is there anything else you would like?"

I wanted him to sit down and tell me more about his life, but I suspected I'd have more luck trying to chat with the pot of fig jam on the tray. "Yes, I'd like to ask you something else. It's not personal, I promise. Did the police find the taxi driver who took Dr. King to the Valley of the Kings?"

"Yes, but he was unable to answer their questions."

"Why not, Abdullah? He didn't do something to her, did he?"

Abdullah hesitated. "They found Sobny in his taxi behind an abandoned house several miles from Luxor. His throat had been slashed. Usually one hears rumors of men boasting or spending more money than they should, but there has been not one word about this crime. Those who have been known to do such things in the past have been questioned by the police and released. It is very curious. People are nervous, afraid to speak about it."

"Was he robbed?" I asked, trying not to shudder.

"He had American money in his pocket, more than two hundred dollars. The police also found Dr. King's room key, which had slipped between the seats." Abdullah bowed slightly. "I will spend the rest of today cleaning the carpet and floor in the hall. It appears that beverages were spilled last night. There is an unpleasant smell."

I followed him to the door and locked it behind him. It was comforting to know I had a bodyguard outside the room, even if he was as ancient as the colossi protecting the temple at Abu Simbel. I went to the balcony and peered down. This side of the hotel was highly visible from the terrace, the sidewalk, and the corniche. Scaling it with ropes and hooks would work only in a mindless action movie.

I took a few deep breaths, poured myself a cup of coffee, and dedicated myself to the dastardly deeds of the vicar's wife, whose pen was as dangerous as her tongue. Caron and Inez joined me and finished the pastries. Inez offered to teach me how to play poker, and I reluctantly agreed.

I'd lost all of my dried figs and was down to a single date when the telephone rang. "Don't touch that date," I said as I went into the sitting room and answered the phone, dearly hoping it was not Peter with an infinitely reasonable explanation why he was stuck in Cairo for another month.

"Mrs. Malloy?" cooed a voice. "This is Buffy. I'm not disturbing you, am I? Now that I've had time to rest and get all clean, I realize that I was hideously ungrateful yesterday. I should have been slobbering all over you like a lost puppy, but I was too upset to think straight. Could I come and apologize in person?"

"You're not going to slobber all over me, are you?"

"Good heavens, no," she said, laughing. "I went to one of the shops by the hotel and bought you a gift. It's not nearly adequate to pay you back for everything you did for me, but those men took my purse and I don't have any credit cards. Maybe when I get back to Rome, American Express will have my replacement card and I can find something extra special for you. If you give me your home address, I'll mail it to you."

"We'll discuss that later. Yes, you may come to the suite. Be careful when you get off the elevator; the floor may be damp."

I told the girls about the call. Caron went to comb her hair, but Inez sat back and said, "You didn't tell us much about what happened to her. Are you sure she wasn't taken to the camp of a sheik with a volatile temper and blazing eyes? Maybe she's afraid to admit she was drawn to his animal passion and they made love on silken cushions beneath a sky of glittering diamonds."

"I'm sorry to say she slept on a flea-ridden blanket the first night, and was then locked in a dingy hotel room the size of a closet. When are you going to finish that infernal book? Your mother's going to blame me if you come home with all these fantasies. As you're so fond of pointing out, she already has reservations about me."

"When I read *Gone With the Wind,* my father claimed my accent was so syrupy that he couldn't understand half of what I said." She wiggled her eyebrows at me. "Vicarious thrills. What's so fascinating about the sheik is that I'm pretty sure he's not truly an Arab. His complexion is lighter, and he buys cases of imported wine and plays operas on a gramophone. The English lady doesn't realize that's why she's in love with him. It's actually very racist. Back when the book was written, it was unthinkable that any civilized woman could get hot and bothered over someone from an inferior race."

"So why is he pretending to be an Arab?" I asked.

"I don't know yet. What's more, I don't think she's really the daughter of a duke or whatever she keeps saying. She's pretending, too. It'd be a lot better if they were honest with each other, but if they were, it would be a very short book."

"And therefore nobody would have bought it and the author would have faded into obscurity, along with a lot of other authors. What a ghastly thought."

CHAPTER 17

Buffy handed me a small cloth pouch with a drawstring. "I wish I could have bought you perfume or jewelry. The American Express lady in Cairo said they'd cover the hotel bill, but they can't advance much cash. I'm going to have to charge everything to the room until I get a new card."

I poured a silver chain and tiny charm out of the bag. "Very nice," I said.

"It's an ankh, the hieroglyph for 'life.' The guy at the shop said it's a symbolic depiction of genitalia, but he was being snide. It doesn't have anything to do with Christianity, even though it looks like a weird cross."

I handed it to Inez, who said, "I should get some of these to give to my cousins. My brother's getting a cockroach I caught in our room. I'm going to tell him it's a scarab."

"It's dead," Caron said. "Wrap it in toilet paper and tell him it was mummified."

Buffy winced. "I'm sure he'll love it. Anyway, Mrs. Malloy, I do want to thank you for everything you did yesterday. I don't know why you risked your life for me, but I am so unbelievably grateful. Those horrible men were going to take me to an oasis way out in the desert. They probably knew some fat old bedouin who'd buy me for a sex slave. Nobody would have ever heard from me again."

"The men spoke English?" I said.

"No. I mean, I don't think they did. I overheard one of them say something about Oasis al-Farafra. Samuel made me go there with him after we arrived in Egypt. It was awful, nothing but mud-brick huts and springs with sulphur water. The bus from Cairo took ten hours. Ten long, sweltering hours with people who hadn't bathed in weeks."

"You seemed to be reluctant to leave Samuel behind at Kharga," I said, trying to sound casual. "That was thoughtful of you, since I was under the impression the two of you weren't the happiest of traveling companions. Didn't he warn you about his plans when you first met in Rome?"

"Sort of, but I didn't pay much attention. I was so bored in Rome with all the lectures and guided tours. It's not like we were a bunch of high school kids"—she winked at Caron and Inez—"who'd get into trouble if we explored on our own. We actually had a curfew, if you can imagine. Once, when we were supposed to have a private audience with the Pope, I was so hungover that I slept till noon. I thought Miss Ripley was going to have a total meltdown and send me home. It's not like I'm Catholic, for pity's sake."

"It sounds like a fabulous program," I said. "What's the name of the college?"

Buffy picked up the chain and ankh and put them back in the cloth bag. "A small private school in California. Nobody's ever heard of it. Oh, and you said something about Sausalito. I made a really dumb mistake on my passport application and mixed up the house numbers. My mother's been married four times. My father was her second, and I use that name. She hardly knows what her last name is anymore. She'll have a new one before I get home. I just hope this husband is older than me. The last kept getting carded when we went out to dinner." She gazed at me like a puppy pleading for a kindly pat on the head. "My shrink says I have a problem relating to men, that I get inappropriately attached. I guess that explains why I was upset yesterday about Samuel. He hasn't come back yet. Chief Inspector el-Habachi told me that the police over there searched the entire town. Did he say anything to you about knowing someone who lives or works there? Could he have recognized someone on the street?"

"Not that I'm aware of."

"If he knew somebody," Caron said, "it might explain why he disappeared the way he did. He could have thought this person could help overpower the kidnappers, so he went to find him. He shouldn't have underestimated my mother."

"Did he know how to find the hotel?" Buffy asked me. "Did you need to stop and ask?"

"Maybe he remembered seeing it earlier," I said. "It's on the main street. I'm surprised your kidnappers didn't choose a place at the edge of town."

"They're not rocket scientists. Samuel told you he was going to check the back of the hotel and never returned? Didn't you get worried?"

"Of course I did," I said, "but I wasn't about to go look for him. I went over to the hotel to ask to use the ladies' room, thinking I might get a better idea about these heavily armed men. The young woman in the lobby gave me the keys and told me which room you were in. The men heard me in the hall and blocked my way, but only for a minute. You told Samuel that they'd threatened to kill you if the police came into the hotel. In all honesty, they seemed more interested in the soccer match on TV than keeping you prisoner. Police could have easily burst into their room and disarmed them."

Buffy licked her lips. "They must have been confused when you showed up. It would have been different with the police."

"Or with Samuel? Were they expecting him?"

"How could they have been?" she said. "Well, I have an appointment for a manicure, so I'd better go. Thank you again for rescuing me, Mrs. Malloy." She left at a brisk clip.

"That was weird," Caron said. "It sounded like she didn't want you to rescue her. She wanted Samuel to, and she was mad that he didn't. I don't think I'd be picky if I were faced with the prospect of a fat old bedouin in bed with me." She shivered. "I mean, icky to the extreme."

Inez nodded. "She didn't claim she was madly in love with Samuel, just 'inappropriately attached.' It was more like she came with him to Egypt because she was tired of all the lectures in Rome. I would have at least asked where he planned to go before I showed up at the airport with my luggage."

"Her three Louis Vuitton suitcases," I said, "and presumably a fourth that she took on the cruise."

"How do you know about her luggage?" asked Caron. "In the hotel basement, right? No, don't tell me. I refuse to be an accessory to whatever crime you committed this time. I want to have a clear conscience if Peter asks me about it."

I suggested that we go down to the restaurant for lunch. Once there, we found a table and ordered from the now-familiar menu. As we were finishing, Magritta loomed over us.

"May I join you?" she asked gruffly.

"Certainly," I said. "I'm surprised you're not at the Valley of the Kings."

"I was earlier, but I came back to visit Nabil's family. The circumstances of his death caused complications. His body was not released immediately, which put a strain on the Arab rituals. Everything is now proceeding. The body has been wrapped for burial, and the house is crowded with mourners." She studied the menu for a moment. "I don't suppose you've seen Jess Delmont, that surly grad student from MacLeod? This is the second day he hasn't shown up. He knows his ancient history well enough, but he doesn't like to get his fingernails dirty. He'll end up being an instructor at some two-bit school, where he'll talk endlessly about his field experience. He and Shannon King are both armchair archeologists. Or were. I don't know which is grammatically correct—or politically correct, for that matter."

"I haven't seen him," I said. "Your excavation is still on hold, isn't it?"

"Yes, but I could use him to sort through the last pile of rubble that was brought up before Shannon died."

"For the *shabti*'s head?" asked Inez. She gave me a frantic look. "I—uh, I don't think he would have found it there."

"No," Magritta said. "It was broken off centuries ago. It's very rare to find one that's intact. They're fragile, and I suspect a lot of them were broken when the priests led the funerary procession to the tomb. The coffins too heavy to be carried on laborers' shoulders were brought on carts. The coffin had to be lowered and made to fit through the doorway. And there is the problem of the step. Wallace and I both recognized its style as eighteenth dynasty. It's in close proximity to Tut's tomb, Horemheb's at KV57, Tutmosis's at KV34, Hatshepsut's at KV20, and the mysterious finds in KV63. All eighteenth dynasty, not twentieth . . ."

"You don't think you've found the tomb of Ramses VIII?" I asked.

"I did not say that, but I'm not at all confident that we did. I do believe Nabil found the *shabti* at the site and brought it to me at the hotel. He was very agitated, according to another of the workmen who crossed the Nile in the same ferry. However, someone gave him a cigarette tainted with that drug. He never had the opportunity to tell me if he was excited because he found it or upset that he did." She beckoned to a waiter. "I wonder how the lentil soup is today. I need a hearty lunch before I return to the site to deal with those petty-minded officials from Cairo."

She and Inez discussed various pharaohs and temples. Caron decided to have dessert and picked at it in morose silence. I sat back and considered what Magritta had said, which fit well with my nascent theory. There were holes in it through which a meteorite could crash. But if I was even partially correct, the meteorite was going to crash very soon.

Bakr was seated in the hall when we came out of the elevator. "Good afternoon," he said, standing up so quickly he almost lost his balance. "Chief Inspector el-Habachi has ordered me to stay with you until Mr. Rosen arrives from Cairo."

"You're our babysitter?" I asked.

"Oh no," he said. "I am here to . . . to make certain that

no one disturbs you. There have been some troublesome events in Luxor. Chief Inspector el-Habachi does not think that you are in danger, but he and Mr. Rosen are concerned."

"This is Mr. Rosen's idea, isn't it?"

"I believe he and Chief Inspector el-Habachi communicated this morning," Bakr said, beginning to squirm. "I will be no bother, I promise. I will stay outside your door, and you will not notice that I'm here."

"Do you have a gun?" Inez asked him.

"Yes, Miss Inez. I am sure I will not have reason to use it. Mr. Rosen will be back in four hours, *inshallah*. Then I will drive the young ladies to Chief Inspector el-Habachi's home, where they can enjoy dinner and be entertained with music."

Giggling, Caron and Inez hustled him down the hall, despite his squeaks, and into the suite. Inez went to fetch a deck of cards, while Caron began explaining the rules of poker. Bakr's wallet was in more danger than we were.

I went out to the balcony, irritated by Peter's highhandedness. I had promised to stay in the hotel, after all. I always kept my word, unless a dire emergency required me to hedge just a bit. I hardly considered those peccadilloes worthy of comment.

A squeal of brakes drew my attention to the corniche. A car ran the stoplight and shot past Luxor Temple. Below, a carriage driver jumped down to comfort his swaying horse. Other carriages stopped so their drivers could shout curses at the now long-gone car. A policeman blew his whistle. People came up from the shops below the pier to gawk. I let out a sigh as it became obvious that the horse was not harmed. Eventually, the driver got back in his carriage and flicked the horse's rump with a whip. The other carriages began to move.

I was leaning on the rail, comparing this minor incident to the chaos that could be created by a herd of camels in a small town, when I saw Lord Bledrock, Mrs. McHaver, and Miriam walking across the terrace to the sidewalk.

Mrs. McHaver carried her cane but was moving at a brisk rate. I expected them to summon a taxi, but they turned in the opposite direction from the temple and continued down the sidewalk. A minute later, Sittermann, who'd been hidden from my view by an umbrella, appeared from the terrace and strolled ever so jauntily in the same direction. He was out of range before I could think of anything to throw at him. He paused for a moment to look up at me and wave.

I recoiled as if he'd pointed a rifle at me. "You insidious, deceitful, slimy worm," I muttered under my breath, savoring each word. I repeated it several times, but its cathartic effect was minimal. I had no idea who he was or why he was skulking around, irritating almost everyone (not Miss Portia and Miss Cordelia) by posturing as a slick Texan mogul. He'd as much as admitted to me that he wasn't, but he hadn't elaborated. How could he, when he was so busy arranging parties in my suite? I tried not to think what Peter's supervisors at the CIA would do when they examined his expense account. He'd been dispatched to Luxor to assist with anti-terrorism tactics, not to make a down payment on Aswan Dam.

The sound of laughter from behind me interrupted my mental tirade. The poker game was well under way, and Bakr was enjoying it, although I doubted he understood the rules. As far as I had been able to tell, wild cards changed willy-nilly and high hands were often low hands. Or something.

I resumed looking over the rail. On earlier occasions, I had walked in the direction they'd gone, and the only destination of note was the odd little mall. Beyond it were office buildings, banks, a travel agency with faded posters of Paris and London in the window, and clothing and furniture stores that catered to middle-class local shoppers. It seemed likely they were headed to the mall possibly to visit Dr. Butros Guindi, proprietor of his little shop of horrors.

It was a mere block away, a little voice in the back of my mind whispered. It would be crowded with tourists contemplating water pipes and T-shirts, but not so crowded that I couldn't keep a prudent distance from my quarries. I'd be there and be back in twenty minutes. If Miriam was trying on scarves and Lord Bledrock was examining silver snuffboxes, while Sittermann bought place mats for the highly theoretical Mrs. Sittermann, I'd be back in ten. A somewhat more pragmatic voice pointed out that I had solemnly vowed not to leave the hotel grounds.

I could not stay on the balcony and weigh my options any longer. If I was correct in certain assumptions, then I would have to find a way to tell Peter and Mahmoud without digging myself into a hole deep enough to bury a pharaoh, his wife, his children—and all his concubines. Tact would be of the essence.

I went into the sitting room. "I'm going to take a bath," I said. "My back is sore after that drive to and from the oasis yesterday. If Peter calls, take a message. If the message involves him staying in Cairo for another day, start packing. You'll have to see the pyramids from an airplane."

Caron, Inez, and even Bakr were too engrossed in the game to respond. I closed the bedroom door, found my sunglasses and a dark blue scarf that I'd bought for Jorgeson's wife, and turned on the tap in the bathtub. I knew from experience that it would take half an hour for the water to approach the rim. I slipped out the door to the corridor, glanced either way in case Abdullah was lurking, and scampered to the stairwell. When I reached the lobby of the New Winter Palace, the scarf covered my hair and the sunglasses obscured my eyes.

I kept my face lowered until I reached the bookstore. I paused in front of a circular rack of paperbacks while I assessed the situation. The mall was less crowded than I had hoped. Sittermann's white jacket was not visible. I went into the adjoining shop and looked out the window. The owner did his best to interest me in chains and bracelets, but I continued to the next shop.

I progressed slowly, scanning the interiors of shops across the walkway for the Brits and Sittermann. I was be-

ginning to think I'd made a mistake and they were all at the
travel agency, booking rooms at a resort on the Red Sea,
when I arrived at a basket shop near the end of the mall. Dr.
Guindi's antiques shop was directly across from me. The
window was as dusty as ever, but through the open doorway
I could see Lord Bledrock and Mrs. McHaver, both standing grimly to one side. Miriam, to my consternation, had
hold of Dr. Guindi's jacket lapels and was yelling at him.
Her face was so close to his that I could see drops of spittle
flying at him like hornets. He shook his head in protest.
Miriam slapped him with her free hand, lightly but with
enough force to sting. Lord Bledrock said something.
Miriam slapped Dr. Guindi again, harder. She still wore a
drab, loose-fitting dress and sensible shoes. Her complexion was pale. A lace-trimmed handkerchief was tucked in
her cuff. And she was slapping the holy bejeezus out of Dr.
Guindi, who had not shown any resistance. If she continued, his head might fly off his neck, I thought numbly. Lord
Bledrock would harrumph, then straighten his tie and offer
his arm to Mrs. McHaver. Miriam would follow meekly,
perhaps using the handkerchief to clean her hands.

A flash of white caught my eye. I forced myself to look
away from the carnage-in-progress and saw Sittermann
partially concealed behind a stack of colorful tablecloths.
He sensed my stare and turned his head. When his gaze
met mine, his eyes widened. He was clearly as appalled as
I was. He shook his head slightly, touched his forefinger to
his lips, and disappeared into the shop behind him.

I looked back at the doorway. Miriam had dropped her
grip on Dr. Guindi's coat and was jabbing him in the chest.
He retreated inch by inch. Mrs. McHaver spoke; whatever
she said startled Dr. Guindi. I eyed the distance across the
walkway. I would be exposed for only a few seconds, and I
was cleverly disguised (despite Sittermann's instant recog-
nition). And what was the worst that would happen if they
did spot me? I had every right to be there. All newcomers
shopped for souvenirs. I could waggle my fingers at them,
smile sweetly, and get myself back to the suite before my

absence was noticed. I could even take a bath. I stared at my watch. In ten minutes, water would begin to dribble onto the bathroom floor. It would seep under the door and into the carpet. It would spread across the bedroom. Once it made it to the sitting room, my goose would be cooked, carved, and ready to be served with chutney and boiled potatoes.

I aligned my sunglasses and prepared to make a dash for the shop next to Dr. Guindi's. Before I could move, an arm wrapped around my neck and a hand clamped over my mouth. I tried to scream as I was dragged backward across the shop. A curtain fluttered against my arm as my assailant pulled me into a back room. I kicked at his shins and tried to scratch his face. The arm tightened around my neck.

"Stop it," a voice whispered, so close that I could feel the warm air on my earlobe. "I don't want to hurt you." The hand was withdrawn, but I could see it poised beside my head.

"Then loosen your arm," I croaked. The pressure eased. I took several deep breaths. "Let me go."

"Can't," came the whisper.

"Yes, you can. Start with removing your arm before you fracture my windpipe. I haven't given up on a career in opera. I promise I won't scream." I didn't add that I had every intention of disabling him with a well-placed jerk of my knee, then snatching up the nearest object and bashing him on the head.

The hand gripped my shoulder so tightly that I bit back a shriek of pain. I was unceremoniously yanked around and carried to a back door, my feet kicking futilely. He released my shoulder long enough to open the door, then shoved me into an alley with such force that I almost fell across a bicycle propped against a crate. The door slammed, but not before I caught a glimpse of a black mustache and a scar.

I closed my eyes and waited for my heart to stop pounding. When I could trust my legs, I walked briskly, if unsteadily, toward the corniche, leaving a trail of colorful expletives in my wake. Had Caron and Inez's purported stalker been following me all this time? With a few small exceptions, I'd been occupied with all the standard tourist activities. As alluring as I was, I had never found myself obliged to beat back admirers.

It had to be Peter's fault, I concluded as I swung around the corner.

And crashed into Peter.

"Hello, dear," I said weakly. "How was Cairo?"

"What do you think you're doing?" he said, making no effort to embrace me and inquire about my well-being. We'd been married less than a month; I hoped he would still recognize me in a year or two.

"I'm going back to the hotel," I said.

He gripped my arm as though he was afraid I might bolt into traffic or dash back down the alley. "You weren't supposed to leave the hotel."

"Something came up. Could we please hurry?"

"I turned off the tap," he said, still speaking to me as if I was nothing more than an acquaintance he'd met at a banquet honoring a civic leader. "Please stop gasping and explain."

"I do not gasp." I pulled my arm free. "I'd explain, but I doubt I can meet your standards. I'm a mere amateur who happens to have been attacked in the last five minutes. Shouldn't I file a report with the CIA first? Is there a manual that'll tell me how to reduce it to a tiny black microdot and glue it to the leg of a pigeon with security clearance? Am I supposed to use your code name and put 'Mrs.' in front of it?"

"Attacked? By whom?"

"If I tell you, I'll have to kill you." I started for the hotel.

He caught up with me, his expression decidedly unfriendly. We went through the lobby and took the elevator. I pulled off my sunglasses and the scarf and handed them to him. He snorted. Abdullah's mouth twitched as he watched us from behind a cleaning cart. When we went into the suite, Bakr dropped his cards and scrambled to his feet, looking at each of us in turn.

"Mrs. Malloy," he said, gurgling, "I see Mr. Rosen found

you. You should not have lied to me. Chief Inspector el-Habachi will be angry at me for failing to—"

"Wiser men than you have tried with less success," I said.

Caron and Inez exchanged looks, then picked up the cards and went into their bedroom. Peter told Bakr to wait outside the door. I retreated to the bathroom, noted wryly that the bathtub was emptying, and splashed water on my face. My hair had been mussed in the scuffle, but there were no marks or bruises on my neck. My clothes felt sullied, so I changed into clean ones.

A bucket of ice had appeared by the mini-bar. Peter handed me a drink and we went to the balcony. Just a stereotypic married couple, I thought as we sat down and looked at the view. He was home from the office, while I'd spent the day lunching with friends and driving the children to soccer practice and piano lessons. Neither of us motivated to inquire about each other's day. Same old, same old. Dog threw up in the backseat on the way to the vet's office. The boss was in a bad mood. Plumber didn't show up as promised. The meeting lasted more than two hours. Don't forget the parent-teacher conference on Thursday.

"How was Cairo?" I asked.

"Oh, fine. I spent a great deal of time being interrogated and lectured because my wife was prowling in the hotel basement and confronting kidnappers at a seedy hotel in an oasis town. My attempts to explain your behavior were met with incredulous stares and derisive snickers. But I really didn't mind, because every man should be humiliated on his honeymoon. It's such a great way to start a marriage."

"Your sarcasm is not appreciated," I said. "I told you about the luggage. As for the excursion to the Kharga Oasis, I had no choice. I tried to get in touch with you, but the only telephone number I had was for the embassy."

"You had Mahmoud's number."

"Samuel convinced me that Buffy would be killed if the police intervened. I decided to wait until we arrived there.

If it was too dangerous, I would have gone to the police and told them everything."

Peter looked at me. "When have you ever told the police everything?"

"This required delicacy, not the local SWAT team," I said, evading the issue. "I presume you already know about Nabil's death, and the murder of the taxi driver who took Shannon to the Valley of the Kings." Peter nodded, not bothering to ask me how I knew. I wasn't sure if I should be flattered or offended. "There is one thing I haven't had a chance to mention to Mahmoud. It happened today."

"Before you snuck out of the hotel, I assume."

I told him about Caron and Inez admitting that they'd found the *shabti* several days before it was discovered in the excavation. "They left it in their room when we went on the Nubian Sea cruise. Someone found it and planted it at the excavation in order to stir up excitement. That implies this particular someone suspected or knew they had it. Sittermann's high on my list."

"It wasn't Sittermann," Peter said. "Would you like another drink?"

He took my glass and went into the sitting room. He knocked on the door of the girls' room and reminded them that Bakr would drive them to Mahmoud's home for dinner shortly, then took his sweet time fixing drinks. I gnawed on my lip and reconsidered my theory. Sittermann was everywhere and knew everything. He'd been following Lord Bledrock and the McHavers (*tante et nièce*). If I'd been less preoccupied at the Kharga Oasis, I might have noticed him peering out through a shuttered window by the Desert Inn or lurking between the camels.

I gave up. When Peter sat down, I said, "How do you know it wasn't Sittermann?"

"If I tell you, I'll have to kill you."

"Oh," I murmured. "One of them . . ."

He grinned. "Technically, one of us."

"Are you sure he's on our side?"

"I'm afraid so."

"The thought makes my skin crawl," I said. "When did you find out?"

"After the cruise, and with great reluctance from certain parties in D.C. and Cairo. I should have been informed before I left the country, but the different agencies don't communicate. The Pentagon has seventeen and a half miles of corridors and more than six and a half million square feet. You can pack in a lot of covert agencies with innocuous-sounding names stenciled on the doors. In order to get a bigger chunk of the budget, they all have to run their own operations and keep their intelligence information to themselves. The idea of cooperating with each other is beyond their comprehension. You shouldn't have a problem with that concept."

"So Sittermann . . . ?"

"Might as well be from another planet. I suspect the only reason he tipped us off was that he was worried about you. Amateurs can get themselves in trouble when they're inadvertently playing with professionals."

"You should have told me," I said, "or at least given me a hint. He's been driving me crazy since we got here, with all his inane jabber about Tut-O-Rama and how he's an ol' cowhand from the Rio Grande. Does he know about your . . . connections?"

Peter shrugged. "I have no idea, but damned if I'm going to enlighten him. Now, will you please tell me why you left the hotel and who attacked you?"

I had no problem with the first part, stressing that my prime motivation was to find out what Sittermann was up to. Peter leaned forward and listened intently when I described the scene in Dr. Guindi's shop. "It was an entirely new side of Miriam," I added, envisioning her cold-blooded demeanor as she swung her hand. "It makes sense, though. She went to extremes to look that dowdy. I wouldn't be all that surprised if she used theatrical makeup for the pallor. At breakfast one morning, she tried to convince me she was a shy orchid pining for Alexander, but she fired a lot of questions at me. We may have a troupe of actors at the other end of the hallway, touring with their show."

"Including Alexander?" Peter asked.

I thought I detected a tinge of jealousy in his voice. I wanted to sit in his lap and remind him that he was more handsome, quite as rich, and came from an upper-crust family as well. He would never be a baron, granted, but I had no desire to live in a drafty manor and devote my energy to snipping flowers and sipping tea. "No, I don't think Alexander is part of the charade," I said. "He really is an indolent, spoiled aristocrat with a cushy job that doesn't interfere with his social life. He either doesn't realize it or doesn't care. That's why I tolerate his company."

Peter sipped his drink. "Or he may be more astute than you think. He has to know his father is buying antiquities on the black market, and Mrs. McHaver as well. Mahmoud has known for years. He'd love to put a stop to it, but they have powerful connections. Lord Bledrock went to Eton with some of the higher echelon in the foreign service ministry. His first wife entertained the Egyptian ambassador's wife in London. Mrs. McHaver funded medical clinics in remote villages. They're benefactors of the Cairo Museum. Mahmoud would find himself at a desert outpost if he dared to even investigate them." He fell silent for a long moment. "And this man that attacked you when you were spying on them in the antiques shop? You're sure you saw the mustache and the scar?"

I was still brooding about his remarks. "You could have told me this, you know. I could have saved myself a lot of energy figuring it out on my own."

"But you're a lowly amateur, remember? You're not supposed to be briefed, especially when some of the information is classified. Scotland Yard does not consult Miss Marple."

"Stuff it, Sherlock," I said.

"Wow," Caron said from the doorway. "Are you guys having a fight? Don't let me interrupt or anything. I just wanted to tell you that Inez and I are leaving for an utterly thrilling evening of making conversation and admiring grubby children. I'll tell you all about it when we get back."

I walked to the door with them and made sure Bakr was waiting. He gave me a chilly look, no doubt blaming me for whatever trouble he was in with his superior. I closed the door and rejoined Peter, who had propped his legs on the rail and was gazing with great innocence at the birds flapping over the Nile.

"Yes," I said, returning to his earlier question, "I saw the mustache and the scar. He must be the man Caron and Inez have been insisting was after them. Is it possible he's part of this terrorist group, whatever it's called?"

"El Asad li-allah, the Lion of God. I don't know why they'd bother with you or the girls."

"Because they're suspicious of you," I suggested. "All these trips to the police station and Cairo, and the other places you went before we arrived. These people are violent. Remember Oskar's not-so-accidental accident in the spring, and now Shannon's. The lethal cigarette given to Nabil so that he wouldn't be able to talk to Magritta about the *shabti*. The taxi driver, poor man, who did nothing more than pick up a second passenger before driving to the Valley of the Kings. Jess Delmont's body is likely to be out in the desert, his throat slashed as well."

"He's in custody in Cairo. They picked him up at the airport, and he hasn't been able to explain why he had ten thousand dollars in his suitcase."

"Well, I'm glad he had enough sense to try to get out of the country before they found him. I think you should call Mahmoud before he sits down to dinner with his charming American guests. The sooner Magritta's taken into custody, the better. Wallace, too."

"And why do you think that?" Peter asked.

I couldn't tell if he was teasing me or not, but I told him anyway. After all, communication is the foundation of a solid marriage.

CHAPTER 18

At breakfast, Caron and Inez announced that they were tired of dead pharaohs and ready to shop. Peter gave them a substantial amount of money, told them to call Bakr to escort them, and watched as they hurried into the lobby.

"Is there anything left to buy in Luxor?" he asked. "They'll need an extra suitcase to haul their loot home."

"They haven't even started on Cairo." I filled his coffee cup and sat back. There were only a few people still eating breakfast, none of them familiar. I was relieved not to have to make conversation with anyone but my husband, who was idly watching the birds fight over crumbs on the floor. If we bought a house in the country, we would put up bird feeders and become experts on rare species of wrens and finches.

"I called Mahmoud while you were in the shower," my future bird fancier said. "He has doubts about this evening's plan, but he also admitted that he didn't have a better idea. I'm going to coach him"—he saw my sudden frown—"here, at the hotel, in an hour. He has to run the show. I can't appear to know anything more than the others."

"You'll do very well as a bartender. Have the invitations been delivered?"

"To everyone in the hotel. Salima's went to the Mummification Museum, where she's giving tours today, and Lady Emerson's to her villa. Magritta and Wallace will be escorted here by police officers. There's been no sign of Samuel. Are you positive he'll show up today?"

"Unless he's buried up to his chin in the desert. It's impossible to estimate how many people are involved in Buffy's kidnapping. If they grabbed him, he's in serious trouble. I doubt they did, though. It's more likely that once he realized that Buffy and I were gone, he found a safe place to hide until he could arrange transportation. Her rescue has been all over the newspapers and TV. His only hope now is to get to her here in Luxor before she does irreparable damage."

"She's been moved to a room on a different floor, and Ahmed has been instructed not to give out her room number to anyone. She accepted the tourism office's kind offer of an all-day spa session at a resort on Crocodile Island. Samuel's backpack is in police custody, and the room is presently occupied by two men from Mahmoud's crime lab."

"That covers everyone but Sittermann. He doesn't need an invitation. This table is probably bugged, and he's listening right now, waiting for us to say what time the party starts." I bent down and whispered into the bowl of sugar packets. "Five o'clock, you sleazebag."

Peter grinned in his endearingly sexy way. "If our suite is bugged, he already knows that and a lot of other interesting things."

"You don't honestly think . . . ?"

"At least my husband will be present at this cocktail party," I said to Abdullah as he stocked the shelf next to the minibar. "You won't have to concern yourself with my unseemly behavior."

"Yes, *Sitt*. Will you need more lemons and limes?"

I waited until he glanced up at me. "You ratted me out yesterday, didn't you?"

"I do not know that word."

"You not only told Peter that I'd left the hotel, you also told him where I was going. Admit it, Abdullah."

"*Sitt*, it was very dangerous. There are evil men in Luxor

who would not hesitate to cut your throat. You're a nice lady, but your curiosity is too great. Americans do not truly understand the passion of terrorists. Suicide bombers beg to sacrifice themselves for their religious beliefs and their countries. Western aggression has bred a generation of martyrs. Secularism has suffered, as have opportunities for education and individual expression. Women will end up in burqas, and boys will study the Koran instead of science and technology."

I was taken aback by his lecture—and his command of English. "Our country is divided, too," I said weakly.

"So I have been told, *Sitt*." He wheeled the cart out of the room.

I went into the bedroom and waited until Peter concluded a hush-hush conversation on the telephone. "Is this a safe line? Aren't you supposed to go to the third pay phone from the left at the bus station, or the emergency room at the hospital?"

"I was confirming our flight to Cairo tomorrow. I heard Abdullah chastising you. I waited for you to counterattack, but you were strangely passive. Are you the same reckless woman who charged into a hotel to tackle armed men and rescue the witless blond princess?"

"She may be blond, but I can assure you she's not witless," I said huffily. "What was I supposed to say to Abdullah in rebuttal—that we're clearly superior because we have drive-through windows and reality TV shows? That almost everyone over the age of twelve has a cell phone glued to his head? That football coaches earn ten times more than professors?"

Peter had the audacity to laugh, and I was considering whether he could continue to do so with a pillow over his face when the phone rang. He answered it, listened, and then said, "Send him up here, Ahmed."

"Samuel?" I said smugly.

"Yes, and according to Ahmed, very dirty and irritated that he no longer has a room here. He was most aggrieved to be told his luggage had been misplaced."

"We don't want him to wander around the hotel lobby, so we need to do something with him until the others arrive," I said. "Maybe he'd like to take a bath and borrow some clean clothes from you. I'm sure he's had an unpleasant time these last few days. I think I'll retreat to the girls' bedroom."

The Savage Sheik lay in wait for me on the bed, and I spent the next hour alternating between flinging myself into his arms and berating myself for falling under his spell. Inez seemed to be correct in theory that he was not a lawless savage, but a rebellious peer tormented by scars from a traumatized childhood. Denial on the Nile. I could hear snippets of conversation between Peter and Samuel, but I stopped listening when I realized that the ravens, falcons, and jaguars under discussion were not Egyptian gods.

A few minutes before five, I went into the parlor. Peter, a gentleman as well as a devoted spouse, stood up and begged the pleasure of making me a libation. Samuel stayed on the sofa, glaring at me. His hair was damp and he was wearing a navy cotton T-shirt that looked much better on Peter than it did on him. It was unfortunate that Peter would never get it back.

"I see you made it back safely," I said to Samuel.

"No thanks to you. Why didn't you wait for me?"

"I did, for half an hour. I finally gave up and went to the hotel, where the desk clerk gave me the room keys and told me where to find Buffy. It struck me as odd, but I was hardly inclined to delve into the motives behind this benevolent cooperation. Rather than risk our lives while you bumbled around behind the hotel looking for a drainpipe or a ladder, Buffy and I left Kharga as quickly as possible." I accepted a drink from Peter and sat down across from Samuel, my smile bright and chipper. "Extricating Buffy from the clutches of her bloodthirsty kidnappers was the goal, wasn't it? I presumed you could take care of yourself.

After all, you are just an American student with an interest in Graeco-Roman ruins. Why would anybody wish to harm you?"

He studied me for a moment. "You're right, Mrs. Malloy. You did the only sensible thing. I freaked out when I went back to where I'd parked and the car was gone. I didn't have any idea what happened to you. I was afraid the men had spotted you and taken you hostage, too. I was trying to figure out what to do when the police descended on the hotel. I didn't want to try to explain why I was there, so I decided I'd better stay out of sight for a couple of days."

"The police searched for you," Peter said, "or so we heard. Where were you?"

"In a hut at the edge of a date palm grove. I paid some kid to bring me food and water."

"So you speak Arabic," I said. "Convenient."

"Only a few words and phrases, Mrs. Malloy. When I was a teenager, I spent my summers as a volunteer for an international relief organization in Palestine. We worked on irrigation projects. I had some free time to travel, and that's when I became interested in archeology and architecture."

"Can you read Arabic, too?" I persisted. "Well enough to study the Koran?"

He was clearly getting annoyed with me. "Only well enough to read a few words on a menu or a road sign. All I know about the Koran is what I learned in a comparative religion course in college. If you wish, we can discuss it, as well as the Torah, the Tripitaka, and the Bhagavad Gita."

Peter gave me a small frown. "Let's stick to the present, Samuel. How did you get back from Kharga?"

"This morning, I hitched a ride with some German guys. They had a couple of cases of Stella, so we had to stop every twenty minutes so someone could . . . urinate on a rock. They headed for a pub after they dropped me off here at the hotel. I was really surprised when I got to the desk. Do you know where Buffy is? All the manager would say is that she checked out of our room and that she's safe. Is she angry at me? You told her what happened, didn't you, Mrs. Malloy? She's not avoiding me, is she?"

"I don't know exactly where she is," I said truthfully. "In Kharga she was more worried than angry. She kept demanding that we wait for you, but I wasn't inclined to linger. One might have suspected she had a grandiose romantic fantasy about you swooping in through the window to rescue her with the panache of Rudolph Valentino."

"Who?" he said blankly.

"You'll have to ask your mother," I said. "No, your grandmother. In any case she was—and still is—very concerned that those brutal men who kidnapped her might have caught and detained you."

"Such a sensitive girl," he murmured. "I can hardly wait to assure her in person that I'm okay."

"It may happen sooner than you think," Peter said. "I hear voices in the hall. Mix yourself another drink, Samuel. You may need it."

I had to agree with my husband. Samuel was smiling, but he was also squeezing a throw pillow with such intensity that its foam entrails were apt to spurt out. He noticed my gaze and put down the pillow.

Peter opened the door. Lord Bledrock came in and shook Peter's hand with such gusto that Peter winced. Mrs. McHaver made a stately entrance, trailed by Miriam. Miss Portia and Miss Cordelia fluttered their eyelashes as they hurried toward the bar. Lady Emerson swept in and made a dash for the sofa before Mrs. McHaver could lay claim to it. Salima shot me a leery look as she came in, then noticed Samuel and stopped in the middle of the room. Alexander bumped into her, caught himself, and sullenly moved away from her. Voices grew louder as our guests clamored for drinks and fought for seats. I hoped those partaking of tea on the terrace would not begin to wonder if a free-for-all was brewing on the third floor.

Magritta and Wallace appeared in the doorway. She

looked very much like the teapot of song—short, stout, and with steam coming out of the spouts on both sides of her head. Wallace was subdued, but brightened when he saw the bottles on the bar. Mahmoud slipped in behind them and stood to one side, ignoring both Peter and me.

"My goodness, Magritta," said Mrs. McHaver, "you're quite the picture of restrained fury. You don't have a pickax behind your back, do you?"

Miss Cordelia giggled. "There was a woman in our village, a baker who made delicious tarts and buns. Her only flaw of note was her propensity to bicycle down back roads in search of elderly gentlemen walking their dogs in the evenings. She'd hack them into pieces and toss the body parts into the nearest pond. Had we known, I would have been disinclined to purchase her cherry pies."

"Or her pasties," said Miss Portia. "One naturally assumed the minced meat was lamb or mutton, but . . ."

Magritta's expression turned darker. "I am not in the mood for prattle. I have been detained and forced to spend almost twenty-four hours in a primitive hotel room with a guard outside the door. I was not allowed to speak to anyone. I would like nothing more than a very dry martini and an explanation for this outrageous treatment. Claire, have you any responsibility in the matter?"

"Detained?" said Lady Emerson. "How can you continue to excavate the site? I've been beleaguered by calls from the media, demanding my learned observations in regard to Ramses VIII. I haven't quite decided how to respond. This morning the site was off-limits to almost everyone. I had no idea you weren't there in conference with the head of the Supreme Council of Antiquities."

"Glad to hear the chap's arrived," Wallace said. "An agreeable sort, although very fond of publicity. He travels with an entourage of minions, military guards, and official vehicles. It can made for quite a traffic jam on some of these narrow roads."

Wallace would have continued had Peter not nudged

him to the bar and inquired about his preference. Alexander joined Peter. Miriam eyed Salima's short skirt and heels, then went out to the balcony.

Mrs. McHaver thumped her cane. "Magritta, you must sit next to me and explain all this. If you're having problems with the authorities, Neville and I will put a stop to it so you can continue work. Have you found someone to replace that local who had the audacity to fling himself on the carpet in Neville's suite? These people should not be allowed inside the Winter Palace."

"Unless they're in uniform," Lord Bledrock corrected her. "We can't get along without waiters, bellmen, and the like. Abdullah brings me tea each morning promptly at eight forty-five. He sees to my shoes if they're dusty, and has my clothes dry-cleaned. He's quite useful. If his English were better, I'd take him home and train him to be a butler."

"He wouldn't take you up on it," Alexander said. "He has a life."

Mrs. McHaver snorted. "What kind of life can any of these people have? All this poverty, filth, disease. I should think any one of the would leap at the opportunity to live in a civilized country."

I didn't dare look at Mahmoud. Thus far he had seemed to be as mild-mannered as I, and certainly had shown more restraint than my husband in matters of temperament and tolerance. If he was moved to start heaving the Brits off the balcony, I might never see the pyramids in the moonlight.

All conversation, pejorative and inane, halted as Buffy came into the room. Her hair was perfectly cut and styled, and her complexion glowed. "Well, hello," she said. "I wasn't expecting to see all of you. Samuel, I'm so relieved you made it back safely. Did you hear about Mrs. Malloy's heroics? If it weren't for her, I don't know what would have happened to me. It was so scary."

"I would have rounded up a posses and come to fetch you," Sittermann said from the doorway. "I was aimin' to do whatever it took, even if I had to go to Cairo and march right into the American ambassador's office. No, ma'am, a Texan ain't gonna allow a gang of foreigners to harm to one hair on the head of a sweet young thing like you."

I gritted my teeth and lectured myself to stay where I was, which was far enough from him to prevent me from throwing a punch. I was unnerved by the ferociousness of my reaction, having never thrown a punch or seriously considered doing so. Peter looked at me as if he could see the repressed fury in my eyes. I took a deep breath and said, "So nice that you could make it, Mr. Sittermann. Would you like a drink before we get started?"

"Before 'we' get started, Mrs. Malloy?" he said.

"I believe Mahmoud has a few remarks planned," I said carefully.

Mahmoud emerged from the corner. "Yes, I do. It may take some time, so please make yourselves comfortable. I can promise you that it will all be very civilized—unless one of you causes a disruption."

"Oh, dear," Alexander drawled. "Have we all been called on the carpet, this time in the parlor? It does make me think of all those uncomfortable sessions in the headmaster's study. All I can say is that Lady Emerson is the culprit. I saw her creeping into the conservatory at midnight, with a candlestick clutched between her teeth."

Lady Emerson bristled. "Where my teeth are at midnight is none of your business, Alexander. I suggest you refrain from further personal comments."

Lord Bledrock harrumphed. "That's right, my boy. Let's have no more nonsense about the location of Lady Emerson's teeth. They're in her mouth now, and that's the important thing." He flapped his hand at Mahmoud. "Get on with it."

"Yes, do," Magritta said. "I'm beginning to yearn for solitary confinement, where the only sound is the rattle of carts on the street. It will be a wonderful opportunity to start writing my memoirs."

"You can't write your memoirs," Wallace protested.

"I'm already writing them. Thinking about calling it *Red Land, Black Mountain*."

"Don't be ridicuious, Wallace," Magritta said. "You can't write *my* memoirs."

"I did plan to ask you about some of the more graphic details about your connubial relationship with Oskar. Thought I'd spice it up a bit."

Mahmoud clapped his hands. "Please, your attention. This is a matter of grave significance. Four persons have been murdered, and many more will die if the culprits are not stopped. If there is an uprising, an attempt to overthrow the government, civilians will suffer."

"Someone's going to overthrow the government?" Salima said. "I should go home and pack. Maybe I can lecture at the Sorbonne. I adore fresh croissants and jam."

Mahmoud stared at her until she bit her lip. "The first victim was Oskar Vonderlochen," he continued. Yes, I realize that I myself investigated his death and was satisfied that it was an accident. I was not aware of the entire situation."

"Oskar?" Magritta said, startled. "What he did was reckless, but he was an excitable man. All those years we dug in the hot sun, uncovering nothing more than the traces of a foundation or a broken jar, a piece of stone with a worn relief. When at last it seemed we were going to find something of great importance, he could not contain himself."

"And he was drunk," Mrs. McHaver said tartly.

"So it seems," Mahmoud said. "I think now it is likely that someone knew where he was going. There were activities that he might stumble upon inadvertently, not at that site but at another one at the far end of the Valley of the Kings, perhaps at the top of the cliff. These activities could only be conducted at night, which required the use of lanterns and flashlights. A necessary risk, but a potentially lucrative one. It could not have been challenging for this second person to come down a goat path, pick up a rock, and strike Mr. Vonderlochen with enough force to crush his skull."

"Balderdash," said Lord Bledrock. "Who'd want to do

something like that? It's not—well, it's not cricket, if you understand me."

"Utter nonsense," Miriam said from the doorway to the balcony. "Everyone liked Oskar."

Salima shook her head. "Somebody didn't. One doesn't bash one's friends."

"That was last spring," I said, doing my best to prompt Mahmoud, who seemed to be confused by the verbal shots being fired from all corners of the parlor. "MacLeod College decided to allow Magritta to continue the work for at least one final season. Shannon opted to use her temporary authority in order to make a deal with Lord Bledrock. Isn't that right?"

"Maybe something to do with exhibiting your collection?" Peter offered helpfully.

"A pesky woman," Lord Bledrock said. "She knew I had great expectations for this excavation, much as Lord Carnarvon had when he backed Carter. If MacLeod College relinquished the concession, it might have been the end of it for me."

"And for Mrs. McHaver," I said. "She had expectations, too, although hers were of a more mercenary nature."

She peered at me down her nose. "I have great enthusiasm for the continued exploration of ancient Egypt. There is a great deal to be learned."

"As well as a great profit to be made." Mahmoud took out a handkerchief and wiped his face. We had warned him to tread lightly until the trap was sprung, but he was unraveling.

Alexander went over to pat Mrs. McHaver's shoulder. "You must be deeply offended by this ridiculous insinuation, Mrs. McHaver. Please allow me to freshen your drink." He took the glass from her hand and hurried to the bar.

"Mrs. McHaver's a generous benefactor, Chief Inspector," Sittermann said, thumping Mahmoud on the back. "I reckon she'll overlook your remark if you move right along. You planning to explain how all this ties in together? We don't have all night."

I held up my hand. "There's something I need to tell all of you. It's embarrassing, and it reflects badly on me as a parent. Last week my daughter and her friend were invited to a party at Salima's home across the Nile."

"A birthday party," Salima said.

"Yes, a birthday party. After the party, they went to a nightclub. I have never allowed them to do that at home, but they felt this was an opportunity to learn more about the modern culture. They did not sample any alcoholic beverages. Due to a rather complicated series of events, they ended up alongside a road on the far edge of Gurna. A donkey cart suffered a minor mishap. After it moved on, they found what they believed was a souvenir like those found in shops all over Luxor. They failed to tell me and Peter, and hid it among their souvenirs. While we were on the cruise, it was taken from their room."

Mrs. McHaver snapped her fingers at Alexander, who'd stopped pouring scotch to listen to me. "Don't dawdle, Alexander. Mrs. Malloy, I do hope we're not to be entertained with a list of their souvenirs. It may be of interest to you, but hardly to the rest of us."

"If we're all guessing," Miss Cordelia said, "then I say a plastic reproduction of Tut's death mask."

"A disposable lighter with Cleopatra's face?" said Miss Portia. "I see them everywhere."

"A clay camel," Wallace mumbled.

Sittermann's reptilian eyes narrowed further. "The *shabti*?"

"Ridiculous!" Lord Bledrock rumbled like a bullfrog. "Can't be the *shabti*. It's invaluable. Only a bloody fool would steal it, then toss it in the pit. What would be the point of that?"

"This is a waste of time." Mrs. McHaver stood up, but somehow the handle of Lady Emerson's parasol was caught on her arm and she sat back with a thud.

Lady Emerson frowned. "So sorry. It has a mind of its own. Mrs. Malloy, I find this most distressing. Are you doubting Magritta's integrity?"

"Absolutely not," I said. "Magritta was as surprised as the rest of you, and initially eager to believe that she was about to discover the lost tomb of Ramses VIII. When the excitement wore down, she began to have suspicions. Am I right?"

"Yes," Magritta said sadly. "It was wrong. You yourself, Lady Emerson, saw the step earlier that day. Clearly eighteenth dynasty. Lord Bledrock and Mrs. McHaver were deluding themselves, perhaps because they have so much invested in the project. I allowed Shannon to enjoy her momentary triumph, but I knew I had to tell her the next day that the *shabti* had come from a different site."

"Which would have ruined everything," Buffy said.

Mahmoud tried to regain center stage. "Yes, it would have, Miss Franz. Professional ethics would have required Shannon to notify the Supreme Council, which would set into motion an intensive search for the true location of the tomb of Ramses VIII. Random remarks heard in the shops and cafés might be taken seriously. When so many people are involved, odds are good that someone will speak indiscreetly. Our informants might find the courage to drop hints in exchange for a few hundred pounds. We in turn would alert certain governmental agencies. Every crate, suitcase, briefcase, and purse would be searched before being allowed out of the country. The military would patrol every road and stop every vehcile."

Salima flapped her hand. "What if Magritta decided to tell someone else?"

"Well," Magritta said slowly, "we very likely have found a tomb from the eighteenth dynasty. Without Shannon's negativity, I may be allowed another season. It would be such a tribute to dear Oskar if indeed the site was designated KV64."

"Here, here," Sittermann said. "I think we should all drink to that! Got any champagne, Rosen?"

Peter gave him a nasty smile. "Put it on your own expense account. You've already done enough damage to mine."

"Well, ain't you the testy one," Sittermann said. "Tut, tut, as we say here in Luxor."

I grabbed Peter's arm and clung to it. "You boys can work this out later. Mahmoud, please continue."

"I'm doing my best," he said, aware he was in the middle of a potential combat zone. "Now we agree the *shabti* was not originally found at the excavation site under Magritta's supervision. I'm not an expert in Egyptology, but those who are seem to agree that it came from the tomb of Ramses VIII. The fact that Caron and Inez found it outside Gurna suggests that the tomb was discovered not by a recognized team of archeologists but by criminals. Tombs have been systematically robbed for three thousand years. This particular tomb, if it had not been previously discovered, could be filled with heretofore unseen treasures of astounding value. The trick was to move them out of the country without the knowledge of the Supreme Council of Antiquities, the Cairo Museum, and authorities determined to preserve and protect Egypt's unique legacy. The media needed to be focused on the Valley of the Kings. This eighteenth-century step intrigued the archeological community, but could hardly warrant major interest from the cable networks and newspapers. The discovery of the tomb of the mysterious Ramses VIII was certainly more likely to appeal to the public."

"But Caron and Inez had proof that the *shabti* came from elsewhere," I said. "They had yet to mention it, but they could at any time."

Lady Emerson pointed her parasol at me. "Then how could someone know they had it in their room? It's impossible to believe that a random thief would realize its significance and subsequently toss it in the pit. That makes no sense whatsoever."

"I concur," Mrs. McHaver said emphatically. "Don't you agree, Neville?"

He nodded. "No reason to think there would be anything of value in their room. After all, they're mere girls."

"That's all true," I said, "but what's important is that someone saw them find the *shabti* in the road."

"That's right," Caron said as she sailed into the parlor from the hall. "A psychotic Arab stalker with a black mustache and a scar across his face. He's been following Inez and me since the day we arrived, waiting for his chance to drag us into a back alley and abduct us. That sort of thing is, like, So Uncool, even if he is a sheik."

CHAPTER 19

Caron's pronouncement was met with reverberating silence. Eyes were round and jaws were dangling. Booze dribbled out of the corners of Wallace's mouth. Mrs. McHaver began to fan herself with her hand, unmindful that she was holding a drink in the same hand. Lady Emerson, having caught the brunt of it, pulled out a handkerchief to blot her face. Miss Portia and Miss Cordelia giggled faintly. Even Peter, who was accustomed to leading gruesome homicide investigations and ordering his minions to scurry about like fleas, seemed dumbstruck.

"Back so soon?" I said brightly.

"I just came up to get some money," she said. "We started playing some peculiar poker game and I haven't figured it out yet." She glanced around the room. "I'll just get some in my bedroom and go back to the lobby. Sorry to interrupt."

We waited until we heard the door from the bedroom to the hall close.

"Well, that was interesting," Sittermann said at last. "Any truth to it?"

"Poppycock, if you ask me," said Lord Bledrock. "Teenaged girls are such histrionic creatures. Best to send them off to school at an early age."

"There is truth to it," I said. "The girls have seen this Arab man with the mustache and the scar several times, including the day we arrived in Luxor. I myself saw him yesterday. What's more important is that someone followed the girls when they fled the nightclub in Gurna and later found the *shabti* in the road. This person, who must have been aware of what was in the donkey cart, later realized that their discovery could be used as a diversionary tactic to muddle up the location of Ramses VIII's tomb."

"And create the opportunity to murder Shannon King," Mahmoud said somberly. "Nabil's loyalty to Magritta was predictable, and he was easily manipulated. The cigarette laced with methamphetamine was given to him during the afternoon, since it was known that he would save it until he left the site. Given to him, I would suppose, by the person who planted the *shabti* at the end of the day. There was too much activity to risk concealing it until then. It might easily have been crushed as endless people descended to examine this eighteenth-dynasty step."

"And that would be Jess Delmont," Magritta murmured. "One of his assignments was to remain until shards and bits of rubble worthy of further study were locked in the truck. He supervised the workmen while they cleaned up the site, gathered their tools, and left. Nabil did not trust Jess to do a thorough job, and usually was the very last person at the site." She ducked her head for a moment, then flicked a tear off her cheek. "I shall miss him. Are you saying, Chief Inspector, that Jess planted the *shabti* and gave Nabil that horrid cigarette? I know the boy wasn't happy to spend the fall season at the concession, but he could have quit. Shannon might have caused problems for him at the college. She wasn't the permanent chair of the department, and he must have had other professors who would help him. Why did he do it?"

"Money," Mahmoud said. "He was paid well. He's already admitted it and begun to claim that he had no idea the cigarette would prove to be fatal."

"Who paid him?" she demanded. "Someone in this room?"

"He hasn't named anyone yet, but he will. The American Embassy tries to help its citizens, but when a serious crime is committed, the country's laws prevail. Once he realizes this, he's likely to try to bargain his way out of a lengthy prison sentence."

"This was all done so somebody could rob a tomb someplace else?" said Samuel.

Mahmoud nodded. "A group, actually. The name of the group, El Asad li-allah, is not mentioned in public, but it is well-known to the security and intelligence organizations. The members have been relatively ineffectual thus far, because they lack funds to purchase weapons from arms dealers in more sympathetic countries. We suspect they've looted tombs in the past. This one was by far the most promising. What they needed was help from unscrupulous dealers and collectors."

"Don't look at me!" Lord Bledrock huffed. "I may not have paperwork on some of the items in my collection, but I don't aid terrorists."

"Nor do I," said Mrs. McHaver.

"Absolutely not," Miriam added firmly. "The last thing we want is chaos. The extremists are unreliable, and capable of destroying any remains of a religious nature that contradict their beliefs. The Taliban exploded those priceless temples carved in a mountain."

Unprepared for this tactical move, Mahmoud looked at me. "It's possible," I said, "that you didn't know for sure with whom you were dealing. Dr. Guindi must have, though. He's your middleman, isn't he? I saw the three of you in his shop yesterday. Were you angry because he mentioned a delay in moving the artifacts from the tomb to his storage—where you could arrange to get them out of the country in your trunks and empty scotch cases?"

"He raised the prices," Mrs. McHaver said, then gulped. "For some jewelry in his shop. He keeps some very nice pieces for his longtime clients. We negotiated a price weeks earlier."

"Just how do you figure there was a delay?" asked Sittermann, grinning at me over a glass of bourbon.

"Yes," said Buffy. "You seem to know everything else."

"Unless she's stealing the Chief Inspector el-Habachi's

thunder," he added. "Then again, he may not be a match for her sleuthing skills, any more than her husband. She casts a big shadow, Rosen. You better watch your step."

Everyone froze and waited for Peter's reaction. Wallace moved to a neutral corner, as did Salima and Buffy. Lady Emerson tightened her grip on her parasol. Miriam held her lace hanky to her mouth. Lord Bledrock eased behind Mrs. McHaver's chair. I must admit I was curious, as well as ambivalent.

Peter nodded. "Sittermann seems bewildered, dear. Please put him out of his misery with an explanation, since he's unable to see it. I guess there's truth in the adage that you can't teach an old"—he paused—"dog new tricks. Some of them need to roll over and drop dead."

"I believe the word is 'play,' Rosen," Lord Bledrock said. "Play dead."

"My mistake," Peter murmured. "Anyone need a drink?"

Disappointed, I continued. "The delay was the result of Buffy's purported kidnapping. It wasn't a kidnapping, but merely an opportunity for her to brief her group and make plans."

"What group?" Buffy asked. "My Triple-A membership lapsed last year, and my college doesn't have sororities."

"You're not in college," I said, tired of tiptoeing around. "Your group is comprised of those trying to stop El Asad from desecularizing Egypt. Moderates, I assume. I have no idea if they have a fancy name as well. I won't ask, because if you tell me, you'll have to kill me."

Buffy gave me a distinctly un-perky look. "I may anyway."

"Whoa," Sittermann said. "She's . . . ?" He made a vague gesture with his free hand. "Really? Well, I've been hornswoggled before, but don't this take the cake? I was beginning to wonder why I couldn't get any information about her past beyond a certain point."

I tried not to look too smug. "Because her identity as bubble-brained Buffy is nothing but a fabrication—an elaborate cover story to allow her to come to Egypt, assess the situation, and decide what to do. She couldn't risk a meeting with her group, so she decided to take a much more dramatic route. If I hadn't seen a picture of her talking to the horsemen, I would have easily fallen for the charade. She dearly hoped Samuel had."

"This is so fascinating," Buffy said, her arms crossed. "Like I really wanted to be dragged across a saddle, spend the night in the desert, and get locked in a nasty hotel room, all the time thinking I was going to be murdered. Doesn't everyone?"

No one seemed able to digest any of this, except for Samuel. His eyes were narrowed and his body tensed. I nudged Peter and pointed, then waited until he'd moved behind Samuel's chair.

"I won't argue that point," I said, "but I doubt you suffered all that much. You've known all along who Samuel really is. Your organization must have been keeping track of him for years. I have no idea when you were first assigned to him, but you decided to move on him after you followed him to Rome. Your cover was a bored, blond girl from California. You persuaded him to let you come to Egypt with him, which wasn't too hard since he realized that you would strengthen his cover story as a casual tourist. To maintain your role, you had to buy designer luggage. Did your supervisors balk at designer clothes as well?"

Salima threw me a kiss. "You are so clever, Mrs. Malloy. I knew it when we first met. I have to admit I was disappointed when you didn't think to go to the storeroom in the basement, but at least you were amenable to my suggestion—and then put it together so neatly."

"You were disappointed?" I said, surprised.

"What in heaven's name is everyone talking about?" demanded Mrs. McHaver. "None of it makes an iota of sense. Why would Buffy have to kill you, Mrs. Malloy?"

"Hush," Miriam said curtly. "We seem to have stumbled into a colony of ants, although they all have wee cloaks and daggers."

Lord Bledrock threw up his hands, apparently forgetting

that he, like Mrs. McHaver earlier, had a drink. The gin splashed on Sittermann, who growled and sidled away. "Sorry, old boy, but you have to admit this is a horrendous muddle. If this is going to go on much longer, I'd much prefer to go downstairs to the restaurant and have dinner. I long for the simplicity of a broiled haddock."

Mahmoud stared at him. "Not just yet, Lord Bledrock. Mrs. Malloy is nearing the end of her explanation. After that, it is possible that no one will be having haddock any time soon."

"Sorry, sorry, sorry," I said mendaciously. "Let's return to Buffy and her group with no name. They decided to yank Samuel out of Luxor before anyone else was killed. Buffy did her best to lure him to the hotel in Kharga, where he would be forcibly detained and interrogated. However, he was deeply suspicious of Buffy by this time. His intention was to arrange for her to be killed in a dramatic rescue attempt, with me as his witness. After we arrived, he went off to polish his plan with his group. This is where I muddled up both their schemes by not waiting politely at the café. The people in the hotel—the desk clerk, the two men upstairs, probably even the old man by the entrance—were prepared for Samuel to show up. My arrival simply bewildered them. No one had any idea what to do, so they numbly cooperated. I suppose I should be flattered that no one considered me a likely terrorist. Buffy was equally startled by my appearance, and she did her best to give Samuel the chance to come thundering down the hall to rescue her. It's rather amazing how a small call of nature can result in the destruction of the best-laid plans."

"You were going to kill me?" Buffy squeaked at Samuel. "After all that crap I had to put up with? Filthy hotels, cockroaches, moldy fruit? You know something—you weren't all that spectacular in bed. Guys like you play with guns and explosives in order to compensate for your sexual inadequacies. You should be dragging a cannon behind you."

"Oooh," Salima said. "Now that's really hitting below the belt."

Miss Portia elbowed Miss Cordelia. " 'Below the belt.' What a quaint phrase."

Samuel ignored them. "The drive through the desert has given you hallucinations, Mrs. Malloy. You need to see a doctor—or a shrink. Aren't you going to accuse me of assassinating Julius Caesar and Attila?"

"I'd like to think not even you could arrange that," I said. "Shannon's another matter. You followed her when she left Lord Bledrock's room, and persuaded her to take a taxi to the Valley of the Kings, probably promising to find a bottle of champagne and go with her. After the taxi driver pulled away from the curb in front of the Old Winter Palace, he picked you up in front of the New Winter Palace. While Shannon either bribed the guard or sweet-talked her way in, you slipped in as well. If she was as drunk as the hotel staff say she was, she couldn't have made it to the site on her own. There was a problem with the taxi driver, however. He couldn't be allowed to tell the police he'd taken two people to the Valley that night. The only solution was to kill him as well."

"I can't believe this," he said, staring at the ceiling. "Next Mrs. Malloy will explain how the aliens in my spacecraft can beam me from one spot to another in a nanosecond."

"I didn't say you killed the taxi driver. You ordered it done. You must have a great power within El Asad. The leader, perhaps? Did you convert to Islam when you were in college?"

He pounded his fist on the armrest. "No one will dare speak against me."

Mahmoud shook his head. "You may have intimidated Egyptian nationals, but these foreigners are not so predictable. After Lord Bledrock, Mrs. McHaver, and Miriam have been charged as coconspirators and accessories to four murders, they may discover they know more than they've said thus far concerning the source of this new batch of precious artifacts. The British Embassy can't protect them. The prisons in their country are unpleasant, but the ones here are even more so."

"And, Father, even if you buy your way out of this," Alexander said, "you'll be booted out of the House of Lords and your club. No one will invite you to their pavilions at Ascot. No more shooting weekends and foxhunts. Neville Bledrock, Baron of Rochland, will be smeared in the press. I may renounce the title. You really ought to cooperate. If you're lucky, you'll simply be sent home and forbidden to ever come back."

"It might be time to take more of an interest in the Persians and the Medes," Miriam said.

Mrs. McHaver gazed at the empty glass on the table. "I've always been fond of porcelain from the early Chinese dynasties."

"Now, wait a minute!" Samuel said. "You're in this up to your necks."

"Hardly." Miriam sniffed, then patted her aunt's shoulder. "We have no illegal artifacts in our possession; nor, apparently, will we have in the future. I can see you're tired, Aunt Rose. We should retire to our room. Chief Inspector el-Habachi, we will anticipate a visit at your convenience."

"No," Lord Bledrock said, "let's go to my suite. I'll have room service bring up some supper. What about you, Alexander? Will we have the pleasure of your company?"

"I don't have anything to do with this," he said emphatically. "I've warned you for years that you'd get nabbed one of these days. You might compile a list of treasures in your collection to donate to the Cairo Museum. I'm sure they'd be most grateful."

"Not my mummy," he blustered. "It's like a dear old friend. Many a night I've sat with him and poured out my troubles. He never contradicts me, or decimates my wine cellar, or gallops across the vegetable garden. The sarcophagi, the scarabs, the necklace from the tomb of Nefertari—all of that can go. I shall never give up my mummy."

"Neville!" Mrs. McHaver said, rising and clutching his arm, "I had no idea you have a necklace from that tomb. How on earth did you acquire it, you sly dog?"

They went out the door. Miriam sighed, then once again

dutifully followed her aunt. Buffy and Sittermann moved out of the way as Mahmoud ushered Samuel to the hall. Magritta realized she was no longer in custody. She caught Wallace with one hand and a bottle of scotch with the other. Nodding, they left.

Salima flopped across the sofa and said, "Bravo, Mrs. Malloy. A devilishly good denouement, replete with wild accusations, betrayals, cringing and whinging. Surely we shall have a bottle of champagne to celebrate."

"I want to talk to you, young lady!" Sittermann snapped at Buffy.

"I have a few words for you, too," she retorted.

They both looked at Peter, who said, "I'm not talking to either of you. I'm fed up with all this childishness. Go away and bug each other's rooms, or just bug each other. I am on my honeymoon. Good-bye!"

They hesitated, then obediently went away. I stroked Peter's knee until he stopped quivering with rage. I would never have married a docile man without the courage to stand up for himself, or meekly stand aside unless he chose to do so; nor would he have married a woman with those traits. I was quite proud of his restraint, although I had been a tiny bit worried that Sittermann had pushed his luck too far. I rewarded my husband with a quick kiss, intending to express my admiration in greater detail when we had privacy.

"Get up, Salima," Alexander said. "If you promise to stop begging for champagne, I'll buy you a damn bottle of the stuff in the bar."

"Just one more thing," I said to Alexander. "I'd like your solemn promise to stop following me and the girls. I won't demand an apology for your unnecessary roughness in the shop yesterday. However, I am sorry I wasn't able to scratch my initials on your face."

"You're the one who pursued Caron and Inez in Gurna?" Salima said. "How brutish."

"I will admit I had been keeping an eye on them and on Mrs. Malloy. Rosen had been acting quite suspiciously since he arrived in Egypt, what with all his abrupt departures and clandestine meetings. It was obvious that he wasn't involved in any development schemes. As for Gurna, I didn't follow the girls there. I was following Samuel, for pity's sake. When they took off running and he went after them, I thought I'd better keep an eye on things. They would have found themselves in serious trouble if they ran into those men with the cart, but luckily they were already hiding from Samuel. He merely observed them from the other side of the road, then left. I made sure they got to the pier. Their attempts to disguise themselves was highly amusing. I think they've learned a few tricks from Claire."

"And yesterday?" I asked.

"I knew what my father and his cronies were up to. I don't think they would have hurt you, but Dr. Guindi has no scruples. I didn't want you to end up in the basement beneath the room at the back of his shop."

Peter grimaced. "You seem well informed. MI6, isn't it?"

"Oh, good god," Salima said. "Bond, James Bond. Are you packing a loaded ballpoint pen and a gold cigarette lighter that doubles as a tear gas cannister? Are you going to take the elevator to the lobby, or scale down the side of the hotel?"

"Don't get smarmy with me, Miss Interpol," he countered. "How utterly absurd."

"I have your dossier in my briefcase. Care to see it?"

Salima's eyes flickered with anger. "Then you know that I am merely a consultant. I pass along tidbits I overhear when escorting foreign dignitaries around Luxor."

"Bully for you."

"Okay!" I said. "That's it. Go elsewhere and spit at each other."

Salima looked at me. "Does that mean you really, truly want us to leave? I'll be much more creative after another martini or two. I can't promise you a fair fight, however. He's inarticulate, which is sad when you consider the price of his education. Perhaps it's adequate to charm brainless debutantes."

"Or yours," Alexander inserted, "to charm Cambridge tutors who can't keep their pants zipped."

Peter opened the door. "Have a lovely evening."

We could hear them bickering all the way to the elevator. I wondered if we'd be invited to the wedding. We retreated to the balcony.

"I suppose Caron and Inez will be back any minute," I said.

"Bakr has orders to drive them to the Hilton near Karnak for dinner. I thought we'd order room service and have a quiet meal."

"No haddock, I hope."

"Not a chance." He stroked my back. "You're not a member of any covert organizations, are you?"

"Just the ACLU and the independent booksellers outfit. Neither of them offered me a decoder ring. Just think how much easier this would have been if we'd had a nice, calm meeting two weeks ago, and everybody volunteered the name of his or her covert agency. Did I mention that Sittermann had my apartment searched? Luanne called to tell me, but I didn't believe her. I do, now. If my bookstore was searched as well, I do hope they straightened the files. I could barely get the drawer closed."

"You want me to do anything about it?"

"No," I said. "I want to sit here and hold your hand and gaze at the mountains and listen to the parties on the ships across the corniche. That's not entirely true. I have some other ideas in mind, but I'm afraid Abdullah will show up and stare disapprovingly at us. 'One hears things, *Sitt*,' he'll intone, in his ominously soft way."

"Mahmoud told him to take a vacation for a few days, so we don't have to worry what he might hear. Mahmoud keeps him on the payroll, since guests have been known to speak indiscreetly in front of the staff. If we turn on the taps in the bathtub, we'll have about twenty minutes to find some way to occupy ourselves before we go for a dip. We can have a leisurely soak, then order dinner and talk about Cairo."

"No more American Embassy?"

"We won't even drive by it in a taxi. I told Mahmoud we didn't have hotel reservations, so I couldn't leave a number. We both knew I was lying. All this murder and conspiracy and stolen antiquities business can wait for a few days."

"Caron and Inez are eager to see the pyramids at Giza," I said.

"We can take carriages and see them in style. Are you going to allow yourself to be photographed on a camel? It's traditional."

I shook my head. "Not in a million years. The last thing I'm going to do is be bullied into sitting atop one of those nasty, flea-ridden, smelly beasts that would spit in my eye given half a chance. I will never be photographed sitting on a camel. Trust me on that."

In Feburary 2005, Dr. Barbara Mertz (aka Elizabeth Peters, author of the Amelia Peabody Egyptology mysteries set in Victorian times) graciously allowed me to trail after her to Egypt. Rumor had it that KV63, possibly the greatest discovery in the Valley of the Kings since Tutankhamun's tomb in 1922, was about to be opened. Although we missed the high drama by two weeks (excavations move exceedingly slowly), I still managed to have many Very Cool experiences.

Because Barbara is so esteemed within Egyptology circles, we were invited inside the yellow tape at the KV63 site to sit under a canvas awning, drink tea, and watch the workmen bring up rubble to be sifted and examined. I was introduced to the key players, who no doubt felt required to be nice to me. No one, by the way, was murdered.

We shopped at cramped, dusty shops, where we were invariably offered tea while various bits of jewelry were presented for our approval. Dr. Ray Johnson of Chicago House gave me a private tour of Luxor Temple and invited us to dinner with the group in residence there (including a Canadian mason). Dr. Marjorie Fisher invited us on a three-day cruise on the Nubian Sea. Bill and Nancy Petty served us a lovely dinner on their *dahabiyya*. Dennis Forbes and I debated the propriety of allowing artifacts to be displayed in museums outside of Egypt. Dear Joel Cole offered a much-needed arm as we walked on rough, rocky surfaces at the sites, saving me from several potentially embarrassing tumbles. Salima Ikram, who has the energy of a well-shaken bottle of champagne, brightened every experience with her wit and knowledge.

On most evenings, we sat on the balcony of our suite at the Old Winter Palace, watching the feluccas drift on the Nile as the sun set behind the mountains. Muezzins wailed from the numerous mosques. Drummers performed on the pier across the corniche. We did not drink tea. We spent a few days at the end of our trip in Cairo, where we attended a reception at the American Embassy. Charles Roberts, an old friend of Barbara's from Maryland, joined us, and he and I rode in a carriage to view the pyramids. I would speak more kindly of him had he not suggested I stand next to the camel for a photograph.

All in all, I had innumerable Very Cool experiences, all due to the graciousness of Barbara Mertz. She introduced me to fascinating people, led the way through the temples and the Valley of the Kings, translated hieroglyphs, made the arrangements to minimalize wear and tear on my bad back, and answered my idiotic questions with patience. She was a perfect traveling companion and will always be a perfect friend.

Joan Hess
October 2007

P.S. I depicted the Old Winter Palace with fairly reasonable accuracy, but there were certain elements that I changed because of the plot. Get over it. Also, there are several ways to spell words taken from ancient Egyptian hieroglyphs and contemporary Arabic words. I relied on my travel guides and several Web sites. Please don't send me letters telling me I got it wrong.

Keep reading for a sneak peek at Joan Hess's next mystery

Busy Bodies

Available May 2009 from St. Martin's Paperbacks

CHAPTER 1

I am not an adept liar, which I think speaks well for my character. However, this deficiency has propelled me into sticky situations in the past, and I had a foreboding feeling it was about to do so again.

"Tea, Miss Parchester?" I said into the telephone receiver. "I'd love to, but I—I simply don't see when I could—well, I was planning on organizing my files, and I promised Caron that I'd drive her and Inez to the mall, and—"

Miss Emily Parchester had taught high-school students for forty years before her retirement and therefore was unimpressed with my sputtery excuses. "Oh, do bring the girls with you. I so enjoy their youthful enthusiasm. I'll see all of you at five o'clock."

Groaning, I replaced the receiver. In that my bookstore was bereft of customers, I received no sympathetic, curious, or even incurious glances. The die was cast: Miss Parchester, a mistress of manipulation, was expecting us for tea. In the past, I'd masqueraded as a substitute teacher in order to come to her rescue when she'd been accused of embezzling money from the journalism accounts *and* poisoning the principal. I'd done extraordinary things (among them being charged with three felonies—a personal best) when her basset hounds were kidnapped by an unscrupulous lout. Although the concept of a cup of tea should have sounded innocuous, it didn't.

I picked up the feather duster and attacked the window display. In the fierce August sunshine, pedestrians ambled by the Book Depot without so much as a look of longing at all the worthy literature crammed inside its musty, cramped confines. Business had been poor all summer, as usual, but it would pick up shortly when several thousand earnest students arrived to improve their minds, as well as their chances for lucrative employment, by enrolling at Farber College. Very few of them would do so in the liberal-arts department. Business and accounting textbooks had spilled onto the shelves once reserved for Mr. Faulkner and Miss Austen. I stocked enough slim, yellow study guides to pave the road to the Emerald City.

It occurred to me that I would be forty years old by the time the semester began. I peered at my reflection in the dusty glass, wondering if said anniversary would coincide with an outbreak of gray hair and the awakening pangs of arthritis, rheumatism, bunions, and all the other maladies that accompany old age.

I concluded I was holding up fairly well. My curly hair was predominantly red, and my mostly svelte body had not yet capitulated to gravity. This isn't to say there weren't some fine lines around my eyes and a few gray hairs. All were the result of being the mother of a fifteen-year-old girl with a propensity for melodrama and an enduring ability to keep me speculating about the quality of life at the nearest rest home. The one occasionally favored by Miss Parchester had seemed congenial, although I doubted they served cocktails in the evening. On a more positive note, visiting hours were restricted.

But not at the Book Depot. Caron burst through the door, accompanied by her ever-loyal sidekick, Inez Thornton. Caron shares my physical attributes but not my imperturbable personality—or my lack of proficiency in matters requiring mendacity. For her, right and wrong are nebulous concepts defined solely by her personal objectives at any given moment. She's not so much immoral as she is ego-centric. Copernicus would have loved her.

Inez is quite the opposite, which is why I suppose they're steadfast friends. She's a composition in brown and beige, all blurred together like a desertscape done in watercolors. Her eyes are leery behind thick lenses, and her mouth is usually pursed in speculation. She has not yet mastered the art of speaking in capital letters, but she has a talented mentor.

"You said you'd drive us to the mall." Caron began accusingly. "I finished doing my hair an hour ago, and we've been Absolutely Sweltering on the front porch waiting for you. I came within seconds of having a heat stroke. Inez had to help me upstairs so I could get a glass of ice water. My face was bright red, and—"

"I said I'd take you at five o'clock, dear," I said. "I can't close the store in the middle of the afternoon."

She rolled her eyes. "And disappoint all these customers lined up at the cash register? I hate to break it to you, Mother, but you could get rid of the books and start selling auto parts—and no one would notice."

Reminding myself of the legal ramifications of child abandonment, I went behind the counter and perched on the stool. "I'd notice," I said mildly. "I can't read a carburetor in the bathtub. In any case, you, Inez, and I have been invited to have tea with Miss Parchester. I'll take you out to the mall afterward."

Inez drifted out from behind the romance rack. "I thought she eloped while she was on that bus trip to the Southwest. Wouldn't that make her a missus-somebody-else?"

Caron was not interested in anyone else's marital status. "Tea?" she croaked, as horrified as if I had mentioned an invitation for a cup of arsenic. "We can't go to some dumb tea party this afternoon. I need to shop before school starts. Otherwise, I'll have to show up Stark Naked on the first day. Not only will I be expelled, but I'll be the laughing-stock of Farberville High School and will have no choice but to kill myself on the steps." Clutching her throat, she staggered out of view to find a book on expediting death in the most gruesome manner within her budget.

I nodded at Inez. "Miss Parchester did indeed elope. She and Mr. Delmaro were married just across the border in Mexico, but he succumbed to a heart attack that very night while they were"—I paused to search for a seemly euphemism, even though the girls had gone through a period of reading every steamy novel in the store and undoubtedly knew more than I—"consummating the marriage. It turned out he already had a wife who'd purchased his-and-her cemetery plots, so Miss Parchester sent the remains to her and resumed her maiden name when she returned to Far-berville."

"They had sex?" whispered Inez "Miss Parchester's got to be as old as my grandmother, or maybe older. I don't think my grandmother . . ."

"That's disgusting," Caron called from the vicinity of the self-help books. "Sexuality is a function of youth. Old people should devote their energy to gardening or playing crib-bage." Her head popped up long enough for her to glower at me. "Or drinking tea."

Inez was edging backward as if she expected her best friend's maniacal mother to come out from behind the counter with an ax. "My grandmother plays duplicate bridge three times a week. She says it's really a lot of fun, especially the tournaments."

"I'd like to think I have a few good years left before I need to find a hobby," I said. From behind the racks came the sound of someone humming "Happy Birthday." This did nothing to brighten my mood. I picked up the feather duster and was preparing to stalk the miscreant when the bell above the door jangled.

Peter Rosen hesitated in the doorway, possibly bemused by the ferocity of my expression and the disembodied hum-ming. He has dark hair, a beakish nose, a perpetual tan, and white, vulpine teeth. He dresses like a very successful Wall Street mogul, from his silk tie right down to the tips of his

Italian shoes. When he chooses, he can be charming. His mellow brown eyes twinkle playfully and, at more intimate times, downright provocatively.

There are other times, alas, when his eyes turn icy and his bite is quite as bad as his bark. These worst of times coincide with my civic-minded attempts to help the Farberville CID solve crimes. Peter Rosen is my lover; Lieutenant Rosen is my nemesis. Frankly, lectures and accusations of meddling do not make for a harmonious relationship.

"Are you under siege by mellifluous hornets?" he asked.

"I wish I were," I said, reluctantly lowering my weapon. I told Caron and Inez to return at five and shooed them out of the store. I then lured Peter into my office, where there was such little space that we had no choice but to press our bodies together. Certain events of the previous weekend were discussed in endearing murmurs, and when we finally returned to the front room, my face was as red as Caron's allegedly had been earlier.

Peter peered behind the racks to make sure the girls hadn't crept back inside the store. "What's the current crisis?"

"We're having tea with Miss Parchester. This ghastly scenario means they won't get to the mall until six o'clock and Caron will be forced to commit suicide in front of the entire student body."

He gave me an odd look before picking up a paperback and pretending to study its cover. "Miss Parchester lives on Willow Street, doesn't she?"

"You should know, Sherlock. You and Farberville's finest staked out her house for three solid days. It's a good thing I found her and convinced her to turn herself in before she was tackled by an overly zealous rookie." I paused in case he wanted to engage in a bit of repartee, and then added, "I'll give you a ten percent discount if you want to buy that book. I haven't read it myself, but according to the catalog, it's the best of the alien slime time-travel fantasies."

He hastily replaced it and took out a handkerchief to wipe his fingers. "So Miss Parchester invited you for a cozy tea party? Did she say anything about the purpose of it?"

"The purpose of a cozy tea party is to drink tea while balancing a plate of cookies on one's knee and making genteel conversation about the weather."

"We've had a lot of complaints from Willow Street residents. May I assume you haven't been to visit Miss Parchester lately?"

I shook my head. "What kind of complaints, Peter? Is she doing something to cause problems?"

Grinning, he headed for the door. "I wouldn't dream of spoiling this particular surprise. Can I come by tonight if I bring a pizza and a six-pack?"

I agreed and watched him as he crossed under the portico and headed up the sidewalk in the direction of the campus. I tried to decipher his cryptic remarks, but I had no luck and was cheerfully diverted when that rarest of creatures, a customer, appeared with a fat wallet and a hunger to put some romantic intrigue in her life.

At five o'clock I closed the store and retreated to the office to wait for Caron and Inez, who were no more than fifteen minutes late. After a spirited argument, I allowed my darling daughter to climb into the driver's seat. Caron's sixteenth birthday loomed as alarmingly as my fortieth; she anticipated not only pink balloons and overnight popularity but also a shiny red sports car. My attempts to save her from debilitating disappointment thus far had been ignored.

"This car is a slug," she said as we pulled out of the parking lot. "Rhonda Maguire's getting a new car. She can't decide if she wants a convertible or a four-wheel drive."

Inez leaned over the seat and said, "The only reason she wants a four-wheel drive is that the boys on the football team are always drooling over them. Rhonda thinks they'll drool over her if she has one."

I closed my eyes as we lurched into the traffic flowing up Thurber Street. "Rhonda ought to be introduced to Miss Parchester's basset hounds. They'll certainly drool over her." I leaned my head against the seat and listened to the ensuing derogatory comments regarding Rhonda Maguire's latest foray into perfidy, which centered as always on her attempts to ingratiate herself with a certain junior varsity quarterback.

"What's going on?" Caron said irritably.

I opened my eyes and frowned at the cars inching around the corner to Willow Street. On the street itself, traffic was barely moving. Those on foot were making noticeably better progress; as I stared, a group of children cut across the nearest yard and jostled a more staid couple in matching Bermuda shorts. Fraternity boys who'd arrived early for rush week were drinking beer and telling what must have been hilarious jokes as they walked up the sidewalk.

"How many people did Miss Parchester invite to tea?" Inez asked with such bewilderment I could almost hear her blinking.

"Just us, as far as I know," I said, equally bewildered by the scene. Willow Street runs through the middle of the historic district. At one time, the mostly Victorian houses were the residences of the highest echelon of Farberville society, including the honorable Judge Amos Parchester. Now some of the houses had been subdivided into apartments, while others struggled like aging dowagers to maintain their facades. I couldn't conceive of any reason why the street was worthy of all this interest, but clearly something odd was happening; something, I amended, that was causing a lot of complaints to be made to the police department.

Caron continued past the corner. "I'm going to park behind the library so we won't get stuck later—when it's time to go to the mall. You Do Remember that we're going to the mall, don't you?"

"Yes, dear," I said, trying not to concoct any wild hypotheses about Miss Parchester's involvement. As we walked up the sidewalk, I was relieved to see that the crowd was gathering in front of the house beyond hers. A great tangle of shrubbery blocked my view of whatever was taking place, but from the expressions of those farther up the sidewalk, it was a doozy.

"Claire," Miss Parchester trilled from her porch, "I've already put on the kettle. Oh, and I see the girls are with you. What a lovely little party we'll have." She clasped her hands together and beamed at us as if we'd done something particularly clever by finding her house.

She may have been impervious to the traffic jam and the swelling crowd, but I wasn't. "What's going on next door?" I said as I herded the girls toward her house.

"It's rather complicated," she said. She ushered us inside and closed the front door. "And annoying, I must admit. As you know, I am a staunch defender of our constitutional rights, but I'm not sure our forefathers took this kind of thing into consideration when they penned the document."

The living room had not changed since I was last there, unless the dust was thicker and the scent of camphor more pronounced. Stacks of yellow newspapers and faded blue composition books still teetered precariously, and the moth-eaten drapes still blocked most of the daylight. Miss Parchester appeared to be wearing the same cardigan sweater, frumpy dress, and fuzzy pink bedroom slippers.

Once we'd been supplied with tea and cookies, I repeated my question. Caron and Inez nodded, one forcefully and the other tentatively.

Miss Parchester sighed. "About a year ago, old Mr. Stenopolis died of a heart attack. He was well into his eighties and quite a neighborhood character. I remember as a child when he and Papa would exchange angry words concerning Mr. Stenopolis's disinclination to keep his grass mowed and his sidewalk swept. Papa was on the state supreme court, as I must have told you, and often entertained distinguished visitors."

"Who lives there now?" I said before we were treated to a lengthy recitation of Papa's accomplishments in the realm of jurisprudence.

"Mr. Stenopolis left the house to his nephew, Zeno Gorgias. The young man moved in two weeks ago. He's certainly charming and personable, but he has some ideas that are . . . unconventional. Mr. Stenopolis once told me that

Zeno is a nationally renowned artist whose paintings sell for
a great deal of money."

"Why did he move to Farberville?" Caron asked. "It's so
utterly middle-class and boring. If I were famous, I'd live in
New York or Los Angeles or someplace where people don't
sit around and drink"—she noticed my ominous expression—
"diet sodas all day."

Miss Parchester smiled sweetly at her. "He said he was
tired of all the pretentious, self-appointed critics of the art
world. He was living in Houston when he learned he'd in-
herited the house and came to have a look at it. It is a lovely
old house, although Mr. Stenopolis never threw away so
much as a tin can or a piece of string. The last time I was inside it, I was appalled. Every room was piled high with rubbish, odds and ends of scrap metal, jars, broken appliances,
magazines, wads of aluminum foil, and so forth. I told Mr.
Stenopolis that it was a firetrap, but he simply laughed. He
had a very infectious laugh."

I tried once more to nudge her into the present. "This
artist named Zeno moved in two weeks ago. What's he done
that has lured such a crowd?"

Miss Parchester's blue eyes watered and the cup clinked
as she placed it in the saucer. "He told me that he's exploring
what he calls 'interactive environmental art.' People are supposed to be startled into reacting to his stimuli." She took a
tissue from her cuff and dabbed her nose, then sniffled delicately and said, "He's been very successful in his goal. So
far he's relied on word of mouth, but he mentioned that he's
been in contact with the local television station, as well as
the newspaper. Before too long everyone in Farberville will
be in our heretofore peaceful neighborhood, trampling flowers, discarding litter, making it impossible for any of us to
take our cars out of our driveways."

"Isn't that a public nuisance?" asked Caron, who has
committed an impressive number of misdemeanors in the
past and therefore been obliged to take more than a cursory
interest in the law.

"I should think so," Miss Parchester said sadly, "but the authorities have refused to become involved. I'm in a muddle myself. I'm adamant in my support of freedom of speech and of religion, but walking to the grocery store is a taxing chore, as well as bending over to pick up litter or trying to salvage my zinnias. Nick and Nora are so distressed by all the confusion that they won't come out from under the back porch. I've considered joining them."

I set down my cup and saucer and gestured at the girls. "Perhaps we'd better take a look for ourselves, Miss Parchester."

Caron and Inez leapt to their feet, and we were thanking our hostess when the front door banged open and a man literally bounded into the room.

"Miss Parchester," he said, snatching her hand and noisily kissing it, "I have come to beg a favor of you. Do you have an extension cord that I might borrow?"

She tried to give him a stern look, but her cheeks were pink and she was twittering like a debutante. "Let me introduce you to my three dearest friends, Zeno. Then I'll see if I can find an extension cord in the garage."

While she rattled off names, I coolly studied him. He had long, black hair that hid his ears and flopped across his forehead when he moved. And move he did, as if he'd been wound too tightly or had imbibed an excessive amount of caffeine. His hands darted through the air and his feet scarcely made contact with the carpet. His expression shifted continuously, which is why it took me a moment to put his age at thirty despite his sweaty T-shirt, sandals, immodest gym shorts—and the Mickey Mouse beanie perched on his head. How it managed to remain on his head was as much a mystery as what he was doing next door.

"I am enchanted," he said to me, lunging for my hand.

I put it behind my back. "Welcome to Farberville, Mr. Gorgias."

He threw back his head and laughed so boisterously that I glanced uneasily at the light fixture above his head. "No one calls me anything but Zeno, my dear Claire. When I die,

there will be only one word on my tombstone: *Zeno*. It will
be the perfect summation of my life." Abruptly sobering, he
spun around and caught Caron's arm. "And what do you
wish as your epitaph?"

"I don't know," she mumbled.

He may have intended to try the same ploy with Inez, but
she was well out of reach and still retreating. "I am sorry I
cannot stay," he continued, "but I must find an extension
cord. Everything is at stake—everything!"

Miss Parchester announced she would look and shuffled
through the kitchen and out the back door. Caron and Inez
clutched each other and warily watched him from behind a
settee. If it would not have been misconstrued as an act of
cowardice, I would have joined them. In a nanosecond.

"So you are a widow," Zeno said, turning back to me. "It
is a crime against nature for a woman to sleep alone, you
know. This is what my grandfather told me when I became a
man." He shoved back his hair and gave me a disconcert-
ingly wicked grin. "Or maybe it's a line from a movie. Who
cares?"

"Why do you say I'm a widow?"

"I love women, from rosy little babies to the oldest
crones with hunched backs and gnarled hands. I study them
very closely. Women are more complex than men, more an-
alytical, more likely to allow an occasional glimpse of their
souls. Also, Miss Parchester told me the tragic story of how
your husband was killed in a collision with a chicken truck.
I wept as I envisioned the bloodstained feathers fluttering
down the desolate mountain road."

Before I could respond, Miss Parchester returned empty-
handed. "I can't think where else to look, Zeno," she said.
"I'm sure I have one somewhere, but it's been years since I
last saw it."

He put his hands on her shoulders and kissed the tip of
her nose. "Don't worry, my darling. After all, art should be
spontaneous, and it has been dictated by fate that I shall have
only one stereo speaker today. Tomorrow I may have two,
three, or even a hundred!"

He bounded out the door.

"Goodness," I said as I sank down on the sofa and took a sip of cold tea. "He's energetic, isn't he?"

Caron snorted. "If you ask me, he's psychotic. He just admitted he doesn't know the difference between real life and the movies." She flung herself beside me and continued making vulgar noises to express her low opinion of Zeno, or, more probably, adults in general.

"I'm glad I don't live near him," Inez contributed, her eyes as wide as I'd ever seen them. "Does he always just barge in like that, Miss Parchester?"

"He said that doorbells limit the spontaneity of the encounter, since both parties are warned in advance. Zeno is enamored of spontaneity, among other things. It's refreshing, but also tiresome. There have been times after his visits when I've taken to my bed to recuperate, or been obliged to pour myself a glass of elderberry wine."

I didn't point out that she found other occasions to seek solace in the bottle, one of which had required some dedicated sleuthing on my part. "I guess we'd better see what Zeno is doing," I said as I stood up.

We were thanking Miss Parchester again when the doorbell rang. It's possible that at least one of us flinched, but the door stayed shut as Miss Parchester went across the room. She opened it, then gasped and stumbled backward, knocking over a pile of old yearbooks and a spindly floor lamp.

A young woman stood on the porch. Her streaky blond hair was cropped at odd angles, reminding me of the roof of a thatched cottage—after a windstorm. Her eyes were large and dark, her lashes thick with mascara, her mouth caked with scarlet lipstick. Her ample body was flawless except for a few freckles scattered on her shoulders and a puckery white scar that might have come from an appendectomy.

I could arrive at this judgment at the approximate speed of light because she was wearing only the bottom half of a string bikini and silky pink tassels on her breasts.